The shadows were long and deep when they found a small dark stain that appeared to be blood buried under the fine layer of sand deposited since the murder. Pashenuro hurried to the river and worked his way along the shore. He soon found a brownish, bloodlike spot on a rock poised an arm's length above the swirling water. The rock would have been an ideal place from which to jettison a body.

Darkness was falling when Bak found the footprint, located half under a rock in a niche so small only a child could have hidden there. From that point, the mute boy Ramose could have peered through a gap between the boulders and watched the slayer at work. They had to find that child—if still he lived.

"I've found something!" Bak called, his voice pulsating with excitement.

A loud crack sounded beside him.

"Get down, Lieutenant!" Pashenuro yelled.

Bak glimpsed something fly past his head and heard another, louder crack. A rock! Someone was using a sling. A deadly weapon in the hands of a trained warrior . . .

Mysteries of Ancient Egypt by
Lauren Haney
from Avon Books

A CRUEL DECEIT
A PLACE OF DARKNESS
A CURSE OF SILENCE
A VILE JUSTICE
A FACE TURNED BACKWARDS
THE RIGHT HAND OF AMON

THE RIGHT HAND OF AMON

LAUREN HANEY

AVON BOOKS
An Imprint of HarperCollinsPublishers

This is a work of fiction. Names, characters, places, and incidents are products of the author's imagination or are used fictitiously and are not to be construed as real. Any resemblance to actual events, locales, organizations, or persons, living or dead, is entirely coincidental.

AVON BOOKS
An Imprint of HarperCollins*Publishers*
10 East 53rd Street
New York, New York 10022-5299

Copyright © 1997 by Betty Winkelman
Library of Congress Catalog Card Number: 97-93173
ISBN: 0-380-79266-4
www.avonbooks.com

First Avon Books printing: November 1997

Avon Trademark Reg. U.S. Pat. Off. and in Other Countries, Marca Registrada, Hecho en U.S.A.
HarperCollins® is a trademark of HarperCollins Publishers Inc.

Printed in the U.S.A.

10 9 8 7 6 5 4

In memory of
George Winkelman
who urged me to "write what you know."

Acknowledgments

First and foremost, I wish to thank Dennis Forbes, editorial director of *KMT: A Modern Journal of Ancient Egypt*, and James N. Frey, who teaches at the University of California, Berkeley, Extension. It's difficult to know to which of the two I owe the greatest debt. From Jim, I learned the craft of fiction writing. Dennis provided moral support and allowed me to mine his vast store of knowledge about ancient Egypt.

Archaeologia's Andrew Gordon and Arthur Richter, sellers of antiquarian books, came through at exactly the right time, allowing me to photocopy some crucial pages I needed while writing this novel.

Though it's not always easy to listen to reason, the critiques given by members of our Saturday writing group, past and present, were and still are invaluable.

Most of all, I wish to thank all those men and women who have contributed to our knowledge of ancient Egypt through study, excavation, and publication. Without their books, this book could never have been written.

Author's Note

Ancient Egypt, circa 1463 B.C.
*18th Dynasty during the dual reign of Maatkare Hatshepsut
and her stepson/nephew Menkheperre Tuthmose, with
Queen Hatshepsut exercising full power*

The characters in this novel are fictitious, creatures of the author's imagination, but the setting is authentic. The Belly of Stones and the ruined fortresses of Buhen and Iken, located about two hundred miles south of present-day Aswan, existed into the twentieth century.

At the time of this novel, the commandant of Buhen loosely administered a chain of at least ten fortresses strung along the Belly of Stones. This was the most rugged, desolate, and arid portion of the Nile valley, and the river was filled with rapids and small islands, making it navigable only during the highest flood stage. Originally built several centuries earlier in the 12th Dynasty, these fortresses lay in various stages of ruin or repair. The garrison troops protected and controlled traffic through this natural corridor, collected tribute and tolls, and conducted punitive military expeditions.

The Medjays were initially desert-dwelling people of Lower Nubia. By the 18th Dynasty, they were men who served as law enforcement officers, maintaining order throughout Egypt and along the desert frontiers.

Cast of Characters

At the Fortress of Buhen

Lieutenant Bak	Officer in charge of the Medjay police
Sergeant Imsiba	Bak's second-in-command, a Medjay
Commandant Thuty	Officer in charge of the garrison of Buhen; has nominal command over the other garrison commanders along the Belly of Stones
Troop Captain Nebwa	Thuty's second-in-command
Seneb	An Egyptian trader just back from Kush, far to the south
Meru	An old fisherman with a vast knowledge of the river
Nofery	Proprietress of a house of pleasure, Bak's local informant
Kenamon	Physician-priest from the capital city of Waset
Pashenuro and Kasaya	The two Medjays who accompany Bak to Iken

At the Fortress of Iken

Commander Woser	Officer in charge of the garrison of Iken
Aset	Woser's beautiful daughter
Lieutenant Puemre	An unpopular infantry officer
Ramose	A deaf-mute child; Puemre's servant
Troop Captain Huy	Woser's second-in-command
Lieutenant Nebseny	Archery officer, a man who loves Aset
Lieutenant Senu	Garrison watch officer
Lieutenant Inyotef	River pilot; a man Bak knows from the past
Sennufer	Proprietor of a house of pleasure
Antef	A besotted potter who dreamed he saw a murder
Senmut	An armorer, a man who mourns Puemre
Mutnefer	Senmut's daughter; Puemre's housekeeper and more
Minnakht	Puemre's sergeant
Amon-Psaro	A powerful Kushite king
Amon-Karka	Amon-Psaro's ill son

Plus various and sundry soldiers, scribes, and townspeople

Those who walk the corridors of power in Kemet

Maatkare Hatshepsut	Queen of Kemet
Menkheperre Tuthmose	The queen's nephew; ostensibly shares the throne with his aunt
Nihisy	Chancellor

The Gods and Goddesses

Amon	The primary god during much of Egyptian history, especially the early 18th Dynasty, the time of this story; takes the form of a human being
Horus of Buhen	A local version of the falcon god Horus
Maat	Goddess of truth and order; represented by a feather
Hapi	The river god
Hathor	A goddess with many attributes, such as motherhood, happiness, dancing and music, war; often depicted as a cow
Osiris	A very ancient fertility god; king of the netherworld; shown as a man wrapped in a shroud
Re	The sun god
Khepre	The rising sun

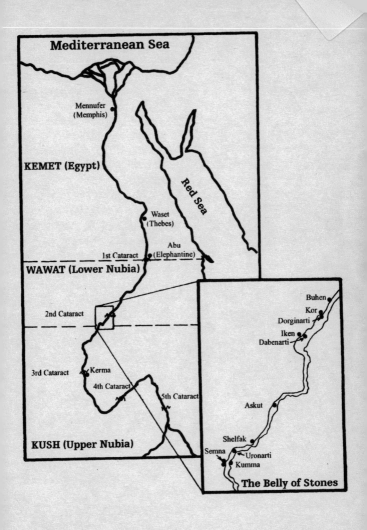

Chapter One

The day was hot, sweltering. The kind of day when predators and prey alike hid among the rocks or under bushes or in the depths of the river. They hid not from each other but from the sun god Re, whose fiery breath drew the moisture from every animal and plant, from the life-giving river itself. Only man, the greatest predator of all, walked about.

Lieutenant Bak, commanding officer of the Medjay police, stood in the sun at the southern end of the long, narrow mudbrick fortification of Kor. Scattered around him were thirty or more donkeys and the baskets and bundles they had carried across the burning desert. A company of spearmen, a few sitting on the collapsed walls of a nearby building, looked on with avid interest, whispering among themselves. Beyond and to the left, four masons repairing a fallen wall sneaked a curious glance each time their overseer's attention faltered.

Sweat trickled down Bak's sun-bronzed face, broad chest, and muscular back, puddled in the crook of his arms, stained his thigh-length white kilt from waist to hem. A fly buzzed around his thick, short-cropped black hair. The sweet scent of cut grain, the ranker odor of manure tickled his nostrils and made him sneeze. He had never in his twenty-four years been so hot. And he had seldom been so disgusted.

"For a single grain of wheat, Seneb, I'd place this load

1

on your back." With his baton of office he prodded several
heavy lengths of ebony bound together with leather cords.
"Then I'd take you into the desert and make you carry it
day after day as you did these poor beasts."

"For every one donkey you see now, I had two before."
Seneb's whine was as irritating as the wounded look he
affected. "Could I leave so many precious objects behind
when the officer at Semna took the other beasts from me?"

Bak's eyes shifted from the trader's round, fleshy face
and portly body to the pathetic creatures around them: donkeys so emaciated their ribs protruded and so travel weary
they could barely stand. All were galled from heavy, ill-
balanced loads and all had long, narrow open sores, the
marks of a whip. The wounds crawled with flies.

His eyes moved on to the children huddled together in
the narrow strip of shade beside the fortress wall. Five girls
and two boys, none over ten years of age, hollow-eyed,
half-starved, dusky skin caked with dirt, too weak and exhausted to show or even feel their terror. Bak had first seen
them tied together in a line like the donkeys had been. A
dark, hulking young Medjay policeman binding an ugly
lash wound on the tallest girl's back glanced up now and
then to give Seneb a look that promised murder. From the
faces of the ten or so soldiers helping tend the children and
animals, he was not alone in the feeling. Bak knew he had
only to walk away and the trader would meet with an unfortunate, no doubt fatal, accident. As much as the thought
appealed to him, he could not do so. His task was to serve
Maat, the goddess of right and order, not balance the scale
of justice as it suited him.

The scribe whose task it was to collect tolls had summoned Bak from the fortress-city of Buhen to the lesser
fortress of Kor. Of no strategic importance, with bleak, unpainted walls in a state of disrepair, Kor was a place of
shelter for troops marching through the area and for merchant caravans. As the river upstream was impassable to
navigation much of the year, ships docked here to off-load

trade goods coveted by the tribal kings living far to the south and to take on board the exotic and precious objects the traders received in return.

"Were the animals confiscated in Semna as unfit to travel as these?" Bak asked the trader. "Is that why you didn't report at Iken as you were supposed to?"

Sweat beaded on Seneb's face, reddened from the sun and the effort of justifying his actions. "I thought it best to come on while the creatures . . ." He clamped his mouth shut, realizing his mistake.

"While they still could walk?" Bak snapped. "Before they and those children died of starvation, thirst, exhaustion?"

Seneb's spine stiffened with indignation. "If anyone is to blame for their disreputable state, it's the inspecting officer at Iken. He looks upon me with hatred and would make any excuse to take what is mine. I dared not stop, though my heart bled for my servants, the children, and these weary beasts."

"I see no blood on your kilt, Seneb, only on your hands."

"You accuse me wrongly, sir. I've dealt out punishment, yes, but only when due and only in moderation."

Bak nudged with a toe the five whips lying on the sand by his feet, leather whips knotted at the end to hurt more. "These speak louder than you, Seneb. And when with kindness we steal the fear from the tongues of the children, they'll speak louder yet."

"You'd accept the word of those wretched savages over that of a respectable man of Kemet?"

Bak beckoned Psuro, the burly, pockmarked Medjay guarding Seneb's four servants, men as dark as Psuro but taller, reed-thin, naked, bought and paid for like the rest of the trader's possessions. Each man stood with his arms behind his back, wrists clamped together in wooden manacles.

"Shackle this swine." Bak eyed Seneb with contempt.

"He'll remain our prisoner until he stands before Commandant Thuty for judgment."

"You can't do this to me!" Seneb cried. "Who'll care for my merchandise, the fruits of my labor through the long months I spent upriver?"

Bak scowled at the contents of the baskets and bundles they had taken off the donkeys: long, heavy lengths of ebony; skins of the leopard and the long-haired monkey and other creatures he did not know; ostrich eggs and feathers; pottery jars filled with precious oils. Two wooden cages held live animals, a half-grown lion in one, three young baboons in another, all emaciated and panting from the heat.

"The donkeys will be cared for here," he said in a hard voice. "The wild creatures and children will go to Buhen for the care they need, and the rest will go into the treasury."

"You can't confiscate all I possess!"

"Take this cur and the others to Buhen, Psuro."

Seneb stretched himself to his greatest height. "I'll have your head for this, Lieutenant."

"Need I point out that my property and yours and that of every man of Kemet belongs in fact to the royal house?" Bak gave him a humorless smile. "I'll not be made to suffer for eliminating you as the middle man between the land of Kush and our sovereign, Maatkare Hatshepsut. You've misused what by right is hers."

Seneb's face paled.

Bak's head swiveled toward Psuro. "If by chance he falls overboard while you take them downriver, so be it." He spoke more for the Medjay's benefit than Seneb's, for by airing the thought, Psuro would be bound to see his charge safe in Buhen.

"No!" the trader cried. "I can't swim! No!"

Psuro shoved Seneb onto his knees and, with the speed of long practice, lashed his wrists within the manacles so tightly he whimpered. Bak caught a glint of satisfaction in the eyes of the five silent children.

He had no time to dwell on his own satisfaction. His Medjay sergeant, Imsiba, strode through the group of watching spearmen, eyed Seneb's animals, and muttered an oath in the tongue of his homeland. Then he spotted the children. The skin tightened across his dark face, he balled his hands into fists, veered toward the bound trader. Seneb saw him coming and cringed.

"No, Imsiba!" Bak lunged toward the sergeant, grabbed an arm bulging with rock-solid muscle. "It's the commandant's task to see him punished, not yours."

Imsiba stared at the trader with smoldering eyes. "I trust he'll not be lenient, my friend, for if he is . . ."

"Lenient?" Bak's laugh held no humor. "You've seen Thuty balance the scales of justice many times. He knows not the meaning of the word." He signaled Psuro to take the prisoners away. Not until the spearmen parted to let them by did he think it safe to release Imsiba's arm. "Now what brought you to Kor?"

The big Medjay tore his gaze from Seneb's back. "So angry was I that I forgot my purpose. The commandant has summoned you." His voice turned ominous. "You and Nebwa."

Bak glanced at the sun, well past midday, and groaned. "Nebwa crossed the river hours ago, Imsiba. I doubt he can stand by this time, let alone appear before Commandant Thuty."

"Tell him you couldn't find me. Say to him . . ." Troop Captain Nebwa teetered, spread his legs wide for balance, grinned across the rim of his chipped drinking bowl. "Say I went off into the desert, so disappointed was I that you and Imsiba, men closer to me than brothers, couldn't share my good fortune this day."

Laughter erupted from twenty or more men lounging on the shade-dappled sand among a grove of date palms. Their

burned and peeling skin identified them as spearmen in
Nebwa's infantry company not long back from desert patrol. The sweetish scent of date wine mingled with the rank
odor of their sweat.

"Nebwa!" Bak wanted to grab one of several thigh-high
pottery water jars leaning against the decaying mudbrick
dwelling behind them and pour every drop over his friend's
head. "Do you want the commandant to strip you of your
rank?"

Nebwa gave him a mournful look. "He has sons. Has
he never celebrated their birth?"

His sergeant, Ptahmose, came through the door of the
building, followed by a wrinkled old man carrying an unplugged jar of the pungent wine. Nebwa held out his bowl.
The short, swarthy sergeant, a balding man with hard,
stringy muscles, took in the scene at a glance and motioned
the old man back inside.

Bak was glad Ptahmose, at least, had imbibed with
greater caution. He reached for his friend's arm. "Come,
Nebwa."

The officer backed away and lifted his bowl high. "She's
my morning star, shining bright, the fairest of the fair." He
stopped, laughed. "She's not fair!" He pivoted, flinging
his arms wide. Wine sloshed from his bowl. "She's as dark
as night and as seductive!" He grabbed Imsiba, pulled him
close, and wrapped an arm around his shoulders. "A
woman of great worth who's just given me my firstborn
son."

Imsiba listed beneath the officer's weight. "The gods
have indeed smiled on you, Nebwa. But not for long, I fear,
if you don't soon report to Commandant Thuty."

Bak eyed the pair. Untidy, coarse-featured Nebwa, second in rank to the commandant of Buhen, was tall and
muscular, as sunburned as his men, about thirty years old.
And Imsiba, half a hand taller, a few years older, was as
dark as obsidian, as lithe and sleek as a lion. Bak thought
of the time not many months before when Nebwa had be-

lieved all Medjays of small worth and Imsiba had looked on the officer with contempt. To see them together as friends was usually a pleasure, but to see Nebwa so besotted robbed much of the joy from his heart.

"Imsiba knows of what he speaks," Ptahmose said. "The commandant is not a man of great patience."

Bak stood before his friend, gripped his shoulders, and shook him. "Do you want your son always to remember his birth as the day his father threw away all chance of reaching the rank of commandant?"

"I've no wish to disgrace myself," Nebwa mumbled.

"Then you must come with us. Now." Bak emphasized the final word with another shake.

Nebwa slipped away from the offending hands and raised his bowl to Ptahmose and the revelers. "Stay, my brothers, and enjoy yourselves. With luck, I'll be back before nightfall." He slugged down the rest of his wine, gave the bowl a last regretful look, and threw it into a clump of dusty, bedraggled weeds.

Ptahmose eyed his unsteady superior. "I'd better come along, too."

"I've no need for a wet nurse," Nebwa growled.

"We've a skiff to return to its owner." Ptahmose winked at Bak. "If I drop you on the quay and take it to the village by myself, you can report to the commandant that much sooner."

Bak caught Nebwa's arm and aimed him toward a small stand of acacias growing beside the river, a glistening stretch of water more than two hundred paces to the west, water they had to cross to reach Buhen. With the two sergeants close behind, they headed across a sun-drenched field covered with the golden stubble of cut grain.

Nebwa stumbled on an unbroken clod, laughed at himself and the world in general. "I've a son, my brothers, a son!" He raised his hands high and whooped, "I've a son!"

A flock of startled pigeons rose from the stubble, their wings whirring overhead. A man kneeling in a nearby field turned around to look, shading his eyes with a spray of green onions.

Nebwa began to hum, droning on and on with no discernible melody. A distant donkey brayed, a dog yipped. The remainder of the oasis, sheltered within a long arc of sandy hills, was silent and still, men and beasts alike escaping from the heat in shady groves and mudbrick houses. Except for a few isolated plots, the fields were bare of produce, the irrigation ditches dry, the weeds limp. Trees and bushes were clothed in dust and brittle with thirst. The sky overhead was white-hot, the lord Re a fiery ball sinking toward the horizon.

The near silence, the dormant land, even the erratic breeze carrying heat and dust from the desert wastes, gave Bak a sense of waiting, of anticipation. The river had begun to swell less than a week before, and he felt as if the land around him, this land of Wawat, had paused to rest before the floodwaters overflowed the earth to bring forth new life.

Regretting the need to tarnish his friend's glow, Bak stopped at the river's edge. The acacias clung to the rim of the steep, crumbling bank, their trunks leaning toward the broad expanse of water as if offering homage to Hapi, the god of the river. On the opposite shore and a short distance upstream, the great fortress of Buhen was barely visible in the haze, its stark white walls melting into the pale sandhills behind them.

A breath of air rustled through the dusty trees, winnowing the dying leaves from the living. Bits of yellow rained down on two sturdy wooden fishing skiffs beached on a strip of dark soil running along the water's edge. Nebwa's eyes lit up the moment he spotted the vessels.

"You owe me a race, Bak." He plunged down the bank, letting the loose dirt carry him to the prow of one of the boats. "Come, Ptahmose! Let's show these men from the north a thing or two about sailing, real sailing."

Bak muttered an oath. When voiced by a besotted Nebwa, the last two words sounded ominous indeed.

"I'll bet a month's ration of grain . . ." Nebwa leaned his weight against the skiff and, with a muffled grunt, shoved it hard toward the water. ". . . against a jar of good northern wine that Ptahmose and I will reach Buhen before you and Imsiba."

"The wager is too large for so simple a voyage," Bak said, nodding toward the haze-shrouded fortress. "The breeze will be dead astern all the way."

Nebwa, stifling a grin, shook his finger in mock disapproval. "No, no, my friend. You don't understand. We'll sail all the way south to the Belly of Stones before we cross the river. That's the way we did it last time, when you won, and that's the way we'll do it today."

Ptahmose laughed at what he took to be a joke. Imsiba spat out a few words in his own tongue.

Bak glared at the man below. "What of Commandant Thuty, Nebwa? Have you forgotten his summons?"

Nebwa gave the skiff another hard shove and it slid into the water. "Make speed, Ptahmose! Do you want me to sail without you?"

With a heartfelt curse, Bak leaped onto the crumbling slope and half slid, half ran to the bottom, setting off a miniature landslide. The two sergeants plunged down the bank a moment later. Bak splashed into the water a step or two ahead of them.

Nebwa, knee-deep in the river, pushing the skiff before him, glanced around and saw the trio coming after him. Laughing like a mischievous child, he hauled himself on board, grabbed the oars, and shoved the vessel into deeper water, well out of reach.

"I'm sailing to the Belly of Stones," he said, making it sound like a royal proclamation. "If you want a race, you can come with me. If not, I'll go alone."

Bak expelled a long, disgusted breath. He hated to admit defeat, especially at the hands of a man too besotted to think straight.

"I'll come!" Ptahmose called. He waded to Bak's side

and lowered his voice so Nebwa could not hear. "There's
no arguing with him when he's like this, as you well know.
I'll take care he doesn't fall overboard."

Bak knew from experience that Ptahmose was one of the
best sailors along this stretch of the river, and Nebwa, when
sober, was equally good. Only through luck had he and
Imsiba won the last race they had run.

"All right, Nebwa, you've a bet!" Bak softened his
voice, said to Ptahmose, "We'll stay as close as we can
should you run into trouble."

The sergeant nodded, waded into deeper water, and
swam toward Nebwa's boat. Bak splashed through the shallows to the skiff he and Imsiba had borrowed after leaving
Kor. The big Medjay was already launching the vessel.

"What folly!" Imsiba gave a mighty shove that sent the
craft into the water. "I'll consider myself a lucky man if I
survive this day without a dunking—or worse."

Bak scrambled on board and, as the vessel rocked beneath him, hurried aft to the rudder. "You should thank
the lord Amon you're not sailing with Nebwa. I, at least,
haven't addled my wits with wine."

"True. But he and Ptahmose know this river through all
the seasons, know its whims as the floodwaters rise. We
don't."

"Surely the path we'll take hasn't changed all that much
since last we raced. It was less than a month ago."

Imsiba, his expression grim, pulled himself aboard. "The
rising waters, I've heard, are already coming with great
force out of the Belly of Stones. The river is shifting the
earth beneath it and along the banks, changing the currents
to fit the new pattern of its bed. And already it's stealing
trees and animals and people from the lower-lying parcels
of land south of the Belly of Stones."

Bak glanced at the other skiff, saw it floating sideways
downstream, Nebwa and Ptahmose fumbling with a snarled
pair of ropes. "Without help, what will Ptahmose do if they

capsize? Is he a strong enough swimmer to save himself and Nebwa as well?''

"Few men would be so strong, my friend."

Imsiba tugged the halyard, drawing the upper yard up the mast. The heavy white linen spread to a rectangle but continued to droop, even when stretched to its fullest height and the yard snug against the masthead. Bak tucked the rudder under his arm and grabbed the oars to send the craft scooting away from the riverbank in hopes of finding a breeze farther out.

"I hope your wife has been frugal, Nebwa," he called. "If she's saved no grain through the months, she'll not soon forgive you this bet."

Nebwa made a rude gesture with his hand.

Bak's laugh rang out as a faint breath of air kissed his cheek. "We must not sail too far ahead, Imsiba, but I think it safe to take advantage of our lead. I'd not like to lose this bet."

Imsiba gave him a wry smile, then adjusted the braces to haul the sail around. The fabric fluttered and sagged in a desultory breeze, billowed out in a gust that sent the boat skimming over the water. Bak waved at the two men they were leaving behind and set the vessel on a southerly course.

The broad, deep river stretched out before them, its waters flowing a reddish brown tinted with green. Far ahead, blanketed in haze, lay the mouth of the Belly of Stones and the first of the multitude of islands, large and small, that made the river impossible to navigate except at the highest flood stage. Bak's duties had never taken him beyond the first island, and, as always, he longed to see the land farther south, a land both praised and cursed by soldiers, traders, and envoys of the queen.

Taking a quick glance backward, he saw Nebwa at the oars, pulling his skiff around, and Ptahmose raising the patched red sail. Farther downstream, the sun-struck river looked like burnished gold, flowing past the oasis to fade away in a tawny wasteland of sandhills and ridges. He adjusted his rear on a beam and rested his back on the hull, confident he and Imsiba were far enough ahead to win yet not too far away should their help be needed.

Squinting into the sun, he eyed the massive fortress of Buhen across the water. High white mudbrick walls, relieved at regular intervals by projecting towers, rose from stone terraces along the river. Atop the battlements, he could see the tiny figures of patrolling sentries. Moored alongside three stone quays, a sleek trading vessel and two squat cargo ships dwarfed the twelve or fifteen smaller skiffs tied up among them. Except for a few hardy trees and shrubs growing along the riverbank, the land around the fortress was barren of life, a sand-swept, desiccated waste pulsating in the heat.

Bak eyed the scene with a fondness which always surprised him. When first he had come, sent as punishment at the order of an angry queen, he had hated the city and his duties as a police officer. How fast he had changed.

The wind held, and they skimmed the water, covering the distance with remarkable speed. The red sail crept closer, narrowing the lead until the vessels were no more than ten paces apart. Bak began to worry. Soon they would have to turn across the stronger midstream current and swing around. Could Ptahmose do it with only a drunken Nebwa to help?

The walls of Kor, an hour's walk south of Buhen, emerged from the haze. Imsiba adjusted the sail while Bak leaned into the rudder, swinging the skiff across the current. Nebwa's craft made a tighter turn and drew up beside them on the downstream side. Red sail and white lost the breeze and fluttered out of control. Bak again grabbed the oars, saw Nebwa do the same in the other vessel. Imsiba tugged a rope to lower the upper yard. The sail ballooned with a snap, tilting the skiff half on its side, catapulting them off course. The hull slid across the water at a dangerous angle, showering them with spray.

"By the beard of Amon, Imsiba!" Bak threw himself against the upward side for ballast. "Do you want to turn us over?"

Muttering something in his native tongue, the Medjay let the yard drop. The vessel wallowed an instant, then leveled out. A glance passed between them, their thoughts meshed, and they laughed with uneasy relief. Bak's eyes darted toward the other craft, now scudding along ten paces ahead as steady and graceful as a great warship. The will to win, it appeared, had prompted Nebwa to shake off a good bit of the wine.

Bak's worry fled, swept away by the excitement of a real race and a firm resolve to reach Buhen first. He aimed the prow downstream and held the skiff steady in the current while Imsiba bundled away the collapsed sail. Ptahmose, more experienced and faster, had already taken up a second pair of oars and settled down to help Nebwa. Their vessel pulled away, setting a course for the western shore and the towering spur wall that projected from the southeast corner of Buhen.

Bak knew he and Imsiba would lose the race if they followed; they were too far behind. So he set a course for the end of the nearest quay, thinking the current farther from shore would carry them faster than Nebwa could travel.

Imsiba, settling himself on a beam, an oar in each hand, grinned. "You flirt with the gods, my friend."

"Our chance of winning is small, I know, but I'll not give up until I must."

"Do you ever?" Imsiba chuckled.

The current and hard, laborious rowing swept them down the river faster than Bak had dreamed possible. Nebwa's vessel lost much of its speed as it approached the shore and soon fell astern. Bak laughed aloud, confident their momentum and a final burst of effort would drive his skiff to the quay before the other craft touched the solid ground at the base of the spur wall.

Imsiba yelled. At the same time, Bak spotted a half-submerged palm tree dead ahead. His stomach knotted, and he shoved the rudder, trying to swing the skiff around. The prow smashed into the short, gnarled roots. The tree rolled, carrying the skiff with it. The masthead arced toward the water. Bak sucked in air and flung himself outward, thought he heard Imsiba's splash not far away. As the river closed around him and he sank to the cooler depths, he had a fleeting thought: Nebwa should have worried about him and Imsiba, not the other way around.

The current carried him downstream, rolling him head over heels. He staved off the urge to panic, willed his muscles into action, forced his arms and legs to move. When he regained control of his body, he looked up through the water, murky with silt, mottled by the sun. Above, he saw the dark silhouettes of the capsized skiff and the tree floating free beside it. And, caught in the tattered fronds, the shadow-figure of a man, arms and legs dangling from a motionless torso. *Imsiba*! he thought, not swimming, too still, probably knocked senseless when he was thrown from the skiff. He shot upward, fear for his friend driving him on.

The light strengthened; visibility improved. The figure, he saw, was not dark like Imsiba, but pale. Relief surged through him. An instant later the palm rolled and the light struck at a new angle. Bak stared. His limbs lost the will to move, but momentum carried him on, propelling him toward the body. It grew larger, closer, hanging over him like a nightmare creature from the netherworld. The face was puffy, unnaturally pallid. The head was thrown back; the mouth gaped round and red; the eyes were wide-open, staring, as if in the man's last moments he had seen or experienced some special kind of terror. Perhaps the terror of being lost in the river through eternity, with no earthly body for his ka, his eternal double, to return to.

Bak's wits fled. He twisted sideways to escape, sucked in a mouthful of water. He broke the surface within a hand's length of those wide-open eyes and mouth. The water roiled around him; the figure rocked. A pallid hand reached out to touch his shoulder. Coughing, gasping for air, he flung himself backward.

The river, closing over his head, brought him to his senses. He resurfaced, heard Imsiba call his name. Waving a response, he watched the palm drift past with its gruesome burden. Not a creature of the netherworld but a man, white and bloodless, bloated, lying facedown in the water. A victim of the river.

As Bak grabbed a frond to halt the tree's downstream journey, an image hovered in his thoughts just out of reach. He had seen something that was not quite right, something about the dead man. He eyed the lifeless back, but saw in his memory the wide terrified eyes and the gaping red mouth he had glimpsed from the depths. His sense of something amiss strengthened. Curious, troubled, he took a deep breath and, clinging to the tree, ducked below the surface of the water so he could see the face as he had seen it before.

The mouth was as wide-open as he remembered. But the red, which he had thought a swollen, distended tongue, was too perfect a circle and flat on the end. He reached out, touched it. It was hard, wood he thought, and embedded so deep a gentle nudge did not dislodge it. He stared, appalled. The object, whatever it was, had been stuffed into the dead man's mouth.

Chapter Two

"Careful!" Bak ducked away from the body dangling between Nebwa and Ptahmose, in the skiff above him. "We've no wish to fish him out again."

"We sped to your rescue fast enough," Nebwa said, winking at his sergeant. "We can surely hang on to your catch."

Bak ignored the gibe. The less said, the sooner Nebwa would stop his infernal crowing.

"Let's pull him in." Ptahmose adjusted his grip on the man's upper arm. "Now!"

The pair gave a mighty heave. The vessel rocked, sending Bak and Imsiba, who were clinging to the hull, bobbing up and down in the water. The body dropped into the skiff with a sodden thump and an expulsion of air that reeked of decay. Nebwa, Bak noticed with a secret smile, swallowed hard. Evidently the taste of palm wine did not mix well with the stench of death.

Nebwa managed a lopsided grin. "The next time you overturn your boat, I pray you'll find a trophy sweeter to the nostrils."

"Stop babbling and move him out of the way," Imsiba growled. "One more mouthful of water and the weight of the silt I've swallowed will sink me to the bottom."

Amid grunts and curses, Nebwa and Ptahmose manhandled the deadweight forward and seated the body high in

16

the prow. While they stared at the swollen, terror-filled face, Bak scrambled on board. He clung to the mast, which stood naked, the faded red sail crudely wrapped around the yards. The stench made him queasy, and he felt water-logged. Imsiba tumbled aboard to collapse on a beam. The effort of removing the sail from the capsized skiff and stuffing it in the hole so the boat could be towed had worn them out.

They had long since drifted past Buhen, but not until Bak looked back did he realize how far. The fortress was nothing more than an indistinct speck of white in the distance. "Commandant Thuty will not be pleased with us today," he said grimly.

Ptahmose, a veteran of many years who valued his lofty rank of senior sergeant, jerked his gaze from the body, hastily changed places with Bak, and began to shake out the sail. Imsiba scooted aft to the rudder.

Turning his thoughts to the more immediate problem, Bak knelt beside Nebwa. The slain man's face he could see with his eyes closed, but he had yet to get a good look at the swollen body. The skin was gray-white. Pale blotches and ragged tears marked flesh scraped by rocks or other obstacles. A foot with three toes and a missing finger marked the passage of hungry fish or some other carnivorous creature, perhaps a crocodile too young and small to hold on to its feast. Bak had seen worse, for the river was a cruel burial place, but the sight never failed to bring a prayer to his lips that he would die far away from its waters.

He aimed a questioning glance at Nebwa, who had served in Wawat for years and knew many of the men in the garrisons strung along the river. "Do you recognize him?"

"Never saw him before."

"Ptahmose?"

The sergeant, who was raising the upper yard, glanced again at the body. "No, sir," he said and turned away to adjust the braces.

Imsiba swung the skiff against the current. The sail rippled in the breeze, caught a stronger gust, and ballooned. The prow sliced through tiny wavelets, holding a course that would carry them to the quay.

Bak studied the lifeless man, picturing him as he had looked when alive and unhurt. The face had been well formed, as flawless as a statue of Maatkare Hatshepsut idealized by the sculptor to make her youthful. Dark eyes, dark regular brows, short red-brown hair curling as it dried in the sun. The body had been of the same perfection, with shoulders and waist and hips, even the height, so well proportioned they would fit a pattern drawn by a master artist. The thigh-length kilt was made of the finest linen and the belt was fastened at the navel by a bronze clasp tangled in the fabric. A ring of gold encircled one finger, its bezel broken and the stone, a scarab most likely, missing.

"A man of quality, from the look of him," Bak said. "A highborn officer?"

Nebwa reached for the hem of the kilt and rubbed the fabric between his fingers. "Maybe a merchant. Some of them, those who have ships above the Belly of Stones and trade with the tribesmen far to the south, have become men of wealth."

Bak rocked forward to take a closer look at the belt clasp. He could see a portion of an embossed design, the profile of a bearded man, a god. "He's no merchant, that I can promise you, but he might be an envoy of our sovereign."

"Wouldn't that make Thuty gnaw his fingernails!"

Curious, Bak untangled the fabric and tilted the clasp so they both could see. The twin-feathered crown of the lord Amon rose above the tiny profile. Framing either side were what looked like sheaves of grain but were actually clustered spears. The design represented the regiment of Amon, Bak's old regiment in the capital.

His eyes narrowed. "Impossible!"

"What is?" Nebwa demanded. "What's wrong?"

"Not long before I left Waset, a few of the officers, men

like me who joined the regiment of Amon soon after Menkheperre Tuthmose took command, began to wear this clasp as a symbol of pride in a military unit we helped rebuild. This man was not one of us.''

"Are you sure? His face is so deformed his own brother might have trouble recognizing him.''

"I left the regiment less than a year ago, Nebwa. I'm not likely to forget my fellow officers so soon." Bak's voice took on a hard edge. "Even if he joined after I left, he'd have no right to wear the clasp.''

He eyed the misshapen face and his anger ebbed. However the man had gotten the clasp, whether by theft or wager or trade, he had surely been repaid a hundredfold for his deceit.

Without allowing himself to think, Bak reached toward the slain man. The task he had to perform was necessary, but one he always dreaded. He pushed his thumb and forefinger into the corners of the cold, clammy mouth, caught hold of the wooden object he had initially thought a tongue, and tugged. The thing resisted and he lost his grip. Swallowing the bile rising in his throat, he shoved his fingers deeper, tugged harder. A wooden handle popped out and a bronze blade followed. The lifeless head dropped forward, chin on chest.

Bak's eyes darted from the gory weapon—a long, slim chisel—to the drooping head. As he realized what had happened, a chill crawled up his spine. The handle, a handsbreadth long and stained red, had filled the man's mouth. The narrow blade, half again as long as the handle, had been plunged deep into his throat. The flattened metal at the end, sharp and ragged from long use, had torn the flesh, making him bleed inside until he could no longer breathe.

Nebwa shuddered. "What kind of man could take another's life in so cruel a fashion?''

"One filled to overflowing with hate." Bak scooted closer to the body to examine the right wrist and the left. Neither showed the bruises or chafing of a rope. "Or so filled with anger he went mad.'' He ran his fingers through the damp, curling hair, but could find no lump.

"We'll soon reach the quay," Imsiba said. "Do you wish Ptahmose and me to off-load the body and see it reaches the house of death while you report to the commandant?"

"Off-load it, yes," Nebwa said, "but find somebody else to carry it away. We vowed to return these skiffs to Meru before nightfall, and that you must do."

Across the prow, Bak saw the northern quay close ahead, glimpsed a sailor relieving himself over the stern of a cargo vessel nestled alongside. Farther upstream, a short distance above the southernmost quay and well out in the current, lay the place where the skiff had struck the tree. His thoughts followed the current up the river to where it flowed out of the Belly of Stones. The man had come from there, he felt sure, but from how far away? How long in those waters could a body remain intact?

Ptahmose groaned. "I'd rather face Commandant Thuty than that old devil Meru. When he sees we've holed his skiff, his cries of woe will be heard all the way to Ma'am."

"All men have to dance to the music of an untuned lyre once in a while," Nebwa said.

Bak glanced toward the lord Re, hanging low on the western horizon, then weighed the commandant's summons against the need for information. "Imsiba and I will return the skiffs. We'll drop you two off at the quay and we'll sail on—with this man's body—to the place where the fishermen beach their boats. I've questions that can be answered only by men who earn their bread on the river."

Imsiba voiced the question in the other men's eyes. "Should you not first report to the commandant, my friend?"

"The days are very hot, Imsiba, and unkind to the dead. This body will soon lose its color and form unless it's dealt with in the house of death. I wish the fishermen to see it now, before any further change takes place."

*   *   *

"Well, Meru, what do you think?" Bak didn't know which was worse, the cloying scent of death, the reek of the grizzled fisherman hunkered on the opposite side of the body, or the rank odor of fish emanating from the half dozen skiffs beached along the shore.

Meru, his mouth puckered in thought, rocked back on his bony haunches and scratched the inside of his thigh. "He died at the hands of another, I'd say."

Imsiba shook his head as if unable to cope with so ridiculous a statement. Three younger fishermen, stark naked, smirked at each other over the nets they were spreading out to dry on rickety driftwood frames.

Bak, well acquainted with the games the villagers played, implored the lord Amon to give him patience. "Your years have given you wisdom, old man, but even I, in my youth, can see how he lost his life."

"Could've been . . ." Meru eyed the body; his torn fingernails worked their way toward his dirty, tattered loincloth. "Could've been thrown from a ship up by the Belly of Stones."

"Don't be an ass, Meru!" Imsiba nudged the old man's shoulder with a knee, not hard enough to tip him over but with enough force to remind him that he could end up sprawled facedown on the ground. "No ships have sailed beyond Buhen all week."

"Look at this man, Meru." Bak pointed to the blotches and tears on the waxen skin. "Read these marks on his body and tell me of his travels upriver."

The old man leaned over his spread knees, scratched a buttock, and studied the injuries. "Came through the Belly of Stones, as I see you've guessed."

"Surely not all the way," Bak objected. "Semna, the southernmost fortress, is several days' march from here. I've heard many crocodiles inhabit the waters between here and there."

"Crocodiles. Boulders to block his path. Trees and brush

to snag him. Quiet pools and backwaters he could float into with no way out." Meru shook his head. "Couldn't have been in the water long. A day and a night at most."

"Where did he come from, do you think?"

"Never gone far into the Belly of Stones, you understand, but from what I've heard from men who have . . ." The old man pursed his lips and drew his brows together, making a great pretense of reaching a conclusion. "Suppose he could've come from as far away as Iken. Water may be high enough now to carry him that far." His skeptical tone negated the words even as he spoke them. "Don't know. The river up there spits out what it swallows as often as not. And what it holds in its mouth, it gives as an offering to the lord Sobek." The crocodile god.

Bak stood up, satisfied Meru had told him all he could. The fortress-city of Iken, he had heard, was as large as Buhen, a trading center where men from all walks of life came together. A good place for a man pretending to be more than he was, or for one who took as his own what belonged to another.

"Do you have anything more to say for yourselves?" Commandant Thuty demanded.

"No, sir," Bak and Nebwa said together.

Thuty rested his elbows on the arms of his chair and scowled at them over pyramided fingers. He was a short man, and broad, with powerful muscles accented by the light and shadow playing on his body from a torch mounted in a wall bracket next to a closed door. His brows were heavy, his chin firm, and the hard set of his mouth had been known to make strong men quake in their sandals.

"You're men who should set an example for those who look to you for guidance. A good example." Thuty looked pointedly at Nebwa. "Neither excessive drunkenness . . ." His eyes swiveled toward Bak, standing beside his friend. ". . . nor foolhardy behavior that leads to the destruction of another's property will lead them along a path of right and order.''

''No, sir,'' his victims chorused.

The commandant frowned at each man in turn, letting the time stretch. To prevent himself from fidgeting, Bak concentrated on the items in the sparsely furnished, but cluttered reception room. Around the commandant's chair stood a half dozen three-legged stools and two low tables. A spear, bow and quiver, and shield lay against one wall; baskets overflowing with papyrus scrolls surrounded the chair; and toys, a few of them broken, were strewn across the floor. Each time Bak entered the room, he was dismayed by its disreputable appearance—and saddened by memories of the previous commandant's widow, who had made the room a haven of quiet elegance for her husband while still he lived.

At last Thuty spoke. ''I see no need to say more. You're men of mature years, old enough to recognize the error of your ways. Now sit down and tell me of the man you found.''

Relieved at getting off so lightly, Bak drew a stool close to a second door, which stood ajar to allow a breath of tepid air now and again to drift down a dark stairwell from the roof. Nebwa shoved the door fully open and rested a shoulder on the jamb. Bak described the way he had found the body and how it looked.

''A man of quality or a scoundrel.'' Thuty expelled a long, unhappy sigh, stood up, and crossed the littered floor to open the main door. Children's laughter and merry squeals sounded in the courtyard outside. A welcome breeze carrying the odors of onions and fish wafted through the room and up the stairwell. ''We must assume the former, I fear.''

Nebwa sneaked a wink at Bak. ''We mustn't risk neglecting a man whose father may have powers far greater than our own.''

''You're an admirable officer, Troop Captain,'' Thuty

said in a wry voice, "but I fear for your future if you don't soon learn respect for the political necessities."

"I've ordered the mortuary priest to do nothing for now," Bak said, cutting off any incautious reply Nebwa might make. "With luck, I'll learn the slain man's name before his condition is such that he must be buried."

"With luck," Nebwa said, "a courier will arrive in the night, bringing news from another fortress of a missing man."

Thuty strode to his chair and adjusted the thick pillow on the seat. As he sat down, a child's laughter turned to shrieks. The commandant's voice took on a sharp edge. "If I don't soon receive a message, his garrison commander will have much to account for."

"He was probably slain no more than a day ago." Bak had to raise his voice to be heard over the wailing child. "No competent officer would report him gone before making a thorough search."

"He may've been sent on a mission outside his garrison," Nebwa pointed out. "If so, he might not be missed for several days."

Bak shook his head. "Neither a desert tribesman nor a villager would leave a bronze chisel in his throat. Even if damaged beyond repair, they find ways to reuse the metal."

"Are you implying his life was taken by a man of Kemet inside the secure walls of a fortress?" Thuty leaned back in his chair, wove his fingers together atop his head, and eyed Bak with a slight smile. "You've not yet learned his name, Lieutenant. Don't you think it too soon to reach so unpleasant a conclusion?"

Bak gritted his teeth to keep himself silent. The guess was premature, he had to admit, but he could think of no other theory that made more sense. "I'll go to the scribal office building at first light tomorrow. If he came south from Kemet on board a ship, he'll have registered his purpose there on his way upstream. The scribes will surely remember him. His face and body were as well formed as those of a god.''

''And if he failed to make his presence known?'' Nebwa asked.

The wailing increased in pitch, betraying a temper tantrum. Thuty's mouth tightened. ''We must assume he slipped around Buhen on one of the desert tracks.''

Nebwa grimaced. The failure of the garrison patrols to prevent nomadic tribesmen from bypassing Buhen without paying the necessary tolls was a sore point with the commandant, one he brought up at every opportunity.

Bak, irritated as much by the child as by the verbal arrows, rose from his stool, crossed the room, and firmly closed the door, stifling the yowling to a whimper. ''If so, he's the scoundrel I took him for when first I saw the belt clasp, and we must worry more about what he's been doing upstream than whether or not he's a man of importance.''

Thuty eyed the door, or maybe Bak, with what might have been a smile of approval. ''Report to me, Lieutenant, as soon as you learn his name. If he was the soldier he appears to be, I must send a courier south to his commanding officer.'' He added, with obvious regret, ''If he was of noble birth, and his slayer remains unknown, I fear you must travel upriver to look into the matter.''

''Me, sir?'' Bak was surprised. Other than one journey to a distant gold mine, his duties had never taken him more than a couple hours' walk from Buhen.

Nebwa frowned. ''That man's death isn't Bak's responsibility! It falls on the shoulders of his garrison commander.''

Thuty laced his fingers across his stomach. ''Late yesterday I received a message from the capital giving me additional authority over the garrisons along the Belly of Stones.'' His eyes shifted to Bak. ''As this includes maintaining order, I've decided to entrust you with the resolution of all major offenses against the lady Maat that occur within my chain of command. Not four hours ago I sent word to that effect to the garrison commanders and the viceroy.''

Bak smiled, delighted with the news and flattered. The commandant had never before shown any special regard for him as a policeman or an officer. "I appreciate your confidence, sir.''

Thuty acknowledged his thanks with a nod.

Happiness gave way to caution and Bak's smile faded. "If I must go upriver, it should be soon. Searching for a man bent on escaping justice is like tracking a wild creature across the desert. The older the signs he's left behind, the fainter they become.''

"Too many questions remain unanswered to make the decision now. And I've another matter to discuss, one equally important if not more so.''

Bak felt deflated. Before he had entered the room, it had never occurred to him that he might be allowed to do more than learn the dead man's name and where he came from. Now that he knew he might have the responsibility of searching for the slayer, he longed to get on with it. What could be more important than balancing the scales of justice?

Thuty bade him and Nebwa be seated, settled back in his chair, and reached for a stemmed drinking bowl standing on the table near his elbow. "About two months ago, a courier came through Buhen on his way to Kemet. He carried a message from Amon-Psaro, a powerful tribal king from the land of Kush. Perhaps you know of him.''

Bak had heard the name but knew nothing of the man, whose sphere of influence lay far to the south, well beyond the Belly of Stones.

Nebwa grew thoughtful. "A man to be watched. One who has great influence over the other kings in that wretched land. I'd not like to face the army he could gather if ever he should find a reason to make war on the land of Kemet.''

"Nor would I," Thuty agreed. "We, with the other garrisons on the Belly of Stones, would be the first to face him. I doubt we'd have the strength to hold him back long enough for reinforcements to come to our aid.''

"Has a trader or someone else with business in the south committed an offense Amon-Psaro can't overlook?" Bak asked.

"Not at all." Thuty's smile came and went in an instant. "His firstborn son, a child of ten or eleven years and heir to the throne, suffers from an illness no physician has been able to cure. The courier carried a message to our sovereign, Maatkare Hatshepsut herself, asking that the lord Amon be sent to Kush to heal the boy.''

"I can well imagine the physicians who live in that vile place," Nebwa scoffed. "Little more than daubers of tainted mud, would be my guess.''

"Not a request lightly refused," Bak said.

Thuty nodded. "The lord Amon and the physicians traveling with him set sail as soon as they could. Almost a month ago.''

No wonder the commandant hopes to avoid the problem of the slain man! Bak thought. The god would pass through Buhen and travel up the Belly of Stones, and the responsibility for his safety and well-being would rest on Thuty's shoulders.

Thuty stretched out his legs, crossed his ankles, and sipped from his bowl. "Even then, couriers came and went, one after another. Because the fortress of Semna lies at the head of the Belly of Stones on the border of Wawat and Kush, it was selected as the meeting place. Ceremonial etiquette was established, and the numbers and ranks of those who would accompany each party were decided." He took another sip and set the bowl on the table beside him. "I chose the two of you to stand among them.''

A broad smile spread across Nebwa's face. "We're to travel to Semna with the god?''

All thought of the slain man fled. Bak's disappointment faded to a shadow, and he imagined himself joining the priestly retinue. Then memory of the body hanging over him in the water intruded. "When is the lord Amon expected, sir?"

"Two days, three at most."

Bak almost laughed aloud at the absurdity of the situation. The god and the dead man would most likely demand his attention at the same time. He could see no way of serving both.

Thuty settled deeper into his chair. "You, Nebwa, will provide the men who'll haul the god's barge out of the water and pull it upriver past the worst of the rapids in the Belly of Stones."

Nebwa's face fell at so menial a task.

"Your men will toil only as far as Iken," Thuty reassured him. "From there, each garrison commander will assign his own men to pull the vessel past his segment of rapids, while the river pilot at Iken will assume the responsibility for towing the barge up the navigable stretches of water." He paused for Nebwa's nod, then continued. "You've a second task of greater importance. You must select thirty of your best men. Your responsibility and theirs will be to guard the lord Amon with your lives. He's the greatest of the gods to us, but to the wild men of the desert he's a statue of gold and a temptation for those who seek easy wealth."

Bak was puzzled. "What am I to do if not provide guards?"

"You're to select ten of your Medjays. During the journey to Semna, they'll stand watch over the lord Amon with Nebwa's men. Once there, they'll serve as guards of honor to Amon-Psaro."

Bak's heart swelled with pride. To be given so exalted a task was an honor indeed.

"You'll stand at the head of your men . . ." Thuty's expression soured. ". . . provided you're not needed upriver to resolve that wretched man's death. If you must search for his slayer, your sergeant, Imsiba, will stand in your place.''

Bak bowed his head in acknowledgment, so torn by his own contradictory wishes he could think of nothing to say. He longed to go to Iken, or whatever fortress the slain man had come from, to prove himself worthy of Thuty's confidence. But he also yearned to travel with the lord Amon, to share his men's joy and honor as they served the god and the Kushite king. Could he somehow manage to do both?

Chapter Three

The sentry, tall and muscular with unruly red hair, rested a sweat-slick shoulder against the wall of the twin-towered gate behind him. He grinned at Bak. "You must've fouled the bellies of every scribe in Buhen, Lieutenant. How's this place going to go on without them?"

"Better, no doubt, than usual." Bak had to smile, though thus far the morning had been disappointing—and frustrating. Of all the scribes who had visited the house of death, not one had recognized the slain man. He had not registered in Buhen.

The sentry laughed. "Never saw so many sallow faces in my life."

His good humor attracted the curious eyes of twenty young, raw recruits marching in ragged pairs out of the passage through the base of the tower. A few slowed, others maintained their pace, stepping on the heels of those before them. Their sergeant barked an order, they re-formed. Marching at double time, they burst out of the broad strip of shade cast by the high citadel wall and hastened up the street in the blinding midmorning sunlight. Bak watched with sympathy, recalling his own experience as a recruit, until they disappeared through the massive desert-facing gate which pierced the outer fortification.

Homes and workshops of civilians who supported the garrison nudged the thoroughfare to the left and right. Un-

like the citadel, where the streets and lanes were straight
and orderly, the outer city was a jumble of cramped structures thrown together in a haphazard manner along narrow,
crooked lanes. Open patches of sand, walled animal paddocks, and encampments for transient soldiers filled the remainder of the vast rectangle.

"I fear you wait in vain, sir," the sentry said. "Nothing
less than a summons from the lord Amon himself could
bring Nofery out on so hot a day. She hides from the sun
as if she fears she'll melt."

"Her curiosity knows no bounds. She'll come."

The sentry laughed. "She might at that. But do you really expect her to recognize him? Those scribes didn't."

Bak's voice turned wry. "It wouldn't be the first time a
man neglected to register, yet visited a house of pleasure."

He offered a silent prayer to the lord Amon that such
would be the case. If not, he would have to cast his net in
ever-widening circles, racing against the time when the
priest in the house of death deemed it necessary to place
the body in a sandy grave or embalm it. With the heat so
great, the decision must soon be made.

A shrill, terrified bray drew Bak's eyes toward a cloud
of dust rising from the southwest corner of the fortress,
where the donkey paddocks lay. The drovers, he guessed,
were branding a new herd driven into Buhen the previous
day. Closer to hand, thin columns of smoke spiraled up
from the metalsmiths' workshops. The sharp smell of molten metal and white-hot fuel mingled with the faint, ever-
present odor of manure and the aromas of fish and onions
and cooking oil.

The soft crunch of sandals on grit drew his eyes to the
passage through the tower. The large white form within
grew more distinct and soon an obese old woman lumbered
out. Sweat dripped from her jowls, formed stained crescents
beneath the armholes of her long white sheath, and glued
the fabric to her back and into the cleft between her heavy,
sagging breasts.

She glared at Bak. "Can you never go about your duties in the early morning or in the evening, as civilized men do?"

"Would you've preferred, Nofery, that I pull you from your sleeping pallet?" His voice was stern, but his eyes twinkled with fondness.

She sniffed. "Little you care what suits me."

The sentry grinned from ear to ear. "Think you can show the scribblers how to hold their morning meal, my little ewe?"

With a coy smile, she patted the front of his kilt where it covered the joining of his legs. "You jest now at my expense, but you'll seek my favors quick enough when next you come to my place of business."

The sentry pushed himself against her as if it was she he visited instead of one of the young seductresses who earned their bread in her house of pleasure.

Laughing, Bak clapped the sentry on the shoulder, caught Nofery's arm, and drew her onto a path squeezed between the jumbled block of buildings and the sunken walkway at the base of the citadel wall. "You can seduce anyone you like when your time is your own, old woman, but now you have a task to perform for me alone."

He could see she liked the inference that she might still be able to lure a man into her bed, especially a strapping young ram like the sentry, but she jerked her arm from his and hid her pleasure in a scowl.

"I rue the day I agreed to be your spy," she said. "If I'd not been so free with my promises, I'd not be obliged to answer to your every beck and call."

She was walking so fast Bak had trouble keeping up with her. For one so put upon, she was wasting no time.

Bak watched Nofery with smarting eyes and a queasiness that always came upon him in the house of death. Hot, sticky air enveloped him like a cloak. The stench of decay, the sweet perfumes used for embalming, and the musty

odor of ceremonial incense assaulted his nostrils. Smoke
from a poorly made wick rose from an oil lamp, sending
tendrils of vapor drifting through the air like wraiths from
the netherworld. He had come to this place many times,
and the oppressive atmosphere never failed to make him
feel that he stood on the threshold of an eternity he was in
no way prepared to inhabit.

Nofery stood beside a thigh-high stone embalming table,
studying the naked body lying in the shallow trough carved
into its upper surface. If she had ever seen the dead man
before, the knowledge was hidden behind the perfume-
soaked square of linen she held over her nose and mouth.

"Do you recognize him?" Bak doubted she did; she had
been silent too long.

"The face, I think, is familiar, yes." Her eyes, narrow
and sly, slid toward him. "If you were to jog my memory,
perhaps with a small favor . . . "

He buried his surprise—and mistrust—in a frown. "This
isn't the market, old woman. You can't haggle with me
over this man's name as you would with a merchant over
the price of an onion."

"I've no wealth to speak of, and I'm no longer in the
prime of life," she said in a plaintive voice. "Yet I must
make my way alone in this hard, cruel land. Have you no
pity?"

Unmoved, he leaned against the empty table behind him
and crossed his arms over his chest. "Before a melon can
be eaten, the vine must be given water in sufficient quan-
tities to allow the fruit to mature."

The wrinkles deepened at the corners of Nofery's eyes,
hinting at a smile. "I saw this man alive and well. Four or
five months ago it was. He must've come and gone all in
one day, for I laid eyes on him only the one time."

She must really have seen him! Bak could barely believe
his good luck. "Go on," he said, keeping his face bland,
his voice level.

"My dwelling is small, but my business grows each

day,'' she said sadly. ''Those who come for beer must sit
on the laps of those who play games of chance. Those who
come for a quiet chat must shout to be heard through the
din. Those who . . .''

Bak tamped down his impatience with a game he usually
enjoyed and strode toward the door. The adjoining room
contained nothing but a basket of clean white linen frayed
at the edges and a few baked clay jars and pots. ''Come
along, old woman. If you've nothing to tell me, I'll find
someone else who has.''

She eyed him, measuring the strength of his will. He
returned her look, saying nothing, waiting.

Her mouth drooped, she let out a long, aggrieved sigh,
and turned back to the table. ''I went to the market that
day earlier than usual. I heard loud, angry curses so I, and
others like me, ran to see. A sailor—I'd never seen him
before nor have I seen him since—was beating his servant
with a staff. The child, a boy of mixed blood no more than
six or seven years of age, lay on the ground, his back, arms,
and face bruised and bleeding. Before those of us inclined
to do so could stop the beating, this officer . . .'' She nodded at the dead man. ''. . . burst through the crowd, tore
the staff from the sailor's hand, and flung it away. Then he
struck the sailor with his baton of office time and time again
until he fell senseless to the earth.''

Bak eyed her long and hard. ''I heard of no such incident.''

''Nor were you meant to, for when the officer knelt to
help the child, he and those of us who watched soon realized the gods had blessed the boy with neither speech nor
hearing. We stood back and allowed this officer, who himself looked like a god, to lift up the child with uncommon
tenderness and carry him to a warship moored at the quay.''

Bak nodded his understanding. A crude form of justice
had been carried out, and, in the eyes of those who witnessed it, the matter was closed. He walked to the table and
studied the grayish face of the man lying there. Would one

who had behaved in so noble a fashion shun the scribal offices, thinking himself too great a man to register? Would he wear a belt clasp for which he was in no way entitled? "Are you certain this is the same man?"

"He is. Ask any of the others who were in the market that morning, and they'll agree."

Bak's final doubt ebbed away, and he gave her a pleased smile. "You've done well, old woman, very well. Now did you ever learn his name and where he was going from here?"

Nofery's smile was no less sly than before. "I'm in great need of a more spacious house. I went to the chief steward, and my plea fell on deaf ears. Only the commandant carries greater weight, but he'll not listen to me alone."

"You tell me all you know about this man, old woman, and I'll convince Thuty of your merits, though that, I fear, will be no easy task."

With a triumphant smirk, she backed away from the table and sidled toward the door. "He boarded a warship carrying replacement troops for the fortresses along the Belly of Stones. I assume they, and he with them, disembarked at Kor and marched on south. How far I don't know."

Realizing she was trying to escape, Bak leaped across the room and caught her by the elbow. "You never learned his name, did you?"

"I wanted to!" She tugged her arm, trying to dislodge the fingers clamped around it. "I thought him a fine man and yearned to know him. But few people had seen him and those who had knew nothing of him."

Mocking himself for letting her trick him, Bak pushed her into the adjoining room. A priest kneeling beside the basket, examining the linen, looked up, startled. Beyond, through another door, an embalmer bent over the body of a young woman lying prone on an embalming table. The wife of an officer, she had died in childbirth during the night. Using a long slim tool inserted through the nose, the embalmer was scraping the soft matter from within the head. A deep bowl with its contents hidden from view contained, Bak assumed, either the body of the unborn child or the organs that had been withdrawn through the gaping slit in the left side of the dead woman's abdomen.

"You'll not go back on your word, will you?" Nofery asked, worried. "You asked only that I tell you all I know."

He wrapped an arm around her shoulders. "I'll go to the commandant for you as I promised. But not until the lord Amon has come and gone."

"Many men will wish to celebrate the god's visit," she pointed out.

"Thuty has too great a burden to listen now. He'd close his heart to your plea, and you'd be out of luck altogether."

Screwing her mouth into a pout, she shook off his arm, trudged ahead down a short passage, and shoved open the door to the courtyard. Hurrying past Imsiba, standing outside with the trader Seneb, the old woman strode to a mudbrick bench shaded by the sycamores and palms lining the high enclosure walls. She flopped down with a grunt that silenced a chirping sparrow and bent over a small fish pool to draw deep into her lungs the sweet scent of white lotus blossoms floating on the surface of the water. Bak smiled to himself. She was not so chagrined that she would return to her place of business before her curiosity was satisfied.

He shut the door behind him and, with the taste of death still on his tongue, eyed Seneb from head to toe. The pudgy trader's hands were tied behind his back; his kilt was rumpled and dirty. Though not a bruise or cut marked his body, his eyes were wary, frightened. It seemed unlikely that the slain man, one whose actions had been so noble they had even beguiled Nofery, would ever have crossed the path of this foul merchant. Yet the question had to be asked, for they had both come from upriver.

"Has this jackal told you of his journeys, Imsiba?"

The big Medjay hefted the long, heavy staff he carried. "With a bit of persuasion, yes."

Bak had little faith in words extracted by means of the cudgel, but in Seneb's case he could think of no more fitting way. "How long ago did he travel upstream?"

"Five months, he claims, as does the pass we found among his clothing."

"Nofery saw our man four or five months ago." Bak spoke with care, preferring the trader remain in ignorance of how little they knew of the slain man. "He failed to introduce himself before traveling south."

The Medjay nodded that he understood. If the man in the house of death had come through Buhen only four months ago, Seneb would already have been far to the south in the land of Kush. If five months, the trader might have crossed his path.

"I'll take this cur inside, and when I'm through, I'll return him to his cell." Bak took the staff from Imsiba's hand. "In the meantime, speak with Nofery. After you hear her tale, send her home. Then go find Hori and see what luck he's had this morning."

Hori was the police scribe. Bak had roused the boy at daybreak and sent him out with instructions to describe the dead man to all the garrison officers and sergeants. A thankless task, but a necessary one.

Imsiba nodded. "I'll find him."

Bak gripped the trader by the neck and aimed him toward the door.

"What is this place?" Seneb demanded. "Why bring me here?"

"Many years ago, when this wretched land of Wawat was ruled by a king not our own, it most likely was a dwelling of the living. Now . . ." Bak jerked the door open and shoved him over the threshold. "Now it houses the dead."

The cloying stench stopped Seneb as if he had run into a wall. "What're you going to do to me?"

Bak dug his fingers into his squirming prisoner's neck

and propelled him through the building to the room where
the unnamed body lay.

At the foot of the embalming table, Seneb dug in his
heels. "Why have you brought me here? What . . . ?" His
eyes landed on the slain man's face. He blinked once,
twice, leaned forward for a closer look. "Lieutenant
Puemre!" A smile touched his lips, spread; laughter bubbled from his mouth.

Bak was so startled he relaxed his grip on the trader's
neck. It took him a moment to realize he had been handed
the name, and even then he was too distracted by the odd
reaction to enjoy his unexpected success.

Seneb walked as if mesmerized alongside the table, staring at the damaged foot and hand, the blotches and tears
on the body. He stopped at the head, purred, "You swine."
And he spat on the dead man's face.

"Seneb!" Appalled, Bak lunged at the trader and
dragged him to the foot of the empty embalming table.
"Are you so low you'd violate a lifeless body?"

"I've harbored hatred in my heart for that man for five
long months," Seneb sneered. "What would you have me
do? Kneel by his side and offer words of forgiveness to his
ka?"

Bak glared at his prisoner, giving himself time to think.
Seneb's caravan had come down the river the same day the
body had. The two men could have met and clashed somewhere along the Belly of Stones. Yet if Seneb were responsible for the man's death, would he have reacted with
such surprise, such pleasure at seeing his enemy lifeless?

"What did this man, this Lieutenant Puemre, do to earn
such loathing?" he asked.

The trader's mouth twisted with malice. "He thought
himself above all mortal men, judging them for faults he
failed to see within himself."

"I want specifics, Seneb, not a bald, flat statement any
man could make. What did he do to you?"

"He . . ." The trader hesitated as if deciding what, if

anything, he should divulge. "He treated me with contempt."

Bak's mouth tightened. He raised the staff, placed the end under Seneb's chin, and forced his head high. The trader tried to step back, but the table behind him caught him just below his fleshy buttocks. Bak increased the pressure. Seneb's spine arced backward. He clung with bound hands to the rim of the trough. His eyes grew large, frightened.

With a contemptuous smile, Bak pulled the staff back until the trader could almost stand erect. "Will you now spit on me? Or will you tell me what I wish to know?"

Seneb, his eyes glued to the pole, tried to swallow. "As I made my way upriver, bound for the land of Kush, he took my pass from me, keeping it day after day for no good reason. He cared nothing for the time I wasted or the goods I had to trade for a mere pittance in order to feed myself and my servants, my donkeys. He'd have bled me until I had nothing left if I'd not finally gained the ear of the garrison commander."

Bak's thoughts leaped back to the previous morning at Kor and the trader's excuse for driving his caravan so long and hard without a stop. The memory brought a dangerous glint to his eyes. "This, then, was the inspecting officer you wished to avoid at Iken when you came back downriver?"

Seneb tried to nod, but the staff held his chin in place. "He was."

"You could've had no children with you at the time," Bak said, thinking of Nofery's story, "and your donkeys must've been fresh. What reason did he have for holding your pass?"

"He had none! I swear it!"

Bak raised the end of the staff a finger's breadth, drawing a fearful moan from the trader.

"My donkeys were laden with ordinary trade goods, I tell you. Pottery, tools, beads, linen. Nothing more, nothing less.'' Seneb's eyes darted in all directions but never once met those of his inquisitor. ''If that Medjay of yours had thought to bring my pass, you could've seen for yourself.''

Bak was well acquainted with the many and varied ways traders, soldiers, and even the royal envoys tried to slip objects through the frontier without paying the required tolls. False passes were not uncommon. He exerted pressure on the staff, forcing the trader so far back his eyes bulged.

''Alright!'' Sweat rolled from Seneb's forehead into his ears and hair. ''Four donkeys were found in the desert, tethered out of sight of the trail. Two carried fine weapons, the others wines from the best vineyards of northern Kemet. He accused me of hiding them—no doubt one of my servants whispered the thought in his ear, meaning to repay me for an imagined wrong—and he insisted I be punished with the cudgel as well as fined. But I knew nothing about them!'' His eyes darted toward Bak and away. ''I swear to the lord Amon, they weren't mine! Would I leave my beasts of burden with no food or water?''

Bak was sure that was exactly what Seneb had done, and Puemre had taken upon himself the task of righting a wrong, just as he had when he beat the sailor who struck the mute child. A man of high principles. Or was he? What of the belt clasp?

Bak eyed the trader with disdain. ''How did you convince the garrison commander to believe you over Lieutenant Puemre?''

''I saw no love between them,'' Seneb said in a sullen voice.

''And you'd already sacrificed . . . What? Half your investment? . . . by denying knowledge of the hidden animals and what they carried?''

Seneb clamped his mouth shut, refusing to admit or deny.

Bak jerked the pole from beneath the trader's chin, grabbed his arm, and swung him around to face the dead officer. ''Did you take this man's life, Seneb?''

"You accuse me of . . ." The trader stared with horrified eyes. "No!"

"Did you come upon him standing alone, somewhere along the river between Iken and Kor? Did you creep up behind him and knock him unconscious, giving him no chance to protect himself?"

"I didn't!" Seneb cried. "Ask my servants. Ask those wretched children I brought from the land of Kush. They'll all tell you. I never left the caravan. Not once."

"We'll ask them," Bak said grimly.

But will we get the truth from them? he wondered. They all hated the trader and no longer had reason to fear him. They would as readily lie now to see him punished as they would have lied to protect him while still he held the whip.

"Lieutenant Puemre, inspecting officer at Iken." Nofery savored each word as if the knowledge was more tasty than fine wine. "I can't imagine why none of the scribes remember him. He was so well-formed and manly."

Bak scooted his three-legged stool closer to the doorway to catch the afternoon breeze and took a sip from his chipped drinking bowl. The beer she had given him was not the best she had to offer, but it was exactly what he needed: thick enough to coat the tongue and pungent enough to chase away the scent of death.

"They never saw him." He took another sip, rolling the harsh liquid around his mouth. "I went again to the scribal offices after I left the house of death. They have no record of a Lieutenant Puemre bound for Iken or anywhere else upriver."

Nofery plopped down on a stool, which disappeared beneath the sagging flesh of her thighs. "Records have been known to disappear through careless filing."

He snorted. "You tell that to the chief scribe."

Tipping his stool back, he rested his head against the doorjamb and eyed the small, cramped room. Since he had come to Buhen he had grown accustomed to its faults and even felt at home within its walls, but he could well understand why she wanted better quarters. Stacks of amphorae and beer jars lined dirty, scarred walls. A table piled high with pottery drinking bowls, most in worse condition than the one he held, stood near the back wall, partly concealing a curtained door leading to a rear room. A dozen or so low three-legged stools were scattered about, one holding a precariously balanced pile of baked clay lamps. After the house of death, the mingled odors of sweat, stale beer, and burnt oil were almost pleasant.

"What a snake that trader is!" Nofery sneered. "To slay so noble an officer was an abomination."

Bak frowned into his nearly empty bowl. "I wish I could be as certain as you are."

Her eyes narrowed. "You doubt his guilt?"

"If you took a man's life, old woman, would you offer as witnesses to your innocence eleven people who despise you?"

Nofery shifted her huge rear, no longer comfortable with her certainty. "I'd like to believe the gods have given me greater wit than that."

Bak lifted a pottery beer jar from the floor between them and refilled their drinking bowls. All in all, he was content with his day, but he felt it a beginning rather than an end. He had found the answers he sought, yet he had more questions now than when he started. Those he felt sure could be answered in Iken. He yearned to go himself instead of sending a courier ahead, as Commandant Thuty wished. But, like the dregs swimming around in his bowl, he was trapped by circumstances.

Nofery broke the silence. "They say the lord Amon travels south to Semna to meet the Kushite king Amon-Psaro, and you're to go with him. You and Nebwa." She stared at the bowl in her hand. "Is this true?"

The abrupt change of subject, a studied indifference in her voice drew Bak upright. "You never cease to amaze me, old woman. I learned of our mission only last night."

"The tale is true then."

"Nebwa will go, yes." Sure she wanted something, he was wary of what it might be. "I may not."

He went on to explain the commandant's decision to make him responsible for all major offenses within Thuty's area of command. While he spoke, a pretty, tousle-headed young woman peeked around the curtain behind Nofery. Her eyes were heavy with sleep, her smile slow and lazy. Bak greeted her with an absentminded nod. He enjoyed the pleasures of the flesh as much as any man, but this was neither the time nor the place.

"So because Thuty chooses to wait," he said ruefully, "I'm sitting on top of a wall, wanting to leap in both directions yet unable to jump either way."

Nofery, grunting at the effort, bent over to pick up the beer jar. She splashed the liquid into his bowl and hers, chuckled. "If I know you, my fine young friend, you're already searching for a way to do both."

With a sardonic smile, he raised his hand to lick off the beer she had slopped over the rim of his bowl. The young woman at the curtain bared one small, shapely breast, fondled it, beckoned. He barely saw her. The old woman's words were like a herdsman's goad, urging him to move, not stand in place.

Nofery was as unaware of his thoughts as she was of the girl behind her. "If you do go upriver with the lord Amon, you'll be in Semna for some time, they say, serving the king himself."

Her tone again was too casual, jerking his thoughts from his own desires to hers. The journey upriver could have nothing to do with her wish to expand, he thought. Unless . . . "What do you want me to do, old woman? Walk through the villages around Semna, looking for a few dusky beauties for this place of business?"

Nofery's face lit up, she chortled. "Now that's an idea! Not one I'd thought of, but . . ." Her laughter dwindled, and she shook her head. "No, I'll speak with Nebwa later. He'll serve my purpose better."

Unable to hold Bak's attention, the girl shrugged her shoulders, stepped back, and let the curtain fall.

He was puzzled. What else could Nofery want? "If you've something to say, spit it out. Imsiba will soon come, and I'll have no more time for your endless demands."

She stared at her hands, lost in some secret memory that softened her heavy features and gave warmth to her mouth and eyes. "I once knew Amon-Psaro, many years ago."

"You, old woman?" Bak asked, incredulous.

"Barely more than a child, he was, yet more of a man than most I've bedded. He was strong and fierce and at the same time kind and gentle. A man above all others even then."

"How can you make such a claim? You've never traveled beyond Kor. You told me so yourself."

Her massive breast rose and fell in an exaggerated sigh. "More than twenty years ago, it was, in our capital city of Waset. He was a prince then, a hostage taken north to Kemet by the soldiers of Akheperenre Tuthmose after their victory over his father in the land of Kush."

Could she be telling the truth? Bak wondered. The war she referred to was the last the army of Kemet had fought in this wretched land. Male children of defeated kings, boys who might one day sit on the thrones of their fathers, were commonly taken to Waset to live in the royal house. Raised with the children of the highest men in the land, adopting their ways, making firm friendships, they more often than not returned to their homelands as staunch allies of the conquering nation.

Hearing voices in the lane outside, Bak tipped his stool back and peered through the door. Imsiba stood a dozen or so paces away, talking with a trio of spearmen. Bak swallowed his beer in a single gulp and stood up, ready to leave.

"As for me . . ." Nofery sneaked a glance in his direction, smirked. "I was young and beautiful then, desirable to many men. Amon-Psaro among them."

The smirk convinced him: she was trying to dupe him for the second time in one day. Giving her his most charming smile, he bent over and pinched her cheek. "You were never young and beautiful, Nofery."

She stared at him with an expression so forbidding he thought for a moment she would slap him. Then she started to laugh, great hearty guffaws that set in motion every roll of fat beneath her long white shift.

Bak, feeling a bit guilty for making fun of her, pulled her to her feet. "Come, old woman. Imsiba is outside. I trust he's spent much of the afternoon questioning those poor wretches Seneb brought from the south. If so, he's earned a reward. A jar of beer should suit him, the best you have."

"You want me to go to Iken." Imsiba's voice was flat, his expression disapproving.

Bak shoved aside a basket of crusty, fist-sized loaves of bread and sat down on the second step of the open stairway leading to the roof. Fine dust drifted aimlessly in a sliver of sunlight falling from above. "The commandant said 'send a courier,' and you're the man I've selected."

"What of Seneb? I've not yet finished questioning those who traveled with his caravan."

Bak had thought out exactly what he wanted, and he was not about to retreat before the Medjay's assault. "Am I not able to question them as well as you?"

Imsiba scowled at the world in general. Bak settled back on the stairs and glanced around his quarters with the unconscious satisfaction of one who had experienced life in a barracks. The room in which they sat was small and plain, with a hard-packed earthen floor and white plastered walls. One stool stood just inside the entrance, the other in a corner amid a clutter of rush baskets overflowing with scrolls, a writing pallet, paint and water pots, all the tools of Hori's trade. One rear door led to Bak's bedchamber, the second to the scribe's room. A large white dog with a broad muzzle and sagging ears sprawled between the two, his legs and bushy tail twitching in response to a dream.

Surrendering to the inevitable, Imsiba dropped onto the stool by the entrance, his back to the narrow, sun-baked lane. "What am I to do once I'm there? Or, more to the point, what are your special instructions over and above delivering the message of Lieutenant Puemre's slaying?"

Bak gave his friend a look of mock innocence. "You question my motives, Imsiba?"

"I know you too well, my friend, to look only on the surface of any task you give me that's out of the ordinary."

Bak plucked a loaf from the basket and, breaking into laughter, threw it at the Medjay, who caught it with ease—and a reluctant smile.

"One day I'll disappoint you, but not today." Sobering, Bak leaned forward, elbows on knees. "If the man who took Puemre's life has been caught, the matter is closed, and all I ask you to do is satisfy my curiosity. Who slew him in so foul a manner and why? For what reason did he fail to register here in Buhen? What story lies behind the belt clasp?"

Imsiba shook his head. "If the slayer has been caught, a message would've come to Commandant Thuty long before now, especially if Lieutenant Puemre was of noble birth."

"You'd think so, wouldn't you? Yet Thuty hasn't even been notified he's missing." Bak raised a cynical eyebrow. "Don't you think an officer's absence would've been noticed by this time?"

"Perhaps you make a mystery where none exists." The Medjay spoke with no conviction whatsoever.

"Go to Iken at first light tomorrow. Speak with the garrison commander and learn all you can. If he can offer no solution to Puemre's death, I must go at once. The slayer's trail is already two days old. By the time you return, three will have passed, and a fourth day will go by before I can get there."

"Are you not leaping too fast, my friend? Commandant Thuty has yet to decide what he wishes you to do."

"The slain man was an officer, Imsiba, and from all appearances a man of quality."

The Medjay muttered a curse in his own tongue. "This Lieutenant Puemre could not have been slain at a worse time. You should journey upstream with the rest of us, not spend your days in Iken, searching for carrion."

"I'm not sure when the lord Amon will arrive in Buhen or how long it'll take him to reach Iken. I'd wager six or seven days, maybe more." Bak's mouth tightened to a thin, stubborn line. "I hope to lay my hands on Puemre's slayer long before that."

Imsiba looked doubtful. "I yearn to believe you can, my friend."

"Thanks to Commandant Thuty, I feel like a man who's been offered two plump pigeons but given no opportunity to eat either of them." Bak's voice turned grim. "I may fail in the attempt, but I intend to try for both."

Chapter Four

Commandant Thuty strode through the door of the room he used as an office. Speculation as to the reason for his summons faded to silence. The dozen officers scattered among the four red columns that supported the ceiling stepped back to make a path to the armchair standing empty against the rear wall.

Nebwa leaned close to Bak and murmured, "Where's Imsiba?"

"I sent him to Iken." Bak kept his voice equally muted. "He left at first light and should be back before nightfall."

"You sly jackal." Nebwa grinned. "What'd you tell him to do? Whisper your praise in the garrison commander's ears?"

Bak snorted. "Questions, Nebwa, not praise." His eyes strayed toward the commandant and an anger born of frustration seeped into his voice. "If I'm to resolve Puemre's death, I've no great desire to report to Iken blinded by ignorance."

Thuty shifted his chair from the wall to stand behind it with his hands resting on its back. "A courier arrived from the north no more than an hour ago," he announced. "If the breeze remains fair, the lord Amon will reach Buhen by midafternoon today."

Murmurs of anticipation, excitement rippled through the room. Even Bak, who had grown to manhood only a half hour's walk from the god's mansion in the capital, was not immune. His joy was soon marred by regret, followed quickly by dismay. Imsiba would not be back in time to watch the holy procession. And the god's arrival at so early a date shrank the number of days that would pass before Amon reached Iken to only four or five. Could he hope to search out Puemre's slayer in so short a time?

Thuty raised a hand for silence. "I assume each of you has told your men what I expect of them when the sacred barge docks at the quay?"

"Yes, sir," the officers chorused.

"I've seldom seen so many kilts and shields drying in the sun," Nebwa muttered. "The rooftops are as littered as the desert verge when an army long away from water rushes to the river for a swim."

Another officer laughed softly. "My men have polished their spearpoints so much they've lost their edge."

Bak's smile was automatic, his thoughts wandering. Since taking command of the Medjay police, he had snared three men who had taken the lives of others. Two had been easy to catch, the slaying done in anger and the slayer too paralyzed by his offense against the lady Maat to cover his tracks. The third death, that of Thuty's predecessor, had taken weeks to resolve. If Puemre's slayer had not yet been caught, such would probably be the case here as well.

Thuty's voice, as hard as granite, broke into his thoughts. "Our sovereign, Maatkare Hatshepsut, thinks of those of us who occupy the garrisons here in Wawat as little more than caretakers of the precious objects passing through on their way to the royal treasury. The chief prophet holds us in no higher esteem." His eyes darted from one face to another. "I can't impress upon you enough how important it is to welcome the lord Amon and his retinue in a manner befitting his exalted status among the gods. Do I make myself clear?"

The officers, Bak among them, spoke as one. "Yes, sir." The chorus was ragged this time, marred by surprise at

Thuty's frankness. The queen's neglect of the army was a constant irritation, a source of many whispers, seldom aired in public. She held the reins of power. For how long, though, was anyone's guess. Her nephew and stepson, Menkheperre Tuthmose, had inherited the crown from his father while still a small child. Hatshepsut, not content to serve as regent, had placed herself on the throne. Many believed the heir, now sixteen years of age, should assume his rightful place above her. He kept his plans to himself, but had several years before begun to rebuild the army into a capable and loyal fighting force.

Thuty eyed his officers at length as if to be sure they understood, then took his seat to discuss the disposition of the garrison troops during the lord Amon's stay in Buhen.

Bak refused to give in to a sense of hopelessness that threatened to overwhelm him. The odds might be against his snaring Puemre's slayer in time to journey upriver with the god, but he vowed to try. Since the only avenue of investigation open to him at the moment was Seneb and those unfortunate children the trader had brought from the south, he would begin with them.

A door slammed at the far end of the old guardhouse, followed by the thud of a heavy wooden bar dropping into place, locking the prisoner inside his cell.

"Spawn of a snake!" Bak snarled at the tiny, barren room in which he sat.

Few men disgusted him as Seneb did, but the more he saw of the trader, the more convinced he was that the man was as innocent of Puemre's death as he was guilty of an endless cruelty to all the creatures he had bought and sold through the years.

Somewhere in the building, Bak heard men's laughter and the clatter of spears. The scent of lentils and onions wafting from the roof vied with the rancid odor of vomit given off by a baker who had passed out in the next room. Midday had barely come and gone, the lord Amon was not expected for another two or three hours, and already the revelers had begun to fall.

Bak rose abruptly from his stool, sending it skittering across the hard-packed earthen floor, crossed the room, and opened a warped wooden door. Its squeak attracted seven pairs of dark, suspicious eyes. The children taken from Seneb's caravan sat in a rough semicircle on the bare floor. Their bodies were clean, their woolly hair trimmed, their wounds bandaged. The stocky Medjay seated in front of them was so intent on his halting attempt to speak their tongue it took him a moment to notice his officer.

"Have they talked yet, Psuro?" Bak asked.

"Not a word." The Medjay scowled. "Each time I leave the room they chatter like birds, so fast I don't understand a word. Each time I come back they seal their lips as if with glue."

Bak was not surprised. The air around the children reeked of mistrust. He studied them one by one, searching for a chink in their wall of silence. Every face was closed to him, every small body stiff with apprehension. Then he noticed the tattoo between the oldest girl's eyebrows, a rough triangle supporting a tiny white crescent. The head of a horned bull, a god of Kush. The child had lived in a pious household. Had she learned respect for gods other than her own?

Praying she had, he asked Psuro, "Have these children heard that the lord Amon will come today to Buhen?"

The Medjay shrugged. "I doubt it, sir. Not one among them speaks our tongue."

Bak nodded, satisfied. "Tell them of his visit. Stress his greatness, his warmth and kindness, his generosity toward those who worship the gods of other lands." He spoke in fits and starts, thinking out a strategy as he went along. "Tell them that soon they'll be sent to our capital city of Waset, where they'll serve the priests who walk the halls of the god's greatest mansion. Then speak no more of the god, but go back to your questions.''

His spirits rose as the plan took form. ''In the meantime, I'll go find Hori and send him to you. Together you must take these children to the top of the fortress wall so they can see the lord Amon for themselves. Perhaps the god, with Hori's youth and good humor to help, will loosen their tongues where we cannot.''

Bak walked across the audience hall, the most spacious room in the commandant's residence with a high ceiling supported by a forest of red octagonal columns. Hori had just rushed off to the guardhouse, as excited by the prospect of playing policeman for a few hours as he was of watching the lord Amon's arrival from atop the wall. *If nothing else*, Bak thought with a rueful smile, *I've made one person happy today.*

The hall and the rooms around it buzzed with life. A youthful scribe stood in front of Thuty's office, explaining to a grizzled sergeant the need for exact records of disbursements rather than rough guesses. Seated on a bench built against the wall, a potter, his hands and arms flecked with dry clay, listened to a stout, balding scribe extolling the virtues of the slim decorated vases from the land of Keftiu, which he wished copied. Near the exit, a young archer dictated a letter to the public scribe, a tired looking man of middle years.

Bak was surprised at the number of people still going about their duties. Although the lord Amon was not expected for another hour or more, the general populace had begun soon after midday to stream out the towered gates leading to the waterfront and the quays. The Medjays and the spearmen Nebwa had lent to help them had already broken up three fights and confined a half dozen belligerent drunks and a couple of petty thieves.

Nodding to the scribe, he crossed the threshold to a long, narrow corridor. The walls had been painted yellow in a

futile attempt to brighten the dimly lit space. A la
figure came hurrying toward him.

"Imsiba!" Bak clasped the Medjay's shoulders as if he
had been gone a month instead of a few hours. "I feared
you'd miss the lord Amon's arrival!" He barely paused for
breath. "How did you get back so soon? What happened
at Iken?"

A wizened old man limped through the audience-hall
door. Bak and Imsiba retreated to the base of a stairway
rising to the commandant's quarters on the second floor.
Light filtered down the steps from the open courtyard
above. Pale dust, streaked by sweat, mottled the big Medjay
from head to toe.

"Well?" Bak demanded.

With a weary smile, Imsiba slumped onto the bottom
step. "The commander of Iken, Woser is his name, saw
me without delay. I knew how eager you'd be for my report, so I stopped only at the barracks for a bite to eat and
the local gossip."

"Have they caught the man who slew Puemre?" Bak
prodded.

The Medjay's smile faded. "Not yet."

"Then I'm to go to Iken."

"Commander Woser thinks your time will be better
spent getting the truth from that vile trader Seneb."

Bak's eyes narrowed. "Did you not tell him my doubts
on that score?"

"I did."

A childish giggle sounded at the top of the stairs. A dark-
eyed girl no more than two years of age stood naked above
them, sucking her thumb, staring.

"Let's leave this place, Imsiba, before all Thuty's children descend on us." Bak eyed his friend critically. "We'll
go to the river, where you can have a bath before the sacred
barge arrives."

In the street outside the building, Bak asked, "While we

waste our time with Seneb, how will Commander Woser spend his time?''

"His officers will look into the matter. He believes they'll have no trouble learning the name of the slayer.''

"If Woser's so confident . . .'' Bak paused; his eyes darted toward Imsiba. "Do you think he's guessed who took Puemre's life and has only to act on the knowledge?''

"I doubt he suspects any one man. Lieutenant Puemre, at the time of his death, led an infantry company. But five months ago when first he reported to Iken, he was an inspecting officer—as that swine Seneb told us. He held the task for only a month. His harsh measures made him many enemies among those who seek to evade the tolls or profit at the expense of their fellowmen.''

Bak muttered an oath. If the slayer proved to be a trader, he might not be snared for months—if at all.

They headed toward the twin-towered gate which straddled the far end of the street and opened onto the quay. The sun god Re, hovering above the rim of the fortress wall behind them, bathed the battlements and towers ahead in a light so bright it hurt their eyes. The thoroughfare was nearly deserted. Only a few stragglers—a woman with a tiny baby, a couple of soldiers, a scribe—rushed toward the gate and the crowd outside. A priest, white-robed and shaven bald, hurried toward the mansion of the garrison god, Horus of Buhen, which dominated the city from a high mound at the corner of the citadel.

"So that's the end of it, my friend.'' A smile played on Imsiba's face. "The problem is no longer yours, and you can journey to Semna with the lord Amon, as is right and proper.''

Bak scooped a rough, fist-sized chunk of milky white limestone from the edge of the street. "Woser doesn't want help, that's plain enough.''

"He's served in Wawat for years; he knows this land and its people far better than you and I.'' Imsiba waved at a soldier peering over the edge of a rooftop. "He's confident he'll lay hands on the slayer sooner or later, and so he'll tell Commandant Thuty in the report he's no doubt preparing even now.''

Woser's reasoning appeared sound enough, Bak had to admit. Yet many men spoke with confidence; more than a few failed. "What of Puemre's belt clasp, Imsiba?''

"The lieutenant came to Wawat from the regiment of Amon.'' The Medjay gave Bak the dour look of one who knew very well he was feeding a fire he had hoped to quench. "Commander Woser told me so himself. How long he'd been with your regiment, he didn't say.''

"It couldn't have been more than a few weeks. I left ten months ago. Take away the five months he's been here, and the time it takes to journey up the river from Waset . . .'' Bak's voice tailed off, he shook his head in disgust. "No wonder Woser assigned him first as an inspecting officer!''

"He probably trained in another regiment. From what I was told in the barracks by those who fought beside him in this foul land, he was skilled in the arts of war and faced the enemy without fear.''

"Nonetheless . . .'' Bak, reaching the only possible conclusion, grimaced. "How lofty a position does his father hold in the land of Kemet?''

A wry smile touched Imsiba's face. "I was told only that his name is Nihisy, but much was made of Lieutenant Puemre's courage and his willingness to befriend his men though he was of noble birth.''

"Nihisy.'' Bak spread his hands wide, shrugged. "The name means nothing to me, but if he's a nobleman . . .'' He had no need to say more. Woser's report would have to be very persuasive to prevent Thuty from sending Bak to Iken.

He twisted the chunk of rock between his fingers, making its many small crystals glitter in the sun. Puemre, he thought, must have been a lot like the stone, never showing the same face twice. Nofery had admired him, and Seneb hated him even in death. He had proven himself worthy to his fighting men, not an easy thing to do, yet he had worn a belt clasp to which he had no right, and he had most likely attained his rank through his father's influence.

"When was Puemre first discovered missing?"

"His sergeant, Minnakht, reported him gone the morning of the afternoon we found him."

Bak was accustomed to the oblique way Imsiba sometimes spoke, but as always he had to struggle to make sense of the words. "Two days before you told Woser we'd found the body. Two whole days, and he didn't send a message to Thuty. How did he explain that?"

"He offered no reason, nor was it my place to ask." Imsiba gave Bak the same dour look as before. "Can you not close your eyes to such a small lapse? You'd be much happier leading me and our men in Amon-Psaro's guard of honor than spending day after day in Iken."

Refusing to admit, even to himself, how tempted he was to heed Imsiba's plea, Bak drew the Medjay off the paved street at the rear of the guardhouse. The sandy plot was cluttered with building materials: drying bricks, wood of varying lengths, a few stone slabs.

He dropped the rock, brushed his hands together to remove the dust, and sat down on a stack of wood. "If Woser neglected to report the absence of a nobleman, what else will he fail to do?"

"The men of the garrison think him a worthy and honorable man. He'll do what he must."

"Will he?"

Imsiba's brow furrowed with disappointment. "If not for you, my friend, I and all our men would still be looked upon with suspicion, as we were when first we came to Buhen. Now that a time has come when we're to be given a place of honor, you must stand at our head, for without you there, our triumph will be hollow."

Bak felt as if he was being torn in two. "Don't you know how much I want to go with you, Imsiba? But I want also to do my duty. And if it takes me to Iken, I must go."

Imsiba shifted from one foot to another, uncomfortable with the decision.

Bak rose from the woodpile and forced a smile. "I can promise you one thing, my brother: I'll do all in my power to resolve this death as fast as I can. With luck, the lord Amon will smile on me, and I'll be free by the time he reaches Iken." He clapped his friend on the shoulder. "Now, go find a place for a swim."

Imsiba gave him a halfhearted smile and hurried down the street to the fortress gate. Bak picked up the chunk of stone, swung around, and hurled it as hard as he could at the mudbrick retaining wall that supported the mound on which the mansion of Horus stood. A puff of dust erupted from the slight hollow it made. Given enough time and a sufficient number of rocks, he could lay bare the temple foundations. He prayed he could gather enough pebbles of information to reveal Puemre's slayer in time to go upriver, as he had promised Imsiba.

Bak stood with his fellow officers on the stone terrace facing the river. His eyes, like those of every man, woman, and child of Buhen, were locked on the sacred barge of the lord Amon, moored at the quay projecting into the water from the pylon gate leading into the mansion of Horus of Buhen. The long, slender hull, the canopied dais rising amidship, and the sacred barque within, all sheathed in gold, glittered in the harsh midafternoon sunlight. The slim and elegant image of a man, the lord Amon, formed of solid gold, as tall as Bak's arm from elbow to fist, stood in a golden shrine atop the barque. As the white-robed priests on board performed their ministrations, the vessel rocked gently on the water; the bright painted ram's heads carved on prow and stern rose and fell in tandem.

Bak closed his eyes and waited for the glowing reflection to fade from inside his lids. Having lived as a youth in the capital, he had seen the enshrined god many times. The sight never ceased to move him, but he no longer felt the single-minded awe of men and women who had never before set eyes on the greatest of all the gods.

With his vision returned to normal, he scanned the river, the crowded quays and waterfront, searching for his men and for possible sources of disruption. Sailors on the warship that had towed the barge upriver were mooring the much larger, heavier craft on the opposite side of the quay. The flotilla of small boats which had sailed out to meet the god trickled back toward shore. A second warship swung around farther out on the water, preparing to dock. The deep beat of the drum that gave rhythm to the oarsmen could now and then be heard above the excited babble of the onlookers. The Medjay police, their spearpoints gleaming in the brilliant light, walked among the crowd to give aid where needed or prevent trouble.

Satisfied all was well, he once again turned his attention to the quay. Commandant Thuty, the priest of Horus of Buhen, and three brightly garbed native princes stood alongside the barge, waiting to greet the lord Amon and his entourage. All wore broad multicolored bead collars, wrist- and armbands of gold or bronze, rings set with bright stones. All but the priest carried spotless new shields, and the shine of their weapons vied with the sun. A dozen soldiers and scribes, shaven and purified to assist the god and his priestly representatives, waited with them.

Red banners, suspended high above the pylon from tall wooden flagstaffs, rustled in a fitful breeze. Bak prayed a tiny puff of air would sneak down from above to cool the sweltering terrace and blow away the smell of too many bodies pressed too close together.

"Swine!" An angry shout from the terrace below.

"Hey! Whattaya think you're doing?" someone else yelled.

Bak leaned over the waist-high wall in front of him. Five small boys, holding hands to form a snake, were weaving a path through the masses of people. The crowd was too thick for such pranks, the terrace too congested. He pursed his lips and whistled a signal. A patrolling Medjay came running. Within moments, the snake was torn apart, the boys reprimanded, the adults pacified.

When he looked back at the sacred barge, the chief priest, wearing a fine white linen robe and decked out in a golden pectoral and bracelets, waved his censer a final time. Lesser priests lifted the gilded barque, a miniature version of the barge, off the dais. Raising the carrying poles to their shoulders, they followed the chief priest down the gangplank, carefully balancing the barque and its precious cargo high above their heads. The moment their feet touched the quay, shouts of joy burst from the onlookers, all jostling for a better view. The words blended into a roar so loud a flock of pigeons took to the air, drawing Bak's eye to the battlements. He smiled. Psuro and Hori and seven wide-eyed children were standing atop the nearest tower, staring down at the god, entranced.

The chief priest, followed by the priest of Horus of Buhen and the commandant, and then the local princes led the procession along the quay. Behind them, two priests purified the lord Amon's path with incense and libation; others shaded his shrine with ostrich-plume fans. Those men borrowed from Buhen carried gilded chests containing ritual equipment and the god's clothing and bright-painted standards symbolizing Amon and Horus and the other gods important to Wawat. As they came closer, Bak could see their mouths move, but their chanting was lost in the clamor and shouting of fervent worshipers. He found himself shouting along with them, felt his breast swell with wonder and adoration.

The procession neared the pylon. Incense wafted through the air. Bak leaned far out over the wall so he could see around his fellow officers. The chief priest waved his censer at the people on the opposite side of the quay, turned, waved it toward Bak and those standing with him. The acrid smoke drifted around the thin, wrinkled face of the priest. Bak's mouth dropped open and he almost lost his grip on the wall. The chief priest was a man he had known all his life, the physician Kenamon, teacher and friend of his father, who was also a physician.

Kenamon disappeared behind Bak's compatriots. The barque of the lord Amon seemed for a few moments to sail above their heads, then vanished through the pylon gate.

Kenamon, Bak thought, a man who had treated the ills of many who walked the halls of the royal house. If Puemre's father was a nobleman, Kenamon would know him.

"My son." Kenamon clasped Bak's shoulders with long, bony fingers. "My heart is filled with joy to see you again. It's been . . . How long?"

Bak gave the priest a broad, warm smile. "Less than a year. Have you forgotten so soon, my uncle, the night I took leave of my senses in Tenethat's house of pleasure?"

The old man, so small and frail he looked as if the faintest breeze would blow him away, chuckled. "Ah, yes, the night you drew attention to the less than honest behavior of certain of our sovereign's favorites."

His eyes grew wide in exaggerated alarm. He clapped a hand to his mouth and peered around as if searching for an eavesdropper lurking in the long evening shadows of the fluted columns which surrounded the forecourt of the mansion of Horus of Buhen. Then they laughed together, the old man with mischievous eyes, the younger with delight. Kenamon's exalted position as the chief prophet's envoy had neither restored his respect for authority nor stolen his sense of the ridiculous.

With their laughter waning, the old priest drew Bak into the broad rectangle of shade cast by the god's mansion. The large painted reliefs of Horus and the queen striding across the facade made his white-robed form appear smaller than ever.

He studied Bak from head to toe and nodded his approval. "Your exile appears to have done you no harm.

You stand as straight and tall as before, with no lack of confidence, and I hear you have your rank back. Yes, I'd say your father has every reason to be proud of you.''

"How is my father?" Bak asked.

"Well and happy, though he longs for your return to the capital.''

Kenamon went on, speaking at length of the news for which Bak hungered. He could have chatted forever if not for the problem of Puemre.

"You know, of course, that I stand at the head of the Medjay police here in Buhen.''

"Yes." Kenamon smiled his pleasure. "The viceroy told me Commandant Thuty named you and your men to serve as Amon-Psaro's guard of honor.''

"It was a great privilege to be chosen, but . . ." He went on to explain the commandant's expanded authority and his own, the finding of a dead man, and his determination to resolve the death quickly so he could travel upstream with the sacred image. At the end, he gave the old priest a fond smile. "Now that I know you're the physician traveling with the lord Amon, I'll look upon the healing of the prince with greater confidence.''

Kenamon's voice grew stern. "When I tend the ill or injured, my son, I'm but an instrument in the god's hands. The fate of this boy, like all I've treated before and all I'll treat after, will rest with the lord Amon alone.''

Bak felt the blood rush to his cheeks. "I understand, sir, but I've noticed through the years that the lord Amon smiles more often on you and those you visit than on those cared for by some of the other physicians.''

"You're as impertinent as your father!''

Bak thought he spotted a twinkle in the old man's eyes, but decided it best he change the subject. "You must forgive me, my uncle, but I've come not only to learn of my father and renew our friendship, but to ask a favor of you, one related to this man I found in the river.''

Kenamon's eyes sharpened with interest. "You intrigue me, my son. What do you wish of me?"

"He was a lieutenant called Puemre, assigned to the fortress of Iken. His father is probably a nobleman whose name is . . ."

Kenamon caught Bak's arm. "Not Nihisy, I pray."

Bak stiffened, alarmed by the concern in Kenamon's voice and face. "What's wrong, my uncle?"

The old priest rubbed his eyes as if to wipe away what he did not want to see. "I must see the body before I know for a fact, but if he's who I think he is, his father Nihisy has just been named chancellor by our sovereign, Maatkare Hatshepsut herself."

Bak sucked in his breath, stunned by the news. "He's one of the most powerful men in the land of Kemet!"

"Puemre was his only son, Bak, the joy of his life. He'll not rest easy until this death is avenged."

A chill crept up Bak's spine. Most violent deaths were crimes of passion, as easily resolved as Commander Woser had told Imsiba this would be. If Woser erred, if Puemre's slayer had struck with care, bent on hiding the truth, even the most diligent investigation might not reveal his name. If that should happen, Nihisy would draw the queen's attention to Wawat. Heads would roll, figuratively if not literally, all the way along the Belly of Stones, beginning with the man who failed to catch the slayer.

"I'd like to break Woser's neck!" Thuty paced across his reception room to the courtyard door, swung around, and glared at Bak and Kenamon as if they were as much at fault as Woser.

"He had no way of knowing Nihisy would be named our new chancellor." Kenamon shifted in Thuty's armchair to set his drinking bowl on the low table at his elbow. "A messenger was never sent south from the capital. I was asked to spread the word as I travel up the river."

Bak, leaning against the jamb of the open stairwell door,

sipped from his drinking bowl. The wine was pungent and heady, the best to be had in the whole of Wawat. The scent of onions, lentils, and roasting beef filtering through the courtyard door promised a feast worthy of a god, a feast he had been asked to share. Yet he could savor neither taste nor smell. He could think only of the decision the commandant was sure to make and the weight that would rest on his shoulders once the decision was aired.

"Woser should've drawn my attention months ago to Puemre's noble birth, yet he made no mention in his reports. And now . . ." Thuty's voice hardened. "Now the wretch has been slain and still he blinds me with silence."

Again Kenamon tried to mediate. "He may have believed Puemre had registered here, as he was supposed to, and assumed your chief scribe told you of his presence."

"Even if true, it doesn't explain why he made no report when the wretch turned up missing." Thuty beat another path across the room, pivoted, scowled at Bak. "Nor does it explain his failure to send back with Imsiba a written account of the whole matter."

Bak was too anxious to hear Thuty's final decision to spend time on useless speculation. "Do you wish me to go to Iken, sir?"

Kenamon gave him a look of worry mingled with pride. He had made his feelings clear during their walk from the house of death to the commandant's residence. He feared for his young friend's future, but was proud of his nobleness of purpose.

"No, Bak, I don't!" Thuty glared. "I wish you to travel to Semna with the lord Amon. But that imbecile Woser has made that impossible. Go! Go to Iken. Get this matter over and done with."

"I'll do my best, sir. That I promise."

Thuty scooped his baton of office off a nearby stool and sat down in its place. "I'll send a courier to Iken tonight with a letter giving you authority over Woser as far as

Puemre's death is concerned. He'll not like it, but I'll leave him no choice.''

What if my best isn't good enough? Bak wondered. *What if this time I fail?* He had already asked Kenamon to speak with the lord Amon on his behalf, but perhaps he should make an offering to the god as well. A plump goose. Maybe more than one.

Chapter Five

"Take care, my friend." Imsiba's eyes were clouded with worry. "I fear danger will greet you at the gates of Iken."

Bak clapped the big Medjay on the shoulder. "I wish you could come, too, but you must stay behind with our men, make sure they're well prepared for the journey upriver. And you must arrange with Nebwa to divide the duties throughout the trek. And offer the physician Kenamon any aid he may need. And . . ."

Imsiba staved off the spate of words with raised hands and a stingy smile. "I've tasks without number, I know, but I'll worry nonetheless."

"You've told me many times our company is the finest in the realm, and I'm taking two of our best men with me." Bak nodded toward Kasaya and Pashenuro, kneeling at the water's edge. "Are they not sufficient to lay your worries to rest?"

Imsiba eyed the two Medjays, who were watching some aquatic creature invisible to their superiors. The youngest of the pair, Kasaya, was the biggest and strongest man in their company, not greatly endowed with intelligence but good-natured and likable. Pashenuro was shorter, thicker in build, clever as well as brave, next in line behind Imsiba. Both men carried spotted black-and-white cowhide shields and bronze spears longer than they were tall. Each wore a dagger at the waist of his kilt and carried a sling. A cloth bag filled with personal items lay at their feet.

"I could not have chosen better," Imsiba admitted, "but they can't stand at your side every moment."

Bak, impatient to be on his way, looked beyond Buhen toward the long sandy ridge that paralleled the river, where ribbons of orange spread across the sky from the rising sun Khepre, a sliver of flame burning the horizon. "I've more concern about Commander Woser than the man who slew Puemre. If he chooses to lay boulders in my path—and from what you say, he will—my task will be ten times ten more difficult than it should be."

Imsiba followed his glance, remembered his own trek south in the heat, and backed off. "You know where to find me should you need me. If no word comes sooner, I'll see you in four or five days' time."

Bak swallowed a final unnecessary order, smiled a good-bye, and turned away. Following the vague footprints Kasaya and Pashenuro had left in the sand, he strode down the slope to the river's edge. The trip to Iken, though only a half day's journey for men unburdened by donkeys and trade goods, would be hot, thirsty, and uncomfortable. Best to get on with it.

Bak and his companions were more familiar with the stretch of shoreline between Buhen and Kor during the cooler months when the river was low. Then, they had fished in the shade of hardy acacias and tamarisks, had cast off skiffs for lazy days of hunting birds in patches of reeds along the shore, had dived into the river from boulders laid bare through the years by swift-flowing floodwaters. But now, with the lord Re burning his hottest, their favored spots were inundated, covered by a river no longer benign. Trees and boulders stood in the silt-laden water; reeds and grassy inlets were vague images beneath the ripples. Vertical banks, undercut by the hungry river, were crumbling, and golden dunes molded by the winds sweeping across the western desert trickled away at the water's edge.

They stopped briefly at Kor, where they spoke with a trader who had arrived that morning, leading a caravan from the south.

"We spent three days at Iken," said the tall, angular man, his skin burned to leather by the sun. "This season's been wicked, hotter than any I can remember in the ten years I've been trading upriver. I had to rest the pack animals. And myself, too, if the truth be told."

"You left when?" Bak asked.

"Yesterday. Late afternoon. My men are well armed and the desert's reasonably safe around here, so we traveled through the night."

"Did you hear anything of a missing officer?"

"Whispers," the trader admitted. "Nothing factual, merely rumors. But I took no note of them. How does one lose an officer in a fortress as large and well run as Iken?"

A good question, Bak thought.

Bak was bartering with a local farmer for dried fowl and fresh vegetables for a midday snack when Pashenuro hurried up with two soldiers who had just been relieved from several days of watch duty, their post a tall, conical hill a brief walk to the south. Their task was to watch the surrounding landscape for intruders, and to relay with mirrors in the daytime or fire at night any critical messages being sent up- or downriver. Bak knew of the place, for the stone-and-mudbrick lean-to that sheltered the men from the sun stood among ancient carvings scratched on the rocks. The hill was not quite a shrine, but a place to visit and stand in awe of the long-ago past.

"Doubt if we'd spot a body coming downriver," said the older of the two, a grizzled veteran forty or so years of age.

"He was caught in the roots of a palm tree," Kasaya said.

The younger soldier, as bald as a melon, laughed. "One tree looks much like another from our post. And a dead man would look little different than a dead bullock.''

The older man, noting the doubt on Kasaya's face, hastened to explain. ''We're too far from the river to see much.
And anyway, our task is to guard the desert trail.''

Bak, though he had faith in Meru's guess that Puemre
had gone into the water near Iken, stepped in to describe
the dead man. ''Did anyone answering to that description
pass by your post?''

''No, sir,'' the bald soldier said. ''We saw no officers at
all, nor any soldiers we didn't know. The only strangers
were traders, men with caravans.''

''Did you happen to see . . .'' Bak described Seneb's caravan in detail, the men and children and animals.

''Sure we did.'' The older man spat on the ground to
show his contempt. ''It was all we could do to make ourselves stay at our post. But since our sergeant would've
served up our heads to Troop Captain Nebwa if we so much
as set one foot off that hill, we had to content ourselves
with a signal to Kor. Hope it did some good.''

''You did well.'' Bak smiled. ''I was summoned from
Buhen, and now the trader Seneb is locked away, awaiting
his turn to stand before Commandant Thuty.'' His smile
faded. ''Now tell me, did he or anyone else in his party
ever leave the caravan?''

''I don't know what they did farther upstream, but from
the time we first laid eyes on them until they walked into
Kor, not a man among them set foot off the trail.''

South of Kor, they found the river obstructed by islands,
some large enough for habitation, others mere boulders,
black granite glistening wet from the frothy waters roiling
around them. On one of the bigger chunks of land, men as
industrious and plentiful as ants climbed among new mudbrick walls rising above the rocks and trees and brush. A
fortress was taking shape, replacing a mudbrick fort built
in the distant past and long ago fallen to ruin.

They plodded on, deeper into the Belly of Stones. There

they found the river wild and angry, as different as night from day to the smooth, sedate flow that passed Buhen. Clusters of rocky islets, many bleak and bare, some green with vegetation, formed a labyrinth of narrow, swift channels and tumbling rapids. Where the channel was clear, the reddish brown water flowed smooth and strong, but across much of the width of the great river, it leaped over boulders and tumbled down falls and whirled in circles around unseen obstacles, whipped into a colorless froth. At times, it collected in quiet pools or rippled through narrow passages or cascaded down steps of glittering black stone. All the while, it whispered and murmured and sang like a living creature, a siren.

Bak was awed by its raw power and its beauty and at the same time he was appalled. A fleeting vision of himself in a skiff, riding these tumultuous waters, sent a chill down his back. He dismissed the thought as fanciful. No sane man would take a boat into bedlam.

Away from the water, a world of golden sand and black rocks stretched out to the west, disappearing in a pinkish haze that blended land and sky. The opposite shore, less encumbered by sand, looked bleak and desolate in the distance, a tortured world of rock eroded by sun and wind, abraded by blowing sand. The rising sun Khepre slowly climbed the vault of heaven, drawing the moisture from their bodies, burning their flesh, searing the barren land. Their feet, shod in reed sandals, burned with every step. They stopped often to dunk themselves in a pool of still water and drink their fill or merely to look at a river gone mad.

Life went on, even amidst the desolation. Crocodiles sunned themselves on a sandy bank; birds chattered in acacias clinging to tiny pockets of earth; waterfowl paddled among the reeds growing in sheltered coves or skimmed the water in search of an easy meal. They saw no people or houses, but each time they came upon a protected inlet, they found neat rows of onions or melons or lentils and sometimes even a patch of grain.

The stony ridge that paralleled the river gradually drew closer, terminating abruptly in a tall, sheer precipice facing the water. Four soldiers, their long spears close at hand, sat on the rocks atop the formation, watching Bak and his Medjays approach. They were watchmen assigned to the signal station located on that highest point in the region.

Leaving his men at the water's edge beside a tranquil pool, Bak climbed a steep skirt of windblown sand rising up the formation. His feet sank deep in the soft slope; the sand clutched his ankles, making his legs feel heavy. It was a relief to reach the naked rock above the drift, to climb the cracked and broken pinnacle of stone. Three spearmen and a sergeant met him at the top, high above the rapids. Bak read curiosity on their faces and the caution inherent to their task.

The sergeant, a short, powerful man close in age to Bak's twenty-four years, examined his traveling pass, then gave him a long, speculative look. "Not many men choose to climb this pinnacle to pass the time of day. And you an officer, too."

"I've a purpose," Bak assured him with a genial smile.

The sergeant remained stern. "And that is?"

The man's duty required him to be suspicious, Bak reminded himself. "I'm in search of information. And since you sit here day after day, high above the river and the desert sands, perhaps you can help me."

The sergeant's eyes darted toward the base of the cliff and the two Medjays lazing in the water. "You must be the police officer from Buhen. The one who's come to find the man who slew Lieutenant Puemre."

Bak stiffened, surprised. "You've heard of my errand already?"

"We saw your Medjay sergeant come and go yesterday, and a courier from Commandant Thuty passed by last night.

Then this morning, when our supplies were dropped off by the desert patrol, we learned of your purpose, for word has spread through Iken like the grains of sand blown in on a storm.''

Bak frowned. The fact that Commander Woser had repeated the message was interesting, for he had essentially admitted publicly that he had failed to satisfy Thuty, his superior officer. But if the admission carried any subtle meaning, it eluded him.

''You must be dry after so long a walk,'' the sergeant said, more amiable now. ''How about a jar of beer?''

Accepting with a nod, Bak followed him to a reed lean-to built against a crude mudbrick hut. The shelter stood just below the summit among the fallen walls of several older ruined buildings. Beyond, on the desert side of the ridge, he glimpsed additional watchmen. Four large porous water amphorae leaned against a shaded wall, and a dozen smaller jars hung from the frame of the lean-to. They swung gently back and forth in a light breeze that drifted across the ridge, providing a breath of air.

The sergeant untied two jars, twisted out the rock-hard earthen plugs, and handed one to his guest.

Bak took a long drink of the warm, thick liquid. Raising the jar to his companion, he smiled. ''An excellent brew, Sergeant.''

The soldier took a long pull, wiped his mouth with the back of his hand. ''You have questions, sir?''

Nothing like a jar of beer to turn strangers into friends, Bak thought. ''How long ago did you hear of Lieutenant Puemre's death?''

''We heard he was missing three, maybe four days ago. We didn't know his ka had fled his earthly body until the patrol passed by this morning.''

''I came upon him floating past Buhen four days ago. Did you or your men see anything in the river that day or the day before? Anything that might've been his body?''

The sergeant laughed, swept his arm in an arc embracing

the great river below. "Could you spot a body out there?"

To the north and south, as far as the eye could see, spread an awesome panorama of cluttered boulders small and large, some fringed with reeds, some tufted with mimosa or crowned with acacia or palm, all with tendrils of water writhing around them or waves leaping over them or falls cascading among them. What might have been a piece of driftwood or a crocodile or a figment of Bak's imagination appeared in a quiet pool, then drifted into a fast-moving stream, dropped over a watery ledge, and was sucked into a vortex of foam.

Bak's eyes darted upward, where he saw a half dozen black specks wheeling in a loose circle high overhead. "Wouldn't a corpse attract vultures?"

"Oh, I've no doubt they spot any likely meal in the water, but as they prefer dining on dry land, they'll look for something that's already washed ashore."

Bak felt like a man banging his head against a stone pillar. "Did you see . . ." Doggedly he described Seneb's caravan for the second time that morning.

"We no doubt saw it," the sergeant said, "but from this distance, one caravan looks much like another. As long as they keep to the trail and behave themselves, we mind our own business. Only if we spot marauding tribesmen or someone in trouble do we signal the patrol. It's their job to keep order on the desert track."

Leaving the lean-to, they walked toward the watchmen hunkered down at the edge of the precipice, looking out over the river.

Bak hated to go with no more knowledge than when he had come. Perhaps if he went on a fishing expedition . . . "How long have you been posted here without a break?"

"Nine days. Tomorrow will end our time on duty, and we'll be relieved by other men until our next stint."

"Do you have much contact with Iken?"

"The patrol comes by each morning to deliver fresh food and drink."

"And garrison gossip as well?" Bak grinned.

"We're no good to anyone if we don't know what's going on around us." The sergeant spoke with a solemn face and a twinkle in his eye.

"I've often found gossip useful," Bak agreed, "but only when filtered through a fine sieve."

"That goes without saying." The humor fled from the sergeant's face, and he grew thoughtful. His eyes darted toward his fellow watchmen; he seemed about to speak but unsure of the ground on which he trod.

"Could it be that you've stumbled onto a chunk of granite which might contain a grain of gold?" Bak prompted.

The sergeant nodded, to himself rather than Bak, and walked on toward the precipice. "One of my men was told a tale two nights ago. It's probably of no merit, for it was based on the ramblings of one too besotted by beer to speak his own thoughts. What you'll make of it, I know not, but I feel you should hear it."

"I'll measure its worth with care," Bak assured him.

The sergeant knelt among his men, and Bak seated himself on a rocky knob beside them. The former spoke to the oldest of the three spearmen, a tall, gaunt man with thick white hair. "This is Meryre. He walked to Iken two nights ago to see his wife. She's young and soon to bear him a child, so he worries needlessly. Since I'm as soft-hearted as he is soft-headed, I let him go some nights to see her."

The older man flushed like a boy talking of his first love.

"Tell this officer the tale you heard in the house of pleasure of Sennufer," the sergeant said.

"I've known Sennufer since we were young and green," Meryre explained. "We soldiered together many years ago, and his wife looks in on my wife each day. I always stop to hear of her before I go home and to share a jar of beer with my friend. That night he told me so strange a tale I truly thought it born in the brewer's froth."

Meryre paused, looked at the sergeant and Bak as if uncertain whether or not he should continue. Both men nodded encouragement.

"A man had come the night before, Sennufer told me. He was utterly besotted, stubbing his toe on the threshold as he entered and stumbling against the other customers. Sennufer took him by the arm and sat him down and half listened to his ramblings while he went on about his business.

"The man claimed the lady Hathor had come to him, offering him pleasure through the night. For privacy, she led him outside the walls of the city to a nest among the rocks and gave him jars of beer without number. At last he closed his eyes and, as goddesses are apt to do, she vanished in his dreams. Voices woke him, he claimed, men's voices raised in anger."

Meryre scratched his nose, remembering. "He told Sennufer that one man turned away, thinking to leave, but the other grabbed him from behind and thrust a knife into his mouth. The injured man struggled to get away, but the other was stronger. Soon he collapsed and the man who stabbed him shoved him into the river."

Bak sat immobile, unable to believe his good luck. If he could find that man, that witness, he'd soon lay hands on the one who slew Puemre.

"I can see by your face, you think this tale a true one," the sergeant said.

"It matches the way I believe Puemre's life was taken," Bak admitted. "Do you know anything, Meryre, of the man who told this tale to Sennufer?"

Meryre shrugged. "He was a craftsman, I think, but I know not who he is or what he does. Go see Sennufer and ask him."

Bak felt like shouting his thanks to the lord Amon. He had done it! He had solved the mystery of Puemre's death before ever setting foot in Iken. Or had he? Would a man so besotted remember the face of the killer five long days after he witnessed the murder?

Chapter Six

The lord Re's solar barque had long since tipped its prow toward the western horizon when they displayed their traveling passes at Iken's northern gate. Continuing along a well-trod path, they crossed an empty stretch of windblown sand before reaching an outer town of stone and mudbrick houses. Many had partially collapsed, some showed signs of burning, and all were blanketed with varying depths of sand. Bak knew they had been built and occupied many generations before, and had been allowed to deteriorate during those terrible years when the armies of Kemet had abandoned Wawat to Kushite kings. Since the Kushite armies had been soundly defeated twenty-seven years ago, the number of soldiers needed to man the garrison was small, and the houses had never been rebuilt.

Flimsy lean-tos and mud-daubed reed mats had been tacked onto structures with broken walls and fallen roofs, providing a modicum of shelter. The dusky-skinned people living there, plainly Kushites, watched the three strangers pass by with shy curiosity. Bak guessed they had come from far to the south to do business in this important trading and manufacturing center, and had set up temporary residence in the ancient dwellings. Thuty had described Iken as "a city as large as Buhen, seven hundred or so people, with half the number of soldiers and twice as many civilians, many of them transients."

They soon entered the lower city, which was more stable in appearance, with warehouses, workshops, and interconnected blocks of white-plastered mudbrick houses. A close look, however, showed as many buildings empty as occupied, some falling in on themselves, others unpainted and neglected.

Making their way along a series of narrow streets, they brushed shoulders with soldiers, sailors, clerks, craftsmen, and traders, less often with women, children, and servants. White-garbed people of Kemet vied for space with brightly clad people from Wawat and Kush. Cooking odors and the ranker smell of burning kilns and furnaces, the nose-wrinkling odors of sour sweat and sweet perfumes, the ever-present aura of human and animal waste, and the musty-fishy smell of the river lay in the still, hot air like an unseen haze. The murmur of voices, the barking of dogs, the squawk of poultry blended together as one. Farther south, the sounds changed to the creak of ships moored in the harbor, the monotonous chant of men carrying bags of grain from vessel to warehouse, and fishermen growing hoarse hawking their day's catch.

Overlooking it all was the huge rectangular fortress whose towered mudbrick walls rose stark white atop the steep escarpment edging the western side of the city.

Bak had heard Iken was a great trading center, but he had had no idea how exotic a place it was, how varied its people, how intriguing its narrow, disorderly lanes and dark doorways. He was struck by curiosity and excitement, a yearning to explore. Hardly able to contain himself, he prayed fervently to the lord Amon that his task would soon be over. The city beckoned.

"I'm afraid I can't help you, sir," Sennufer said. "I don't know who he is."

Bak dropped onto a low, three-legged stool, his spirits utterly deflated, and frowned at the short, wiry man, whose thin hair was so fiery red it had to be hennaed. "Have you any idea why he came here to bare his thoughts?''

Sennufer shrugged. "A drunken whim, most likely."

"A dangerous whim. If by chance he was overheard and word reached the wrong man, I'd not give a handful of grain for his chances of surviving to an old age."

"I wouldn't worry overmuch." Sennufer glanced outside, where Pashenuro and Kasaya were standing in a narrow lane, chatting with four spearmen. "Meryre heard the tale wrong. Or maybe I twisted it without meaning to, leading his thoughts astray. The besotted man didn't claim he saw a murder; he said he dreamed one man killed another."

Bak scowled at Sennufer, then turned his face away lest he seem unappreciative. He eyed this place of business: two cluttered rooms looking out on the lane and the blank wall of a warehouse. The rear of the room in which he sat was stacked waist-high with beer jars. Stained reed mats covered the hard-packed earthen floor. A basket of drinking bowls, four low tables, and a dozen battered stools stood around the room. Game boards had been painted on the upper surfaces of the tables, providing customers with an opportunity to wager while they drank.

The second room, which reeked of bread and beer, was abustle with activity. Two male servants, sweat pouring off faces made ruddy by heat and effort, chattered together. One crumbled half-baked bread into vats containing a sweetened liquid. The other stirred and strained the fermented brew, poured the thick liquid into large jars, and stoppered them with mud plugs. Sennufer was a frugal man, it seemed, one who manufactured the merchandise he sold. Bak was glad he had not been tempted. Home brew was ofttimes worthy of the gods, but also could be so strong it would lay low a bullock. With Sennufer's business so near the waterfront, the stronger type would no doubt be more in demand.

"You've surely heard of Lieutenant Puemre's death," Bak said. "Doesn't it stand to reason that your drunken friend witnessed that murder?"

"He may have, I grant you. Or he may've been seeing the creatures born in a beer jar: snakes, scorpions, crocodiles, even a murder or two."

"Can you describe this man who dreamed of murder?" Bak asked in a wry voice.

"He was of medium height, neither fat nor thin. He had dark hair cut short and dark eyes. He wore a short kilt, had a flint knife at his belt, and wore no sandals." Sennufer noted the bemused look on Bak's face. "I know. Half the men in Iken could answer to that description."

"Meryre said you thought him a craftsman."

"I had that impression, yes."

"Why?"

Sennufer rubbed his earlobe, thinking. "His hands, I guess. The fingers were short and broad, as were the palms, and his nails were dirty. Or maybe stained. They were strong hands, the hands of a man who uses them to earn his bread."

"If he should come again to your place of business, would you recognize him?"

"I would." Sennufer hesitated, frowned. "I think I would."

Bak stood up to leave. One thing he knew for a fact. His interview with Commander Woser could not possibly turn out any more disappointing than this one had.

Bak and his men, unable to spot a path that climbed the escarpment to the fortress of Iken, approached one of a dozen or more spearmen guarding the harbor. The man pointed out a cut in the cliff face and gave directions to a steep path he assured them they would find there. The route was well traveled, taking them straight to the fortress and a broad, towered gate. After they displayed their passes, Bak led the way inside a city that looked much like Buhen, with blocks of white-plastered buildings lining narrow, arrow-straight streets.

"Go to the garrison stores," he told Pashenuro and Kasaya. "Get food and drink, enough for three or four days, and bedding and a brazier and whatever else we'll need. Talk to all who approach you. Maintain a frank and open face and don't push too hard for news of Puemre's death, but learn what you can. After I talk with Commander Woser, I'll send a message, telling you where our quarters will be."

Bidding them farewell, he hurried to the commander's residence, a large house with a pillared court surrounded by rooms astir with scribal activity. When he identified himself, the men who overheard pretended indifference, but examined him as closely as a physician studies an open wound. A scribe sent him up a flight of stairs to the second level which, like the commandant's residence in Buhen, served as the living quarters.

Commander Woser, a medium-sized man with a slight paunch, was seated in his reception room in an armchair over which the tawny skin of a lion was draped. From his build, the wrinkles at the corners of his eyes and mouth, and thick graying hair cropped below his earlobes, Bak guessed him to be in his late forties.

Without rising, he welcomed Bak with a smile so reserved it chilled the room. "So you're Thuty's policeman. Lieutenant Bak, is it?"

His tone rankled. He made it sound as if Bak should be on a leash, sitting at Thuty's feet.

"So you're Woser," Bak said with no smile at all. "An able commander, I've been told, but one too lost in the day-to-day business of his garrison to report a man missing to his superior officer."

Woser flushed. "An oversight, I admit."

Bak, forced to stand until bidden to sit, glanced around the room. A stack of scrolls lay on a table at Woser's elbow. Several low tables, wooden chests, three-legged stools, and camp stools competed for space with weapons and armor piled against the wall and a variety of products from Kush, confiscated perhaps or merely obtained in trade:

a basket of ostrich eggs and feathers, a pile of bright skins, and an open chest filled with gaudy bead jewelry.

"Commandant Thuty was not even aware you, and therefore he, had a man of lofty birth within your command."

"I shoulder no blame for that," Woser said stiffly. "I assumed Lieutenant Puemre registered in Buhen, as he was supposed to do. I had no knowledge of his failure in that regard."

Bak knew if he pushed too hard, he would be treading on shaky earth, but Thuty had given him authority over Woser in the matter of Puemre's death, so he pressed on. "Would it not have been politically expedient to make special note of a man like Puemre when you made your reports to your commandant?"

Woser leaned forward in his chair, his eyes as dark and intense as his voice. "Puemre was a good officer, a talented man of arms, but so are my other officers. I didn't wish to raise him above them simply because his father happened to be a nobleman."

Bak felt stirrings of approval for the commander. "I sympathize with your purpose, but one must be realistic."

"Is it realistic to hold one man who has no greater experience than practice warfare above others who've fought for the lives of themselves and their men, proving themselves valiant on the field of battle?"

"Not many ranking officers would act upon such strong convictions."

Woser waved off the compliment. "In a little over a year I'll return to Kemet, leaving soldiering behind to live out my days on the small plot of land I was given long ago for service to my country. I no longer stand in awe of men of lofty birth."

"Puemre's father is now chancellor of Kemet," Bak pointed out, "a man who has the ear of our sovereign. To call him lofty would seem an understatement."

"A misfortune," Woser admitted with a faint, but definitely cynical smile. "A development I never anticipated."

Bak concealed his own smile. It was time he moderated his attack, but not so much as to give Woser the offensive. "Commandant Thuty didn't send me here because he mistrusts you," he said, skidding along the edge of the truth, "but because he feels I might more quickly be able to lay hands on Puemre's slayer. After all, you've many other tasks, and I'll have only the one. He doesn't want this death to lay a shadow over the lord Amon's journey through the Belly of Stones."

Though Woser's expression remained guarded, he pointed to a convenient stool. "Take a seat, young man. I missed my midday meal. Late it may be, but would you care to join me in a light repast?"

A short time later, with a jar of beer, a flattish loaf of bread, and a bowl of thick, savory vegetable stew on a low table beside him, Bak felt more comfortable with Woser but no less wary.

"I've heard of you," Woser said, dunking a chunk of bread in his bowl, "and I know of the high regard in which Thuty holds you. It's said you not only laid hands on the man who slew Commandant Nakht, but at the same time you stopped the theft of gold from one of the desert mines and led a skirmish that saved a caravan."

Maatkare Hatshepsut herself had ordered the stolen gold to be kept a secret, but it had been inevitable that rumors would leak out.

"I know of no gold leaving Buhen in anything other than an official shipment," Bak said truthfully, for the thief had had no time to carry away his hoard.

"You did lay hands on Nakht's slayer," Woser insisted. "That's common knowledge all along the Belly of Stones. As is the success of your battle with the tribesmen."

Bak fished a slice of celery from the stew, uncertain what to say, unsure of Woser's purpose. "I was lucky. The lord Amon stood by my side, guiding my thoughts and my actions."

"No need to be so modest, lieutenant. You're an exemplary soldier, a fine and . . ."

"Enough!" Bak smiled to take the sting from his words. "Too much flattery will make me suspicious of your motives."

Woser chuckled. "I'm just trying to point out that this task Thuty gave you is unworthy of your talents. If, as I believe, Puemre's death was an accident, you've nothing to investigate."

Bak's eyes narrowed. "An accident?"

Woser wiped the inside of his bowl with a crust of bread, finishing his stew. "According to Thuty's message, Puemre was found in the river with his throat cut in such a way he suffocated on his own blood. My guess is that he slipped and fell into the water, which carried him downriver to the rapids where his throat was torn by a sharp rock. To assume his death a murder seems an overcomplication of a simple situation."

Bak set his bowl down, rocked back on his stool, and gave Woser a long and hard look. "It was I who found the body and I who pulled the murder weapon from his throat. That weapon was a chisel jammed hard and fast into place, too deep to be easily removed. Lieutenant Puemre's death was not an accident."

Woser did not actually squirm, but he looked decidedly uncomfortable. "If not, a trader must've slain him, as I believed initially. One of the many Puemre alienated during the month he served as inspecting officer."

"I doubt Chancellor Nihisy will be satisfied with so simple an explanation and no evidence to back it up." Bak noted the flush spreading across Woser's face. "Now tell me, sir, who, as far as you know, was the last to see Puemre alive?"

"I was. I and my senior officers." Woser's voice was as stiff as his spine. "We met here the night he disappeared, here in this very room. We spoke of the lord Amon, discussing the duties each man would perform when they accompany the god upriver to Semna. They left long after nightfall.''

Bak stared at the older man. Woser looked drained, which in itself gave him away. He believed, Bak felt sure— or perhaps he knew for a fact—that one of the officers who had attended that meeting had committed murder. No wonder he preferred to sweep Puemre's death under a floor mat!

''I blame myself,'' Woser said as if he guessed Bak's thoughts. ''I should've called them together earlier in the day, made sure they left before dark. At so late an hour, only men up to no good prowl the streets.''

Bak nodded, letting him think he agreed. But he had read the monthly reports of crime in Iken, and they did not bear out the charge. ''I must talk to all who were here that night, learn what they saw, if anything.''

''I understand.'' With an obvious effort, Woser met Bak's eyes. ''I'd prefer you to wait until tomorrow. I can summon them then, when they're not so busy with their garrison duties.''

Bak could see the commander wished to keep him at arm's length until . . . What? Until he and his officers had time to think up a collective tale designed to deceive? Bak thought it best he go along with the game, let them assume he was easily led. ''I'd prefer today, but tomorrow will do as well. In the meantime, I need quarters for myself and my men, somewhere apart from the barracks.'' He stood up, preparing to leave. ''And I wish to see Puemre's quarters. Can you tell me where he lived?''

Puemre's house was in the lower city not far from the small house the chief scribe had allocated to Bak and his men. This residential sector, close to the base of the escarpment, was slowly being enveloped by the shadow of the fortress towering above it. The sole occupant of the narrow lane was a slick-haired yellow cur sprawled in an open doorway, its tongue hanging out, its thin chest heaving to catch a breath of air.

"We'll not find much here," Kasaya said, wading through a drift of sand the serpentine wall outside the sector had failed to keep out of the lane. "If Commander Woser is protecting one of his officers, he'd have long ago sent men to clean out anything that would point a finger."

Bak stopped before the last house in the lane and a wooden door latched to discourage entry. "We must begin somewhere. Besides, I want Woser to know I'll sweep up every grain of sand, if I must, to look at the dark, clean earth beneath."

"I thought you wished him to believe you can be deceived."

"If he knows I'm serious about this investigation, he'll fret. If he thinks I'm stupid, he may be careless."

The young Medjay's expression lingered somewhere between confusion and skepticism.

Bak lifted the wooden latch and shoved open the door. The house was small, a single room five paces by ten, whitewashed for cleanliness, and a small kitchen at the rear lightly roofed with branches and palm fronds. Beyond a low platform covered with a sleeping pallet, a ladder led to an opening in the roof, closed now with a palm-leaf mat. A second pallet, much smaller than the other, lay on the floor in the opposite corner. A stool and three reed chests completed the furnishings. Several dried mud animals, a toy crocodile carved of wood, and a broken doll, lay clumped together on the smaller bed.

"He must've kept the boy with him!" Bak was surprised, though not sure why. "The mute child Nofery talked about."

Kasaya, little more than an overgrown child himself, had been intrigued by Nofery's tale. "Maybe Puemre kept him as his servant. A boy of six or seven years can do many small tasks to ease life's path."

"How did they manage to talk to each other?" Bak wondered. "More important, where's the boy now?"

The two men studied the room, looking for signs of recent occupation. The brazier was cold, the pottery dishes clean and neatly stacked against the wall. Both sleeping pallets were smooth and tidy. One chest contained men's clothing: tunics and kilts of fine linen, all clean and folded. Another was filled with sandals and armor and hand weapons: dagger, mace, and sling. A smaller chest held Puemre's razors, eye paint, and other toilet articles. An examination of the contents of several pottery jars large and small disclosed a bare minimum of foodstuffs.

"I fear the child's run away," Bak said. "With so little food remaining, I doubt he'll return." He was not unduly concerned. The boy was probably close by, living in the home of some soft-hearted, motherly woman with a brood of her own.

Kasaya hurried to the door to study the sandy lane. "He hasn't come this way since the last strong wind. How long ago was that, I wonder?"

"Go find a neighbor."

Within minutes Kasaya came back, bringing with him a dusky young woman of fifteen or so years holding a tiny baby to her breast. Her eyes were heavy with sleep, as if the Medjay had disturbed her afternoon nap.

"The wind blew hard three nights ago," Kasaya said. He nodded to the woman. "Speak up, mistress. Tell the lieutenant what you told me."

She lowered her eyes, too shy to speak in more than a murmur. "I've not seen the boy since the night before the sergeant came, looking for Lieutenant Puemre."

Bak's interest quickened. "The child was already gone before Puemre was found to be missing?"

Her eyes flickered to his face and away; she nodded.

Bak's thoughts tumbled over each other, searching through the possibilities. Somehow the boy must have learned of his master's death. Was it possible that he saw Puemre die? Would it be stretching credibility to assume the murder had been witnessed by two people? One a drunk who might not remember and one a mute who could not repeat the tale? Both of whom had disappeared.

"Tell me of that night," he urged.

"My man was on guard duty, so I lay alone on the roof. The air was hot and my baby restless. I couldn't sleep. I saw the boy climb up from this house and stand for an instant in the starlight. He carried a bundle on his back. A sheet, I thought, filled with I know not what, a burden so heavy it bent him double. He looked around like a puppy lost from its mother, searching for the terrors of the night. Finding no threat—he didn't know I watched him—he walked from roof to roof until he reached the far end of the block, where he disappeared from sight."

"And he's not been back since."

She hugged her baby close, gaining courage from its warmth. "No, sir."

Kasaya nodded in agreement. "I found sand on the mat above the ladder, so he didn't sneak in from the roof."

Bak eyed the room, noting how neat it was, how abandoned it appeared. If the boy had seen Puemre slain, he would never come back. Nor would he be easy to find, as Bak had initially assumed. He let out a long, frustrated sigh. "Who's come to this house since Puemre's death?"

The girl nuzzled the dark fuzz on her baby's head. "The sergeant returned again and again, looking more worried each time. The woman came, the one heavy with child who cared for the house and cooked. Other men came, soldiers they were, but I know not how many for they all looked much alike to me."

Bak had expected no less, but his spirits sagged even further. With so many people coming and going, any clues Puemre might have left had long ago vanished. The search he must make would be fruitless.

He asked a few more questions that led nowhere and dismissed the woman. "You may as well go, too, Kasaya. This house has been swept clean. I see no point in wasting your time as well as mine."

*   *   *

The lord Re hung low in the western sky, stretching the shadow of the escarpment across the lower city. The harbor was still and quiet, its waters a sheet of molten gold reflecting a cloudless sky. A soft breeze stirred the air, rousing the city's inhabitants to their evening endeavors, giving voice to animals and fowl and men.

Bak descended the ladder from the rooftop and glanced around the room. He had yet to search the sleeping pallets, then he could leave. As he knelt beside the child's bed, he wondered what Pashenuro had managed to glean from the garrison stores. A plump duck would be pleasant, he thought, and a jar of beer, treats to counterbalance his failure to find a single clue to Puemre's death. Or life, for that matter. Puemre had lived well enough, but austere, as if trying to prove to his fellow officers—or maybe himself— that he could turn his back on his noble heritage.

Lifting the sheet, shaking it out, he thanked the lord Amon that he would soon be finished and on his way. He had barely peeked inside the house Woser had assigned to him and his men, but it seemed ideal: two rooms, located like Puemre's house at the end of a quiet lane. He eyed the pallet on which the mute boy had slept. The pad had been doubled, making it thicker and softer, more like a nest. He raised it, looking without hope for a hiding place in the hard-packed earthen floor.

A broken piece of grayish pottery fell from the folds of cloth, clattering to the ground, a shard with some kind of drawing in black ink on its smooth outer surface. Picking it up, he saw lines rough and uncertain, a sketch by an untrained hand. People with round heads and pointed, bird-beak noses, shapeless bodies, and stick-like arms and legs. Then his eyes widened and he pursed his lips in a silent whistle. The sketch showed a man with the tall crown of a king bending over a small figure lying on a bed. A second man stood behind the king, knife in hand, arm poised for a deadly thrust. The meaning was clear: the Kushite king

Amon-Psaro with his ailing son, and someone . . . Puemre
maybe? . . . intending to slay the king.

He took a long, deep breath to calm his pounding heart.
Was he leaping to a conclusion based on faulty evidence?
Why would Puemre want to slay Amon-Psaro, a man who
had not set foot on the soil of Kemet for many years and
probably never would again? No, the idea was ludicrous.

He heard a sound, the faint crunch of sand underfoot.
Swinging around, he glimpsed a deeply tanned leg and a
short white kilt. Something struck him on the head, rocking
him back, and he felt himself falling. The world around
him turned to night.

Bak opened his eyes, tried to lift his head off the floor.
The room tilted at a frightening angle, making his stomach
churn. His skull felt about to burst. He closed his eyes,
swallowed. After a while, he tried again to rise. This time,
he managed to lift his shoulders onto Puemre's clothing
chest, empty now, its lid askew. When the room stopped
spinning, he looked at the mess around him and cursed with
all his heart. Whoever had struck him senseless had torn
the place apart. The chests were empty, their contents
strewn around the room, along with the sleeping pallets and
sheets. The food storage jars had been tipped over, leaving
grain and flour, lentils and dried dates, dumped on the floor.
His eyes landed on a grayish mass of grit close to his knee
and he muttered another, harsher curse. The shard with the
drawing had been crushed to bits.

The chunk of pottery could have been accidentally trod
on during the search—but he did not believe it for a moment. He quickly sorted through his thoughts, finding a new
possibility. Maybe Puemre was not the man who wanted
Amon-Psaro dead; maybe instead he had caught someone
else plotting against the Kushite king.

Bak heard a noise, a faint crunch of sand underfoot exactly as before. He swung around and at the same time
grabbed an empty storage jar, not much of a weapon but

better than nothing. Glimpsing a man peering through the doorway, a long scar deforming his cheek and a wide-eyed look of shock and fear, Bak hauled himself to his feet and lurched toward the portal, the world unsteady around him. The man ducked away and began to run. Bak crossed the threshold on legs too shaky to carry him farther. Clinging to the doorjamb, he watched the man race around the corner at the far end of the lane and vanish from sight.

He scowled, more at his own infirmity than at his failure to catch the man. It should be easy enough to find one with so terrible a scar.

Bak walked along the lane, careful to make no quick movements that would goad the dull ache in his head into a full-fledged throbbing. He half listened to the voices on the rooftops, families relaxing in the cool of the evening while the women prepared the last meal of the day. A tiny brownish monkey chattered at him from a doorway. Dogs barked in the distance and a donkey brayed. A rat shot up the lane and through an open portal; an orange-striped cat raced after it. Iken might wear brighter colors than Buhen, he thought, but it was no different, a frontier city made up of men, women, and children, soldiers and civilians. Ordinary people going about their ordinary tasks.

As he neared the end of the block, the aroma of braised beef wafted from the open doorway of his new quarters. A broad smile spread across his face, and he hastened forward. The commissary, it appeared, had been generous indeed to Pashenuro.

He strode inside and followed the scent to a small, square courtyard at the back of the house. Stopping short on the threshold, he gaped at the attractive young woman kneeling at the burning brazier.

"Who're you?" he demanded.

She looked up, startled by his sudden entry, and gave him a sloe-eyed smile. "I'm Aset, daughter of Commander Woser."

For an instant, he wondered if the blow on his head had addled him so badly he had come to the wrong house. Impossible. "What're you doing here?" The question was too abrupt, he knew, and lacking in tact.

She rose to her feet, her elegant figure visible through a calf-length white sheath so diaphanous he could see every curve, every shadow and light. "You've had a long, hard day, Lieutenant. I thought to ease your evening hours with food and drink and . . ." She hesitated, shrugged. "With whatever pleasures strike your fancy."

He swallowed hard, trying to ignore the warmth in his loins. She was about sixteen, ripe for the plucking. But common sense told him to be wary of this woman. "Where are my Medjays, Kasaya and Pashenuro?"

She raised an eyebrow as if surprised he should care. "I sent them to my father's kitchen."

The warning signals grew stronger in his thoughts, helping to quench the fire in his groin. The barracks would have been a more logical place to send them, especially if she meant them to spend the night away from this house.

With a sultry smile, she reached out to take his hand and led him to the mudbrick bench built onto the back of the house. Near the bench, he saw a reed basket overflowing with two wine jars, stemmed drinking bowls, and several bundles wrapped in leaves, food prepared by her father's servants, he guessed. A neatly folded bundle of cloth lay on the end of the bench, a robe, he assumed, something to cover her nakedness while she walked the streets between the commander's residence and this humble abode. A pleasant breeze floated off the roof, blowing away the heat from the brazier.

She picked up a jar and a bowl. "Shall we drink and be merry while our food cooks?"

Bak took the jar from her, noted the vintage on the plug, and nodded his approval. Whatever her game, she was playing it with style. Or was it Woser's game? "I assume your father believes you to be with friends, mistress Aset?"

"Oh, he never questions my actions."

I'll bet, Bak thought. *A lovely thing like you would be the bane of any father's life.*

She sat beside him, so close he could smell her sweet-scented hair and see the tiny brown mole tucked in the cleft between her lush, round breasts. "Will you open the wine?" she asked.

Squashing the moment's temptation, he broke the plug and filled her bowl. The wine was a clear, deep red, heavy with the scent of a delicate yet indefinable fruit.

Taking a sip, she smiled and turned the bowl so his lips would touch the same spot. "Drink, my brother, and enjoy. Let's make this a night never to forget."

My brother, she had said. The endearment was as disconcerting as the invitation. "I'm most flattered that you've come to me, mistress. You're as lovely as a gazelle, too perfect a creature to waste on one as undeserving as I."

"You're far too modest." She ran her fingers down the muscles of his arm, making his skin tingle. "My father has told me you're a man of great courage."

"Your father exaggerates." He rose to his feet, distancing himself from so tempting a morsel.

She looked up, surprised, and gave him a pouty smile. "You don't find me attractive?"

"You know I do." Kneeling beside the brazier, he picked up a stick charred on one end. "You're as lovely as any woman I know." He made a pretense of stirring the fire, his thoughts flitting in all directions, searching for a way out. The last thing he wanted was to be expelled from Iken by an irate father.

"Come to me," she urged, patting the seat beside her.

He formed what he hoped was a regretful smile. "I'm sorry, mistress Aset, more sorry than you'll ever know. But I've pledged my heart to another."

The excuse was bittersweet, not altogether true, nor was it untrue. He had, many months before, given his heart to a woman too recently widowed to love him or anyone else.

She had gone to faraway Kemet, taking her husband's body for burial in his tomb. He had heard nothing from her since, nor was he sure he ever would. Still he yearned for her.

Aset's smile hardly wavered. She bent toward him, her shapely breasts bulging at the top of her dress. "She's not here. I am."

He eyed the plump offering. True, he had some time ago turned his back on abstinence. After all, yearning was one thing; remaining faithful to a faint hope was something else again. Not now, though, not with Commander Woser's daughter.

Quick footsteps sounded in the house. Leather sandals, Bak thought, not the reed-sandaled steps of Kasaya or Pashenuro. He offered brief but fervent thanks to the lord Amon for giving him the wisdom to leave the bench.

A gangly young man burst through the door, his hand on his dagger, his face an angry scarlet. He stopped short. His eyes darted from Aset to Bak and back again. Confusion supplanted anger.

"Nebseny!" The girl's face paled; she sprang to her feet. "What brought you here?" If her show of surprise was an act, it was a good one.

"Your father sent me. He told me he thought this man . . ." Nebseny glanced at Bak, far more than an arm's length from the girl, and took in her dress. "What're you doing in this house?" he demanded of her, "and in so revealing a gown!"

"What I do is none of your business," she snapped.

Without a word, he grabbed her arm and shoved her out of the courtyard and into the house. Scooping up the folded robe, he hurried after her.

Bak followed as far as the front door. As they disappeared from sight at the end of the lane, he let out a long, relieved breath. Thanks to the lord Amon, a great deal of luck, and a healthy suspicion, he had missed entrapment by a hair. He walked back to the courtyard and dropped onto the bench, not sure who had been doing what to whom.

Had Woser thought up the game? Or Aset? The young man Nebseny had seemed genuinely angry, but appearances could be deceiving.

He glanced at the meat, so brown and fragrant it was worthy of the lord Amon. The wine, too, was special. Yet he did not enjoy eating and drinking alone. He cocked an ear, heard children playing on the rooftops. One of the boys would surely be willing to carry a message to Pashenuro and Kasaya at the commander's residence.

Chapter Seven

"You understand what you must do," Bak said, looking first at Pashenuro and then Kasaya.

Pashenuro slipped the loop of his leather sheath onto his belt and retied the strip of linen. "I'm to follow Lieutenant Puemre's company onto the practice field—or to whatever task they have today—and I'm to speak with the sergeant, Minnakht, working my way into his confidence. With luck, and if the lord Amon smiles on me, he'll not only talk with an open and honest tongue, but he'll encourage his men to tell me what they can."

Bak fastened the clasp of his wide multicolored bead bracelet, tugged at the hem of his kilt to smooth it over his hips, and sat down on the sleeping platform, converted now to a bench cluttered with his neatly folded sleeping pallet, his sandals, Kasaya's shield, and a basket of bread so fresh it perfumed the room. The few other furnishings were the Medjays' sleeping pallets on the floor, two folding camp stools, and a basket of nonperishable provisions. A smaller basket containing writing implements and a few scrolls sat near the doorway to the second, empty room.

"Your purpose?" he asked Pashenuro.

"I'm to learn what I can about the dead man and . . ." The thick-bodied Medjay slid his dagger into the sheath, adjusted the weapon for greater comfort, and picked up his shield and spear, lying along the base of the wall. "Using all the guile I possess, I'm to learn what I can about the other officers without anyone guessing my purpose. Especially how they and Lieutenant Puemre worked and played together, whether friendly or as foes.''

Bak grinned unexpectedly. "That should keep you busy through much of the morning."

"Much of the week, I'd guess." Pashenuro laughed.

Bak sobered, his eyes darted toward the younger man. "What have you to do, Kasaya?"

The hulking Medjay, sitting cross-legged on his sleeping pallet, poured a dollop of oil into his hand and spread it over his arms and torso. "I'm to start with Lieutenant Puemre's neighbors, learning what they know of him and of the people he knew and the places he went. Of the people they name, I'm to go only to the civilians who knew him outside the garrison."

"I'll be talking to the men in the barracks," Pashenuro reminded him.

Kasaya frowned at the unnecessary offering. "If I find the mute child, I'm to bring him back here and guard him with my life. The same is true of the craftsman who drowns himself in beer. As for the scarred man, once I learn where he lives and toils, I'm to stay far away, letting him think he's safe from your questions."

"What of the woman heavy with child?" Pashenuro asked. "The one who cared for the dead man's house."

Bak slipped a foot into a sandal, his thoughts turning to the sketch he had found in the mute boy's bed. He had been convinced of a plot when he found it, but in the light of a new day, the idea seemed ridiculous. Why would any man of Kemet want to slay Amon-Psaro? He was a powerful king, yes, but he ruled a distant land. A land so far away, it seemed more mythical than real.

Still, a tiny suspicion lurked, an irritant like a minute grain of sand lodged in the corner of an eye. "If she cleaned the house for him and the boy, she also washed their sheets and made their beds. I should talk to her myself.''

''Amon-Psaro's courier passed through on his way to Buhen soon after nightfall last night,'' Woser said. ''He came again at daybreak, carrying Commandant Thuty's answer and instructions for me as well.''

''The king's entourage is within a few hour's march of Semna!'' Bak slumped onto the nearest stool, one of several scattered around the courtyard. ''I don't want to believe it!''

''They'll march through its gate before dark. There they'll remain, awaiting the lord Amon.''

''The young prince must've taken a turn for the worse.''

Woser strode across the courtyard, pivoted, and strode back. Worry clouded his face. ''The long journey and the heat of the desert at this time of year would be a strain on anyone. For a frail and ailing child . . .'' He shook his head, the wrinkles on his brow deepened. ''I pray Amon-Psaro understands that the lord Amon can sometimes be whimsical in his cures.''

I pray Kenamon's skills as a physician are worthy of the challenge, Bak thought, sharing the commander's concern.

''The god's barge must already have left Buhen,'' Woser said, taking another turn across the court, narrowly missing a basket of white thread wound into balls. The container stood at the foot of a loom on which a length of finely woven linen was stretched. ''The vessel should reach the gates of Iken by dusk tomorrow. The lord Amon will spend but a single night here in the mansion of Hathor before journeying on, directly to Semna.''

''He won't linger at the other garrisons along the Belly of Stones, visiting the gods as originally planned?'' Bak whistled softly. ''For time to be so critical, the prince's life must truly be threatened.''

''The boy can't breathe in the life-giving air, so the courier told me. Each day that passes seems his last.''

The two officers looked at each other, awed by a course of events they were helpless to alter, their mutual mistrust momentarily forgotten.

Woser was the first to turn to more practical matters, to tasks he could control. "All our plans for the lord Amon must be revised. The procession when he arrives will go on, but the presentation of gifts, the distribution of food and drink, the merrymaking, must be curtailed. We must assign additional sentries without delay and send more troops to patrol the desert track. We must..." He went on, listing the many and varied tasks that had to be done, squeezing four days' work into half the time.

Bak let his thoughts stray to his own pressing needs. If he was to take his place at the head of his men while they served as Amon-Psaro's guard of honor, he had only two days to lay hands on Puemre's slayer. An impossible task unless the witnesses, the mute boy and the besotted man, were found. As for the sketch, he prayed the child could somehow explain it away.

A new thought came to him. Perhaps Puemre had for some unimaginable reason taken a dislike to Amon-Psaro. Maybe he had made the sketch, hoping to bring misfortune to the Kushite king by means of sympathetic magic. If so, it had worked; the prince's health was failing daily. *But what if I'm wrong?* Bak wondered; *what if there is a plot afoot?* Tiny fingers of fear ran up his spine. Amon-Psaro would soon be encamped at Semna, a bare day's hurried walk from Iken. Too close by far.

"I must quickly get on with the task Commandant Thuty assigned me," he said. "Are your officers here, as promised?"

Woser scowled, the moment of mutual regard lost. "I trust you understand how much they have to do in too short a time."

"I'll not keep any of them long," Bak assured him.

*   *   *

Troop Captain Huy leaned over a broken section of battlement and eyed the rooftops of the lower city. Bak stood beside him, high above the escarpment on a partially fallen spur wall that projected from the eastern face of the fortress. In the distant past, the spur had served a purpose. Now, with the armies of Kush long ago defeated and warfare limited to desert skirmishes, with a powerful girdle wall in place, the spur had lost its value and had been allowed to crumble. Bak had demanded privacy, and he could think of no place more private in this or any other garrison.

"According to Puemre's personal record, he spent much of his youth on his father's estate near Gebtu." Huy spat a seed over the parapet and popped another date into his mouth. "One servant taught him to read and write. With another he learned to hunt and fish. A brave and respected veteran, a man I once knew, passed on the arts of war. The estate manager, of course, taught him the business of farming."

The tall, slender infantry officer was close to fifty. His eyes were a startling blue, his gray hair cropped even shorter than Bak's. He spoke in a wry voice, not quite poking fun at the dead man's upbringing, but letting Bak know the contempt he held for those who thrived on advantage and privilege. A long, ugly scar on his right shoulder left no doubt that he had earned his position, second only to Woser in the garrison hierarchy.

A breeze not yet heated by the sun rustled their hair. Swallows darted away, soon to return to their twittering young hidden in nests bored in the weathered mudbrick. The view was glorious—and enlightening—showing clearly the tactical significance of the fortress and its island outlier.

In the hazy distance, the river made a sweeping bend through the desert, flowing broad and relatively free of obstacles. Below the bend, Iken's two white stone quays reached into the water to shelter the surprisingly large number of vessels that plied the hazardous waters of the Belly

of Stones. The fortress loomed over the harbor and, a short
walk north, the crucial point where the river literally broke
apart, torn asunder by rocks and islands to form a multitude
of swift-flowing, foam-shrouded rapids. A calm, smooth
channel dammed downstream by a rocky cascade separated
the lower city from a long tear-shaped island that supported
only the most tenacious and water-tolerant brush and trees.
Beyond, rising from the rocks of a second, higher island, a
smaller fortress gave a second important advantage over an
attacking army.

With no time to linger on details, he turned his attention
back to Huy. He shared the troop captain's conviction that
a man should earn his way, but he kept the thought to
himself. "You've just described a life of bucolic gentility.
That doesn't explain how Puemre qualified for service in
the regiment of Amon."

Huy gave him a cool glance. "The trouble with the army
these days is boredom. And boredom leads to impatience.
You young officers have never had to face another army.
All you do is sit in the garrison day in and day out, wearing
calluses on your backsides, maneuvering for promotion."

Bak wanted to shake the man for his condescending attitude and at the same time he silently thanked him for the
opening he had offered. "Are you suggesting we slay
Amon-Psaro so the other Kushite kings will join forces and
march against our army, giving our officers an honest opportunity to gain experience?"

Huy snorted. "You'd not make jokes if you'd ever faced
them in battle as I have." He ran a finger down the scar.
"The man who gave me this was outnumbered four to one,
yet his courage never flagged. They're worthy foes. More
than worthy. Fearsome and deadly."

Bak was impressed by his sincerity, or at least the appearance of sincerity. "Until ten months ago, I was an officer in the regiment of Amon. I knew my fellow officers.
Lieutenant Puemre was not among them."

Huy eyed him with interest. "You were infantry?"

"No, chariotry."

"Humph." Huy's interest flickered out, and he stared across the lower city, hiding his thoughts in a frown. "When barely a man, Puemre was sent by his father to Iunu, where he labored as a scribe in the great mansion of the lord Ptah. He later moved on to Byblos to serve as chief scribe to our royal envoy there. Upon his return to Kemet, he joined the regiment of Ptah as an officer. Two years later—soon after you came to Buhen, I assume—he moved to Waset and the regiment of Amon. There he stayed a mere three months before coming south."

"His life was filled to the brim, it would seem." Bak's voice was as wry as Huy's had been. "Was he born a wanderer, I wonder, or did he go from one task to another for a reason?"

Huy seemed about to speak, but changed his mind and answered with a shrug.

"Troop Captain Huy!" Bak spoke slowly and deliberately, leaving no room for misunderstanding. "What you don't offer voluntarily, I'll read for myself in Puemre's personal record. Or learn from another source. Preferably not from his father, Chancellor Nihisy, when we're all standing before the viceroy, charged with dereliction of duty—or worse."

Huy swung away, his back rigid, his hands balled tight. He strode a few paces along the parapet, stopping at a place where a tall, heavy tower had fallen away from the wall and crumbled. A wasp flew past his head unseen. A swallow dived and scolded, protecting its nest from a man unaware of its proximity. Two sentries patrolling the battlements atop the main wall met at a distant tower. They paused to stare at the officers on the spur wall—and probably to gossip about Puemre's death and the mission of the man talking so privately with their troop captain.

"Puemre was a highly respected scribe, you'll read in his record, and he was a good officer: brave, talented in the arts of war, a creative tactician. So we found him here in

Iken.'' Huy pivoted, showing a face dark with suppressed anger. "He knew few men had his ability, and the knowledge gave him an arrogance that knew no bounds. He wanted the moon and the stars and the sun for himself, and anything he wanted he got, no matter what the cost to those around him.''

"He used people?''

"He trod on us.''

"What exactly did he want? Your position?''

"Mine. Commander Woser's.'' Huy laughed bitterly. "I've no doubt Commandant Thuty would've been in his way, for he made no secret of his desire to sit in the viceroy's chair.''

Bak whistled. "Few men set their sights so high.''

"The men in his company believed he would one day walk with the gods. His fellow officers, I among them, thought him a demon.''

Bak parked his rear against the parapet and studied the older officer. Huy's aversion to Puemre was palpable. Not many men harbored so intense a dislike without a particular reason. "What specifically did he do to you?''

The older officer's mouth tightened. "I didn't like his attitude, that's all.''

Bak expelled a long, irritated sigh. "I didn't like the fact that he wore a belt clasp of the regiment of Amon. A clasp entitled only to those who helped rebuild the regiment, not upstarts like him. Yet I don't despise him the way you do.''

"I didn't slay him!''

"Have I accused you? No! I'm merely trying to identify the man who did.''

Huy picked up a mudbrick clod and hurled it at the main wall. The missile slammed into the white-plastered surface, shattering. A patrolling sentry gave a little start and swung around, looking for the source of the sudden noise. Recognizing his superior officer, he raised his spear in salute and marched on.

"Puemre's first skirmish was with a band of desert

tribesmen who'd been stealing cattle from the riverside villages.'' Huy brushed his hands together, dislodging bits of dirt. ''When I assigned him the task, I advised him to waylay them where they'd least expect it, take them captive, and bring them back to Iken.'' The officer shook his head in disgust. ''Naturally he knew more than anyone else. He felt it wasn't manly for one army to ambush another, so he marched across the desert, raising a dust cloud that could be seen as far away as Semna. Instead of him waylaying the tribesmen, they ambushed him among the dunes and a pitched battle resulted. Five lives were lost on our side, and twice as many of the enemy, who were poorly armed as usual. If he'd done as I told him, none would've died on either side.''

Bak noted the angry flush on Huy's face, a failure to forgive a mistake any newly arrived officer might make. ''There it should've ended, but it didn't, I assume.''

''How right you are!'' Huy picked up another clod and heaved it, this time well away from the sentry. ''When taken to task for losing so many unnecessary lives and, worse yet, risking the loss of his entire company, he laid the blame at my feet.''

''He surely didn't get away with it!''

''Fortunately, the gods smiled on me. I'd given him his orders in front of other men, men who could and did pass the truth to Commander Woser.''

A valid reason to hate a man, Bak thought, *but is it reason enough to kill?* ''What happened the night of Woser's meeting? The night Puemre disappeared?''

''Nothing out of the ordinary.'' Huy almost smiled. ''Other than our reason for the meeting, of course. It's not often the lord Amon honors us with his presence.''

''When did you meet and for how long?''

''We entered the commander's residence soon after dusk, the five of us together. I remember seeing a servant lighting the torches in the courtyard. We discussed for over an hour the duties we had to perform during the god's visit and the journey to Semna. After we came to an agreement as to who would do what, we left.''

"Does Woser customarily call meetings so late?"

"Only when he feels the need, as in this case.''

Bak could not remember a time when Commandant Thuty had called a meeting after dark. "Did you disagree on any matter of importance?"

Huy's laugh held not a speck of humor. "Puemre never agreed to anything, significant or otherwise, that didn't show him in a praiseworthy light, especially when men of importance were involved.''

"As in this case.''

Huy gave him a scornful glance. "If you think to lay Puemre's death at our feet simply because we saw him last, your fame as a clever policeman will be as fleeting as the morning mist over the river.''

"I'm searching for answers, not pointing a finger.'' Bak gave him a long, speculative look. "Who do you believe took his life?"

"We've a city filled with people who come to do business and leave when they've finished, many whose feet he trod on while serving as inspecting officer.'' Huy nodded toward the buildings below the escarpment. "He probably came upon one of them in a dark lane, a man who hated him. Or he might simply have been slain by chance, his life taken by a stranger who was frightened away before he could steal whatever jewelry Puemre wore that night.''

A plausible theory, Bak thought, *except for the fury that drove the murder weapon.* "When did you last set eyes on him?"

"We left together, the five of us. We separated outside the commander's residence, each man going his own way. I saw Puemre walk down the street—alone—heading toward the main gate. I trod a different path, one that took me to my quarters and a much-needed evening meal. I've no wife, but my concubine and servants will vouch for me.''

Later, as Bak threaded his way along a busy street, heading toward his meeting with the watch officer, he mulled over his interview with Huy. Could the officer have taken Puemre's life? He had certainly hated him enough, and with good reason. He had an alibi of sorts, but the members of his household would be sure to say he went straight home, whether or not he had. His theory about Puemre's death had come close to echoing Woser's, but otherwise he had been, with a bit of prompting, reasonably forthright. A good man trying hard to paint a true picture. Maybe.

Lieutenant Senu so closely resembled a monkey that Bak had to smother a smile. In his late forties, he was short and thick, with broad shoulders, narrow hips, and short bowed legs. Cropped orange-red hair standing on end framed coarse, heavy-browed features. His skin, too light to accept a tan, was mottled and peeling, a perpetual state, Bak imagined.

"I don't know what Troop Captain Huy told you," Senu said. "He has a tendency to forgive and forget. But Puemre was a swine. Plain and simple."

The watch officer, professing too many pressing tasks to take time out to answer questions, had suggested Bak come along while he inspected the sentries on the battlements. So Bak found himself once again on the wall, not the old crumbling spur wall, but the new girdle wall that ran north from the fortress, following the escarpment for many paces, then turning toward the river to form an outer enclosure around the city as well as the garrison. The freshly plastered walls were stark white, the walkways smooth, the towers and crenels sharp-edged, as yet unsullied by blowing sand.

Though the heat had climbed through the early hours of morning, the breeze had stiffened, easing the fire of the sun but filling the air with tiny needles of sand. Bak, tasting the grit, feeling it beneath his kilt and in his eyes and nose and ears, thanked the lord Amon he did not have to patrol these walls throughout the day, as did the sentries.

"Huy mentioned problems," he admitted, keeping his voice noncommittal, hoping to invite confidences.

"Problems!" Senu laughed, his voice harsh and cynical. "To walk alongside Puemre was to become a victim."

"What of the mute boy who lived with him? Did he misuse him?"

"Little Ramose?" Senu shook his head. "No, he was good to the child. Treated him like a son. Of course, that was different."

Bak eyed the officer with interest. "In what way?"

They approached a sentry, a tall, sturdy young man wearing a thigh-length kilt similar to that of the officers. A dagger and sling hung from his belt and he carried a long spear and a pale brown cowhide shield. Stopping the man, Senu ordered him to stand at rigid attention, examined his appearance and the readiness of his gear, and sent him on his way.

Striding on toward the next sentry, roughly two hundred paces away, Senu explained without prompting, "Puemre got along well with ordinary mortals. Men and women of lesser rank who posed no threat and offered no obstacle. Besides, Ramose worshiped him. The boy would've given his life for him, and any man or woman who saw them together could see it."

Bak offered a silent prayer to the lord Amon that such was not the case, that the child still lived. "I've been told Puemre's men thought him a fine officer."

"Oh, they liked him alright. With good reason. He was brave and clever on the field of battle, a natural warrior if ever I saw one." Senu scanned the desert to the west, with its rolling dunes shrouded in a dirty yellow haze. His gaze lingered on a denser column of dust that marked the approach of a caravan. "Except for one time when first he came to Wawat, he never lost a man or a skirmish. The troops like that; it makes them feel safe—and proud."

"And the spoils of war are greater," Bak said in a wry voice.

"None came back empty-handed," Senu admitted, pausing to scratch his ankle with the tip of his baton of office. "Don't get me wrong. They had to abide by the rules. Puemre wasn't willing to risk his precious reputation so his men could fill their barracks with booty. They turned in everything of value, as they were supposed to."

From the size of the dust column, Bak guessed the approaching caravan was small, like Seneb's had been. "I've been told he was a hard and unforgiving inspecting officer."

Senu let out a short, bark-like laugh. "He gave many a trader a lesson in honesty. Few got by him without paying the proper tolls." Barely pausing for breath, he added in an off-hand manner, "If you ask me, that's where you should look for the one who slew him."

Too offhand, Bak thought, as if schooled by Woser. "Have you ever heard of a trader named Seneb?"

Senu's face took on a disdainful sneer. "A man rotten to the marrow of his bones. One who trades in flesh and blood, in the misfortunes of others, two-legged and four-legged alike."

Bak waved off a fly buzzing around his head. "I've been told Puemre made his life a misery when last he was here."

"A few months ago." The sneer gave way to a cynical smile. "I despised Puemre, but in that one thing I applauded him. Seneb would be here yet, starving most likely, if Woser hadn't crumbled to his pleas for a new pass so he could journey on upriver."

"He hasn't stopped at Iken on his way north to Kemet?" Bak asked, double-checking the trader's movements. As watch officer, Senu would be the first to know who passed through the gates of the city.

"Not yet, but soon he will." Senu's eyes suddenly darted toward him, his voice grew defensive. "Why question me about that swine? Has he been found in the river, too? I swear I've never touched him."

Bak saw no harm in setting the officer's mind at ease,

and hearing of Seneb's plight might loosen his tongue. "He bypassed Iken, so he claims, and I first saw him at Kor. I confiscated his caravan, and we're holding him in our guardhouse in Buhen. He's to stand before Commandant Thuty, charged with as many offenses against the lady Maat as I can prove."

Senu stopped at a crenel and stared out across the desert wastes. "Sometimes the gods are too forgiving and justice is slow to come, but when at last the evil among us are brought to their knees, there's nothing more satisfying." He turned around and a smile spread slowly across his face. "I thank you, Lieutenant Bak, for renewing my faith."

Bak was beginning to like this odd-looking man. "What vile deed did Puemre do to hurt you?" He knew he was taking advantage of Senu's newfound goodwill, but he had no choice. Time was too pressing.

The watch officer nodded, as if he understood, and walked on. "When first he came to Iken, I stood at the head of the infantry, not here with the sentries. He made no secret that he coveted my task. But Woser insisted he start as an inspecting officer where he could prove himself worthy before leading men whose lives would depend on his ability."

"A sensible decision."

"Not the way Puemre saw it," Senu snorted. "One day a scroll came from the royal house in Waset. Suddenly I found myself a watch officer, and that swine stood at the head of my men." He looked away, but not before Bak saw the hurt in his eyes. "I spent a lifetime in the army, facing the enemy on the field of battle, and I worked my way up from common recruit to lieutenant. All he had to do was write a letter."

"I understand." The words sounded lame to Bak's ears, but his heart ached for a man so ill-used. "Will Woser soon right the wrong he had no choice but commit?"

Senu stopped twenty paces from the next sentry, too far away to be heard. "He told me the day we learned of

Puemre's death that as soon as the lord Amon comes and goes, I can again lead my company. For now, my task as watch officer is more important.''

Bak allowed him time to inspect the sentry before asking his final question: "I must know when you last saw Puemre and how you account for your time after Woser's meeting.''

Senu accepted the question easily; Bak was sure he had expected it. "I parted from him and the others outside the commander's residence and never set eyes on him again. From there, I went directly to my home in the lower city, where my wife and children awaited me.''

Another man whose patience Puemre had stretched beyond endurance, Bak thought. Another man who claimed to be with people who would willingly repeat any story he told them.

Bak hastened along the lane, plowed past a half-dozen spearmen walking away from the commander's residence, and hurried inside. He was late for his next interview, this with the lieutenant who led the archery company. A scribe directed him to the living quarters on the second floor. He dashed up the enclosed stairwell, taking the steps two at a time.

"You never learn, do you?" A man shouting, his voice familiar yet unfamiliar. "First Puemre and now this snake Bak.''

Bak stopped so abruptly he came close to stubbing his toe on the next step.

"Can I help it if men find me beautiful?" Aset's voice.

Bak had no use for eavesdroppers, and his conscience urged him not to listen further, but he did. Shamelessly.

"You have eyes for every man in Iken except me!" The man's voice again.

"Can you take me away from this garrison? This awful place of endless sun and heat, where my face will wrinkle and my skin turn to leather before I'm twenty? Can you offer me servants and a fine house and give me beautiful dresses and jewelry?''

"You know I can't!''

"Then go away and leave me alone.''

"Aset! Few men have that kind of wealth.''

"Puemre did, and Lieutenant Bak has the same confident demeanor, a self-assurance born of wealth and security.''

Me? Bak wondered. *Can she really be so naive she sees nothing beneath a man's skin?*

"If riches are all you want, go to him!'' The man's voice cracked, betraying his pain and anger. "Give yourself to him! See if I care!''

"I will. You just wait and see!''

Rapid footsteps came toward the stairwell. Bak shot upward, refusing to be caught listening. As he hit the top step, the man burst through the door. They slammed together, knocking the breath from them both, and fell to the floor, arms and legs entangled across the threshold.

"Oh, no!'' Aset, wide-eyed and gaping, ran toward them.

She knelt at their heads and, paying no heed to Bak, bent over the other man, her look of surprise and shock melting to concern. Both men struggled to sit erect, forcing her back, and stared at one another. The man with whom she had quarreled was Nebseny, the one who had dragged her away from Bak's quarters the previous evening.

"You!'' Nebseny spat. "I should've known.''

Aset, seeing he was unhurt, deepened her look of concern and turned to Bak. Placing a hand on his arm, she gave him a gentle and worried smile. "Are you alright? Did this clumsy oaf hurt you?''

Bak, noting the fury on Nebseny's face, scrambled to his feet, distancing himself from both of them. He reached out to the gangly young man, offering to help him stand. Nebseny spurned the hand with a resentful glare and rose without aid.

Aset stood up and strode across the courtyard, her back

stiff with purpose. Two servants, watching wide-eyed from a portal opening to the rear of the house, hastily withdrew lest she spot them. She stopped before a bow and a leather quiver filled with arrows leaning against the wall beside the door to Woser's reception room. She picked up the bow, almost as long as she was tall, and the heavy quiver and brought them back.

"Take this trash with you and get out!" she commanded, shoving them at Nebseny. "I never want to see them or you in this house again."

Bak cursed the gods and Aset, too. Nebseny was the man with whom he had come to talk.

"This is a place of business as well as your home, you selfish . . ." Nebseny controlled himself, and added with a sneer, "Don't worry, my sweet. I'll not darken the door again except when summoned by your father." Shouldering his quiver and bow, he pivoted toward the stairwell.

Bak stepped into his path, barring his way. "I've come to speak with you about Lieutenant Puemre's death."

"Get out of my way!"

"Commander Woser promised you'd talk with me."

Nebseny spoke through gritted teeth. "I had nothing to do with that snake's death, nor do I know who slew him. I wish I did, for he did us all a good deed by cleansing this garrison of scum worse than that found in a stagnant pool."

Bak knew jealousy was speaking, but what else? "Was he an accomplished archer as well as infantryman?"

"His skills with a bow were adequate, that's all."

"You were fortunate then. He had no basis to usurp your men and duties."

Aset slipped around Nebseny to stand beside Bak. She stood so close he could feel the heat of her shoulder next to his, her hair brushing his arm. Her voice was honey-sweet. "Lieutenants Nebseny and Puemre had much in common. One was a mere soldier who wanted the good things in life; the other had the good things but wanted more to be a good soldier."

Her words were designed to goad the archer, as was her proximity to Bak. What did she want? he wondered. To set one against the other?

Nebseny affected to ignore her. "You've talked to Huy, I see, and to Senu. I can add no more."

Shouldering Bak aside, shoving him against Aset, the archer hastened down the stairwell, never looking back. The girl clutched Bak's arm as if for support and looked up at him with the large brown eyes of the lady Hathor in her guise as a cow. She raised moist red lips toward his, inviting intimacy. He was too angry with her for ruining his chance to talk with Nebseny to feel any kind of warmth. Nor did her father's proximity entice him, nor her determination to escape Iken with wealth and position.

Gently but firmly, he pushed her away, pivoted on his heel, and followed Nebseny down the stairs. He left the building with a sigh of relief and a rueful laugh at his own expense. For the first time in his life, he was running away from a beautiful woman.

Not until he was halfway to the towered gate did he realize how much he had learned without exchanging more than a dozen words with Nebseny. The young officer was in love with Aset, crazed with jealousy. He had implied that the girl had, at the very least, encouraged Puemre's attentions. If that wasn't a reason for murder, Bak did not know what was. As for Aset, could she have slain Puemre, he wondered? She might well have had reason, especially if he spurned her, but she was too slightly built, he felt sure, and not strong enough.

Chapter Eight

"Haven't seen either man this morning." Sennufer lifted a crumpled cloth from the top of a game table and wiped away the sweat rolling down his face, neck, and wiry torso. "If they show up, I'll tell them you're looking for them."

"They'll come," Bak assured him from the doorway. "We were to meet here sometime after midday."

The house of pleasure reeked of sweat and fermenting bread. The heat hung thick and cloying in the air. A half dozen men, sailors from the look of their sun-toughened skin, sat on the hard-packed earthen floor, playing a game of chance. Each time one threw the gaming sticks, they yelled or cursed according to their luck.

"Have you seen the craftsman who dreamed of murder?" Bak asked. "Or remembered anything more about him?"

Sennufer, his mouth screwed up in thought, threw the cloth over his shoulder. "I keep seeing his hands, a grayish dirt under his nails, but I told you that before." He removed a beer jar from the stack against the wall and, donning a genial smile, held it out. "Come on in, Lieutenant. May as well enjoy a brew while you wait."

Bak smiled his thanks, but edged backwards, beating a tactful retreat from the heat, the stench, and the noise. "I've a man to see at the harbor. Tell my men to come to me there."

Grayish dirt. Sennufer had initially described the besotted man's hands as dirty, but had given no color. Now he claimed the dirt was gray. Bak could think of no specific craft where a gray material was regularly used. Maybe Sennufer erred, with time adding color to his imagination.

He swallowed the last few bites of fish and threw the broad leaves in which it had been wrapped into the river. For an instant they remained cupped together, floating like a miniature green boat, but the current soon caught them and swept them downstream, tearing them asunder. He left the shade of a tamarisk, its roots teased by the rising waters of the river, and climbed the bank. Upstream lay the harbor, where he was to meet the last of the four officers who had attended Woser's meeting, the river pilot Lieutenant Inyotef.

He strode along a sandy lane poorly populated in the midday heat by a few sailors, a trader or two, and a housewife with her young female servant. Three men walked past in the opposite direction, leading a donkey caravan. The heavy scent of hay piled high on the animals' backs made Bak sneeze. A dozen or more warehouses faced the harbor, along with a few small places of business and homes. The tumbled walls of several abandoned warehouses stood among them, reminders of a more industrious time long ago when more grain was needed to feed a large and hungry garrison. Two squat cargo ships and a narrow-hulled trading vessel nestled against the quays. Several small skiffs were tied among them.

Bak sat in the shade of a stand of acacias near the harbor, his knees drawn up beneath his chin, his eyes on the ships and the men toiling in and around them.

"Lieutenant Bak?" A male voice behind him.

Bak hastened to stand, then turned around and gaped. "Inyotef?"

The man standing before him, a man of medium height, slender yet broad-shouldered with curly graying hair, broke into a smile. "By the beard of the lord Amon! Never would I have dreamed the police officer I was told to meet would be you!"

Bak clasped Inyotef's shoulders. "Nor would it ever have occurred to me that the river pilot Inyotef was in actual fact Captain Inyotef of the royal fleet."

"No longer, my boy." The older man stepped back to look at the younger. The movement was awkward, one of his legs less nimble than the other.

Bak sucked in his breath, his eyes darted toward the weaker limb and away. The puckered brownish scar and misshapen bone below the knee struck him like a blow to the stomach. He was responsible for the injury that had crippled this man.

"I now see ships safely through the Belly of Stones." Inyotef smiled, either unaware of Bak's dismay or ignoring it. "The task may not be as glamorous as captaining a warship, but it requires more thought and skill."

"How long have you been in Iken?" Bak managed.

"Three years this time."

He must have come soon after his leg healed, Bak thought. *Had he been sent south because a man so deformed was believed unworthy to sail one of the great royal ships of the line?* "This time?" he echoed.

"I've a skiff tied up at the northern quay. Come, we can talk there." Ushering Bak along the waterfront, his pace rapid in spite of his pronounced limp, Inyotef explained. "My first command, long ago, was in Wawat. I learned then to bring the ships through the rapids at Abu and twice I brought vessels through the Belly of Stones. So when I heard a pilot was needed here, I asked to come."

Bak tried not to see the limp, tried not to remember, but the nightmare would not go away. The regiment of Amon had been sent to Mennufer to practice maneuvers on the great sweep of sands west of the pyramid-tombs of the early kings. They had sailed from Waset by boat and were to return the same way. Bak's chariot horses, among others, had been assigned stalls on the deck of Inyotef's ship. He and the captain had become friends of sorts, talking as men do about anything and everything during the long, idle hours of the voyage.

On the morning of departure for the return trip, he had led his team, two fine bay geldings, to the gangplank. Four men stood two or three paces away watching the loading, among them Captain Inyotef. One of the horses was highly strung at the best of times. The gangplank terrified him. Bak calmed him with words and caresses and led him to the narrow bridge. As his front hooves touched the wood, someone laughed, a hearty guffaw that boomed across the wharf. The horse flung its head back, jerking the halter from Bak's grip, and swung around, striking Inyotef, knocking him to the pavement and stepping on his leg.

Bak had gone with his company back to Waset but, thanks to a physician friend of his father, had kept track of Inyotef's progress. The break had been bad; for many days the doctors held little hope he would survive the pain and infection. Willpower alone had pulled him through the crisis. After the worst was over, he had improved daily until he was once again on his feet. Bak had heard no more. He had assumed, or wanted to believe at any rate, that Inyotef had fully recovered.

"You've no need to ache with guilt, Bak," Inyotef said, reading his thoughts. "During those days while once again I learned to walk, I realized I'd never command another warship. It wasn't in me, and I'm speaking of my heart as well as my body." He stopped before a sleek white skiff bobbing on tiny swells washing against the quay. "I'd wanted to return to Wawat from the day I left, but the power and thrill of command held me in Kemet. My injury gave me the excuse I needed."

"I'd like to believe that." The words sprang forth from deep within Bak's soul.

"I swear by all the gods in the ennead, it's the truth." Inyotef clapped him on the shoulder. "Now let me show you my pride and joy, and then we'll talk of murder."

Bak searched Inyotef's face, looking for blame. He found none. He wished he could so easily forgive himself.

The skiff was much like any other rivercraft, as far as Bak was concerned, except better cared for than most. Inyotef talked of the mast and fittings, the halyards, the sail like a man speaking of his love. The pilot caressed the prow, held the rudder with a tender grip, admired the curved lines of the hull with his eyes. Of greater importance to Bak, who cared more for living creatures than inanimate objects, Inyotef moved about the vessel with the agility of a monkey, his infirmity diminished by familiarity.

"I spend much of my free time here." Inyotef raised a reed awning over the open hull and motioned Bak to sit in the prow. "My wife could never accept the frontier life of Iken, so she went back to Kemet some months ago. I've no one now to go home to."

Bak squashed another tug of conscience. Through his fault, Inyotef's life had been torn asunder, but that was no excuse to turn his back on the task he had been given. "You were one of the last to see Puemre alive, I've been told."

The pilot pulled a torn sail from a basket near the stern. "As you surely know by now, I and the others who attended Woser's meeting parted outside the commander's residence." He draped the sail over his lap, covering his legs, and threaded a large bronze needle. "I went to the bathhouse, but at the door I decided to go home instead. As I walked along the street to the main gate, I fell in behind Puemre. I thought of catching up, but as he was no particular friend, it wasn't worth the effort of rushing after him."

Bak realized he was being handed two distinct paths to follow. He chose the most obvious. "How long were you behind him?"

"All the way to the lower city." Inyotef poked the needle through the heavy cloth and pulled the thread through.

"At the base of the escarpment, he turned north, taking a lane to his house. I went my own way, going first to the river for a walk before making my way home."

Bak was puzzled. "Huy lives inside the fortress, yet you and Senu don't, nor did Puemre. Why is that?"

"I can't speak for Puemre, but most women prefer the lower city, where the houses are in better condition and the market closer to hand." Inyotef smiled. "Woser would like us inside the garrison, but he'd have a general uprising if he insisted. The strongest man is only as strong as the women in his household."

"Does mistress Aset complain?" Bak grinned. "Or is she content to hold court in the commander's residence?"

Inyotef laughed. "Her complaints never end. Woser long ago grew deaf to those he can do nothing about."

Bak's smile broadened, but soon he sobered. "Your fellow officers called Puemre a swine and a snake. I take it you agree."

Inyotef's laugh turned wry. "Either name will do. As I said before, he was no friend of mine."

Bak studied the pilot, looking for a sign of deceit. He saw nothing but a bland innocence overlying contempt for the dead man. The contempt he could accept; the bland innocence was suspect, especially since Inyotef had gone out of his way to make sure Bak understood he did not like Puemre. "Each had an unhappy tale to tell. Do you also have one, Inyotef?"

"Puemre was arrogant, self-centered, and unprincipled. What more can I say?"

"You can be more specific."

The pilot snorted. "Why would he bother with one such as I? I had nothing he wanted."

Bak decided to call his bluff—if he was bluffing. "I thank you, my friend, for the information." He stood up, preparing to disembark. The vessel bobbed on a swell, forcing him to grab the mast. "I've many men still to interview, but I'll talk with you later when I have more time."

Inyotef's eyes flickered. "Oh, I suppose you'll hear sooner or later." He sounded and looked truly resigned.

Bak had to smother a smile. The pilot, like his fellow officers, had a sound reason for slaying Puemre, and he was not about to be cheated out of admitting it.

Inyotef lowered his eyes to the torn sail, hiding his expression in his task. "Puemre thought me unworthy, a man who'd given up, and he looked upon me with scorn." His voice took on an edge of anger. "He told all who would listen that I was old and unfit, that instead of guiding vessels through the Belly of Stones, I should be sent back to Kemet. He said perhaps I could run a ferry across one of the smaller channels of the river where it flows through the marshlands of the north."

"And you a former warship captain."

"It hurt." Inyotef's mouth tightened. "If he'd lived long enough, I might've . . ." His eyes met Bak's and he gave a humorless smile. "Who knows what a man can do when driven too far?"

"So you see," Bak said with a scowl, "any of the four, or Commander Woser himself, could've slain Puemre. Each man had a reason and each the opportunity."

Pashenuro stood at the edge of the water, peering into its shallow depths, his light harpoon poised to strike the first good-sized fish to swim by. "Would the innocent officers protect the guilty?"

Bak grimaced, disgusted with the lot. "It looks like it, doesn't it?"

After leaving Inyotef, he had found the stocky Medjay waiting for him beneath the stand of acacias, the harpoon beside him and a reed basket for the fish he meant to catch for their evening meal. Kasaya had not yet shown up. They had left a message for him with two boys playing on the quay and had walked downstream, following the irregular row of tamarisks and acacias growing along the river's edge, searching for a low spot already underwater.

"What of the plot to slay King Amon-Psaro?" Pashen-uro asked.

Bak eyed what looked like a long, brownish chunk of driftwood beached in the sun on the rocky island across the channel. Or was it a crocodile? "If such a plot exists—and I'm not yet convinced one does—and if they're in it to-gether, they'd have to protect each other, whether guilty or innocent of Puemre's murder."

"Try as I might, I can think of no good reason for of-ficers in the army of Kemet to slay a Kushite king."

"Nor can I." Bak waded out knee-deep into the water. The thick rich mud bubbled up between his toes and the current tugged on his legs. "I'd bet a month's allotment of grain that Puemre was slain for a personal reason."

The Medjay thrust his harpoon, catching a perch midway along its body. The creature writhed in the water, stirring up the mud. Pashenuro jerked it off the long, narrow point and killed it with a quick blow.

Throwing his prize into the basket with two smaller fish, he said, "The men of the garrison think highly of Com-mander Woser. They'll listen to nothing bad about him. If his officers are equally devoted, they'd protect him, espe-cially if they, too, hated Puemre."

"I've a feeling his daughter Aset tempted Puemre as she did me." Something cold touched Bak's leg. He jerked back, startled. A good-sized catfish darted away, perfect for the brazier if he'd had a harpoon. "I've no doubt she cared less for the man than for his nobility, but if in some way he threatened her well-being, Woser would've had good reason to slay him. As would the archer Nebseny. He har-bors the jealousy of a spurned lover."

"There's a rumor going round the barracks . . ." Pash-enuro's eyes darted across the channel toward the island. "The crocodile has had enough sun. He's on the move, heading for the water."

Bak followed his glance. The log had grown short, stubby legs and a long snout edged with teeth. He wasted

no time wading back to the sandy shore. "A rumor, uh?"
He grinned. "I knew your morning with the troops would
be time well spent."

Pashenuro's smile vanished half-formed. He plunged into
the water and thrust his weapon. His leading foot slid forward; he staggered and came close to falling. The fish flitted away unscathed. Muttering a curse, he waded back to
dry land.

"They say mistress Aset is with child and the father unknown."

Bak whistled softly, surprised yet not surprised. "She's
too set on living a life of luxury and ease to have played
with just any man. Who does the rumor call the most likely
sire?"

"Lieutenants Nebseny and Puemre lead the race. A
trader has been suggested, but no one remembers seeing
her outside her father's house with any man other than a
servant or an officer."

"Probably not a trader then." Bak knelt to splash water
on his face, arms, and chest. "How's Woser supposed to've
reacted?"

"They say he's filled with rage."

Bak had never seen the father and daughter together. He
vowed, when finally the opportunity arose, to pay close
attention to the way they behaved with one another. He
also renewed his determination to stay far away from Aset.
"What else did you hear?"

"I heard much talk of Puemre's talents as a soldier. Even
the sergeants, the most critical of men, spoke highly of his
abilities. He erred a single time, they say, losing a few of
his men because his ideals were so high he couldn't bring
himself to ambush the unwary enemy. There was some talk
that Troop Captain Huy was at fault there, but in general
he's regarded as a good and honest man and few I talked
with hold the blame as true."

Bak rose to his feet. A faint breath of air touched his
dripping shoulders, cooling them for an instant. "Are the

men aware of how much Puemre was disliked by his fellow officers?''

Pashenuro studied the water intently, his eyes on a school of fingerlings. ''They know, but they don't understand. Especially since they respect and admire them all.'' He clutched his harpoon tighter, but the larger fish he expected never appeared. ''You may or may not know, but every man you suspect of murder—except Lieutenant Nebseny—long ago received at least one golden fly.''

Bak stood dead still, startled by the news and humbled. Golden flies were awarded only to men of proven valor and presented by the sovereign herself. Or, more likely in this case, her deceased husband or her father before him. ''How long ago?''

''Twenty-seven years. They fought in the army of Akheperenre Tuthmose during our last war against the Kushites.''

Maatkare Hatshepsut's husband and brother. Not as great a warrior as his father before him, but one who had vanquished the Kushites once and for all. Bak was glad he had not known about the gold of valor when he spoke with the officers. The knowledge might have weakened his resolve to think of them as suspects.

''The news is a blow,'' he admitted. ''How can I accuse men so valiant of slaying a fellow officer?''

''There's worse,'' Pashenuro said grimly.

Bak closed his eyes for a moment, resigning himself. ''Go on.''

''According to several men I spoke with, Troop Captain Huy and Lieutenant Senu came upon Puemre in a house of pleasure one night. They left before he did and were seen later, waiting in the shadows of the lane outside. The next morning, Puemre showed up at his men's barracks, bruised and battered from head to toe. He'd been beaten, he claimed, by men he never saw.''

Bak leaped to the obvious conclusion, as every man in the garrison must have.

"Another time," the Medjay went on, "Puemre mysteriously fell overboard when on a ship piloted by Lieutenant Inyotef. Thanks to the lord Amon and the fact that he could swim like a fish, he saved himself."

Men of valor, Bak thought cynically. "What of Nebseny?"

"He once threatened publicly to castrate Puemre, but I heard of no instance where he tried to follow through. One reason given for the threat was mistress Aset. Another was an accusation Puemre made, saying Nebseny's archers failed to support his infantry during a riverside skirmish a month or two ago."

"With the officers divided, were not the troops also divided in their loyalties?"

"Not yet, thanks to the good sense and strength of purpose of their sergeants, but I felt an undercurrent of unease. A breach would soon have come, I think."

"Puemre's death came at a most opportune time, it seems."

Bak picked up a handful of small stones and pieces of broken pottery. One by one he threw them at the river, skipping them across its surface, giving his body something to do while he put Pashenuro's gleanings into perspective. Two facts leaped out from the rest: First, the officers had told him nothing more than every man and woman in Iken already knew. Second:

"Did Amon-Psaro lead the Kushites when our soldiers faced them in battle twenty-seven years ago?"

"I thought the same," Pashenuro smiled, "but no. He was a prince then, only ten years of age, too young to go to war."

With a sigh, Bak transferred the last bit of pottery from his left hand to his right—and stopped to stare at the squarish lump. The shard was a greenish gray. And gray ware was made in Iken for trade upriver. The besotted witness must be a potter.

*   *   *

"I didn't see a thing!" Antef sprinkled a small handful of fine chaff on the lump of wet grayish clay and kneaded it in with all the power in his thick, stubby fingers, taking out his distress on the material. "I didn't! It was too dark! I swear to the lord Khnum!"

Bak controlled his impatience with an effort.

The chief potter had explained that Antef had once been a skilled craftsman, but was no longer trusted to form the clay into the mediocre ware shipped south to the land of Kush. The reason was apparent. Antef's hands shook uncontrollably, not so much from fear as from too much beer over too many long years.

Bak knelt beside the short, grizzled man and laid a soothing hand on his shoulder. "I'm accusing you of nothing, Antef. I merely want to know what happened that night."

"I saw the lady Hathor. She came to me, offering me the pleasure of her body."

Antef looked around as if to assure himself his fellow potters were not listening. From the studied way they concentrated on their respective tasks, Bak could tell they were. The potter talked on, his tension receding as the goddess filled his thoughts. He told the same story Meryre had repeated but with many and sundry details, most of which, Bak suspected, had crept into the tale not from memory but through frequent repetition.

While the potter spoke, Bak glanced around the workshop, which he had found among the broken walls of an ancient house in the lower city. It was a good-sized enterprise employing four potters, each with an assistant to turn his wheel. Spindly wooden frames covered with reed mats shaded them and their work through the heat of the day. Another man puddled the clay, treading it out with his bare feet, adding sand or chopped straw or dung as required, while Antef kneaded special batches by hand. A younger man, maybe sent by his father to learn the craft, carried the formed pots into a roofless room, lining them up to dry.

The chief potter stoked a cylindrical brick oven as tall as he was.

"Saying she wanted me alone, with no other man to see or hear, the lady took my hand and led me outside the walls of the city." Antef was deep into his story, his eyes locked on some distant place well out of reach of men with less imagination. "We stopped many times to kiss, and she fondled me and I, her. When at last we found our nest among the rocks, we fell to the earth together, starved for satisfaction."

Bak hated to interrupt so vivid a tale. "Where was this place, Antef?"

The potter shook his head, dragging himself back to reality. "North of here it was, among the rocks overlooking the far end of the long island." He pointed vaguely toward the river. "The place is rough and lonely, but the sand has made a bed as soft as the fuzz on a newly hatched duckling."

Bak remembered seeing the low rock outcrop some distance downriver from where he and Pashenuro had talked. It would have been a long walk for a man besotted by beer. "You've more to tell, I know."

Antef went on, describing in lurid detail every man's dream of a night with a goddess. His coworkers sneaked glances at each other and at Bak, their mouths twitching with silent laughter.

"When at last she wore me out," Antef said, "I closed my eyes and slept. When next I awoke, a sliver of moon was showing and she was gone."

"What woke you?" Bak asked.

"Nothing." Antef's eyes darted to his inquisitor's face and fell away. "Nothing, I swear!"

"You heard two men talking, didn't you?" Bak kept his voice hard, his tone positive, as if he himself had been on the spot instead of hearing the tale thirdhand from Meryre. "You saw them arguing. One man turned away, preparing to leave. The other grabbed him from behind. I know what happened then—one man stabbed the other—but I must hear it in your words."

"No! I saw nothing!"

"I don't enjoy using the cudgel, but I will if I must."

"It was dark, but . . ." Antef's voice broke; he dropped his chin to his breast. "Yes, he slew him. I could tell from the sounds I heard and what little I could see. He stabbed him in the face or maybe the neck, dragged him to the river, and pushed him in. It happened so fast . . . I could do nothing to help, I swear!"

Not that fast, Bak felt sure, but even if Antef had interceded, Puemre would have died. And the potter would probably have died with him. "What did the murderer look like?"

"I never saw his face. If I had, I'd have told." Antef began to sob. "I fear him greatly, and I'll not rest until he's caught. But I can't help you. I saw only his back."

Bak believed him. He was too frightened to lie.

"I asked everyone I met to tell me of the boy," Kasaya said, "but no one has seen him. He was like a shadow to Lieutenant Puemre. Now it's as if the sun has gone and the shadow with it."

"Was he slain and thrown into the river like Puemre, I wonder?" Pashenuro asked.

"Antef saw no child." Bak's voice turned grim, reflecting the dread lurking in his thoughts. "We can only pray he wasn't slain somewhere else at another time."

The trio hurried along the row of trees hugging the river's edge. Kasaya, the best tracker of the three, scanned the earth to right and left, searching for tracks or objects that might have been left behind by a child or by a man intent on throwing aside the remnants of murder.

They slowed their pace as they approached their goal, a mound of tortured black granite, broken and cracked by oven-like heat and midnight cold, by blowing sands and raging waters. Rising from a blanket of dun-colored sand blown off the western desert, the mound reached out toward the northern end of the elongated island that lay in the water below the fortress. The channel between mound and island was confined to a passage no broader than ten paces, where the water raged down a series of shallow, foaming falls and swirled around jagged and torn boulders.

They climbed the mound, searching first for the sheltered spot where Antef had dreamed of the lady Hathor. The wind had blown with strength at least twice since Puemre's disappearance, so their chances of finding signs of murder were slim at best. Nevertheless, they had to try.

Bak stood on the tallest chunk of granite and, hands on hips, surveyed the tumbled stones and raging waters below. To the west, the lord Re was resting on the horizon. "The scarred man, you say, is an armorer?"

"If he's the man you saw, and he must be, his name is Senmut." Kasaya knelt on a low, snaggle-tooth boulder to study a likely pocket of sand. "The chief armorer told me he makes and repairs spears, sharpening points and setting them on the shafts."

Pashenuro stole Bak's next question. "What was his connection with Lieutenant Puemre?"

Kasaya moved on to another nook. "Senmut's oldest daughter, a girl of fifteen years, was the one who cleaned and washed and cooked for him and the boy."

Bak scowled. "If she did nothing more than housework, why would her father knock me senseless to search the building?" He stepped across a gap to another, lower boulder. Glancing at a small sandy pocket, he let out a grunt of satisfaction. "Here's Antef's nest, I think. Or someone else's secret drinking place."

The Medjays hurried to his side to look at four empty beer jars lodged in a crack between two weathered boulders. A yellowish stain on another rock reeked of urine. After Kasaya searched the area and found nothing further, they stood where Antef must have and looked down on the sandy waste below the mound. Somewhere there, Puemre had been slain.

The Medjays clambered down and set to work, examining the sweep of sand while Bak searched the rest of the mound. The shadows were long and deep when Kasaya found a small dark stain he thought was blood buried under the fine layer of sand deposited since the murder. Pashenuro hurried to the river and worked his way along the shore. He soon found a brownish spot on a rock poised an arm's length above the swirling waters. It might or might not have been blood, but the rock would have been an ideal place from which to jettison Puemre's body.

Darkness was falling when Bak found the footprint, located half under a rock in a niche so small only a child could have hidden there. From that point, the mute boy Ramose could have peered through a gap between boulders and watched the slayer take Puemre's life. They had to find that child—if still he lived.

"I've found something!" he called, his voice pulsing with excitement.

A loud crack sounded beside him. He glanced around, uncertain what had made the noise. He noticed a faint smudge on the rock next to him, like a bruise.

"Get down, Lieutenant!" Pashenuro yelled, ducking into a crack too narrow for his bulk.

Bak glimpsed something fly past his head and heard another, louder crack. A rock! Someone using a sling. A deadly weapon in the hands of a trained warrior, a weapon often used by the soldiers of Wawat. He ducked, rolled between projecting stones, and peeked out to check on his men. Kasaya was hunkered down next to a boulder at the base of the mound, staring out toward the water. Pashenuro's refuge was closer to the river.

Another missile about the size of a goose egg flew over Bak's head, smashed against the boulder behind him, and burst.

"There he is!" Pashenuro called. "Behind the ridge on the island."

"I see him!" Kasaya yelled.

Bak squirmed around until he could see. As if on demand, a man popped up, swung his arm, and let fly another rock that smacked against a boulder within arm's length. He vanished as fast as he had appeared. The way the light was failing, Bak had seen nothing but a vague, colorless silhouette.

He felt no sense of danger—he and his men were safe as long as they remained where they were—but he hated being pinned down, waiting to be saved by the dark. And he longed to catch the assailant. He studied the channel between the mound and the island, thinking he might swim across. The flow was fast and the low falls, if the foam gave any clue, were pounding on hidden rocks. The risk was too great.

"I might be able to swim across." Kasaya's voice was tentative, as if he too thought the risk unwarranted.

"Let the swine go." Bak glanced at the print of the small, bare foot, making sure he had not scuffed it in his rush for safety. "I've a footprint you must see before the light goes."

They walked back to their quarters in the dark, too intent on making their way through the unfamiliar city to talk of their experience. Bak was puzzled by the attack. Why had the assailant used a sling when a bow would have been a far more effective weapon? Only one reason made sense: a bow and full quiver would have been impossible to transport if the attacker swam to the long island.

A second question troubled him. He and his men had learned almost nothing about Puemre's death. Every tale they had heard since arriving at Iken had been common knowledge. So why would anyone try to slay them? Or had he alone been the intended victim? Most of the rocks had come his way. Had he learned something unique, something no one else knew? Or had one of Woser's officers simply been trying to frighten him off? He worried the problem like a dog frets over a tough piece of leather, but found no satisfactory explanation.

The answer came in the dead of night while he lay on his sleeping pallet on the roof, wide-awake, staring at the stars, letting his thoughts drift. Only he had seen the sketch on the broken piece of pottery. If someone thought it important enough to try to scare him off, the drawing must be factual. Which meant Amon-Psaro's life must be at risk after all. A chill flooded his body, making the hairs on his arms stand on end. If Amon-Psaro was slain by a man of Kemet, war would be inevitable.

He could be wrong. He prayed he was. But he had to assume the worst.

Chapter Nine

"Find that boy." Bak hurried up the gully to the fortress, through the main gate, and along the street to the armory, repeating the words over and over in his thoughts, the orders he had given Kasaya and Pashenuro. "If he still lives, we must make sure he stays alive. If he's been slain, we must learn how and when and by whom."

The Medjays had left their quarters with the same sense of urgency he felt. The mute boy Ramose had to be located and, if still living, Bak had to find a way to communicate with him. He had to know for a fact the significance of the sketch on the pottery shard. The fortress of Semna, and therefore Amon-Psaro, was too close to Iken for comfort. Even worse, all Bak's suspects would be traveling upstream to Semna with the lord Amon. The god's entourage would provide an ideal refuge for a potential assassin, allowing him to make his play and slip back among the others camouflaged as one among many.

Bak strode into the armory, a building too spacious for the number of men toiling there, its once whitewashed walls now worn and dirtied to the dark brown of river silt. Long ago when the fortress had been fully manned, the structure had bustled with craftsmen striving to arm a large and active force. Now, with the garrison small and the battles reduced to skirmishes, with most weapons brought in by ship from the north, the need was limited to minor manufacture and repairs.

Pausing on the threshold, he nodded a greeting to the chief armorer, a swarthy, muscular man of thirty or so years, and glanced around in search of the scarred man. The hot, stuffy room rang with the sound of two men hammering bronze points to harden the edges. The acrid smell of molten metal filled the air around a thick pottery furnace nested on a bed of charcoal. Quick, sharp clicks and the sound of broken stone skittering across the hard-packed earthen floor betrayed the presence of someone in the next room flaking flint for an arrowhead or some other implement of war. The stench of wet leather drifted through an open door, beyond which several men were stretching reddish hides onto wooden frames, making or repairing shields.

A barrel-chested man of medium height, his cheek deformed by a long scar, strode through the rear door. He spotted Bak, his eyes widened with recognition, and he swung around as if to run. He had nowhere to go; the armory had only a single exit.

"Senmut!" Bak snapped, silencing the pounding and chipping, drawing a dozen gawkers from the surrounding rooms.

A look of craven fear washed across the scarred face. "I didn't slay Lieutenant Puemre! I swear it!"

Bak had expected a denial, but one of lesser consequence. "If you're as innocent as you claim, why did you knock me out? Why search the house?"

The chief armorer scowled at the watching men, sending them scurrying back to their tasks, then hunkered down near the outer door, listening to every word, every shade of meaning. He would no doubt report what he heard to his family and probably to half of Iken as well.

"I've done nothing!" Senmut said. "I swear!"

"Why did you run two days ago, when you found me in Puemre's house?"

"Wouldn't you? Would you want to be blamed for something you didn't do?"

"You're open to blame until you explain yourself." Losing patience, Bak caught Senmut's arms above the elbows and shook him. "Now talk! I want no more denials."

Senmut backed up, his steps clumsy, his eyes fearful. "I went looking for the boy, that's all. I swear it! Then I saw you on the floor, Puemre's belongings strewn around you, and I ran."

"The boy . . ." Bak's ears took in the silence of the tools, the idleness of craftsmen too busy listening to work. "You need a jar of beer, Senmut." To the chief armorer he added, "I'll not keep him long."

Senmut, startled into obedience, led the way to a house of pleasure in the next block, where the proprietor sold beer so thick it clogged the strainer. The establishment was neat and clean, with walls freshly whitewashed and a floor sprinkled with water to keep down the dust. Beer jars and drinking bowls stood in tidy stacks, and a few low three-legged stools were scattered among straw-stuffed pillows for seating. The brew was strong and tasty, ideal for breaking down a wall of defense and loosening a tongue. A large helping of patience might also be in order, Bak reminded himself.

"You went looking for the boy," he said, keeping his voice kind, conversational. "The mute child Ramose, you mean?"

Senmut eyed his interrogator with suspicion. "He needs a new home. I thought to take him to mine, to make him part of my household." He drank from his bowl, taking several healthy swallows. "I've no wife to mother him. She died two years ago. But my children like him, and my oldest daughter is a mother to all."

Bak studied the armorer's face, searching for a lie. "The neighbors haven't seen the boy since the night Puemre disappeared. I fear for his safety."

Senmut's work-hardened hands fidgeted on the bowl.

"He's a tough little fellow, a born scavenger. He can get by where most others would starve."

"Puemre was slain," Bak said, spelling it out. "The child might well have suffered a like fate."

The armorer's voice turned gruff, despairing. "Puemre was a son to me, and Ramose a son to him. I'll care for him as I will my daughter's unborn child." Bak's last grim words must have sunk in then, for he shook his head and gave a pathetic imitation of a smile. "The boy ran away, that's all. He came to my daughter yesterday morning to let her see he was alive and well. In the market, it was, soon after the fishermen brought in their catch."

Bak's emotions leaped to surprise and delight, and gratitude to the lord Amon. Yet he was confused by Senmut's mixed signals, by so deep a despair. "Your daughter cooked for Puemre and cleaned his house?"

Senmut wiped his nose with the back of his hand, sniffed. "She cared for him, yes, and one day soon she'll care for his child." His voice broke, and he covered his face with his hands. His shoulders trembled with silent sobs.

Puemre's child? Bak laid a kindly hand on his arm. "I must speak with her, Senmut. Where can I find her?"

Mutnefer, Bak guessed, was close to Aset in age, but there the resemblance ended. Where Woser's only daughter was delicate and lovely, Senmut's eldest child was graceless and plain. Where Aset was girlish and fanciful, Mutnefer was a woman heavy with child and the responsibility for her father's household, six children between the ages of two and twelve.

"Puemre loved me, and I him." Mutnefer rested her hand on her unborn child, and her voice trembled. She wore a loose dress of ordinary linen, a single wristlet of bronze, and the merest touch of kohl on eyes red-rimmed from crying. "He meant to take us with him when he went back to Kemet."

Bak, seated on a stool in the roofless cooking area behind the three-room house, was touched by her faith in Puemre's promises. Hiding his compassion, he watched her drop a lump of well-kneaded dough into a round pottery baking dish, setting it in a mound of hot coals. She covered the dish with a conical lid. A naked two-year-old boy played in the shady doorway and a girl of eight or so bent over a stone mortar, pushing the grindstone back and forth, making coarse flour from grain. He had seen two other small children, the oldest about five, playing on the roof under the sharp eye of a ten-year-old. The child next in age to Mutnefer, a boy of twelve or so, had gone to the river to fish. All who were old enough had to earn their bread in Senmut's household.

"Without your help, how did your father plan to care for so large a brood?"

Her smile was as tremulous as her voice. "They, too, were to go to Kemet: my father, my brothers and sisters. Puemre promised us a house on his father's estate, a parcel of land, and even a servant, a woman to care for the small ones. Instead of making weapons, my father would make tools for the men who worked the fields of the estate."

A promise easily made, Bak thought, and equally easy to forget. "What was to become of you? Were you to wed him or . . . ?"

She laughed, incredulous. "I have no noble blood! He loved me, yes, and he meant to take me into his household. I would've been his favorite for all time, he vowed, but his concubine, not his wife."

Bak thought it best to drop the subject before she guessed how skeptical he was. He did not want to hurt her. "When did you last see Puemre?"

"The evening he disappeared." Her voice dropped to an unhappy murmur. "He walked me home before reporting to the commander's residence."

"What did he say? Will you tell me of his mood? Was he happy or sad or angry, for example?"

Mutnefer retrieved a portable camp stool from the house. The legs were carved and painted to look like the delicate heads of river birds, the seat made of finely woven leather. Bak could imagine a piece of that quality in the commander's residence, not in this poor household.

She noticed his interest. "Puemre saw the trouble I had getting off the ground once I sat down, so he brought this stool to ease my life." Blinking back tears, she placed it in the shady strip next to the wall and sat down heavily.

He wondered what he would do if she had the baby then and there. The thought was unsettling—until he recalled seeing women on the roofs of several houses in the block.

"Puemre came home that day long before dusk. I always cooked his evening meal and ate with him and Ramose, then brought whatever was left back to my family." She closed her eyes, swallowed. "He picked me up and swung me around in a circle, so excited he spoke in riddles. He mentioned the king Amon-Psaro, the prince, revenge, and a great battle with the Kushites. He said our sovereign, Maatkare Hatshepsut herself, would give him the gold of valor and more."

Bak felt like hugging her. She had supplied the motive for Puemre's murder, far exceeding his expectations. Puemre had somehow discovered that Amon-Psaro was to be slain at the hands of an avenger. He should have shared the knowledge with someone in authority, but had kept the matter to himself so he alone could bask in glory. Now he was dead, silenced forever. His secrecy was unforgivable. Even if he mistrusted his fellow officers and his commander, he should have sent a message to Commandant Thuty.

Bak questioned Mutnefer further, but she could tell him nothing more. Puemre had babbled, filling in no details. If he had not opened his heart to her, Bak wondered, with whom had he talked? An image of the sketch on the pottery shard leaped into his thoughts. The mute child. Who better to confide in than one who could neither hear nor speak?

"Your father said Puemre's servant, the boy Ramose, came to you in the market yesterday."

Mutnefer stared at her hands, her fingers entwined over her bulging stomach, her face bleak with worry.

"If he can name the man who slew Puemre, and I've reason to believe he can, he's in grave danger." Bak leaned toward her, willing her to speak. "I must find him, mistress, before the killer does."

"I don't know where he is." Her hands writhed. "I can't talk to him. Puemre never taught me how. But I could tell how afraid he was."

"Did you give him food?"

She bit her lip, nodded. "What I could spare."

"How much did he take from Puemre's house the night he ran off."

"Not much. He's surely finished it by now."

He's probably stealing to survive, Bak thought, *and what better place than at the market.* "If you see him again, will you bring him to me?"

"If I can." She swallowed hard, striving to be strong. "He didn't trust anyone but Puemre, and now . . . Well, he came to me yesterday, but he ran off again."

Bak rose to his feet, preparing to leave. The gritty whisper of the grindstone drew his eyes toward the thin, silent girl laboring over the mortar. He prayed to the lord Amon that no child of his would ever have to live so hard. "My men and I have more rations than we can use this week. Will you accept a few items in return for what you've told me?"

The pleasure he saw on her face was as great a reward as the information she had provided.

As he walked the narrow lane outside the house, another thought surfaced. If only one officer was stalking Amon-Psaro, why were the others covering his tracks? Could the reason have something to do with a shared experience in the war against the Kushites twenty-seven years ago?

*   *   *

"Lieutenant!" It was Kasaya, running down the lane from the fortress. "I've been looking everywhere for you, sir. Commander Woser and his officers have gone out to the slipway." He stopped in front of Bak, his massive chest heaving. "The barge of the lord Amon is approaching Iken, with Sergeant Imsiba, Troop Captain Nebwa, and half the garrison of Buhen."

Bak broke into a smile, delighted at the news. "It'll be wonderful to see a friendly face again and to speak for a change with officers who're straightforward and honest."

Kasaya grinned. "First you must speak with Commander Woser. He wants to see you right away."

"No more bad news, I hope."

"He didn't bless me with knowledge."

Bak's laugh was short-lived. He recounted his interviews with Senmut and Mutnefer and told Kasaya to go find Pash- enuro. They should take all the rations they could spare to Mutnefer, get her description of the mute boy, and go on to the market. The child, he felt sure, would turn up sooner or later and he wanted at least one of them there when he showed his face. The boy had to be found and any secrets he held somehow released. Only then would he be safe.

"I've seldom seen men work so hard," Imsiba said, his eyes on the crowd massed in the distance. The glitter of gold could be seen above their heads, the elegant, upswept prow of the god's barge towed now by men rather than a warship. "I pray the lord Amon makes the effort worth- while."

"You've heard Amon-Psaro is already in Semna," Bak said.

Imsiba's face turned dour. "How can a man expect a god, no matter how great and powerful, to heal a child so ill?"

"What does Kenamon have to say?"

"He speaks with the unflagging faith of a priest, not the practical physician he is. But the closer we come to Semna,

I've noticed, the more often he kneels in prayer.''

The big Medjay's gloom was contagious, filling Bak's heart with grim and unwanted thoughts.

They strode across the sandy waste, neither in a mood to talk yet comfortable with the shared silence. Bak's eyes darted ahead, tracing the course of the slipway along which the lord Amon's barge was being dragged past the most formidable of the rapids below Iken. The route stretched across the sandy desert flat, a road paved with logs, slightly curved to form a cradle, lying side by side on a bed of dry and cracking silt.

As they neared the barge, Nebwa stepped back from among the soldiers surrounding the vessel and shouted an order. The men standing in front, well above a hundred troops from Buhen, took up the slack on heavy ropes attached to the craft, while others alongside did the same, their task to prevent the barge from tipping to the right or left as well as to aid with the tow. Several men carrying large round-bottomed jars hurried forward.

Commander Woser and the officers Huy, Senu, Inyotef, and Nebseny stood off to the side with Kenamon. The lesser priests and a couple of soldiers purified for the occasion knelt beside the lord Amon's golden barque, waiting to lift it onto their shoulders and move it forward with the barge. The doors of the shrine were closed and sealed, protecting the image of the god from the noise and dust of the outside world.

A second shout from Nebwa. The water carriers tipped their jars, soaking the silt in front of the barge, making it as slick as the grease taken from a fat roasted goose. A foreman counted off the rhythm in a singsong voice, and the tow-men began to pull. Muscles bulged. A few men grunted, others cursed. Sweat poured forth beneath the heartless sun. The lower hull, gently rounded, bare of paint and gilding, slid forward on the bed of logs, its wood creaking and moaning with the strain.

A great golden barge traveling across the barren desert. *Amazing!* Bak thought.

Nebwa walked alongside, watching with a wary eye, alert for snarled ropes, a fallen man. Ten paces and he shouted again, bringing the barge to a halt, giving the men a chance to rest.

Bak let muscles that he had not realized were tensed relax and looked farther afield, searching out his men. A mixed guard of Medjay police and the spearmen Nebwa had selected formed a rough oval thirty or so paces around the barge. Others stood on higher ground off to the west, widely spaced yet not so far apart they could not communicate with a whistle or a shout. Their task was to watch the desert for marauding tribesmen.

"You've done well, Imsiba. I wish I could say the same."

"I've had no opportunity to speak with Commander Woser." Imsiba stared toward the officers with Kenamon. "Have you learned yet why he raised so high a wall around the news of Puemre's death?"

Bak laughed ruefully. "If he were the only obstruction I've found in Iken, I'd think myself lucky."

The big Medjay gave him a curious glance.

"I'll explain tonight. After the lord Amon is safe within the mansion of Hathor. Now I must talk to Woser." Bak grinned. "I've been summoned."

While Imsiba struck off to the west and the line of guards watching from afar, Bak circled around the weary tow-men. The officers and priests were too intent on their conversation to notice his approach.

Woser was saying, "You surely don't believe Chancellor Nihisy will come all the way to the Belly of Stones!" The commander looked worried, Bak noticed with some satisfaction.

Nebwa raised his hands palm forward, staving off the words. "You misunderstand. All I said was that I wouldn't want to walk in Thuty's sandals, or yours, if the man who slew Puemre isn't brought to justice in a timely manner.''

"The chancellor won't come," Inyotef said. "He's too new to his task, too busy slipping into the palace bureaucracy. He'll send someone else in his place.''

"Worse yet," Nebwa snorted. "A lesser man who represents a great one is always harsher than his master. Especially when the master is too far away to learn the true facts and soften his agent's decisions.''

"Do you always look on the dark side, Nebwa?" Huy kept his voice light, teasing almost, but he looked as worried as Woser.

"I call the score the way I see it." Nebwa spotted Bak and a broad grin erased the gloom. "Now here's the man who can save you from Nihisy's wrath!" He clasped Bak's shoulders in greeting. "No man yet has escaped his justice.''

"You exaggerate." Bak spoke automatically, his eyes darting around the group, noting their reactions.

Woser's face was taut; tired eyes betrayed nights made restless by anxiety. Nebseny's mouth was a thin, tight line. The wrinkles etching Huy's forehead had deepened. Senu's eyes searched Bak's face and Nebwa's, as if he suspected a plot to spread fear among him and his fellow officers. Inyotef smiled, a trait Bak remembered from the past, the pilot's way of hiding tension, worry, fear, or any sign of weakness.

Nebwa eyed the barge and the men around it, some drinking beer from a goatskin, others oiling themselves to prevent their skin from drying, the rest sitting and talking or lying on the sand with their eyes closed. He gave no hint of whether or not he noticed the officers' reactions. "You're too clever by far," he told Bak. "A man impossible to deceive.''

"You make me sound like one who walks with the gods," Bak joked.

"You walk with the lady Maat, that I know." Nebwa clapped him on the shoulder, grinned at Woser. "You'll see. When he's in search of justice, he's like a dog with a bone. Once he sinks his teeth in, he never lets go. I wouldn't tread in the slayer's footsteps for all the gold in Wawat and Kush.''

Bak was delighted with Nebwa and the reactions he had brought forth, but he wondered if his friend had not gone too far. A cornered criminal, like a trapped animal, was apt to strike out with uncontrolled fury. If he knew from which direction to expect an attack, he could guard against it, but here, where one man seemed as guilty as another, he had no defense.

Kenamon gave the pair a disapproving scowl, patently unhappy with Nebwa's game and suspicious of Bak's part in it. ''Have you heard the news, my son?''

Bak caught the censure in the elderly priest's voice, and a deeper worry. ''What's wrong? Has something happened to Amon-Psaro?'' The moment the words popped out, he knew he had made a mistake. If, as he believed, one of the officers standing with him was determined to slay the king, he had revealed what he knew in one short, ill-conceived question.

Woser gave him an odd look. ''Not the king. It's the prince.''

''A courier came to Commander Woser not an hour ago,'' Kenamon explained. ''He carried a message from Amon-Psaro, who's gravely worried about the life of his son. He no longer has the patience to wait in Semna while the lord Amon makes his slow progress up the river. He's bringing the child to Iken.''

''May the gods save us all.'' Bak's voice was flat and lifeless, his thoughts stalled.

''As the river is still too low to sail all the way uninterrupted by rapids, Amon-Psaro will come by the desert route. His entourage is large, more than a hundred men including servants, so they'll not be able to travel fast, but they should arrive in two days' time.''

Bak did not bother to hide the dismay he felt. No one,

with the exception of the would-be assassin, could possibly guess its true source: the Kushite king on his way to Iken, walking onto the home ground of a man who wanted him dead. Like a honeybee buzzing toward a gossamer web, with a spider poised to strike.

He looked toward the golden shrine and offered a fervent prayer to the god dwelling inside. *Let us soon find the mute child,* he implored, *for we've no other trail to follow.*

Chapter Ten

"We searched the market from end to end." Kasaya towered over Bak, sitting on the roof of a warehouse facing the river. "No one is harboring the boy, nor did we miss any hiding places."

"Then tomorrow you must search farther afield," Bak said doggedly. "We have to find him before Amon-Psaro marches into Iken."

They spoke loudly so each could hear the other over the excited babble of voices, the crowds lining the riverbank, jostling for a better view of the approaching flotilla: the golden barge of the lord Amon and the vessels escorting it during the short voyage from the slipway to the harbor.

"I see no problem, sir." The young Medjay's eyes and thoughts were on the procession of rivercraft sailing slowly upstream, fittings polished, banners flying from masts and stays, crews decked out in their spotless best. "With Sergeant Imsiba here and half our men, we should be able to search all of Iken between dawn and dusk."

Bak snorted. "How blessed you are, Kasaya, to be able to sleep with your eyes open and dream while you go about your daily tasks."

A puzzled look flitted across Kasaya's face, to disappear with a flush. "They must stay with the lord Amon?"

"That's where their duty lies."

"Yes, sir." Kasaya's eyes darted back to the glittering

barge, the longing to stay and watch the spectacle written clearly on his face. "I must go to the market. I'm taking the first watch and Pashenuro the second, so he'll want time to find a hidden place to sleep."

"Sit!" Bak commanded. "If I know Pashenuro, he long ago found a bed and now he's searching out the fattest and plumpest fowl and fruits for his evening meal." *And maybe a tasty morsel to share his bed,* he thought.

With a delighted smile, Kasaya sat next to him on the roof. Elevated above the trees scattered along the riverbank and the many people standing at the water's edge, their view of the flotilla was unobstructed.

The people, though deprived of much of the customary pomp, were as thrilled by the god's arrival as the residents of Buhen had been—and they were far more colorful. Standing among the unadorned soldiers of Kemet were men and women bedecked with feathers and tattoos and exotic jewelry, symbols of tribes upriver to the south and from the deserts to the east and west. They wore costumes of every color and shape and size, from the skimpiest of loincloths to elaborate multicolored robes. As the barge drew near, they pressed forward as one, their voices louder, more excited.

Once the lord Amon was safely housed in the mansion of the lady Hathor, where he would remain throughout his stay in Iken, the spectators would disperse, Bak knew. The market would be far more crowded than normal and the child Ramose almost impossible to find. A wearisome thought, not one designed to lift the spirits.

The men standing on the quay—Commander Woser, his officers, the priests who ministered to the lady Hathor, five local princes, and two desert chieftains—shuffled their feet, adjusted kilts and tunics and weapons, brushed dust from sandals. Bak could guess their thoughts. Instead of the overnight stay initially planned, the lord Amon was soon to become a semipermanent guest for an unspecified length of time. Each had to put on his best face—and keep it on for the duration. A mixed blessing at best.

Inyotef stood at the prow of the lead vessel, a warship gaily decorated with long, fluttering pennants of red and white. He stood tall and erect with no sign of infirmity, Bak noted. His face was expressionless, his baton of office clenched in his hand. Next came the lord Amon's gilded barge, the long, slender hull attached to the warship by towropes thicker than a man's wrist. The golden vessel glided over the water, turned to molten copper by the last rays of the sun. The white-robed figure of Kenamon stood before the dais on which the golden barque rested; the lesser priests stood with him. The shrine, mounted atop the barque, was open on all sides, allowing the people to see and adore the slender gold image standing within. The murmurs rose to thundering shouts of adoration.

Two sleek trading ships, one on either side of the glittering barge, served as escort vessels. Imsiba and the Medjay police stood in the near ship, Nebwa and his contingent of guards in the craft on the far side. At the sight of his men, so tall and straight and noble, Bak's heart swelled with pride. And, he had to admit, his head swelled, too. They were the best police force in the world, he was convinced, worthy guards for the lord Amon, the greatest of all the gods.

"You've a rare talent, Bak." Nebwa, glancing around Sennufer's house of pleasure, wrinkled his nose at the stench of beer, sweat, and a faint odor of dead mouse. "You can walk into any city and, at the speed of a swallow, nose out the worst establishment there and make it your own special place."

Bak laughed. "Nofery wishes to turn her house of pleasure into a palace. Will you enjoy it more when you must dress like a kingfisher and smell like a lotus so she'll admit you through her door?"

"Nofery? Running a house fit for royalty?" Laughing,

Nebwa pulled a lumpy, straw-filled pillow into the corner where Bak was ensconced on a stool, sat down, and signaled Sennufer for a jar of beer. "Imsiba's not yet come?"

"He should be here soon." Bak thought of telling him of Nofery's claim that once she had loved Amon-Psaro, and he had loved her, but dismissed the temptation as frivolous. Nebwa had to return to Buhen the following morning, and they had other, more pressing matters to discuss. "He had to stay until the lord Amon was safe and content in the mansion of the lady Hathor and Kenamon and the other priests settled in the house they've borrowed from the chief scribe."

"The old man's getting tired." Nebwa smiled. "In spite of his exhaustion and an uncertain future, I truly believe he's enjoying himself. He's seen nothing like this land of Wawat in all his life, and his curiosity knows no bounds."

"After the lord Khnum formed him on his potter's wheel, he threw away the pattern," Bak said with a fond smile.

Imsiba strode through the door. "My friends!"

His tall, muscular figure and the confidence in his voice drew the eye of every man there: a dozen hardened sailors, some from the south and the rest from Kemet, and four soldiers newly back from desert patrol, their faces and bodies ruddy from windburn and sun. The majority were playing games of chance and drinking a brew so new it smelled more of bread than beer.

Imsiba accepted a jar from Sennufer, toed a stool toward Bak and Nebwa, and sat down. They talked of nothing, waiting for the other patrons to lose interest. The lane outside turned dusky. Sennufer lit several oil lamps, scattering them around the room. The game soon grew exciting, the voices loud and raucous, sailors and soldiers alike forgetting the officers among them. Bak told his tale, omitting no details of his stay thus far in Iken. By the time he finished, the black of night enveloped the land and the air inside was thick with smoke.

"If Puemre was slain because he knew of a plan to slay Amon-Psaro, why would the other officers protect the one who slew him?" Nebwa shook his head vigorously. "It makes no sense."

"Do you have any idea how many times I've come to the same conclusion?" Bak glared at nothing, disgusted at his failure to come up with a better idea. "They all faced the Kushites in battle twenty-seven years ago. Would that not be enough to quench their thirst for blood?"

"Did you see that war firsthand?" Nebwa asked Imsiba.

The tall Medjay shook his head. "My village was raided the year before. I was brought to Iken, I think, and here the soldiers took me away from the tribesmen who stole me. When the armies of Kemet marched on Kush, I was already in Waset, living as a child on a country estate belonging to the lord Amon."

"I, too, was a boy." Nebwa swirled a thick layer of dregs around the bottom of his drinking bowl. "My father was a soldier, a sergeant like you, and we lived in northern Wawat—in the fortress of Kubban. He marched south with the army of Kemet and came back a hero."

"I wasn't yet born." Bak had seldom felt as youthful and innocent, protected by circumstances and birth from his friends' more exciting childhood. "Was the war so special men would kill at the memory?"

Imsiba shrugged, queried Nebwa with a glance.

"My father spoke often of the war, of heroism and booty. My mother spoke only of the sadness in Kubban when the men sailed south. And the fear." Nebwa stared into his cup, recalling his father's tales of the distant past. "Akheperkare Tuthmose, our queen's father, had died in his sleep, leaving the throne in the hands of his son, Akheperenre Tuthmose. The wretched men of Kush, thinking our new king too weak and unsure of himself to defend his birthright, stirred the pot of discontent among the chieftains of southern Wawat, urging them to rebel. Buhen stood at risk, as did the fortresses along the Belly of Stones, and even those of us living as far north as Kubban feared a siege.

"The king sent an army, and the rebels of Wawat dropped like grain falling before a scythe. Our soldiers marched on to the land of Kush, slaying the warriors, laying waste to the villages, and taking prisoners and booty. Many men died on both sides before the most powerful of the kings who had urged rebellion, a tribal chieftain of much courage but no common sense, was captured on the field of battle. His warriors threw down their arms. Our army marched into his capital and took all of value within. The king was put back on his throne, a broken man. His first-born son was sent to Kemet as hostage, and peace has reigned to this day."

Bak had heard the tale before, but it had never held such significance. "Was his son Amon-Psaro, do you think?"

Nebwa shrugged. "Maybe." He thought a few moments, nodded. "Probably."

Bak leaped at the straw. "Except for Nebseny, all the officers who attended Woser's meeting the night Puemre died fought in that war: Woser, Huy, Senu, and Inyotef. If Amon-Psaro's father was their foe . . ." He shook his head, rejecting his idea even before it was fully formed. "No. If that were the case, Amon-Psaro would be bent on revenge, not them."

"The answer must lie elsewhere," Imsiba said.

A sailor roared as if struck by a scorpion, scrambled to his feet, and lurched out of the building. Laughing at his misfortune, the other gamblers spread a dozen small ivory carvings across the floor and began to haggle over who had won what. Bak, Nebwa, and Imsiba sat in silence, each working out a theory to present to the others.

Bak expelled a long frustrated sigh. Every path they ventured down took them further from a solution. "Nebwa, you've served in Wawat for years and you know most of the officers along the Belly of Stones, or at least their reputations. Tell me what you can of Woser and his officers."

Nebwa frowned. "I go back to my original question: If one slew Puemre, why would the others protect him?"

"If I knew the answer to that . . ." Bak shook off his irritation, grinned. "Alright, I admit it. I'm desperate. Now will you humor me and answer my question?"

Laughing at the admission, Nebwa waved to attract Sennufer's attention, pointed toward the stack of beer jars, and held up three fingers. "Woser's always outranked me, so my dealings with him have been limited. I know nothing of his personal life; I didn't even know he had a daughter until you mentioned her." He paused, waiting for Sennufer to hand around the jars and walk away. "By reputation, he's an exceptional officer, one who should be promoted to commandant, but he's spent too much time on the frontier to attract the attention of those in the capital who make the decisions. I've heard he long ago was awarded a golden fly, but I don't know when or where he earned it."

"Speaking of Commander Woser . . ." Imsiba nodded toward the door.

Bak glanced around, muttered a virulent curse. The commander was standing on the threshold, his mouth tight and determined, his body stiff with suppressed tension. He stepped inside and the room went dead still, the sailors and soldiers startled by the arrival of so lofty an officer.

What is he doing here, Bak wondered, *in this lowly place where one would never expect him to set foot?* "Tell me of Nebseny," he said to Nebwa.

"Woser's coming this way."

"If you exert enough pressure on the strongest of metals, it'll break."

"Not always where you want it to."

"Tell me of Nebseny," Bak repeated, sensing Woser coming up behind him.

Nebwa wiped the skepticism from his face. "I've never met him and know nothing about him as a man." He toyed with his drinking bowl as if unaware of the silence in the room or the reason for it. "He's reputed to be a fine archery officer, cool under pressure, one not afraid to stand at the head of his men in the heat of battle."

"Lieutenant Bak." Woser's words came out hard and fast, betraying his leashed anger. "Troop Captain Nebwa and Sergeant Imsiba. Are you merely drinking together, or am I interrupting a meeting?"

Bak formed a genial smile. "We've little time for pleasure tonight, so we brought our business with us. Will you pull up a stool and join us, sir?"

Nebwa glanced pointedly around the room and chuckled. "Police officers, you'll notice, concern themselves less with their surroundings than those of us accustomed to the more formal life of a garrison."

Imsiba turned away, hiding a smile, and asked Sennufer to bring a stool. Woser eyed the place, its wiry proprietor, and the other patrons with a stony disdain. The sailors and soldiers sat tongue-tied and stiff beneath his cool gaze.

"I've asked Nebwa to tell me what he knows of some of your officers," Bak said, deliberately prodding the commander.

Woser dropped onto the proffered stool and leaned toward Bak. "My officers are worthy men." He spoke close to a whisper so his words would not carry, but his voice was hard and edged with anger. "You've no right to treat them as potential murderers, and you've no reason to consider them as such."

"Commandant Thuty gave me the authority to do as I see fit." Bak's voice was equally firm. "Do you wish to sit here and listen to what Nebwa has to tell me? Or would you rather remain in ignorance until at last I lay hands on the man who slew Puemre?"

Woser turned half-around and his eyes raked the other customers. "Get on with your business or get out."

A sailor scooped up the throwsticks, made a call, and flung them across the floor. A soldier called out to Sennufer and held up a finger for a jar of beer. Other men gulped from their bowls. They spoke to one another, their voices too loud, nervous. Woser swung back around to glare at Bak.

Nebwa gave his friend a quick look of comprehension, as if for the first time he fully understood the obstacles Bak faced. "I've known Troop Captain Huy for years, though not well. He's been assigned to duty in Wawat off and on for as long as I can remember. Our paths have crossed often, but we've never lived in the same garrison at the same time. My father always spoke of him with respect, and I've always liked him and believed him an honorable man and officer. He knows the whole of Wawat better than anyone else I know. If war should come to this part of our empire, his knowledge could make the difference between victory and defeat."

While Nebwa spoke, Bak watched Woser surreptitiously. The commander looked surprised and pleased at the words of praise. His jaw came unclenched, his fingers uncurled from tight fists, his shoulders relaxed.

"Huy's a stiff-necked old boy," Nebwa added, "and as stubborn as they come. Once he forms a thought, it turns to stone. He'd fight to his death, so they say, for whatever he believes."

"An admirable trait, I'd say." Woser gave a disgusted snort. "I fear for today's army and the well-being of the land of Kemet. You younger men have no sense of duty, no loyalty to ideals."

Bak clamped his mouth shut, refusing to argue the point. The regiment of Amon was the best fighting force Kemet had ever known, and he suspected the other newly rebuilt regiments shared its excellence. Was Woser baiting him to sidetrack him? Or did he truly believe the past better than the present? He glanced at Nebwa. "What of Lieutenant Senu?"

Nebwa's eyes shifted toward the commander, then dropped to his beer jar. "Like Huy, he's spent much of his life in Wawat, but he's also been assigned to duty farther upriver. I've never lived at the same garrison, and, until today out at the slipway, I doubt I ever met him.''

"He's an upright, decent man." Woser waved off Sennufer's offer of a brew. "A good, solid officer."

"No doubt," Bak said under his breath.

"I've heard of Lieutenant Senu," Imsiba broke in. "The tale may or may not be true but, considering the circumstances, it's worthy of telling." He spoke to Woser rather than Bak. "They say he once found a sergeant trading with a local chieftain, handing over weapons made in Kemet and getting in return young and untouched girls stolen from desert nomads. Senu killed both men and left them in the village for all the world to see."

Woser's eyes met Imsiba's and held. "It's a tale, no more. Senu's record is clean."

A minute smile flickered on the Medjay's face, and he bowed his head in acknowledgment. "As you say, Commander Woser."

Bak could almost read his friend's thoughts: Senu deserved a golden fly, not censure. He was inclined to agree.

With reluctance, he turned his thoughts to his final suspect, Inyotef. *Why,* he wondered, *must I feel so guilty each time I think of him? The injury to his leg resulted from an honest accident, not from any fault of mine.* "Can you tell me of the pilot Inyotef?" he asked Nebwa.

Nebwa gave him a sharp look, as if wondering how he could bring himself to ask the question. "I've met him four times, each time the men in my company helped tow a vessel along the slipway. I can't claim to know him any better than I know Senu, but I've often heard him praised. He's considered the best pilot on the river between Abu and Semna."

"He should be," Woser said irritably. "He's plied the waters of Wawat off and on for years. Long before he commanded a vessel, he served here as a seaman."

"I've heard he first came on one of the ships carrying the army of Akheperenre Tuthmose," Nebwa went on.

"He's gone home to Kemet many times, but has always come south again, though rarely so far. This is his first assignment to a garrison on the Belly of Stones. He lived before in Abu."

"Does he have any reason for shame?" Bak asked, closing his heart to a second surge of guilt.

Nebwa gave him another quick glance. "They say when his feet touch dry land, his tongue grows sharp and he sometimes strikes out with his baton of office. His wife left a year or more ago, taking their children with her, and some believe he struck her once too often."

Bak could not remember Inyotef losing his temper. Had he grown bitter after the accident? Bitter and vindictive? Bak prayed the cause lay elsewhere—or, better yet, that the tale was untrue.

"She denied the charge," Woser said as if in answer to Bak's thoughts. "She told me she hated Iken and wanted to live again in a richer, gentler land. How could I fault her when my own daughter shared the wish to leave?"

"You seem never to find fault in anyone, sir." Bak eyed the commander thoughtfully. "An unexpected trait in a man who's reached the lofty rank of commander."

"I find fault with you, young man." Woser sat stiff and straight, his eyes level and unflinching. "You're so anxious to lay hands on a murderer here and now that you refuse to look farther afield at far more likely suspects."

"An anonymous trader?" Bak's laugh held no humor. "Can't you see my intent? The sooner I eliminate the innocent, the faster I'll lay hands on the guilty."

Woser eyed him for several moments, his face bleak and closed. Abruptly, as if he had come to a sudden decision, he stood up. "I can waste no more time on Puemre's murder. I've a most important task to assign, one well suited to you."

Bak glanced at Nebwa and Imsiba. They looked as startled as he was, and as wary.

"As you've surely noticed, Lieutenant Bak . . ." Woser's

sarcasm was designed to sting. ". . . habitable space in Iken is limited. I've therefore decided to house King Amon-Psaro and his entourage—more than a hundred people, you've no doubt heard—in the old fortress located on the island across the channel from this city. It's not much more than a shell, and it's cluttered with bricks fallen from the walls and trash left by traders and herdsmen who've camped there through the years. I've no other officer to spare, so you must assume the responsibility for making the structure habitable and secure. I'll give you as many men as you need."

Bak was staggered by the assignment—and by the cleverness of Woser's move. The task could take much of his time, stealing the hours he would otherwise be spending on his investigation.

"I realize I'm taking you away from your other duties, but for a few days at most." Woser almost smiled. "After the fortress is clean and safe, you'll have nothing further to do except look to Amon-Psaro's safety while he's on the island. Troop Captain Huy will ensure his well-being each time he comes within the walls of the city."

Bak yearned to refuse, but in all good conscience he could not. If Amon-Psaro's life rested in his hands, the only way he could feel confident in the security precautions was to set them up himself. "The lord Amon, I assume, will move to the island to be near the royal party?"

Woser looked at him as if he were addled. "The god must live in the mansion of the lady Hathor. We can't flaunt a long-established custom to satisfy the needs of a Kushite king."

"What of the prince?" Bak asked, his voice made grim by an answer he feared he already knew. "From what I've been told, he's too ill to be moved so great a distance day after day."

"He'll live in the house we've loaned Kenamon. There he can receive constant attention from the physician and he'll be only a few paces from the mansion of the goddess, an easy journey even if he must be carried.''

Bak muttered a heartfelt curse. Each time Amon-Psaro wished to see his son, he would cross the channel by skiff and march through the lower city, up the gully to the plateau, and along the streets of the fortress. He would be vulnerable coming and going, twice a day if not more often. And Huy, the man in charge of security, might well be the one planning to slay him.

''The swine,'' Nebwa spat.

Imsiba shook his head in disgust. ''Never would I have expected so shrewd a way of tying your hands from a man as hidebound as Woser.''

Bak, seated on a stool in the front room of his temporary quarters, scowled at the pair in the flickering light of three palm-sized oil lamps he had scattered around. He refused to dwell on Woser's perversity. ''Nebwa, when will your task be finished in Buhen?''

''Two days, three at most.'' Nebwa knelt to tidy Kasaya's sleeping mat. ''I'll travel home tomorrow, the gold and tribute items will be transferred the following morning from the treasury to the ship, and it'll sail as soon as the loading is finished.''

''You must tell Commandant Thuty all you've heard today and ask if he'll let you come back to Iken.''

''That was my intent.'' Nebwa stripped down to his skin and sat on the pallet. ''How many men should I bring? Will a half company be enough?''

Bak's spirits began to lift. If Woser thought to hobble him, he would be sadly disappointed. ''Of those who towed the barge along the slipway, leave twenty behind. They, with Pashenuro at their head, will give me a good solid core of trustworthy men on the island. I doubt I'll need more.''

''And what of me?'' Imsiba asked, gathering his spear and shield from the floor so he could return to the fortress for the night. ''I must stay with the lord Amon, I know, but is there not some way I can help? Perhaps ask Kenamon to intercede with Woser?''

"Say nothing to Kenamon. I don't want to worry him further unless I have to." Bak waited for Imsiba's reluctant nod, then, "At first light tomorrow, I'll examine the island. As soon as I see what must be done, I'll come to you and tell you what I've found. Kasaya and I will go on with our search for Puemre's slayer, so you must be prepared to advise Pashenuro should I not be available when he needs help."

Imsiba's eyes glinted with mischief. "Woser won't be happy when he hears you've divided the task he gave you, laying it on the shoulders of other men."

Bak grinned. To circumvent the commander's orders was a joy. "I doubt he'd have thought up this task if Nebwa hadn't struck fear in his heart, speaking so highly of my powers as a policeman that the gods themselves couldn't live up to the praise."

Nebwa stretched out on the pallet, his wrists crossed beneath his head, untroubled by the charge. "I know, my tongue runs away with itself at times."

"I must go," Imsiba said. "Our men will fear I've had too much beer and have lost my way." He bade them good-bye and left.

Bak pinched the wicks of two lamps, leaving the third burning while he undressed. Each time a breeze tickled the flame, shadows danced around the near-dark room. "Tell me of your newborn son, Nebwa. How was he when you left?"

"He's a perfect child. Handsome, smart . . ."

Bak half listened, his thoughts far away, his hands and body going through the motions of undressing, laying his clothing across a stool, lying down on the sleeping platform. The night was too hot for a sheet, so he threw it aside. By the time he reached across to quench the third lamp, leaving the room in velvety darkness, Nebwa was snoring.

Bak closed his eyes and let himself drift off. Something moved, something in his bed, some other creature perhaps. His eyes popped open. He lay still, saying nothing, feeling his heart thud in his breast. Except for Nebwa's soft snores, the room was silent. He must have been dreaming.

He started to turn onto his side, felt another movement, the pressure of something round and cold and damp against his arm. Like a snake. A snake? He shot out of bed with a yell.

"Wha . . . ?" Nebwa mumbled. "What? What is it?"

"Get outside! Quick!" Bak leaped toward the door, a vague rectangle slightly lighter than the room. With eyes accustomed to the dark and the sky bright with stars, the lane was like a long, straight, dry riverbed, empty and barren.

"What happened?" Nebwa demanded, a pace or two behind.

"I felt something in my bed," Bak said grimly. "A snake, I think."

"You don't suppose . . ." Nebwa let the sentence hang in the air between them, the unspeakable thought.

"The house was empty when we moved in," Bak said, thinking aloud. "No, Nebwa. It's probably been inside all along, hiding from us." He clapped his friend on the shoulder. "I'll go get a light so we can see. We can't go back to bed with that thing crawling around, looking for a warm body to cuddle up against."

He trotted down the lane, as naked as the day he was born. As far as he could tell, his yell had not awakened any of the neighbors sleeping inside the nearby houses or on the cooler rooftops. He stopped at the first intersection he came to. In the distance, he spotted a spearman assigned to night patrol, torch in hand. The watchman, a chubby young man barely old enough to shave, was not unduly surprised at the tale he told; snakes often invaded the old houses.

They loped back to Bak's quarters side by side. The soldier held the torch just inside the door and they all peeked

in. As far as they could see, the snake was not on the floor.
Grabbing a spear leaning against the wall, Bak sucked in
air as if it were courage and crept toward the sleeping platform. Nothing moved; the bed looked empty. He nudged
the wrinkles with the spearpoint. The creature caught in the
folds of the sheet came to life, writhing to free itself, hiss-
ing. The whole bed seemed to move and then the sheet and
snake, tangled together, fell off the platform. Bak leaped
backwards, his heart locked in his throat.

A small flat head slid out of a fold of linen and a brownish body followed. The head rose off the floor, its upper
body swelled to form a hood. It hissed at Bak and the men
in the doorway. A cobra. One of the deadliest of all reptiles.
Bak took the torch from the watchman and stepped closer
to the snake. Holding the flame toward the creature, dis-
tracting it with fire, he muttered a quick prayer of forgiveness to the lady Wadjet, the goddess whom the cobra
represented, and struck out with the spear. He drove the
point through the hood, pinning the snake against the sleeping platform. The watchman killed the flailing creature with
his spear.

"I've lived in Wawat more than thirty years," Nebwa
said, staring at the broken body, "and I've never before
seen a cobra this far south."

The watchman prodded it as if checking to make sure it
was truly dead. "I saw one a month or two ago. It came
south in a shipment of grain. I thought someone killed it,
but maybe it got away."

"More likely someone kept it for himself," Nebwa muttered.

Bak felt chilled to the bone. So dangerous a pet would
have made a good weapon if one wished to slay a king like
Amon-Psaro. Or a nosy police officer.

Chapter Eleven

Bak woke up with what one of his Medjays, a man slain in the line of duty the previous year, would have called a burr in his loincloth. He itched to lay hands on the one who had left the cobra in his sleeping pallet. If the goal had been to stop his meddling, it had failed miserably.

He bade Nebwa good-bye at sunup, sent the twenty borrowed spearmen to the garrison stores for tools and supplies, and hurried to the market to tell Pashenuro of the new task he must shoulder. Following narrow, winding paths between stalls already drawing customers, he searched for his two Medjays. He traded a few faience beads for breakfast—a flat loaf of bread and a bowl of thick lentil stew—and ate as he walked along.

As early as it was, the proprietors of woodframe stalls roofed with reed or palm-leaf mats had set out bowls filled with fragrant herbs; amulets and good-luck charms; lentils and beans; bronze tweezers, razors, and knives; and a multitude of other small objects. Larger items were piled along flimsy walls: flint-edged scythes and wooden plows, lengths of linen, large pottery jars filled with beer or oil or salted fish or meat, smaller jars containing wine or honey. Local herdsmen and farmers were building red and green and yellow mounds of fresh fruits and vegetables on rush mats spread on the ground. Men and women set out baskets filled with succulent dates or sweet, sticky cakes or bread or eggs

159

or grain. Several men had hung unplucked fowl from the wooden frames of lean-tos, while others were spreading fish on the ground.

He liked best the stalls of the men and women who had come from far upriver. Seated cross-legged on the ground or perched on low stools, the people were as exotic as the products surrounding them. Short and fat, tall and thin. Painted, tattooed, scarified, greased, smeared with red clay or white ashes. Some nearly naked, others elaborately robed, a few dressed no different than men of Kemet. Their offerings included tawny or spotted animal skins, ostrich feathers and eggs, lengths of rare woods and chunks of gemstone, caged animals and birds, shackled slaves.

The customers, though sparse at this early hour, were equally intriguing: local farmers and villagers; soldiers, sailors, and traders from Kemet to the north; and herdsmen, farmers, and villagers from far to the south. Each man and woman had brought objects to trade, foodstuffs and luxury items common to them yet desirable or rare to others.

Across a stretch of barren, hard-packed sand, he found Pashenuro sitting on the mudbrick wall of an animal paddock filled with a mixed herd of sheep and goats, talking with a bald, potbellied farmer. A fine dust rose in puffs above the bleating creatures, trotting this way and that for no good reason. Other paddocks contained donkeys, a lone mule, rare in this part of the world, and long- and short-horned cattle, snorting or lowing or braying in protest of their entrapment. Dust drifted through the air, carrying the smell of animal and the stench of manure.

"The boy's been seen," Pashenuro said after the farmer walked away, "but he's like a wraith, here one moment and gone the next. Today we'll search for a hideaway outside the market, looking into houses both empty and occupied, and the storage magazines as well."

Bak glanced at the rows of warehouses between the market and the harbor. If the buildings were fully used, two men would need a week to search through the objects stored inside. He yearned to shake Woser until his teeth rattled. "I must tear you away from this task and assign you to another. In the meantime, I've borrowed some men from Nebwa, and I'll send four to help Kasaya."

"Another task?" the Medjay asked, surprised. "I thought finding the child more important than anything else."

Bak gave a short, hard laugh. "To us, yes, but Commander Woser has his own priorities. He's ordered me to make habitable the island fortress so Amon-Psaro can live there in comfort and safety. I've no choice but to make you head of the men who do the work." He swatted at a fly buzzing around his face. "Come, let's find Kasaya, and I'll explain to you both at once."

Pashenuro could not stop shaking his head. "How can the commander do this, sir? Why is he doing it?"

"You didn't have to borrow men from Buhen." Huy shaded his eyes with his hand so he could watch the boat carrying Nebwa's spearmen draw away from the quay. "With Puemre gone, the men in his company are without an officer. I thought to hand them over to you until you're recalled to Buhen, or until Commandant Thuty sends someone else to fill the vacancy Puemre left."

Another time-consuming task, Bak thought. To lead a company of spearmen was a full-time job. "Nebwa offered men and I accepted," he said, keeping his voice noncommittal. "As for an entire company . . . I doubt I'll need so many, but I can't know for sure until I see the island."

"Shall we go?" Huy asked, stepping into the skiff he had made available for Bak's use. The craft rocked beneath his weight, its hull scraping the stone revetment that prevented the riverbank from eroding between the two quays.

Bak untied the vessel, jumped in, and shoved off. Sitting at the rudder, he took up the oars and rowed across the glassy surface of the harbor. The boat was small and compact, easily handled by one man, a pleasure to use. He

longed to try out the sail, but that would have to wait until
the return trip. The prevailing breeze at Iken, as at Buhen,
blew from the north.

He had to admit Huy was doing all he could to ease the
task of preparing the fortress for Amon-Psaro. He had given
freely of tools, supplies, and food. He had promised as
many men as needed, had arranged for two supply boats to
ply the waters, transporting men and food and building supplies from Iken to the island, and had found the skiff. He
had even volunteered to accompany Bak on this, his first
journey to the island, guiding him across the perilous currents upstream of the rapids. Would a man bent on mur-
dering the Kushite king be so helpful? Certainly—if
cooperation would be to his advantage.

At the end of the quay, the current grabbed the vessel
with surprising force, carrying it swiftly downstream.

"Row well out into the channel," Huy advised. "You
don't want to be swept onto the long island. You want to
go around it."

Bak nodded, recalling the lay of the islands as he had
seen them from the girdle wall high above the river the first
time he and Huy had talked. Upstream to the south, the
main channel flowed broad and relatively free of obstacles.
Immediately in front of the city, however, the river spread
out in multiple channels, flowing around and over rocky
islands and outcropping rocks that formed swirling, raging
rapids impossible to navigate. The island closest to the Iken
waterfront was the long, narrow tumble of broken rocks
from which the man with the sling had harried him and the
Medjays. Pockets of earth gave a foothold to sparse but
tenacious trees and brush, much of which, he guessed,
would vanish under water as the flood deepened.

A second channel separated that island from another, divided now by the rising waters into two chunks of land
connected by a narrow isthmus. The ridge to the north, tall
enough to remain above water through the highest flood,
supported trees, brush, and the island fortress. He had to

swing the boat around the long, narrow island and sail down the second channel.

Following Huy's advice, he dug the oars into the water, his powerful strokes driving them across the current. As they passed the southern tip of the long island, Bak could see water lapping over the low spots, sneaking onto land that a day or two ago had been dry. He swung the skiff into the second channel and drove it across the current toward the island on which the fortress stood. A third current caught the skiff, pulling it to the right toward a pair of craggy islets rising from the mouth of a side channel. Beyond, he heard the growl of angry water and spotted jagged rocks rising above a swath of foam.

"Careful!" Huy warned.

Bak was already working the rudder and oars, turning the skiff midstream. He was glad Huy had come along. To a man reared in Kemet, where the river flowed smooth and broad and the greatest hazards were shallows, these wild waters were a new and unsettling experience.

Ahead, the channel flowed clear all the way to the landing stage. The fortress, he saw, was an uncomplicated structure of plain mudbrick walls built on a stone-revetted base that followed the contours of the island. The fortification was protected at intervals by stubby spur walls. The vessel on which Nebwa's men had sailed was moored against the rocky shore, and the last few men were disembarking. The others, each laden with baskets or tools, formed an irregular line, hauling the supplies up a steep slope and through a partially collapsed gate.

As they drifted downstream, the growling waters behind subsided to a whisper and another, throatier roar sounded ahead. Awed by the power he heard, Bak stood up to look. A hundred or so paces beyond the fortress gate, the channel turned white and vicious. The width of the river from one island to the other was a wild tangle of rocks and water and froth. A rainbow twice the height of a man leaned over the water, trembling in the spray rising from the maelstrom.

"Now you see why we drag the ships overland," Huy said.

"They'd be beaten to pieces in that water." Chilled at the spectacle, Bak dropped onto his seat and turned the skiff toward the shallower water alongside the island. "I saw those rapids from the girdle wall, but at so great a distance they lose their impact on the senses."

"The rocks get worse downriver before they get better."

The tall, lean officer caught up the rope and looped the end, preparing to moor the vessel. As the skiff bumped the shore, he threw the loop over a post grayed by the sun and made shiny from use. They followed the last soldier in line up the steep, rocky path and into the fortress.

Bak paused at the gate to look around. His first reaction was one of dismay. To call the place a fortress, he thought, was a gross exaggeration. It was nothing more than a fortified wall enclosing a roughly rectangular space over two hundred paces wide and four times as long, a place to shelter farmers and their livestock during an attack. From the poor condition of the walls and the amount of debris covering the floor, it had been neglected for years, probably since the war against the Kushites—if not before.

Nebwa's spearmen were equally disheartened. They stood in the middle of the fortress, looking around, their faces long, their usual banter silenced.

Pashenuro issued an order, spurring them to action, and strode across the rubble-strewn floor, glancing around the filthy, dilapidated structure, frowning. "Not a place where I'd house a king, sir."

"A palace it'll never be," Bak agreed, scowling at the disarray. "The question is: Can we make it not merely habitable, but attractive by midafternoon tomorrow?"

The Medjay managed a weak smile.

Huy eyed the crumbling walls. "I've not set foot in this fortress for many months. It's in worse condition than I remembered."

"Alright, let's see what's here." Bak hoped he sounded

more hopeful than he felt. "Then we can decide what must be done."

The trio walked along the base of the walls, veering around trees, overgrown bushes, and mounds of fallen bricks, stumbling over hidden roots, stepping across suspicious holes in the earth, avoiding piles of waste, most of it dry and hard, left by humans and animals. They examined fallen sections of the fortification, calculating the effort needed to make temporary but effective repairs. At the end, they climbed a stairway eroded by wind and water until it was little better than a steep, irregular ramp. Standing on the wall not far from the gate, they looked out across the fortress. Nebwa's spearmen, clearing a space for their camp, were now laughing and chattering as if they had not a care in the world. It must be pleasant, Bak thought with envy, to be free of responsibility.

Vaguely aware of the crash of water in the channel behind him, he thought over the task ahead. To finish in time would be difficult, he decided, but not impossible. "The floor will have to be cleared and cleaned," he told Pashenuro. "Leave all the trees and bushes where they are, at least for now. They'll give life to this place, make it seem less harsh and abandoned. Save all fallen bricks that still remain whole and whatever else you find of value. Dump the rest into the river."

"Yes, sir," Pashenuro said.

"The walls will be your greatest problem," Huy said, staring at a large irregular gap at the northwest corner. "You've no time to make new bricks."

"We'll fill the holes with rubble," Pashenuro said.

"And have Amon-Psaro laugh at so crude a fortress?" Bak shook his head. "No. If no one objects"—he queried Huy with a glance—"we can mine the old, abandoned houses in Iken, prying out bricks that are whole, and sail them across the river for reuse here."

"An excellent idea!" Huy smiled his approval. "With

enough men, you might well turn this fortress into a place
befitting a king.''

"I must accept your offer of Puemre's company," Bak
said reluctantly. "Pashenuro will need half the men here
on the island and four or five masons to show them how
to lay the bricks. The rest should remain in Iken, gathering
bricks for shipment across the river."

"Done!" Huy nodded. "Puemre's sergeant, Minnakht,
is a good and trustworthy man. You can look to him with
confidence to head those who'll work in the city."

With the worst of his difficulties resolved, Bak allowed
himself to breathe more freely. He did not deceive himself
that the task would be easy, but he was certain it could be
done. If the lord Amon smiled on him—and on his work-
men—it should be finished before Amon-Psaro marched
into Iken.

Bak stood at the gate, looking back at Nebwa's spearmen, the core of his work force. Their lean-to tents had
been set up, a hearth built, tools distributed, food and supplies stowed away. One man knelt at the hearth, dropping
vegetables into a pot, and another was kneading bread. A
half dozen men were spread out across the northern end of
the fortress, cleaning the stone and hard-packed earthen
floor, while the rest carried baskets of debris through a far
gate to the river. They had accomplished a lot in their short
stint on the island, yet the task ahead looked endless.

"We'll go to the barracks the moment we get back to
Iken," he promised Pashenuro. "You should have help by
midday and bricks long before nightfall."

The Medjay nodded and hurried back to his crew. As
Bak turned away to follow Huy down the path to the skiff,
his eyes drifted unbidden toward the roaring maelstrom
downstream. From where he stood, he could see no water-
fall, but he guessed from the gathering speed of the river,
the distant roar, and the amount of foam hurling into the

air that the riverbed fell substantially, not all at one time, but in a series of cascades.

Ships sometimes traveled those rapids, he knew, when the river rose to its greatest height, laying a protective depth of water over many of the rocks. Using sturdy ropes, men standing on the islands or on unsubmerged boulders man-handled the vessels upstream or guided them through the deepest channels while the current carried them down-stream. His feeling for Inyotef swung from pity to admi-ration; the pilot was responsible for guiding the ships through the rapids as well as along less troubled waters.

Bak saw an object in the mist, a vague image emerging from the steaming, roiling water. It looked for an instant like the head and shoulders of a man. No, he thought. Im-possible. Abruptly the figure vanished from sight, a figment of his imagination he was sure. Then he saw it again in the smoother water above the rapid, moving slowly across the current, aiming toward the long island. A second figure emerged from the foam, and a third. The first reached the shallow water along the shore and stood up. A man. No, a boy!

He stared hard, unable to believe any human being could survive so great a turbulence. "Are my eyes deceiving me?"

Huy, halfway down the path, glanced downstream and laughed. "The local men and boys swim these waters with ease, using goatskins filled with air to lift them to the sur-face each time the lord Hapi pulls them under. I, too, when first I saw them, thought my eyes played tricks on me."

"They've more courage than I have, or are more fool-hardy."

"The river is the center of their lives, Lieutenant, from birth to death and from dawn to dusk. They know all its habits through the seasons and how to use them to their advantage."

Bak watched the last boy wade onto the island and shake off the water like a dog. "I count myself a fair swimmer, and I like the water, but those boiling rapids hold no appeal."

"You're fortunate you can swim. I'd drown in a quiet pool."

"You've never learned how?"

"Why do you think I sail with such care?"

Noting Huy's discomfort, Bak allowed the subject to die. He did not want to humble the officer, nor could he afford to alienate him.

As he unfurled the sail, a bright yellow rectangle of heavy fabric, and raised the upper yard, he said, "Nebwa tells me you've spent much of your life in Wawat."

Huy settled into the prow of the skiff, facing forward. "I've lived in Kemet, serving in the fortresses along our eastern frontier, and once I served as envoy to the land of Keftiu, but I think of Wawat as my home."

"You won the gold of valor, I've been told, while fighting in this barren land."

"Twenty-seven years ago, it was, far to the south in the land of Kush." Huy smiled at the memory. "I was a young man then, a raw recruit with more courage than good sense. I fought without thought, risking my life as if I were immortal." He glanced at Bak, chuckled. "Though often foolish, I acted the hero, and won a golden fly to prove it."

Bak saw pride on the officer's face and the humility of a truly brave man. He hoped Huy was not the murderer he was seeking. "Did you have occasion to see Amon-Psaro's father?"

"Only at a distance, and not until we won our final battle. He was a prisoner, his arms shackled, his head bowed with grief at the loss of his army, hundreds upon hundreds of good and valiant men."

"What of Amon-Psaro? Was he there, too?"

Huy shook his head. "He was a child, too young to stand with his father on the field of battle. I didn't get to know him until later."

"You actually knew Amon-Psaro?" Bak was so surprised he almost forgot to adjust the sail so they could pass the southern tip of the long island.

Huy eyed him with curiosity. "We took him hostage. Did you not know? He grew to manhood in the royal house in Waset."

"Is that where you met him?"

"I was among the party who took him north." Huy's voice grew distant, following his thoughts into the past. "We spent many days together, sailing downriver to our capital. First, I served as a guard, ordered not to let him escape and flee back to his father. Later, when we were far away and he could no longer think of returning to Kush, we played games together and wrestled and fished and hunted. I like to believe I made him forget the loneliness he felt and the sadness of leaving his home and family."

Bak felt as if he had found a lump of gold in a long-dry desert watercourse. Huy had not simply known Amon-Psaro; he had known him well. Well enough to become his enemy? "You were good friends, then."

"He was my brother." Huy's smile turned wry. "I was very young, at heart only a child. When we bade good-bye at the door of the royal house, I left with tears on my cheeks. I knew I'd never see him again, and I didn't."

He was telling the truth, Bak felt sure, but was it the whole truth? "You must be looking forward to meeting him again."

"He'll not remember me. Too many years have passed."

Huy spoke in an offhand manner, but Bak heard something else in his voice: a hope that Amon-Psaro would recognize him. As the friend he had lost so many years ago? Or as a long-standing foe?

"Lieutenant Bak!" A boy of seven or eight stood on the end of the northern quay, shouting. "Lieutenant Bak!"

"What is it?" Bak lowered the yard and let the vessel's momentum carry it into the still waters of the harbor.

"I've a message for you, sir. From the Medjay Kasaya."

"Tell me."

"He found the one he's been looking for. You must go to the market right away. To the animal paddocks."

Bak paused at the edge of the market to look across the sandy waste toward the paddocks. Somewhere behind, he had lost Huy. The officer had insisted on coming along, saying he wanted Bak with him when he spoke to Sergeant Minnakht and the men of Puemre's company.

Bak spotted Kasaya instantly. The big Medjay stood beside a paddock in which a lanky Kushite in a skimpy loincloth was trying to rope a huge, long-horned bullock. The enraged creature was wheeling around, bellowing, raising a cloud of dust that half hid Kasaya, three of the spearmen who had helped with the search, and a small dusky boy. Kasaya towered over the child, his huge hands gripping the boy's skinny shoulders. Bak loped toward them.

The boy watched him draw near, his eyes wide, terrified. *Kasaya must surely have made it clear that we pose no threat,* Bak thought, *that we are in fact trying to keep him alive. Why then is he so afraid?*

Without warning, the boy jerked free of the Medjay's grasp, ducked beneath a spearman's outflung hand, and raced away from the paddock through the dust, aiming for a row of stalls at the edge of the market.

"Catch him!" Bak yelled, frantic to keep him isolated from the crowd, where he would be almost impossible to find.

He sprinted across the sand, determined to head the boy off. Kasaya and the spearmen spread out, forming an arc to drive him into Bak's arms. Bak ran to within ten paces of the child and slowed, poised to lunge. Kasaya and the spearmen closed in. The child, looking as desperate as a gazelle held at bay by a pack of wild dogs, veered straight toward Bak, startling him. Bak reached out to grab. The boy ducked low and sideways. Bak's fingers touched hot, sweaty flesh and the child slipped from his grasp. Moments later, he plunged into the throng of shoppers.

Bak swung on his men, furious at the loss. "Imbeciles! How could you let him get away like that?"

"I couldn't hold him, sir." Kasaya looked devastated. "I swear I couldn't. He's as slippery as an eel."

Bak took a long, deep breath, controlling his anger and frustration. He, too, had had a hand in losing the child. "Where's the other man I sent to you?"

"We left him in the storage magazine where we found the boy." Kasaya pointed toward the center of five interconnected warehouses fifty or so paces away. "I told him to guard the child's belongings."

"The boy'll not go back there." Bak glared at the market and the near-hopeless search they faced. "Let's spread out and find him."

With Bak in the center, they plunged into the throng. The aisles were jammed with men, women, and children from all walks of life, people who lived along the Belly of Stones and those who had come from afar to see the lord Amon. Some haggled over prices. Others wandered from stall to stall, squeezing fruits and vegetables, shaking jars, lifting the uppermost layer of a basket in search of hidden perfection—or rot—below the surface. A few gazed at the merchandise in quest of a special bargain or looked wistfully at objects too dear for their meager means.

Heat and a multitude of odors enveloped food stalls, metalsmiths' braziers, and crowded humanity. Shouts and laughter rose above a buzz of voices. Bak shouldered a man aside and was shoved in turn by another man. Bumped from behind, he stubbed his toe on a brick holding down a corner of linen and stumbled into a donkey that swung its head around to snap at him. Sweat poured down his back and chest. Anger and frustration clouded his face, discouraging sharp comments from men whose feet he trod on.

Someone screamed. A woman's high-pitched wail of horror and loss. Silence fell all across the market, as if the

people awaited another scream. A curious murmur swelled
to a cacophony of speculation and fear.

Bak raced in the direction from which he thought the
scream had come, shoving people out of his way. He seldom carried his baton of office, but now he was sorry he
had left it behind in Buhen. Sobbing broke out ahead, pulling him toward his goal, a ring of people already collecting
around someone else's misfortune.

He burst through the ring and stopped dead still. "No!"
he cried, the words torn from him as he took in the scene.
"No!"

The armorer's daughter Mutnefer was on her knees,
bending over the small dusky child. Her body shook with
sobs drawn from the depths of her being. The boy lay on
his side in the dust among a dozen fallen jars and a puddle
of blood. His bony arms and legs were flung askew, his
eyes and mouth open wide, as if he were as afraid in death
as he had been in life. A last drop of blood clung to the
lower end of a long, deep slit across his throat.

"Troop Captain Huy remained with the body as you
asked him to, sir. It was he who ordered the crowd away."

Kasaya stared straight ahead, unable to meet Bak's eyes.
Nor could he look at the straw nest hidden behind a store
of pottery ewers, braziers, and bowls in a rear corner of the
warehouse, illuminated by a flaming torch mounted on the
wall. The sheet was dirty and stained; an unwashed bowl
had drawn ants. A larger bowl was filled with childish
treasures: a wooden crocodile and dog, a ball, a boat, a
sheathed knife that must once have been carried by Puemre,
and a small ivory scribal pallet with shallow wells containing red and black cakes of ink and a narrow slot holding
two reed pens.

Bak, kneeling beside the makeshift bed, could barely
look at them himself. He felt as guilty as Kasaya and the
spearmen did. If they had not searched out the child, he

might never have run into the arms of the one who slew him. "What of the others?"

"They were all in the market, sir."

"All of them?" Bak asked, incredulous.

"Yes, sir." Kasaya swallowed hard. "Commander Woser came soon after you left to see what the trouble was, and his daughter, mistress Aset, was with him. It was she who realized the shock was bringing forth the baby and led Mutnefer away. Lieutenant Nebseny came running, as did Lieutenants Senu and Inyotef, each from a different direction."

Bak rubbed his hand across his eyes as if to wipe away the images stored there. No one had witnessed the murder, nor had anyone noticed the boy, not even Mutnefer, until he grabbed the back of her dress as his legs gave way beneath him.

Bak stood up, clasped Kasaya's shoulder, and gave the Medjay a wan smile. "Go find me a basket, and tell Nebwa's men to report to Pashenuro at the island fortress. We'll take the boy's possessions to Mutnefer's house. Her brothers and sisters will like the toys; the rest she can keep as memories."

After Kasaya hurried away, Bak cleaned the bowl with a handful of straw, shook out the sheet and folded it neatly, and laid them with the other objects in the basket. Each item tore at his heart, deepening his determination to lay hands on Puemre's slayer, a man so low he had slain a helpless child. Seething inside, he glanced around, making sure he had everything and searching for . . . What? A broken chunk of pottery with a sketch on its surface? He poked around in the straw, found nothing.

Rocking back on his heels, he studied the spot where the bed had been and the pottery stacked around it. He noticed, within arm's reach of the boy's nest, a wide-necked ewer lying beside a pile of bowls when it should have been stacked with the other jars. He picked it up. Something rattled inside.

Muttering a quick prayer to the lord Amon, he turned
the ewer upside down. Four shards fell out, each covered
with rough sketches in red and black ink, sometimes three
or four images one on top of another, the red figures mixed
with the black, making it hard to tell them apart. One picture, a bolder black than the rest, showed two men of Kemet, one thrusting a weapon down the other's throat, above
a wavy line, water. The figures were so much like those in
the sketch he had seen in Puemre's house that he was sure
they had both been drawn by the same hand.

The boy must have drawn the pictures, not Puemre. What
better way to communicate when you can neither speak nor
hear? Had he drawn the sketches solely for his master? Or
had he intended to give them to someone, Mutnefer maybe,
to pass along a warning? The truth would never be known,
but Bak liked the latter idea.

Chapter Twelve

"So that's my tale." Bak wiped the last tender morsels of stewed duck from the inside of his bowl and popped the chunk of bread into his mouth. "All I've seen and done from the time I walked into Iken three days ago until I found these sketches in the boy's hiding place." He nodded toward the four pottery shards lying beside him on the hard-packed earthen floor.

Kenamon, seated cross-legged amid a clutter of cloth and papyrus packets, small jars, and bowls, looked up from the grayish quartz bowl he held on his lap. "Commander Woser has much to account for."

"He does. But is he guilty of murder with plans to slay a king? Or merely hiding some personal secret?"

They sat in the courtyard of the spacious house the elderly priest and his staff had borrowed for their stay in Iken. Next to the mansion of Hathor where the lord Amon was living, it offered comfortable and convenient quarters for Amon-Psaro's son and the priest-physicians who would tend him. A pavilion had been erected over half the court to shelter its occupants from the sun. Seven large water jars leaned against a shaded wall, but all other signs of the family who normally occupied the building had been removed.

Kenamon untied the corners of a cloth packet and shook out a handful of small, pointed leaves, pale green and crispy dry. He dropped them into the bowl, retied the knot, and laid the packet aside. "I'll speak with him, if you wish, and remind him of his duty to the company of gods and our sovereign, Maatkare Hatshepsut."

"I won't trouble you yet." At any other time, Bak would have smiled at the powerful figures, both human and divine, Kenamon could summon to his lips at any given moment, but he was too upset about the slain child Ramose. "I think it too soon to reveal what I've guessed about a possible attempt on Amon-Psaro's life. If I know no more by mid-morning tomorrow, I'll come for you then, after you've performed the morning ablutions for the lord Amon."

Imsiba came hurrying through the door. "My friend! You wish to see me, I've been told."

Bak knew of no way to soften the news. "We found the mute child, Imsiba, and now he's dead."

The tall Medjay muttered something in his own tongue. The grim look on his face left no doubt as to the meaning. "How did it happen?"

Bak told him. While he spoke, the frail old priest crushed the brittle leaves with a wooden pestle, bringing out a tangy odor that cleansed the air of other smells. He added several black seeds, from a poppy Bak thought, and sprinkled a few grains of malachite into the bowl. He crushed the substances further, wrinkled his nose, sneezed.

Bak finished his tale, then had to calm Imsiba with assurances that Kasaya had been no more at fault than anyone else. "If you're eager to lay blame, look to me. I thought it more important to find the boy than to keep our search a secret. Now all we have to show for my haste is a dead child and a few tangled sketches."

Imsiba knelt in front of the shards. "These?" he asked, picking them up, studying them one by one.

Bak nodded. "I thought to leave them in Kenamon's hands. My quarters are like a woman in a house of pleasure: open to all who wish to enter."

Imsiba held out the shard showing one man slaying another near water. "You were right, my friend. The child witnessed Lieutenant Puemre's death."

And the knowledge killed him, Bak thought bitterly. "The others are harder to understand." He picked up a fragment and studied the multiple pictures, trying to distinguish the red figures from the black. "I thought, among the three of us, we might sort out at least a few of the sketches, separating each one from all the rest."

"First let me finish this poultice." Kenamon unplugged a small jar and poured honey onto the mixture, added three reddish drops from a glass vial, and enough beer to form a thin paste. Stirring the concoction, he added, "The scribe who loaned us this house has an abscess on his neck. After I open it, this should help him heal."

"I see an empty boat." Imsiba scowled at the shard in his hand. "And here's a soldier fighting the enemy on the field of battle. No. A man marching, more likely."

"This one also has a boat, but with a crew." Bak eyed a thick black arc holding stick-like men with paddles. "It has no sail, so it's traveling downstream."

Kenamon covered the quartz bowl with a square of linen and tied it in place. Setting the medication aside, he picked up the other two pieces of pottery, glanced at the one showing Puemre's death, and laid it back down to examine the remaining shard.

"This may be an army." Bak held his shard for Imsiba to look and pointed at a red stick figure. "You see the multiple profiles of this man?"

The Medjay tilted his head, studied the sketch. "Men marching side by side. Yes, an army. But whose? Did you notice the headdress?"

Bak eyed what looked like an untidy clump of red grass atop the egg-shaped head. "That's not a headdress; that's hair."

"Why could not the child have been a better artist?" Imsiba grumbled.

The elderly priest twisted his fragment of pottery a quar-

ter turn, studied it closely, and chuckled. "His figures are
neither neat nor attractive, but he had a talent. I've no doubt
of the message he wanted to convey here." He held out
the sketch, a confused mass of red and black lines and
curves, and traced with his finger the outer edge of the
figures, inked in black, that he had identified: a crudely
drawn man wearing a crown entangled with a woman in a
lewd embrace.

"The male figure looks like the one in the drawing I
found in Puemre's house," Bak said with satisfaction.
"That sketch also showed a man wearing a crown. I
thought then, and I still do that he was meant to be Amon-
Psaro."

"The female figure wears the broad collar of a woman
of Kemet," Kenamon said.

Bak hated to disillusion the old man, but . . . "Those collars are no longer unique to Kemet, my uncle. I met a trader
only last month who was traveling south to Kush, taking
with him a chest full of beaded jewelry, collars included."

"How old was the boy who drew this?" Kenamon per-
sisted. "Only six or seven years, you told me. Too young,
I'd think, to create this image without seeing for himself a
man and a woman entwined together."

"He did not see Amon-Psaro," Bak said doggedly. "The
king hasn't set foot in either Kemet or Wawat for . . ." He
hesitated, then admitted, "I don't know exactly how long,
but for many years."

"Mutnefer is even now giving birth to Puemre's child,"
Imsiba reminded them. "Where was the boy when they lay
together? Not far, I'd guess."

Kenamon raised his hands, palms forward, and smiled a
surrender. "I admit I didn't think out the problem before I
provided an answer. But I believe the boy too young and
innocent to create a lie. He saw a crowned man with a
woman, either with his own eyes or secondhand through
those of someone else."

"Puemre knew how to speak with him," Imsiba said.

"According to Nebwa . . ." Bak stood up and took a turn across the courtyard, giving his thoughts free rein. ". . . when the Kushite king learned of the death of Akheperkare Tuthmose, he fomented rebellion among the people of southern Wawat. Maybe a woman of Kemet who lived in this area, a mother or sister or daughter, a lover perhaps, of one of the officers now assigned to Iken, was carried off by the rebels and taken south to Kush as a gift to the king— or a youthful prince close to manhood."

Imsiba nodded. "Did not the girl Mutnefer say the lieutenant talked of revenge?"

"Not long before he died." Bak paced again across the courtyard, swung around, strode a third time to and fro. "We know why Puemre was slain: to silence his tongue. And if that sketch is a valid clue, we know—or think we know—why someone wishes to slay Amon-Psaro: to avenge the death or rape or some unknown violation of a female relative or lover."

"Twenty-seven years is a long time to hold a grudge," Imsiba pointed out, "especially over a wartime incident, no matter how indecent."

"Far-fetched, to be sure." Bak scowled, as dissatisfied with the theory as Imsiba was. "But no more so than Woser and his staff blinding me with ignorance. Revenge is personal, one man against another, not a communal effort."

Bak found Kasaya on the roof with four of the Medjays who had traveled upstream with the lord Amon. Sitting in a strip of shade from the fortress wall, they were sharing a stewed duck, a pot of lentils and onions, and a melon. As their usual diet was far less sumptuous, they were thriving while on their temporary assignment. Bak accepted a chunk of sweetish green melon and hunkered down to wait until the men finished the succulent fowl.

After the quartet filed down the stairs, Bak and the young Medjay crossed the roof to the front of the house, where they could look down on the broad north–south street that connected the two massive towered gates of the fortress. A slick-haired yellow dog lay sleeping in a shady doorway. A child two or three years of age played in a dusty lane too far away to overhear. Heat waves rose from the rooftops. The odors of burnt charcoal and cooking oil and manure were carried on a breeze too soft and gentle to dry the sweat trickling down their bodies.

"I need a weapon, Kasaya, something I can use to break Woser's wall of silence."

The bulky young Medjay frowned, puzzled. "You would go to a garrison commander, dagger in hand?"

"You misunderstand me," Bak smiled. "In this case, I speak of knowledge as a weapon. The more I know about Woser, the better armed I'll be when I go to him for the truth."

The light dawned on Kasaya's face. "Oh! Information!"

Smothering his smile, Bak studied the young Medjay. Tall, broad at the shoulder and narrow of waist, a handsome yet innocent visage. "I can think of no one better able to help than you."

"You think me worthy after . . ." Kasaya stared unhappily at his large, naked feet. ". . . after I let the child die?"

Bak laid his hand on the young man's shoulder. "We failed this morning, you and I both, and we can in no way make amends. But let's not let his death go unavenged. Let's find the man who slew him."

Kasaya raised his chin and stiffened his spine. "How can I help, sir?"

"I don't know how many servants toil in the commander's residence. From what I've seen of mistress Aset, I doubt she lifts a hand to care for the household, so the number may be large. Servants move back and forth through the rooms, seeing and hearing much and saying little."

A donkey squealed in terror or pain outside the northern gate, drawing Bak's attention and Kasaya's. A man yelled, hooves clattered on hard-packed earth, and the creature burst through the portal, the baskets it carried bouncing to the rhythm of its trotting hooves. A portly man clad in a knee-length kilt raced after the animal, stick raised, chasing it all the way to the southern gate, where a guard stepped into its path and grabbed its halter.

The pair on the roof could not help but laugh. Bak was grateful for the young Medjay's resilience—and his own, for that matter.

"Go to the commander's residence." Bak stared across the rooftops toward Woser's house. "Be friendly. Especially with the women: those who are older and motherly and those close to you in age. Ask no questions. Say, if you think it would help, that I removed you from your duties because you failed in some small task. If you confide in them, gain their sympathy and trust, they may confide in you, telling you all they've seen and heard in Woser's household."

Kasaya thought over the assignment, and a smile wiped the gravity from his face. "I feared, when I saw you coming, that I was to be punished. Instead, it seems, I'm given a reward."

"They all hated him," Minnakht said.

Puemre's sergeant, a large, heavy man in his late twenties, with a crooked nose and an ugly scar on his thigh, stood beside Bak, hands on hips, legs spread wide, watching his men cutting bricks out of the partly collapsed wall of an old warehouse. Not a man among them looked happy with so menial a task.

"I don't like to think they envied him," he went on. "I respect them all. But what else can I think? Oh, I know Lieutenant Puemre sometimes trod on other people's toes, but he was raised a nobleman. Aren't they all like that?"

"My contact with the nobility has been limited," Bak said, keeping his voice neutral, uncritical.

Minnakht gave him a quick, amused glance. "I've heard you were exiled to Buhen because your fist made contact with a nobleman's chin. Or was it his nose?''

Bak was always amazed at the way useless information spread along the southern frontier. As a police officer, he thought it best to let this particular item die a natural death from lack of attention. ''More than half the bricks are coming away broken, I see. Has that been the case since you started this task?''

The smile faded from the sergeant's face. ''The mud hasn't been moistened for years and the straw that binds it has rotted away. Here, let me show you.'' He strode to a mound of bricks so broken they looked like the clods in a newly plowed field. Picking up a chunk, he crumbled the black earth between his fingers, turning it to dust. ''You see?''

Bak's voice grew firm, an officer speaking to a lesser man. ''Have you tried other walls in other parts of Iken?''

The sergeant stiffened at the unexpected tone of command. ''No, sir, but I doubt . . . ''

''Do it. The buildings in this city couldn't have been raised all at one time or by a single brickmaker or mason. The binder will be different, the consistency, the way they dried. They'll have weathered in different ways, depending on their location.''

Minnakht's eyes narrowed in thought, then a look of approval passed over his face. Without another word, he selected five men and sent them to various ruined sections of the city.

Bak watched the nearest man slowly, painstakingly extract a brick from a wall. ''Tell the men here to cut bigger blocks from these poor walls. The island fortress has many large gaps as well as small ones.''

''Yes, sir.'' The sergeant strode through the ruined building, issuing the new orders. By the time he came back, his men looked more cheerful and he more content with this new and untried officer to whom they must report.

Satisfied with the tentative acceptance, Bak let his voice return to normal. ''Puemre served for a short time in my

old regiment, the regiment of Amon. Why did he transfer
so soon to Wawat?''

"The officers there, he told me, were youthful men
firmly settled in their ranks, leaving few opportunities for
a newcomer. He thought promotion would come faster on
the frontier.''

"So he came to Iken, where all the officers were older
men, firmly settled in their ranks.''

Minnakht stared straight ahead; his voice turned defensive. "If the truth were known, the officers in the regiment
of Amon probably turned their backs against him, as they
did here.''

Yes, Bak thought, *like most men of courage and integrity,
they had no time for a man who thought himself more de-
serving than he was.* "You got along well with him, I've
been told.''

"He wasn't the easiest man to please, but he was a good
officer—the best I've ever known.'' The sergeant turned
away so Bak could not see his face, and a huskiness filled
his throat. "When any of us needed help, he was generous
with both his time and his wealth. When we marched into
battle, he was the first to face the enemy, and he was the
bravest. Once he understood the ways of the frontier, he
never planned a skirmish that failed.''

Bak was surprised at Minnakht's depth of feeling, like a
man grieving for a friend rather than an officer. "What of
mistress Mutnefer? Did he speak to you of her?''

"Many times. He thought her a kind and gentle woman,
one to love through eternity. He meant to take her with him
when he went back to Kemet.'' Minnakht's eyes spilled
over. With an annoyed grimace, he brushed away the tears.
"He planned to make her his wife.''

Bak gave him a sharp look. "His wife? She told me he
meant to keep her as his concubine.''

"He talked many times to me of facing his father over
the matter, but he never told her. He wished to surprise
her.''

Bak had seldom heard so sad a tale. No wonder Minnakht was upset. "It's best she never knows. Her life's already filled with toil and poverty. To add the knowledge of what might have been would double the hardship."

"She'll not hear it from me, of that you can be sure." Minnakht glanced at Bak as if searching for approval. "I mean to take her for my wife, if she'll have me."

"Mutnefer?" Bak asked, startled by the admission.

"My wife died in childbirth two years ago. I've felt no great need for a home and family since her death, but now the time has come. I want Mutnefer, and I wish to take the child as my own."

"You're certain Minnakht was in the barracks when Puemre was slain?" Bak asked.

"Yes, sir." Pashenuro's eyes darted along the line of men carrying old, dry bricks up the path from the supply boat to the island fortress. "He stayed the night, as always."

They stood at the gate, watching the men work with an ant-like patience and tenacity. The sun was dropping toward the western horizon, the shadows lengthening, the northern breeze carrying away the intense heat of the day. The sharp chirp of a sparrow sounded above the roar of the rapids. The mound of bricks on deck shrank rapidly as crewmen shifted their cargo onto trays suspended from yokes across the shoulders of the infantrymen. They, in turn, plodded up the steep path, balancing the unfamiliar load with care, and deposited the bricks at the base of the walls, where they were raised to the scaffolding or ramparts for use by men repairing broken sections of wall.

"Would his men lie for him?" Bak asked.

"Others were there, too," Pashenuro said. "Outsiders who'd have nothing to gain by saying they saw him when they didn't: eleven guards traveling north with a royal envoy and three spearmen journeying upriver for assignment at Semna."

"I see the sense in Minnakht's taking Mutnefer as his wife," Bak admitted, "but when he confessed he coveted her, I was sorely tempted by the obvious conclusion. If I thought Puemre's death an ordinary murder, I'd have locked him away then and there."

"I like him." Pashenuro's eyes darted toward another cargo boat coming around the end of the long island, an idle craft Minnakht had searched out after his men had found several productive sources of brick. "Lieutenant Puemre was lucky to have him in his company."

"Pashenuro!" A mason perched high on a scaffold beckoned.

Bak could see his presence was an added burden the Medjay did not need. "You've much to do before nightfall, so go on about your business. I can check the repairs without dragging you around with me."

Bak was more than satisfied with the work that had been done. The repairs on the long eastern wall, which had suffered the least through the years from natural and human erosion, were completed. The fresh plaster holding the patches together could not entirely be disguised, but the wall was whole, with no sign of neglect except for damaged spur walls invisible from the interior. He strode back to the much shorter northern wall and the gaping hole at the west corner, where most of the men were working. Pashenuro had vowed the whole span would be fixed before nightfall.

"Those men deserve a reward."

Bak swung around, startled more by the echo of his own thoughts than the unexpected presence behind him. "Senu! What brings you to this island outpost?"

The short, stocky lieutenant watched a tray of bricks being raised to a broken section of battlement. "I came upon Sergeant Minnakht and his men, tearing down a block of ancient buildings and carrying them away from Iken brick by brick. I wanted to see for myself where all those bricks are going."

What's a watch officer doing way out here? Bak wondered. *Especially so near the end of the day when he must soon inspect the sentries assigned to night duty? True, Senu had commanded most of these men before Puemre was given the company, but to come so late?* ''We'll leave a few buildings standing''—he grinned—''those dwellings that are fully occupied.''

Senu laughed. ''There's a warehouse not far from my quarters I wouldn't mind seeing pulled down. It was long ago used to store grain; today it holds nothing but rats.''

''If you're serious about its destruction, speak with Minnakht.''

''I will. The pests are everywhere.'' Senu eyed the long eastern wall with a studied interest. ''How's your search progressing for Puemre's slayer?''

A fishing expedition, Bak thought. *Why am I not surprised?* ''I've been side-tracked today and have faced a major setback, but I'm confident I'll soon lay hands on the guilty man.''

If Senu noticed how meaningless the words were, he gave no indication. ''Now there's been another death, I hear. The murder of an innocent child. Did the same man slay him, I wonder?''

''I've had no time to tie the threads together, but could his death so soon after that of his master be a coincidence?'' Giving Senu no time to form an answer, Bak took his arm and ushered him along the finished wall. ''Come, let me show you the work we're doing.''

As they walked, he pointed out several repairs, then said, ''I've been told you once fought with our army in Kush, winning the gold of valor.''

''That was a long time ago, twenty-seven years.'' Senu's face clouded. ''I was a callow youth, more foolhardy than brave. I did what I had to do to survive, and the king handed me a golden fly.''

Bak glanced at the officer, surprised by his disparaging tone. ''You take no joy in the award?''

"Joy?" Senu's laugh was hard and bitter. "I wear the fly only when I must. Only on the most ceremonial of occasions."

Senu was a scarred man, Bak saw, the wounds deep within his heart. What had happened? Was the incident sufficient to fuel a plot to slay Amon-Psaro? "You faced Amon-Psaro's father in battle?"

"Faced him?" Senu scoffed. "He chased us into a narrow valley blocked by sand and hunted us down like vermin. Not one man in four survived." His mouth tightened; he visibly shook off the wrath clouding his visage. "Has your quest for the murderer taken you in any special direction?"

"We're narrowing down the possibilities." Bak saluted the cargo vessel's master, standing at the gate having a final word with Pashenuro before sailing back to Iken. "What saved you from the Kushite army?"

"Woser came with his company." Senu's snort reflected the bitterness of memory. "He was a lieutenant, greener than I was but with fresh troops and the courage of the lady Sekhmet. When the Kushite king saw he might soon become the victim of his own trap, he withdrew, leaving those of us still living cowering among the rocks."

"You must've done something right, Lieutenant. The gold of valor isn't awarded lightly."

"In our desperation, we took many lives." Senu's laugh was sharp and brittle. "Does the number of dead make a hero? No, it's the way one stands up to the enemy."

Bak agreed, yet he could not understand so complete a rejection of the golden fly. A portion of the tale was missing, he was sure. "I've been told you've served in Wawat for many years and even far to the south in the land of Kush."

"My wife came from this part of the world, and my children were all born here." Senu's eyes darted toward the two men at the gate. "I think of the Belly of Stones as my home."

The ship's master waved a farewell to Pashenuro and hurried down the path to the landing.

"Did your duties ever take you to the court of Amon-Psaro?"

Senu's eyes darted toward the departing sailor. "Wait!" he called. "I must go!" he told Bak. "The men assigned to the evening watch could even now be awaiting me."

He swung away, loped to the gate, and rushed outside. Bak followed as far as the empty portal and watched him hurry down the path toward the soon-to-depart vessel. Another supply boat, the last of the day, was moored a short distance upstream, waiting to take its place at the landing, where it could more easily be unloaded. Bak turned away and went back inside. He had no doubt Senu had to inspect the watch, but he had a feeling duty had very little to do with the hasty retreat.

Chapter Thirteen

After a final discussion with Pashenuro over additional supplies and rations needed for the following day, Bak hurried out the gate, eager to be on his way before darkness fell. He had no wish to sail those treacherous waters in the fading light of dusk, and to make the attempt in the dark would be suicidal.

He stopped short at the top of the path. His skiff was gone, no longer tied to the post. Muttering a curse, he glanced upstream, thinking someone had borrowed it. He saw the supply boat, rounding the southern tip of the long island on its way to Iken. Other than that, the channel was empty. He swung around, looking downstream. There he saw the skiff, fifty or so paces away, about halfway between the landing and the tumbling rapids. The empty vessel bobbed on the water, its prow aimed upstream, its stern bumping the rocky shore. The mooring rope was snagged on something below the surface, the boat anchored in place, but with the current so strong it was only a matter of time before the vessel broke free.

Bak snarled an oath and plunged down the path. How could that accursed boat have broken loose? At the river's edge, he ran north through the sparse brush, following a line of trees whose roots were washed by the rising waters, risking a twisted ankle on the rough stony terrain. A sparrow darted from limb to limb, scolding him, but its voice

was lost in the thunder of the rapids. He drew even with
the small craft and, giving no thought to possible hazards
such as sharp rocks or old, discarded spearpoints, he
stepped into ankle-deep water and reached for the hull. The
aft end swung away, tugged out of his grasp by a whim of
the current. Or the perversity of the gods.

He took another step into the river, knee-deep now with
the current pushing his legs, trying to shove him downstream. Another step, thigh-deep and chilly, the pressure of
the current more insistent. He reached for the skiff. It
ducked away, darting downstream at least two paces and
edging farther from the island, then jerked to a halt. Its
anchor, a rock most likely, was shifting on the bottom. He
had no time to waste. The rope could break free at any
moment and the vessel be carried into the rapids.

Still he hesitated, thinking of the boys he had seen
emerge from the rapids that morning, wishing he had one
of their goatskins to help him stay buoyant. Erasing so useless a thought from his heart, he gritted his teeth and dived
into the water with a mighty shove of his feet. The current
caught him, and at the same time his momentum carried
him to the skiff. He grabbed the prow. His added weight
tore the rope free and the vessel began to swing around,
moving swiftly toward the boiling waters, sweeping away
any vague idea he might have had about climbing aboard.
With a renewed sense of urgency, he caught the rope and,
summoning forth his most powerful strokes, propelled himself toward the shore. The skiff seemed to come alive, trying to jerk out of his grasp, but he was a strong swimmer
and the distance was short.

As he closed on the row of trees, he found the bottom
and stood up. He had been swept so close to the rapids, he
could feel the mist carried on the northerly breeze. He
waded to dry ground, his knees shaking from effort and
tension. The skiff was like a fractious colt, tugging and
bucking behind him. Wiping the water from his face, he
pulled the vessel close against the shore, where the current

was not so strong, and sat on an outcropping rock. He
needed to catch his breath—and to offer thanks to the lord
Hapi for allowing him and the skiff to reach dry land and
safety.

"Lieutenant!" A shout muffled by the rapids.

Bak glanced around, thinking for an instant he had imagined the call. Pashenuro was scrambling down the steep
slope behind him. Three other men, one carrying a coiled
rope on his shoulder, were hurrying after the Medjay
through the brush and water-torn rocks clinging to the incline below the fortress wall. A rescue mission.

"Are you alright, sir?"

"How did you know . . . ?"

Even as he formed the question, his eyes traveled up the
tall mudbrick wall towering behind them and came to rest
on the broken corner where most of the men were working.
At least half the crew was perched on the scaffolding and
parapet, yelling and clapping, though no sound reached him
over the booming rapids. He had to laugh. He had been too
intent on rescuing the skiff to notice he had an audience.

Pashenuro waved, signaling them to get back to work.
"We tried to reach you sooner, sir, thinking we might help,
but you were too fast for us."

The mooring rope tugged at Bak's hand, reminding him
that his task was not yet over. The breeze blowing across
his wet shoulders urged him not to tarry; night would soon
be upon them.

He hastened to thank them for coming to his aid, added,
"I'm too close to the rapids to attempt to raise the sail. I'll
need this man's help . . . " He nodded at the man with the
coiled rope, a lanky spearman named User. ". . . to walk
the skiff up the channel as far as the landing. The rest of
you can go back to your tasks. You're needed more inside
the fortress than here."

Pashenuro and his companions hurried away. User se-
cured his rope to the skiff and splashed knee-deep into the
river. With Bak beside him, they waded upstream, boat in

tow, stepping with care, probing the depths for hidden rocks or roots or cavities. They stumbled and slipped and once User would have fallen headlong if Bak had not caught him. The boat snagged on flooded bushes and rocks. A snake swam by. A pair of brownish geese skimmed the water's surface.

How many times Bak glanced at the rope in his hand, he had no idea, but suddenly he stopped, giving it all his attention. Much of the end was smooth and even, not frayed and ragged as it would have been if it had worn through. The chill that radiated from his spine had nothing to do with the fact that he was wet from head to toe. Someone had cut part way through the rope, releasing the skiff. For what purpose he could not imagine. To keep him on the island? Or had a mistake been made? Had the knife been too sharp, cutting deeper into the fibers than intended? Had someone meant him to climb into the skiff and, before he had time to raise the sail, the rope would snap and he would be carried to his death in the rapids?

He plodded on, saying nothing to his companion. He saw no need to plant worry and fear in User's thoughts and therefore in the whole of Pashenuro's work crew, nor did he want word to spread far and wide that someone was trying to slay him. First, he thought, the warning had been issued: the man with the sling. Next a definite attempt on his life: the snake in his bed. And now this. Puemre's slayer had come a long way in only three days.

At the landing, Bak spotted a short length of rope hanging from the post where he had moored the skiff. He thanked User and sent him on his way, untied the bit of rope, and threw it into the vessel. Before climbing in, he checked the boat thoroughly, looking for signs of tampering. The halyard, he discovered, was snagged in the block at the masthead, making the sail impossible to raise until the tangle was cleared. The rope could have snarled on its own, but he was too suspicious now even to consider the possibility. Finding nothing else amiss, he cast off, raised the sail, and headed back toward Iken, every sense alert for trouble. Not until he had passed the southern tip of the long island did he relax enough to give his full attention to the bit of rope he had thrown on board. As he expected, the end was smooth and even, with a clump of frayed fibers looking like the whiskers of a cat poking out of one strand.

He adjusted the sail, filling it with air, and settled down beside the rudder to think. The skiff had been tied to the post when the next-to-last supply boat was being unloaded. He remembered seeing it there. No one would have cut the rope then. The landing had been like an anthill, with dozens of men on deck and on the path to the fortress gate. The last supply boat of the day had been anchored upstream, waiting for a mooring closer to the path. The rope must have been cut as the first boat was sailing away and the second moved into its place. Both crews had been busy then, preoccupied with their tasks and less apt to notice.

As for who had cut the rope, only one of his suspects had been on the island: Senu.

No, Bak thought, too obvious. Senu was too intelligent a man to point a finger at himself. Or had he deliberately made himself look guilty, hoping Bak would suspect everyone but him?

As Bak adjusted the sail and shifted the rudder, aiming the skiff toward the calm waters between the two quays, the lord Re bade his final good-bye to the world of the living and sank into the netherworld for the twelve hours of night. Red and orange streaks rose upward, lighting the sky, darkening the long shadow of the escarpment that cloaked the lower city. The burst of light brightened the vessels moored in the harbor, turning the cedar hull of a sleek traveling ship a rich red-brown and bringing to life the gaily painted forecastles and cabins of three cargo vessels.

In the reflected light, which gave the water's surface a golden glow, Bak spotted a dark figure swimming near the end of the quay. An arm emerged and waved. He waved back, though he had no idea of the swimmer's identity. Spotting an opening between Inyotef's skiff and a fishing boat, he went about the business of docking his own small vessel.

By the time the skiff was secure for the night, the sun had set and the sky was turning gray, revealing a pale crescent moon amid dim specks of light. He prayed Kasaya had thought to bring food to their quarters from Kenamon's kitchen. The youthful Medjay had no talent for cooking; even a simple stew was beyond his ability. After the strenuous and stressful day, Bak had no desire to cook for himself or to search out something to eat, yet he yearned for a large and sumptuous meal.

Inyotef's head popped up from the water between the skiffs. "You've had a long day, Bak. Didn't I see you at dawn, sailing out of the harbor with Huy?"

Bak grinned. "So you're the one who waved a greeting from the watery depths, making me think the lord Hapi had sprouted arms."

Inyotef laughed. "You were sailing as if born to these waters, a joy to watch."

"Coming from you, that's a real compliment." Bak knelt and offered his hand. "Are you ready to come out? I've beer at my quarters and, with luck, there'll be food as well."

"And questions, I assume?" Inyotef swam close to the quay and raised his hand for the proffered help. "Woser tells me I'm high on your list of suspects."

Bak grabbed the hand and heaved. Inyotef was heavier than he looked, his muscles dense and compact. As he scrambled to his feet, Bak wondered if he could have swum to the island and cut the skiff free of its mooring. The distance was not impossibly far, with the long island breaking the journey into two laps, and a strong swimmer who knew the river well could use the currents to his advantage.

No! Guilt flooded Bak's heart. The idea was absurd! Inyotef had a weak leg. "I suspect everyone." He smiled, turning it into a joke. "But some people more than others."

Inyotef studied him in the fading light, and finally gave an odd little laugh. "I've done nothing I'm ashamed of. Ask anything you like."

"I feel better now." With a contented smile, Bak set his empty bowl on the rooftop and picked up a fresh jar of beer. Breaking the dried-mud plug, throwing the pieces aside, he filled his drinking bowl and tasted the brew with caution. Since the beer sold at Iken was as likely to be made by men who came from far to the south as by those from the north, the quality varied drastically from one jar to the next.

"A feast fit for Maatkare Hatshepsut herself." Inyotef gnawed a healthy bite from the end of a thick leg bone. "I've not often tasted a chunk of beef this tender."

"We have the lord Amon to thank, no doubt. The steer was probably an offering divided among the priests and my Medjays after the god's evening meal."

Kasaya had been nowhere in evidence when they reached the house, but they had found three stools stacked one on top of another, supporting a basket laden with food and drink. The precaution had been wise. They had surprised a mouse, darting in and around the stubby legs of the lower stool, searching for a way to reach the basket.

They had carried the food up to the roof and watched the night fall while they ate. The stars were glittering specks in a sky as dense and black as obsidian. The air was cooled by the northerly breeze, chilling the sweat on Bak's breast and ruffling the hairs on his arms. A jackal howling in the distance raised a chorus of barking, yowling dogs. Now and then, he could hear the skittering of tiny claws, rats waiting in the shadows for a scrap of food. The sweet scent of some fragrant wood, perhaps cinnamon, souvenir of a past offering to the god, wafted from the basket, com-

peting with the fading smells of the city: animal dung, burnt
cooking oil, food, and sweat.

"I understand you once battled in Kush, winning the
gold of valor," Bak said, easing his way into his questions.

"That was long ago," Inyotef smiled. "In the carefree
days of my youth when the living was all-important and
life itself taken for granted as eternal."

Bak remembered Huy saying something similar, or had
the speaker been Senu? "Most men shout their successes
far and wide," he said, forming a smile as genial as the
pilot's, "yet I was surprised to learn of the award. You
didn't say a word through those many long hours of talk
while we sailed north to Mennufer."

"Nor did I speak of a second golden fly I earned during
a voyage to the land of the Keftiu." Inyotef's smile cooled,
and his voice took on a sharp edge. "I'm no braggart, my
young friend."

Feeling his face grow warm, Bak busied himself with
selecting a thick slab of meat and wrapping it in bread.
"You faced Amon-Psaro's father on the field of battle?"

"I've always served the royal house from the deck of a
ship." The chill left the pilot's voice and a wry smile
touched his lips. "You've not pried into my past as much
as I thought. If you had, you'd know me as well as I know
myself. My successes, my failures. My wealth, my habits,
how often I defecate and where."

Bak recalled from the past how adept the pilot was at
putting a man in his place, how quickly he could grab the
offensive and control the conversation. His mouth tightened; he would not be manipulated. "I must earn my bread,
Inyotef, and so must you. When I report back to Buhen,
Commandant Thuty will listen avidly to each word I say,
each reason I give if I never learn the truth."

The implied threat hung in the air between them, unseen
but potent.

Inyotef broke the silence with a quick, hard laugh. "Your
exile in Wawat has made you hard and intractable, Bak,

like this arid and empty land. But I suspect you're a better man for it, a better officer."

Bak smiled at what he chose to take as a compliment. "You sailed on a warship plying the waters above Semna twenty-seven years ago?"

"A cargo ship. I was an ordinary seaman then. The vessel was heavy with weapons and food bound for our army in the land of Kush." Inyotef stopped, gnawed on his bone, forcing Bak to probe where probing should not have been necessary.

Bak did not bother to hide his impatience with the ploy. "How did you win the gold of valor?"

Inyotef's expression was lost in the dark, but his tone was suspiciously like that of a man enjoying a small victory. "Our vessel went aground on a sandbar. A troop of Kushite soldiers, seeing us trapped and unable to free ourselves and greedy for our cargo, came racing out of the sandy wastes, firing flaming arrows. Our sail burned like a torch and we lost our mast. We had few men to spare to hold off the enemy; it was all we could do to smother the many small fires blazing from prow to stern. I and three others who could swim slipped into the river and dug away the sand, working beneath the water until our vessel broke free."

"Admirable," Bak said, picturing the scene, imagining the desperation of men trapped on a burning ship. "You earned the golden fly and more."

"A path was cleared for me, and I soon became an officer." Inyotef's voice again turned wry. "You didn't draw me to your quarters to speak of my youthful adventures. What do you really wish to know."

"I see an irony here, a situation that interests me greatly." Bak took a bite of bread and meat, chewed, and swallowed, washing it down with beer, making the pilot's ploy his own. "Not only you, but Huy and Senu and Woser fought bravely against the Kushite army. Now the four of you are together, officers assigned to this fortress of Iken.

And Amon-Psaro, a great tribal king in present-day Kush, will soon arrive with the future king. The son and grandson of the man you faced in battle.''

"Irony?" Inyotef snorted. "It's the reality of empire, Bak, where a shared interest in trade wipes out years of mistrust and mutual enmity.''

Bak had no intention of allowing himself to enter a debate on that well-worn subject. "Huy told me he was one of the men who escorted the hostage child Amon-Psaro to Kemet after our victory in Kush.''

"He was, and so was I.''

"You sailed downriver with them?" Bak gaped.

Inyotef laughed softly. "Funny, I'd forgotten that journey. But I'm not surprised Huy remembered; it was a far from happy experience for him.''

Bak's eyes darted toward the pilot. "He told me he enjoyed the journey, befriending Amon-Psaro, playing games with him, fishing and hunting.''

"Like most mortal men, he prefers to remember the good rather than the bad." Inyotef examined the bone, searching for a fragment of meat he might have missed. "He's a poor sailor, terrified of rapids and rough waters.''

"So he told me.''

"Then you can imagine his reaction when our ship rode the floodwaters downriver through the Belly of Stones. I've never seen a man so frightened.''

"I, too, would be afraid," Bak admitted. "It's hard to believe the water could rise so high it would cover those crags and boulders enough to cushion the hull of a great warship.''

"In many places, it won't. But there are paths of greater depth through the rapids. When the flood is at its highest and with the ship controlled by men with ropes standing on the taller islands, it's . . ." Inyotef laughed. "It's an exciting journey, but reasonably safe. Amon-Psaro thought the voyage as much of an adventure as I did, but Huy . . ." He let his voice tail off, shook his head. "Last year I saw

Huy standing alone, facing four armed men. Smugglers, they were. Desperate and vicious killers. He never showed a moment's fear. But his feet were planted firmly on the sand. Put him on a boat, let the craft rock on the swells, and he turns pale with terror.''

Bak swallowed the last bite of bread and meat. Brushing the crumbs from his lap, he asked, "What was Amon-Psaro like?''

Inyotef shrugged. "In many ways, he was no different than any other boy of ten or so years. Curious about everything, easily impressed, innocent, fun-loving. Yet he was a prince to the core of his being, a regal creature who knew himself to stand above mere mortals.''

Bak sipped from his bowl, recalling Huy's words. "He was my brother,'' the group captain had said. Could an ordinary soldier, a guard, be like a brother to a royal child? One who walked with the gods? "Did Senu and Woser return to Kemet at the same time?''

"Other ships traveled north with ours, forming a convoy. I didn't know them then, so I don't know if they were on board.''

Bak eyed the pilot, wishing he could see his face better. "I have one more question, Inyotef, perhaps the most important I've asked this evening. As an old friend, I beg you to be frank in your answer.''

Inyotef laid the bone on the leaves in the basket with the care and precision of a man sorely tried. "Have I lied to you thus far?''

"I mean no offense,'' Bak said, raising his hands as a sign of appeasement. "My words were careless, I know. But your fellow officers have been far from open with me.''

Inyotef chuckled. "You're a policeman.''

The gibe stung, especially from a man Bak considered a friend. "It's been clear from the outset that Commander Woser and the other officers, specifically Huy, Senu, and Nebseny, don't want me to identify Puemre's slayer. In fact, they've gone to great lengths to stand in my way. Why?''

The chuckle grew to a full-fledged laugh. "You're imagining obstacles where none exist, Bak. They're as eager to satisfy the lady Maat as you are."

My good friend, Bak thought, disgusted, *a man whose indignation knows no bounds when I even hint he might not tell the truth.* He wondered how many of Inyotef's other answers had been equally deceptive.

Bak lay stretched out on his sleeping pallet, staring at the stars. Soon after Inyotef's departure, he had gathered his bedding from the sleeping platform, shaken it out thoroughly in search of any deadly creature that might have been hidden among the sheets, and carried it up to the roof. He wondered why Kasaya had not yet returned from the commander's residence, thought of all the work Pashenuro and the men had done at the island fortress and all they had yet to do, worried that his search for Puemre's slayer and therefore an assassin seemed to be going nowhere.

He was close to sleep, yet awake enough to hear the sounds and smell the scents of night. The soft patter of reed sandals in the street and the odor of burning oil identified the spearman assigned to patrol that sector of the lower city through the hours of darkness. The terrified squeak of a mouse and a throaty growl announced a cat's capture of a late-night snack. Snarling dogs spoke of a fight over a bone or a bitch or a small animal caught by one and desired by all. A crying child and the stench of excrement told of a baby suffering from an illness of the stomach. A woman giggling on the next rooftop and the soft murmurs of a male voice preceded a rustling of bedding, heavy breathing, and moans of ecstasy. Familiar, comfortable sounds. Bak's eyelids grew heavy and he slept.

"Lieutenant Bak. Are you asleep, sir?"

Bak opened his eyes, shook himself awake, sat up. "Kasaya! What is it? What's wrong?"

"Nothing. But I thought you'd want to know." The burly Medjay hunkered down beside him and spoke in a murmur so his voice would not carry to the occupied roof-tops close by. "I've found a woman in the commander's residence who'll speak with you, a servant called Meret."

"She wants to talk now?" Bak asked, his voice dubious.

Kasaya shook his head. "At sunrise tomorrow. At a place not far from the river where the women gather to do their washing."

"Isn't she afraid her master will hear of the meeting from the other women?"

"Most feed their families before washing their linen, but she has more sheets and clothing than all the others combined so she must start early. The place she mentioned is sheltered by a row of trees. It's easy to see all who approach and impossible to be seen from the lower city or the fortress."

"Why has she offered to help? Is she seeking vengeance for some real or imagined slight on Woser's part or on the part of Aset?"

"No, sir." Kasaya stared at his knees, fidgeted with his hands. "She's . . . Well, she's a widow, sir, and lonely."

Bak reined in the urge to grin. "And you're going back to her bed tonight."

"Yes, sir."

Clapping him on the shoulder, Bak sent him on his way. As the Medjay's soft footsteps faded away in the street below, he lay back down. He regretted the need to use the woman in so shallow a way, but he had no choice. All he could do was pray she would provide the breakthrough he so desperately needed.

Amon-Psaro would march through the gates of the fortress before nightfall the next day, yet the identity of the man who wished to slay him was as elusive as it had been from the beginning. Many signs pointed to a conspiracy among the officers, yet he rejected the theory. The idea that four senior officers, all stationed at a single garrison, hated

Amon-Psaro enough to wish him dead stretched credibility. The fact that they all were assigned to the garrison at Iken when Amon-Psaro decided to come to Iken was a joke played by whimsical gods, not an occurrence planned in an organized plot. The idea that they all would risk a war to settle a personal grudge was as totally implausible. If he could get the truth from Woser, maybe once and for all he could settle the matter.

Chapter Fourteen

Bak walked along the water's edge, staying close to the trees, blending as much as possible into the long shadows of first light. Should Woser learn of this meeting, he would not thank Meret for speaking of his private affairs, especially with the police officer whose efforts he had done all he could to obstruct. She would no doubt be beaten, and Bak did not want that on his conscience.

The morning was soft and gentle, the land not yet heated by the lord Re. The air was sweet, the sky a clear, vibrant blue. The trees were alive with birdsong, too loud to hear the leaves rustling in the breeze or the murmur of the rapids, whose voice was softened by distance.

Kasaya stepped out of the trees twenty or so paces ahead and waded into the river. He cavorted in the water as if born to the lord Hapi, diving, rolling, leaping, letting the current carry him downriver, battling the flow to return upstream. He was showing off to the woman, Bak guessed, flaunting his youthful vigor, his large well-formed body, his good spirits.

As Bak approached the spot where the Medjay had entered the water, he paused. Ahead, the row of trees curved away from the river's edge and back again, forming a sandy half circle dotted with weathered boulders and bushes growing from patches of rich black soil. A backwater during the height of the flood, he guessed, but now an ideal place for the local women to do their laundry. Sheets so white they burned his eyes were already draped over several boulders and bushes, drying in the sun.

A thin-faced woman of about seventeen years knelt at the edge of the water, looking often at Kasaya, laughing with delight at his performance, while she scrubbed a wine-stained dress with a whitish substance Bak assumed was natron. Her long white shift was hiked up to her thighs, revealing legs as slender and muscular as her bare arms. Her hair was pulled back and hidden inside a bag-like protective cloth. Sweat poured from her brow and stained the back and underarms of her dress.

Bak scuffed his sandal, alerting her to his approach. She glanced his way and flushed, then scrambled to her feet, clutching the dress to her bosom, and attempted an awkward bow.

Suspecting Kasaya had exaggerated his importance, Bak waved off the formality. "Go on with your task, mistress Meret." He knelt at the edge of the trees, letting her know he respected her wish for secrecy. "Kasaya has told me you're willing to speak of Commander Woser's household."

She nodded, tongue-tied by shyness—or maybe shame at what she was about to do.

"No one will know you've talked to me, that I promise."

"Kasaya says you're a man who keeps your word," she murmured, dropping to her knees, bending over the stained dress. "Ask what you will."

Since Meret had been given the lowly task of washing linen, he guessed she was one of the lesser servants, helping in the kitchen, making beds, and dusting and sweeping in addition to doing laundry. In a frontier fortress, however, where households were small and informal, she would also sometimes help Aset with her toilet. And she would certainly gossip with the other servants.

"How did mistress Aset behave with Lieutenant Puemre? Did she act as if she cared for him?"

"The mistress is a child." Meret's smile was tender, forgiving of Aset's faults. "Her mother died when she was very young, a babe. If her father had taken another wife, she'd have learned to be a woman. Instead, he's always given her all she desires and shelters her from care and worry. She plays with his affections, and because she knows no better way, she flirts with all men, hoping to bring them to their knees as she does her father. Lieutenant Puemre was no different than the rest."

She stopped abruptly, the color spreading across her face, evidently realizing her tongue had been running away from her.

A long speech for a shy woman, Bak thought, and a strange one. Two women close to each other in age, one a household drudge, the other her pampered mistress. An ideal nest for jealousy, yet the one with nothing plainly adored the one who had everything. Kasaya must have bewitched her to get her to speak.

"What of Lieutenant Nebseny?" Bak glimpsed the Medjay leaving the water to settle down at the base of a tree, where he could watch the path from the fortress and also eavesdrop. "From what I've seen of him, he appears to be her slave, though a reluctant one."

"They're betrothed."

Bak whistled his surprise. "I'd not heard a word. Why does no one speak of it?"

"She refuses to wed." Noting Bak's raised eyebrow, Meret hastened to her mistress's defense. "She has no desire to hurt the lieutenant; she looks upon him with fondness. But she wishes above all else to live in Kemet, while he likes serving on the frontier. She fears they'll not be happy."

Bak snorted, incredulous. "Woser lets her play that game?"

"Not willingly," Meret admitted, sprinkling more natron on the fabric and scrubbing the stain between her knuckles. "The betrothal was his wish. He and the lieutenant are as close as father and son." A thought struck her, and she smiled. "That's why Aset flirted so shamefully with Lieutenant Puemre. She thought it amusing to defy her father while at the same time she teased her betrothed."

Not tease, Bak thought, manipulate. Or, more likely, she cared not a grain of sand for what either man thought. She wanted only to wed a nobleman and live a life of wealth and ease on a great estate in Kemet. "How did Puemre respond to her?"

"He flirted, but at a distance." Her expression clouded. "Those of us who serve in the commander's residence knew of the woman he had, the armorer Senmut's daughter. We tried to warn Aset, but . . ." Again the tender, forgiving smile. "She's always been certain of her own charms."

"Did your mistress win him at last?"

Meret lifted her eyes to Bak's. "I don't know."

The look she gave him was open and direct, free of guile or shyness. The false look of a liar, he felt sure. "I'm not asking if she won a vow of marriage, Meret. If she had, she'd have shouted her victory to all the world. I want to know . . ." He paused, giving his words greater emphasis. "I must know if she lay in his arms, letting him fill her belly with child."

"No!" Her eyes widened, dismay replacing the mock innocence.

"That's what the men are saying in the barracks."

"Maybe that's why . . ." She clapped her hand to her mouth. "No, it's not true!"

He saw he had touched a raw spot. "The common soldiers, the traders, others as well, say she's with child, and Puemre was the father."

"He never touched her! She teased, that's all. I should know; I wash her sheets and clothing." Her face reddened at the oblique reference to her mistress's monthly cycle. She lowered her eyes and murmured, "Why must you men always believe the worst?"

Bak stared, his thoughts jolted by her words. True, he

had been assuming the worst, but not the way she meant. He had been thinking of Woser's lack of cooperation, and Nebseny's, in terms of a plot against Amon-Psaro. Now this lowly servant had unwittingly reminded him that the obvious explanation was ofttimes the real one, something closer to home and more personal.

He stood up, strode to her, and caught her by the shoulders, lifting her to her feet. "Listen to me, Meret! You must be open and honest with me. If you aren't, many men may die, men innocent of wrongdoing."

She stared, her eyes huge, frightened.

He shook her none too gently, forcing a nod from her. "Tell me how Woser and Aset and Nebseny behave when they're all in one room." He could see she didn't understand. "Do they tread lightly around each other? Do they each seem to have a guilty secret, but look with suspicion at the other two?"

"How did you guess?" she whispered, overcome by awe.

He planted a big kiss on her sweat-salty forehead and released her. "Kasaya," he called, striding toward the trees and the path that led back to Iken, "take good care of this woman. Unless I'm sadly mistaken, she's halved the number of questions I've been asking myself."

"I pray you've guessed right," Kenamon said. The elderly priest hurried along the street at Bak's side, walking in the shade of a row of white-plastered buildings. The deep shadow gave added depth to the lines of worry spanning his brow. "If each of the three is protecting the other two, perhaps none are guilty."

Bak drew the old priest into an open doorway, getting out of the way of a sweaty gnome of a man and his clattering train of five donkeys laden with burnished red pottery jugs. "If I can eliminate one man from my list of suspects, I'll think myself smiled on by the gods. If I can eliminate two, I'll feel as if the lord Amon himself has taken me by the hand.''

"And if one of the two, either Woser or Nebseny slew Puemre?''

Bak smiled. ''I doubt I'd survive the shock of so easy a solution.''

"What of mistress Aset?''

"If my thoughts have led me down a true path, she's served as the idol around which her father and her betrothed have danced.''

"The commander should long ago have handed her over to a sterner man.''

The last of the donkeys trotted by, and they hurried on. The street was busy at this early and cooler hour, buzzing with the chatter of soldiers and traders, people with business inside the fortress. They strode past only two women, an officer's wife and her servant, the latter carrying an empty basket, on their way to the market.

Reaching an intersecting street, they edged past a contingent of new recruits, ten young men so raw they still smelled of the farmyard, and a grizzled spearman rushing them along at double pace. Beyond, the garrison officers and their sergeants were streaming out of the commander's residence, leaving a meeting Bak had heard had been called to discuss the presentation of arms when Amon-Psaro's entourage marched up to the gate of Iken. Bak greeted those he knew with a nod: Huy, Senu, Inyotef, and Nebseny. The archer looked through him as if he did not exist.

"I wish you better luck with Woser than you'll have with him,'' Kenamon murmured, nodding toward Nebseny. "He's a stubborn young man, and protective of his own.''

"Aset is the key, my uncle, of that I'm convinced.''

Bak and Kenamon entered the building and hurried down a long hall to a stone-paved, pillared courtyard on the ground floor. A lanky guard stood near the doorway, yawning, eyeing all newcomers with the disinterested look of a man who had never faced trouble and never expected to do so. Several scribes could be seen through an open portal, scrolls spread across their laps, pens scratching on the smooth surfaces. Woser stood in the doorway of the room he used as his office, glaring at a trader who was plainly disgruntled, a lithe young man wearing a broad beaded collar, bronze bangles, and a glittering ring on every finger.

"I'll listen to no more of your complaints," Woser said. "You must find another place for your animals, and that's final."

The trader's face reddened, his eyes flashed anger. "I have forty-eight donkeys, Commander, weary from their long journey north. I'd hoped to rest them here. Now I'll have to push them further, all the way to Kor."

"So be it." Woser was plainly in no mood to sympathize with man or beast. "King Amon-Psaro's entourage travels with a large number of pack animals. They'll need every paddock we can provide."

With an irate grimace, the trader pivoted on his heel and stomped away.

Woser glared at Bak, noticed the elderly priest behind him, formed a tired smile. Beckoning them into the office, he slumped into his armchair. "I must admit, I'd like nothing better at this moment than to turn Amon-Psaro's entourage around and send them back where they came from. One would think the lord Amon would be more trouble to entertain, but no. He stands in the mansion of the lady Hathor, silent and regal in his shrine, while we turn this city upside down for a savage king from a savage land."

"Amon-Psaro was raised to manhood in the royal house in Waset," Kenamon pointed out. "I doubt he's any less civilized than we are."

"We'll soon see." Woser eyed Bak. "Huy tells me the island fortress is rapidly becoming habitable. You're to be commended."

"I've a willing and hardworking crew." Without waiting for an invitation, Bak drew a stool from among a clutter of scroll-filled baskets and offered it to Kenamon, who sat

down in front of the commander. He preferred to stand, so
Woser would have to look up to him. "We've not come to
speak of the fortress; we wish to talk of the night Puemre
was slain."

Woser's fingers tightened for an instant around the arm
of his chair, then relaxed. "What can I tell you? I met with
my officers to discuss the lord Amon's journey to Semna.
After we made what plans we could, they left, and I went
to my bed and slept."

"What of your daughter? Was mistress Aset in her
bed?"

"Certainly." The answer came too quickly. The justifi-
cation required more thought and an abashed smile. "She's
long been a woman, but I still think of her as a child. I
look in on her each night, just as I did when she was a
babe. I pray you won't tell her. She'd not be pleased if she
knew."

Bak could imagine the scene Aset would create if she
caught her father peering at her during the night, snooping
she would probably say. He walked to the door and called
out to the guard. "Go upstairs to the residence and bring
mistress Aset to her father's office."

Woser leaped to his feet, eyes smoldering. "You
can't . . . !"

"Sit down, Commander!" Kenamon's usually placid
voice resounded with authority. "Lieutenant Bak must do
his duty as he sees fit, and you must allow him to proceed."

Woser dropped into his chair, his face pale and tight.
Kenamon was a highly placed priest, one whose wishes
could not lightly be denied. "You've no right to question
my daughter, Lieutenant, no reason. She had nothing to do
with Puemre's murder."

Hearing the soft patter of sandals in the courtyard, Bak
looked around. Aset was hurrying along the row of pillars,
her eyes on him, her face as tense and worried as her father's. The guard followed close behind. Either he did not

quite trust her to obey the summons or, more likely, he was consumed by curiosity.

Bak turned on Woser, his voice barely more than a whisper, his tone rock-hard. "If you utter one word before I say you may, I'll charge you with murder and treason."

"Murder and . . ." Woser, looking startled, glanced from Bak to Kenamon. "What?"

"He has every right," Kenamon said grimly, "and sound reason."

Aset edged past Bak, half-blocking the door. Spotting the strain on Woser's face, she barely looked at the priest. "What's wrong, Father? What's he . . ." She glanced toward Bak. "What's he been saying?"

"Go find Lieutenant Nebseny," Bak told the guard. "Bring him here as quick as you can."

"Yes, sir." The guard, whose face had come to life, his boredom displaced by curiosity, excitement, and purpose, pivoted and strode away.

Aset looked at first one man and then another. The summons of Nebseny in addition to herself had clearly unsettled her, undermining her confidence. When her eyes landed on her father, searching for support, he shook his head, his meaning unclear. From the confused look on her face, the message was as lost on her as it was on Bak.

"Mistress Aset, your father claims you were in your bed the night Lieutenant Puemre was slain." Bak raised his hand, cutting off a response, and guessed, "You weren't, I know, nor were you even in this building."

"Who told you that? One of the servants?" She raised her chin in defiance, belying the tremor in her voice. "It's a lie. I was here through all the night, as was my father."

Kenamon gave her a somber look and seemed about to speak but, like Bak, he heard the quick footsteps on the stone pavement outside. Whatever he meant to say, he reserved for later.

Bak, watching Aset, saw out of the corner of his eye a grim-faced Nebseny veering around three scribes standing in the middle of the court, arguing about the meaning of an obscure glyph. The temptation to trample on the young officer's feelings was too great to resist.

"I suppose Lieutenant Nebseny slept here that night as well," he sneered. "Did he share your bed, I wonder? Or did Puemre come back to keep you company?"

Nebseny burst through the door, grabbed Bak's shoulder, and swung him around. "You swine!" He drew back his fist, murder in his eyes, and swung.

Bak, only a little surprised by so foolhardy a reaction, blocked the fist with an arm. Moving with a speed born of many long hours of practice, he grabbed Nebseny's wrist, jerked him off-balance, and twisted him around, shoving his hand high between his shoulder blades, forcing a moan from his lips.

Kenamon sucked in his breath, shaken by the sudden violence. Woser slid to the edge of his chair, poised to aid his young friend. The scribes in the courtyard, chattering like jays, scurried across the pavement to peer through the door. The guard stood paralyzed and confused, not quite sure who was in charge.

"Don't hurt him!" Aset cried. "Please!"

Bak recalled the way she had hovered over Nebseny when he and the archer had crashed into each other several days earlier. He was fairly sure that if he hurt the young man badly enough, she would tell the truth. But that was not his way. He pushed the hand higher, eliciting another moan, and shoved Nebseny hard. The archer stumbled across the room and fell to his knees at Woser's feet.

Bak noticed the scribes at the door and the guard. "Leave us. There's nothing here to see."

"Go back to your duties," Woser said, standing, giving them a strained smile. "This is a misunderstanding, nothing more."

The scribes drifted away, whispering among themselves. The guard relaxed, choosing to take his commander's

words at face value. Bak stood grim and silent, waiting until
they could no longer be overheard.

"You've been lying from the outset," he said at last, his
eyes darting from one stunned face to another. "Not just
to me, but to each other. Now I demand the truth."

"I beg you to speak up," Kenamon said. "If you don't
soon talk with honesty and candor, I fear for all of Wawat
and the land of Kemet itself."

Woser, his face clouding with worry and puzzlement,
dropped into his chair and eyed the old priest. Nebseny,
scrambling to his feet, glanced at Bak, his commander, and
Aset, confusion vying with the anger and shame of his pre-
cipitous defeat.

"We were all three here in this house," Aset said, the
challenge clear in her voice. "You can't prove otherwise."

Bak wanted to shake her good and hard. She was forcing
his hand, making him go further than he had meant to go.
"Commander Woser, Lieutenant Nebseny, I'm charging
you both with the murder of Lieutenant Puemre, with the
intent to commit treason against the royal house." He kept
his voice hard and cold, grating almost. "Mistress Aset,
you'll stand with them before the viceroy, charged with
assisting them in their crimes."

Nebseny snorted. "You must be mad."

"Don't scoff, young man," Kenamon said quietly. "We
know Puemre had knowledge of a plot which could
wrongly be laid at the door of the royal house—and cause
all manner of mischief in this barren land of Wawat."

"The charge is a sham." Woser glared at Bak. "You're
so fearful of Puemre's father, so desperate to lay hands on
his slayer, that you're striking out in all directions."

The old priest shook his head sadly. "My heart bleeds
for you, Commander. You'd willingly give your life for
your daughter, yet you blind yourself to the truth."

"How can I know what's in fact the truth? This so-called
policeman has given me no specifics."

''Have you earned my confidence?'' Bak demanded.
''You failed to report Puemre's death, and you've blocked
my path to his slayer from the instant I stepped through the
gate of this city.'' He took a turn across the room, swung
around, strode back to stand in front of the commander,
towering over him. ''I'd like to think you're merely protecting your daughter, a foolish young thing who always
gets her way by bending your affections to her will, a silly
child who would lie to the lady Maat herself to protect both
you and her betrothed.'' He swung toward Aset and
snapped, ''Can you deny my charge, Mistress?''

She flung her head high, refusing to answer. Nebseny
eyed her, a flush spreading across his face, as if for the first
time he realized she might actually care for him. Woser
squirmed in his chair, ashamed of so great a weakness in
his own heart and household.

''The penalty for treason is death, Commander.'' Bak
made his voice ominous, and at the same time prayed
Woser would not call his bluff.

''I've not betrayed my gods or my land, and I see no
way you can prove I have.'' Woser closed his eyes and
spoke with resignation. ''But to be charged with so heinous
an offense would ruin what's left of my life, and that of
my daughter and the man as close to me as a son. I'll tell
you what you wish to know.''

''Father!''

Woser silenced the girl with a wave of his hand. ''As
you've guessed, Lieutenant, on the night Puemre was slain,
I left this residence soon after my officers departed. I went
to a woman I know in the lower city, one who'll tell you
I stayed with her through the night. Her servants know of
my coming and going. They, too, will vouch for me. As
will the watchman assigned to that sector of the city.''

Aset stared openmouthed. If Bak had not expended so
much effort in getting Woser to talk, he would have
laughed, but he smothered the urge, fearing he would risk
his hard-won advantage.

Woser gave the girl a wry smile. "Even I must have a life of my own, my daughter."

She managed a limp smile. "Oh, Father, I was so afraid! I knew you didn't sleep in your bed that night, and I thought . . ." She lowered her eyes, flushed. "I thought you'd heard those awful rumors about . . ." Her voice tailed off, she swallowed hard.

His expression turned grave. "When I came through the southern gate at dawn, I saw you hurrying through the streets, with no other woman to see you home safe and well." His voice roughened, betraying his unwillingness to ask a question whose answer he feared. "Where had you been?"

"I went to the barracks, looking for Nebseny."

It was Nebseny's turn to gape.

"I waited for more than an hour, talking with the men on watch." She shot the young officer a guilty look. "I'd heard you argued again with Puemre and came close to blows. I learned later he accused you of backing away from a skirmish when his men needed help, but at the time I thought . . . Well, you surely can guess what I thought. That's why, in the end, I made them promise not to tell you I was there."

Nebseny gave her a bitter smile. "You thought me so low I'd creep up behind him to take his life instead of facing him like a man."

"I didn't!" she cried. "I only knew you weren't where you were supposed to be: in the barracks, asleep."

"I was on the fortress wall, pacing back and forth the length of the city. I'd heard those rumors flying through the barracks. I was trying to build the courage to tell your father I didn't want to spend the rest of my life with soiled linen."

Aset bowed her head, covering her face with her hands.

"The sentries must've seen you there," Bak said.

Nebseny nodded, his eyes on his betrothed, distracted by what to him was far more important than an alibi. Hesitantly, he went to the girl and took her in his arms. "Don't cry, my beloved. Your servant Meret has since come to me. She's assured me the tales were untrue."

Aset turned her face into his breast and clung to him.

Woser, watching the pair with open relief and a weary satisfaction, must have felt Bak's scrutiny. He looked up at the man who had so recently bedeviled him and offered a tentative smile. "I owe you more than answers, Lieutenant. How best can I help?"

"The prince's health seemed better while they camped through the night, but soon after the caravan set off this morning, he had another attack." The courier, a short, wiry young man, stood at rigid attention, repeating the message he had been given. Sweat trickled down his face, making runnels in the dust clinging to his cheeks. "King Amon-Psaro looked forward to reaching Iken by nightfall. He was most disappointed at the need to break the journey so close and yet so far away."

Bak scowled, trying to look disappointed, hiding the relief he felt at his own reprieve and that of the men toiling on the island fortress. Kenamon, he feared, would worry himself sick at the delay in seeing his patient, but almost everyone else in Iken would welcome the respite.

Woser, his face solemn, looked south across the desert, as if far in the hazy distance he could see the Kushite encampment. A puff of wind drove a dust devil up the narrow walkway along the battlements and whipped a dry and torn leaf over the parapet.

They stood atop the massive outer wall of the fortress. As Bak had preferred to discuss the threat on Amon-Psaro's life in more privacy than the commander's residence provided, Woser had suggested the younger officer accompany him on one of his periodic surprise inspections of the sentries. Bak had readily agreed, but if he had known how hot and thick the air had become, he would have suggested a walk along the river instead.

"You must tell King Amon-Psaro that my heart is filled with disappointment," Woser said to the courier. "I'd hoped to see him in Iken today. However, as the prince's health is all-important, I understand the need to postpone his arrival. I'll make haste to the lord Amon and offer my heartfelt prayer that the child will feel more like traveling tomorrow."

"Spoken like a true diplomat." Bak grinned after the courier had hurried away.

Woser gave him a quick smile. "Too many years on the frontier, greeting the envoys of kings and queens, have made my tongue as oily as that of a palace hanger-on."

His eyes darted toward an approaching sentry, the last he had to inspect, a tough-looking man of close to forty years burned a crisp brown from many years in the sun. The man halted before his commander and stood at attention, his eyes fixed on some far-off point. Looking stern and competent, Woser examined clothing, weapons, and physical well-being.

While Bak waited, he rested his elbows on the thick mudbrick wall and looked out across the desert. The tawny plain stretched as far as the eye could see, its sandy blanket torn here and there by dark ridges and knolls of protruding granite. The stiff westerly breeze stirred the desert surface, filling the air with fine sand, coloring the sky a pale yellow and cloaking the sun with haze. The distinction between earth and sky was lost in the distance, where individual features blended and blurred. A sweaty slick of fine dust coated Bak's body and he could taste the desert on his tongue, minute bits of parched and stale rock carried on the wind from far-off lands. His wrists itched beneath the wide bead bracelets he wore. He yearned for a swim, and mercifully he might now have the time.

The sentry strode on, and Woser joined Bak at the wall. "I like to believe nothing can pass by me unseen in this garrison." His face was shadowed with worry and self-reproach. "How did I fail to see a plot against Amon-Psaro?"

Bak eyed him with something less than sympathy. "Did you actually tell Huy and your other officers to stand in my way?"

Woser had the grace to flush. "I made it clear I thought the slayer had done us all a favor. I went no further."

"In other words, you made it easy for them to justify their failure to help, their unwillingness." Bak heard the accusation in his voice, knew he must drop the matter or risk alienating once again an officer whose cooperation he badly needed.

"How many men do you believe are involved?" Woser asked.

"One, if the mute child's sketches are to be believed. And I'm more inclined than ever to think them true." Bak could not prevent himself from adding, "Especially now that I've verified your alibi and Nebseny's and know for a fact you're both innocent. The idea of a conspiracy has always troubled me."

Woser turned away, his shoulders hunched, his hands locked behind his buttocks, and strode the few paces up the walkway to the corner tower. Bak stared at the commander's back, suddenly doubting himself, wondering how one man alone could hope to slay a king, a man always surrounded by guards and lackeys. *Could I be mistaken?* he wondered. *Did I sort out one conspiracy of silence, leaving another yet to be found?*

Woser strode back, his expression unhappy yet resolute. "I've known my staff officers for many years, Lieutenant, and I call each and every man my friend. But if you wish, I'll give you a private place and send them to you one by one. I give you leave to ask them what you will. Use the cudgel if you must."

Any doubts Bak might have had about the commander vanished altogether. "With Amon-Psaro's caravan stalled in the desert, I've a day's reprieve. Perhaps the gods will smile on me and I can narrow my suspects to one before he marches into Iken. If not, I fear I'll have to accept your offer.''

Chapter Fifteen

"Amon-Psaro should never set foot inside these walls." Bak spoke as if voicing the thought would make it a real possibility. "There are too many rooftops, too many unoccupied and ruined buildings."

Standing halfway up the open stairway that connected the commander's residence with the battlements, he scowled at the city laid out below, a geometric patchwork of white rooftops, narrow sun-struck streets, and small, shadowy courtyards. Several of the blocks looked as if a gigantic mouse had nibbled away random chunks of mud-brick and plaster, leaving a broken wall here and a collapsed roof there. Heat radiated from the flat white roof below him, drying the beads of sweat forming on his flesh. The stench of the watery depths wafted from a nearby rooftop, where a neighbor's morning catch of fish had been laid out to dry.

Kenamon, standing at the base of the stairs with Woser, Imsiba, and Nebseny, shaded his eyes with his hand and studied the tall citadel wall looming over the mansion of Hathor and the small figure of a sentry patrolling the battlements above the temple. "The walkways atop those walls bother me," he said, apprehension turning his voice querulous. "They look an ideal place from which to fire off a quiverful of arrows."

"None but the most reliable men will patrol the battlements.'' Woser's face was set, determined. ''He'll not be threatened from that quarter, I can assure you.''

Bak plunged down the stairway to the roof. ''You'd do well to station a few archers up there,'' he told Nebseny, ''men with stout arms and a long reach. Men you'd trust with your life.''

The young officer flushed, not yet accustomed to the sudden change in his attitude toward Bak, or Bak's toward him. ''I've just the men: twenty archers and a sergeant newly arrived from the faraway land of Naharin. You can be sure they've no grudge against the Kushite king.''

''Perfect.'' Bak walked to the edge of the building and looked down on a grayish striped cat sprawled in the shade of a doorway, suckling five fuzzy kittens not yet old enough to see. He and the other officers had identified one precaution that would avert the need for many of the others, but they needed Kenamon's consent to break a religious convention. They had been skirting around the issue since they had gathered in Woser's office, and Bak still wasn't sure how best to ask. ''I doubt the prince is in danger . . .'' His eyes darted toward Imsiba. ''. . . but you must guard him well, you and our men.''

Imsiba had seldom looked so somber. ''We'll stay with the child through all the hours of day and night, my friend. He'll never be left alone.''

''It's Amon-Psaro I'm worried about,'' Woser grumbled, careful not to look at Kenamon. ''We've taken every precaution, yet gaps remain in our security.''

''As there always will be unless . . .'' Nebseny let his voice tail off and glanced at Bak, dropping the burden fully onto his shoulders.

Bak could avoid the issue no longer. ''Amon-Psaro will be safe in the island fortress. We've nothing to worry about there. The weak link in our chain of defense—and, believe me, my uncle, it's very weak—is the journey from the island to the harbor and the march through the city to the

temple. Back and forth day after day for as long as the
prince is ill, the king's life will be at risk.''

Kenamon's mouth tightened. "What are you asking of
me?''

From the resolute look on the old man's face, Bak could
tell he had already guessed what the officers wanted. "Will
you allow us to build a shrine on the island and house the
lord Amon there?" His voice grew passionate with conviction. "I beg you, my uncle, to agree. Then the king and his
son can be together day and night, safe from threat, without
the need for the twice-daily march along streets difficult if
not impossible to secure.''

The elderly priest, his face grave, shook his head. But
instead of voicing an immediate rejection, he clasped his
hands behind his back and paced the length of the rooftop,
his head bowed in thought.

A snarl sounded in the street below. Bak glanced around,
saw an orange tom skulking up the lane toward the striped
cat and her helpless kittens. She faced him, her back arched,
the fur on her tail standing on end, snarling to protect her
brood. The tom crept on undeterred, his tail whipping back
and forth, bent on stealing one of the tiny, blind creatures.
Bak scooped up the nearest object to hand, a stone spindle,
and flung it at the wall above the tom's head. He leaped
upward, twisting around in midair, and scooted away.

"I'm sorry, my son." Kenamon, his face grim and unhappy, patted Bak's shoulder as he would a favored puppy.
"The lord Amon must remain in the mansion of Hathor.''

Why? Bak wanted to ask. *Is a shrine not good enough
now that he's a great and mighty god?* "We'll recruit the
most accomplished carpenter in Iken to build it and the
most talented goldsmith to sheathe it. Set up in a private
corner, the lord Amon will be safe and well protected from
man and beast and the elements. He'll be more comfortable
there, for all the fortress will be his, not one small room in
a temple he must share.''

Kenamon gave him a fond smile. "You speak with a

golden tongue, my boy, but I was told by the first prophet himself that the god must dwell with the lady Hathor.''

Muttering a curse under his breath, Bak glanced at the other officers and Imsiba. Woser looked disgusted, the Medjay and Nebseny helpless to come up with a better idea. He knelt at the edge of the roof and stared into the lane below, giving himself time to think. There had to be a way around that order. The kittens were alone, he noticed, and only three remained. Where was the mother? Had the tom sneaked back to steal the other two while he looked away?

All rules could be broken. One simply had to find a way where no blame would fall on anyone's shoulders. The mother cat trotted out of the shadows of the house, lifted a kitten by the nape of the neck, and pattered back inside. She was moving her litter to a new and safer place.

A broad smile flashed across his face, and he offered a silent prayer of thanks to the lady Bast, the cat goddess. ''What if we also built a shrine on the island for the lady Hathor?'' He picked up another spindle, this one broken, and glanced often along the lane, making sure the tom did not return to stalk his innocent and now-unprotected prey. ''A new mansion it would be, but of modest proportions. Would you then agree to move the lord Amon?''

Imsiba and the other officers, trying hard not to laugh at so brazen an idea, stared at Kenamon, willing him to agree. The priest, his mouth twitching with stifled humor, walked to the edge of the roof and looked into the lane. The mother cat stalked out of the house and caught up another kitten. Kenamon burst into laughter. ''Not even the first prophet himself could argue with so fortunate an intervention by the lady Bast.''

Pashenuro rolled his eyes skyward. ''First you give us another day so we need not push so hard, and now you ask us to build a shrine. Will this task never end?''

Bak laughed at the Medjay's hangdog expression. ''You should be overjoyed—as I am—that we're getting off so easy. Once this fortress is habitable and Amon-Psaro in residence with the lord Amon, most of our worries for his safety will be over.''

''We'll be toiling far into the night, I fear.''

Bak sobered, fully aware of the enormous responsibility he had laid on Pashenuro's shoulders. ''Woser is even now explaining the task to a carpenter and a goldsmith. Minnakht is searching out the finest woods in the city, and Nebseny is raiding the treasury for gold. All you have to do is provide a firm and flat foundation in the most sheltered corner of this fortress.''

Their eyes automatically followed the little drifts of fine sand blowing across the open floor. With the northern wall repaired, that end was the least touched by the breeze.

After they had decided where best to situate the shrine, they walked around the walls, examining the finished work and discussing the effort yet to be made. The floor had been cleaned from one end to the other, the debris hauled away. A half dozen men were smoothing rough spots and filling holes. Two men were trimming bushes and cutting branches that hung too low. Other than the cook and his helpers, the rest of the men were scattered over the long, western wall, hanging from scaffolding, suspended from ropes, standing on ladders. They laughed and joked, chiding each other, Pashenuro, even Bak. They were men enjoying a job they would soon see over and done with, a job to be proud of and one never to be repeated.

Bak was delighted with the men and their effort, and he told them so. As for Pashenuro, he made a silent vow to plead his case to Commandant Thuty as soon as they returned to Buhen, asking that the Medjay be promoted to sergeant.

''I thought you should be one of the first to know.'' Bak, bursting with self-satisfaction, raised his drinking bowl to Inyotef. ''As the man responsible for ferrying Amon-Psaro across the river day after day, you'd have been at his beck and call throughout his stay in Iken.''

A raucous yell exploded from a rough circle of sailors and soldiers sitting on the floor of Sennufer's house of pleasure, gambling with knucklebones. Laughter rippled through the group. Someone banged his fists on a wooden stool, beating out a hasty tattoo. A woman's giggle sounded behind a heavy curtain drawn across the door to the brewing room.

Inyotef gave the gamblers a distracted glance. ''I owe you another jar of beer, it seems.''

Bak picked up his jar, sloshed it around, and found its contents wanting. Holding it high, he signaled Sennufer to bring more. ''Having the god and the king in one place is more convenient for everyone—and safer.''

Inyotef's eyebrow shot upward. ''I wouldn't think safety would be a factor, not here in Iken. The only place in all of Wawat where there's less to fear is Buhen.''

Bak wished he could tell his friend of the threat to Amon-Psaro's life, but he could not do so until he somehow cleared him of suspicion. ''Haven't you heard of the child whose throat was cut while he ran through the market? I'd hate to think of the consequences should Amon-Psaro or any member of his entourage suffer a like fate.''

''I heard about the boy.'' Inyotef expelled a long, regretful sigh. ''Terrible that one so young must lose his life like that. He was the child who served Puemre, I've heard.''

Bak sensed a question rather than a simple comment, but he had not brought Inyotef to the house of pleasure to hand out information. ''Tell me what you know of Senu.''

A befuddled and naked man, shielding his privates with a dirty kilt bunched in his hand, shoved the curtain out of his way and stumbled through the door from the brewing room. Tagging close behind was a scraggly young woman pulling a rumpled dress down over her substantial rear. While the pair made an unsteady trek across the room and out the door, the gamblers roared, slapped their knees, jeered.

"Your taste in houses of pleasure has never been dull," Inyotef laughed, "but I'm honor-bound to tell you, it's far from refined."

Bak grinned. "As you pointed out yesterday, I'm a policeman."

The pilot eyed him over the rim of his drinking bowl as if he suspected Bak was needling him. Then he shrugged, dismissing the thought, and sipped from his bowl. "If you think Senu slew Puemre, my young friend, you must think again. He's a good man and a good soldier. I can think of no one I'd rather stand beside when facing combat."

"High praise indeed." Bak shifted his stool so he could see his companion's face better through the gloom. "Do you know him as well off duty as on?"

The knucklebones clattered onto the floor. A gambler yelped with glee, his companions groaned.

Inyotef's mouth tightened with disapproval, whether because of the disturbance or the question was unclear. "Senu wed a woman from this wretched desert. He's sired children who know no other place but Iken and the Belly of Stones. He's even taken one of the taller and more fertile islands as his own and raises crops like a native." Inyotef gave a sharp, cynical laugh. "We've nothing to talk about but his duties and mine. I don't claim to know him."

Bak heard bitterness in Inyotef's voice, and envy. Traits that made him uncomfortable, especially when found in a friend. "Like the rest of you, he's made it clear he hated Puemre. And with good reason, it seems to me."

Inyotef snorted. "His home is his life. Soldiering is merely the task he performs to place bread on his table. If he'd not been so involved with his family, he'd have seen the way Puemre coveted his company of spearmen and taken precautions."

From what Bak had heard of Puemre, he doubted any defense would have stopped him for long. "Senu makes no secret of his dislike for the duties of a watch officer. Is he equally dissatisfied with the course of his life, his career?''

"I respect him," Inyotef said carefully, "and within the limitations I've mentioned, I like him. He's not a man who'd slay another from behind, that I can assure you."

Bak could already hear the "but."

"But," Inyotef went on, "Senu, like all of us, has been the victim of whimsical gods, especially in his early years."

"Good fortune follows bad as surely as day follows night," Bak said, spouting a platitude an elderly aunt often repeated, a banality he hated though at times found useful. "But you speak of Senu as a victim, which makes a lie of the promise of good fortune."

"He won a golden fly, but the joy of it was short-lived."

Bak eyed his friend narrowly. "Tell me straight out, Inyotef. Don't dance around the edges of the tale, teasing me with hints."

"It happened a long time ago in our war with the land of Kush. He was a sergeant, new to the rank and inexperienced." Inyotef stared into his drinking bowl as if reluctant to speak, swishing the beer around, bringing the dregs to the surface. "He . . . He disobeyed orders, I heard, and told his unit to charge the Kushite army. Most of his men were slain, but they held off the enemy long enough for a fresh and superior force to move into the area and come to their aid, winning the battle." The pilot paused, glanced at Bak with a sad smile. "His bravery won him a golden fly, but his disobedience curbed what could've been a brilliant career. Now you see why he's bitter."

The tale was much as Senu had told it, but with a different slant, one that made him seem more foolhardy, a danger to his troops. Bak had heard bitterness in Senu's voice, but he had thought at the time the feeling was more worthy than Inyotef believed, a bitterness over the loss of lives rather than a damaged career. The truth was no doubt somewhere between the two. As for whether or not Senu

had reason to slay Amon-Psaro, Bak felt no closer to an
answer now than he had been before.

"When do you meet Huy?" Inyotef asked.

"Midafternoon." Bak glanced upward, checking the
time. The sun, a golden orb magnified by the yellowish
haze in the air, had not long ago passed its highest point,
leaving him an hour or more to hustle Minnakht and his
men off to the island with a final load of used bricks. He
added, with a laugh, "Woser told him this morning how
close to finished the men are with the work. He wishes to
see this miracle for himself."

A quick smile flickered on Inyotef's lips. "I thought to
sail across with you, but you're leaving so late I haven't
the time."

Bak, with the pilot by his side, veered off the path and
strode to the river's edge a few paces downstream of the
northern quay. He nodded toward a squat cargo vessel
moored close in, its broad-beamed hull riding low in the
water. "You're taking the grain ship upriver to Askut?"
Askut was an island fortress about halfway between Iken
and Semna.

"Not for a day or two yet." Inyotef flashed another
smile. "The captain and his crew wish to see Amon-Psaro
march into the city. I can't say I blame them. With so large
and colorful a following spread out across the desert, the
procession should put to shame the lord Amon's arrival."

Bak was glad Kenamon was not around to hear the god
coming off so short when compared to a tribal king from
the wretched land of Kush. He knelt at the river's edge and
splashed water on his face and shoulders and chest. It was
not the swim he had hoped for, but it would have to do.
"If you've no ship to pilot, what's so important you can't
come with us?"

Inyotef stepped out of his sandals and waded to his knees
into the water. "I wish to study the rapids downstream.
When I see how high the river has risen, I can estimate

how many days will pass before the water covers the rocks to a sufficient depth to carry a ship.''

Nodding his understanding, Bak stood up. "Tomorrow morning then. I doubt Amon-Psaro will arrive before midday, so you'll have plenty of time to examine our handiwork before you're needed to transport him."

"I'll look forward to it."

"The swine!" Bak glared at his skiff, beached above the stone revetment midway between the two quays. The small vessel lay on its side, the interior damp and in places puddled with water that had flowed in through a small, ragged hole in its prow. "Someone took an ax to it! Who? And why?"

"To keep us from sailing to the island?" Huy snorted at so ridiculous a thought. "Surely not! We've too many other ways of getting there."

A dozen onlookers standing on the slope above them talked among themselves, offering wild speculations as to who the culprit might have been. A spearman assigned to harbor patrol held them at a distance while his partner knelt at the prow, looking as mystified as Bak and Huy.

"You didn't see anyone?" Bak demanded, eyeing the sailor who had rescued the vessel.

"No, sir." The short, muscular man, clad in an ill-fitting loincloth, scratched his unkempt head. "I was alone on the cargo ship, sitting in the shade of the forecastle, fishing, dozing. It was nice there, breezy, not too hot. Maybe I heard something, something that woke me. I don't know. When I noticed your skiff—half underwater, it was—I bellowed like a bullock trapped in a marsh. They came running." He nodded toward two local farmers who had hurried to his aid. "We dived in and between the three of us dragged it out just in time."

"When I find the man who did this . . ." Bak let the threat hang in the air, allowing those around him to imagine any number of worthy retributions.

Huy knelt beside the spearman and probed the hole with his fingers. "I know a carpenter, one who's built several small boats, who might be able to fix it, but not before nightfall."

"Send for him."

With a nod as curt as Bak's voice had been, Huy strode up the slope. He spoke a few quiet words to the spearman, who dismissed the audience with a sharp command and a display of spear and shield. As soon as the last man had vanished from sight, he hastened away on the troop captain's errand.

Bak stood, hands on hips, glaring at the hole. He was angry, but more than anything he was puzzled. This was simple destruction, not a threat to his life, so what was its purpose? His thoughts darted hither and yon, searching for an answer. He could find none.

The sun was sinking toward the western desert by the time the two officers sailed out of the harbor. Huy's skiff was older than Bak's and needed a fresh coat of paint, but it was serviceable, the officer explained, for the short journeys he often made to the islands south of Iken.

Bak, seated in the prow, watched with approval while Huy raised the sail and searched out an erratic breeze, letting the wind shove them out of the harbor. As soon as they were midstream in the channel, he spilled the air from the sail, took up the oars, and let the current carry them north toward the long island. Bak recalled Huy saying he could not swim and Inyotef describing the officer as terrified of the water. In his experience, few men so afraid could—or would—make themselves into accomplished sailors. "You handle the vessel with admirable skill. It's hard to believe you fear the water."

Huy gave him an ironic glance. "You've heard my worst-kept secret, I see."

Bak laughed. "Each of us has a weak spot. The trick is to overcome it, as you obviously have."

"As long as my feet are dry, I'm fine." Huy, keeping a wary eye on a shaggy tamarisk branch floating along beside them, rowed with strong, sure strokes across the current. "I realized when first I traveled as a soldier that I must control my fear or look the fool. As I hadn't the will to learn to swim, the next best way was to learn to sail."

"Inyotef said the two of you and Amon-Psaro sailed through the rapids on a warship." Bak eyed a cluster of rocks to their right and the churning waters racing through a gap between an island and a low-lying segment of land slowly being engulfed by the river. "That must've been an experience never to forget."

"An understatement if ever I heard one." Huy's laugh held not a speck of humor. "Did he tell you he came close to drowning me that day?"

Startled, Bak's head snapped around. "With what intent?"

"Oh, he meant no harm." The same humorless laugh. "As we neared Kor, he pushed me overboard, thinking necessity would force me to swim. Instead I panicked, gulped in water, and sank like a stone. Inyotef stood paralyzed, too surprised and distraught to act. It was Amon-Psaro, then only a child, who saved me from certain death." He adjusted the rudder, turning the skiff eastward to pass the upstream end of the long island. The vessel nudged the tamarisk branch. "Inyotef was filled with remorse. He begged my forgiveness, and I forgave him. But if ever I had the will to learn to swim, I lost it then."

Bak was jolted by the tale and annoyed with Inyotef's silence. He could understand the shame the pilot might feel, but he was too irked to sympathize. If he had known of the incident earlier, he would have saved many steps on the long path to discovering who might wish Amon-Psaro dead. Huy owed his life to the Kushite king. The likelihood that he would wish to slay him was close to nil.

Something cool tickled his foot, jerking his thoughts from speculation to reality. He glanced at the hull where

his sandals rested. An elongated puddle was sloshing back
and forth along the keelboard, its source a thin stream of
water pouring through a crack between two boards higher
up the hull. He cursed softly to himself, suddenly very
much aware of Huy's fear, acutely conscious of the officer's potential to panic.

The branch still clung to the skiff, he noticed, close to
the seam that was leaking, as if a cluster of leaves was
caught on a rough spot below the waterline. Yet the outer
surface of the hull should have been smooth the length of
the vessel. Working hard to keep his face expressionless,
his motions unhurried lest Huy notice, he reached into the
water and explored the hull with his fingers. The branch
broke free. Where it had been, he felt a ragged edge of
broken wood and, probing deeper, a rounded hole that paralleled the surface of the hull instead of breaking through
the wood. For an instant he was puzzled as to its purpose,
but the answer was not long coming: the hole should have
contained the dowel that pinned the two boards together.

With a growing sense of urgency, he leaned farther out,
reached deeper, and ran his hand over the wood. He soon
found a second hole, one seam lower than the missing
dowel and triangular. His stomach lurched. A butterfly-
shaped wooden cramp had been knocked out of the opposite edge of the board from which the dowel was missing.
At the first hint of pressure, that section of board would
pop away from its mates, leaving a hole in the hull as big
as his lower arm.

He glanced around, searching for a safe haven. They had
passed the upstream end of the long island and Huy was
leaning into the rudder, swinging the craft across the current
that would carry them downstream to the landing of the
island fortress. Bak doubted the skiff would stay afloat that
distance.

Opening to their right was the channel that formed the
back side of the island where the fortress stood, its course
split at first by two small islands, rocky outcrops too low

and craggy to support more than a few scraggly bushes.
Beyond the larger of the two flowed a single channel, its
waters boiling and angry, tumbling over and through and
down a fresh set of rapids.

"Swing us in close to those islands." Bak kept his voice
cool and calm, soothing he hoped.

"Is something wrong?" Huy demanded.

"We've a small leak. I'd like to . . ."

A sharp crack of breaking wood cut him short. The stanchion holding the rudder collapsed. The rudder twisted in
Huy's hand, breaking the notch holding it against the stern.
The boat took on a life of its own, swinging sideways in
the channel, out of control. Huy stared appalled at the useless rudder, the color draining from his face.

Staving off his own terror, Bak tore the oars from the
officer's hands and dipped them in the water, trying to right
the vessel before the added strain on the hull tore the damaged joints apart. He was too late. With an eerie groan, the
loosened board pulled away from its mates and water
flooded into the skiff. Bak lunged toward Huy, offering him
the oars, thinking they might help keep him buoyant.

"No!" Huy screamed, flailing out with his arms.

The vessel dropped away from their feet, spilling them
into the river. Bak glimpsed Huy, mouth open, eyes wide
with terror, sinking beneath the surface. The tamarisk
branch entangled an oar, and at the same time the current
caught Bak's body and swept him downstream. An instant
later, his head went under.

Chapter Sixteen

Through the murk, Bak saw, close overhead, the broken stanchion and loose rudder clinging to the stern by a few turns of a torn rope. He saw the oar he held, entangled among the leaves and spindly branches of the tamarisk bough. He saw a school of tiny fish and a broken chunk of pottery. He saw Huy, his arms and legs thrashing, his wide-open eyes and mouth magnified by the water, his terror out of control. He felt the current carrying them downstream, rushing them toward the maelstrom at the north end of the island fortress.

His heart leaped into his throat, choking him. He panicked, opened his mouth for air, sucked in water instead, gagged. The grit, the fishy taste, the water he swallowed, kicked in his sense of self-preservation. He let go of the entangled oar, shoving it and the branch away so the tough, springy shoots could not ensnare him. His other hand was empty, he realized, the second oar lost. Raising his arms, he kicked out, pushing himself to the surface, to clean, fresh air.

Coughing, breathing, he glanced around, trying to orient himself. Then he remembered Huy. Terrified. Panicked. Drowning. Twisting his body, he dove beneath the surface. If he didn't locate the older officer soon, while they were close together and—he hoped—at a safe distance upriver from the pounding rapids, he might never find him—or find him too late.

With no sense of where he was or in what direction he had last seen Huy, he turned slowly around, searching the murky depths for the tall, slender figure. Close by and higher in the water, he spotted the dark shadow of the skiff, held upside down by its mast and waterlogged sail. Unburdened by its human cargo, the vessel was rising slowly upward. A good-sized perch flitted past, its scales an iridescent silver. Something that looked like the hindquarters of a donkey drifted downstream, the target of a ravenous school of fish. He imagined he could taste death in the water he had swallowed.

Unable to spot Huy, he swam toward the skiff, where he had last seen him. With luck, the officer would not have drifted far. He tried not to think of the current, which was flowing faster and stronger than when he went overboard, or the crocodiles he had seen in the calmer waters on the opposite side of the long island, or how he would manage a panicked Huy. He refused to think he might not find the older man. The dappled light above tempted him to surface for air, but he resisted the urge. The longer he stayed under, the more likely he was to remain in Huy's proximity.

The skiff bucked like a playful colt. Bak glimpsed a patch of white and what he thought was a thrashing leg. He lunged toward the vessel. The distance was short, two or three paces at most, but far more of an effort than he expected. He needed a good, deep breath of air.

His head broke the surface and at the same time the prow popped up to reveal Huy scrabbling at the hull, trying frantically to cling to the overturned vessel but unable to grasp the smooth boards. Bak saw terror on his face—and desperation.

Drawing in air, he swam toward the older officer and reached for his arm. Huy flung himself upward, too terrified by the unexpected touch to notice its source, and tried again to scramble onto the skiff. Whether he knew his weight

was pushing it down or, in his panic, thought it was fully
afloat, Bak could not tell. Bak ducked beneath the surface
and again swam to the other man, meaning to catch the
flailing legs. Huy stepped on his head and pushed himself
upward, grabbing for the prow, shoving Bak deeper underwater.

With a silent but heartfelt curse, Bak ducked away. His
chest hurt, and he needed to cough. His legs and body felt
heavy and ungainly, too awkward to battle the ever-swifter
flow of the current. He swam toward the light, aware his
time was running out. Yet he was too near his quarry to
give up without another try. He angled his ascent to close
again on the officer.

Huy saw him that time and identified him. He swung
away from the hull and dove toward him, wrapping his
arms around Bak, pinning Bak's arms to his sides. Together, they began to sink. Conscious of the fire in his lungs
and his rapidly waning stamina, Bak struggled to free himself. Huy clung with a strength born of utter terror. With
growing desperation, Bak tore his lower body away from
Huy's and kneed the older man in the privates. The water
cushioned the blow, but it was solid enough to hurt. Huy
jerked back and doubled up with pain. Bak caught him by
an arm and, forcing his weary muscles to one last effort,
propelled himself upward.

Huy was like an anchor. Bak's arms and legs were
leaden, the temptation to breathe almost beyond resistance.
He felt sure they were both going to drown.

And then his head broke the surface.

He raised the older officer's head out of the river, gulped
air, coughed, took in more air. The water he had swallowed
rose into his throat, threatening to erupt. Half-sick and
bone-weary, Bak felt the strong pull of the current and
heard the roar of rapids. He glanced around, saw they were
racing toward a narrow churning waterway below two small
islands, little more than outcropping rocks. The side channel, he thought, south of the island fortress. The rapid ahead

was smaller than the one below the fortress but equally dangerous. As tired as he was, as unable to fight the maelstrom, they would both be pounded to death if they were sucked into its swirling waters.

At the speed they were traveling downstream, they would reach the first of the eddies within moments.

Huy moaned, coughed up water, and glanced around bleary-eyed. His body tensed, and he grabbed Bak, his terror renewed by the roar of the rapids and the speeding water. Too exhausted for a long, drawn-out fight and closing on the turbulence, Bak hit him on the jaw. Huy's head snapped back, his eyes closed, and he went limp.

Across the channel to the north lay the large island on which the fortress stood. The structure, built on the higher ground at the far end, was hidden from view by protruding rocks and brush. It was too far away and the rapids too loud for its occupants to hear a shout for help, too far away for an exhausted man to swim, especially one burdened by a senseless man. Feeling the pull of friendly faces and hot food, Bak turned with reluctance toward the tiny barren island to the south. He took another deep breath of air, more for moral support than from need, and began to swim, towing Huy behind him. Bits of foam washed toward them, beckoning. Spray filled the air.

He was so tired he did not realize they had reached the island until he stumbled onto solid rock. He struggled to his feet, dragged Huy to safety, and collapsed on his knees. Bowing his head to the ground, he offered a silent prayer of gratitude to the lord Amon.

"I owe you my life." Huy, his face pale, greenish almost, sat with his back against a large rough boulder not far from the river's edge, letting the sun dry his clothing and heal his abused body. "If I had a daughter, she'd be yours. But I've no daughter, and nothing less would be of sufficient value to repay you."

"In a way, you have repaid me. I know now for a fact you're not the man I've been seeking."

Bak sat on a jagged chunk of rock, the highest point on the island, keeping an eye on the channel the boats traveled when going back and forth between Iken and the island fortress. He was tired and bruised, his knees abraded. His arms and legs were weak and shaky. His kilt was filthy and torn from hem to waist. The hour was late, the sun close to setting, but with luck and the lord Amon's favor, another boat would make the trip before darkness fell. He had no wish to spend the night on this rocky outcrop, an irregular mass of jagged, water-worn stone.

Huy managed a wan smile. "I tried to drown you. How can you be sure my terror wasn't pretense?"

"I doubt the lord Amon himself could turn a man into so accomplished an actor," Bak said in a wry voice, "but I've a more substantial reason as well."

They both spoke louder than normal to make themselves heard above the tumbling waters.

"And that is . . . ?" Huy asked.

"When we reached the harbor, we found my skiff holed for what seemed like no good reason. So instead of my vessel, we used yours. It, too, had been damaged, though in such a way we wouldn't notice until too late. You'd never have set foot on it if you'd done the dirty work yourself."

If possible, Huy's face turned paler than before. "My skiff was damaged deliberately?"

Bak described the damage to the hull, the missing dowel and butterfly cramp. "And from the way the stanchion broke, it must also have been weakened."

Huy's face turned grim as the truth began to dawn. "We were meant to die together."

"Exactly." Bak rubbed the back of his neck, trying to banish the soreness from his muscles. "I might've taken my boat out alone, but with a hole in its hull, I couldn't. You were busy through much of the day, watching your officers and their men practice the drills they'll perform for Amon-Psaro, so you couldn't take your skiff out until they'd finished.''

Huy muttered a savage oath. ''I worked the men like oxen, making no secret of the fact that I wanted to quit early because we planned to sail to the island.''

''Many things could've gone wrong.'' Bak's voice was as grim as Huy's face. ''For example, I could've taken a barge to the island, though I've never done so before, and waited for you there. But I didn't. Everything fell into place for our would-be slayer, just as it was meant to.''

Huy eyed a heron wading in a shallow backwater across the channel and scowled. ''I can understand Puemre's murderer wishing you dead, especially if you're treading close on his heels. But why slay me?''

Bak gave the older officer a speculative look. ''What do you know of Puemre's death that you've failed to tell me?''

''Why would I hold anything back?'' Huy snapped. ''Puemre was a swine, true, and I've no reason to grieve for him, but his death—any death—is an offense to the lady Maat. A lie only magnifies that offense.''

''You must know something,'' Bak insisted.

Huy scrambled to his knees—not for the first time—and leaned out over the river. He wretched once and again and again, vomiting water yellow with bile, his body racked with pain and exhaustion. When he finished, he leaned back against the boulder and closed his eyes. Bak allowed him to rest. Huy was a strong and determined man, but no longer young. He had spent the heat of the day standing beneath the blazing sun and had come close to drowning. He had earned Bak's respect, and he had earned the right to be left in peace while he collected himself.

''I know Puemre's father is the chancellor,'' Huy said, his eyes still closed, ''a favorite of Maatkare Hatshepsut herself, and laying hands on his slayer would naturally be important to you. But you seem driven by the task.''

''I'd forgotten Nihisy,'' Bak admitted, laughing softly at

himself. "I've been too worried for Amon-Psaro."

Huy's eyes snapped open. "Amon-Psaro? What are you talking about? Have you been holding secrets within your heart that bear on the workings of this garrison?"

Bak hastened to tell him all he knew. "So you see now why I dared not trust you," he concluded, "and why I've asked the questions I have."

"Woser told us he was certain a trader slew Puemre. I took him at his word." Huy snorted. "Because it was easier, I guess, to look to a stranger than to a friend."

"The commander was laying a false trail. He feared Nebseny slew Puemre, and he even worried that mistress Aset might've done it."

"Woser loves Aset above all others. After her mother died, he made her his sole reason for living." Huy rubbed his eyes, red-rimmed from the water. "Maybe now that you've cleared the air between them and between her and Nebseny, he can enlarge his life, perhaps wed Sithathor, the widow he's been visiting since he took command of Iken."

A pair of crows swooped down, landing on a rock protruding from the river a few paces above the rapids. One bird, its wings fluttering for balance, hopped down to the water to pluck out the sodden carcass of a rat. Its mate squawked, calling to a third crow perched on an acacia on another small island.

"As for me," Huy went on, "I disliked Puemre for blaming me for the lives he lost during the first skirmish he fought, but as all the world knew his accusation had no substance, I carried no burden of anger, no wish for revenge."

"You came too close to drowning for me to suspect you any longer," Bak reminded him. "If my thinking is right, the man I seek is either Inyotef or Senu."

"I can't believe either man an assassin."

"I'm convinced I'm right," Bak said, his tone as unyielding as that of the older officer.

"And if you err?"

"I'll have no choice but to look at every man in this garrison, far too many for the few short hours until the Kushites march into Iken. The thought is intolerable."

"We can and will surround Amon-Psaro with guards, every man in the garrison if need be." The certainty evaporated from Huy's voice. "But if one of those two happens to be the guilty man . . ."

Bak had no wish to go again through the various options available to protect the king, each and every one faulted. Fruitless speculation gave birth to frustration and depression, two feelings that could only get in the way of clear thinking. "Will you tell me of Senu and Inyotef, sir?"

A tiny smile flitted across Huy's face, probably because of the formality from a man who had not long ago kneed him in the groin and knocked him senseless. "Senu made a mistake when young, as many inexperienced men do. He saw his company winning a battle, and he urged them to charge forward, forgetting to notice the men to left and right, the way the front line wavered, the numbers of wounded falling. Carried away with success, he urged his men well ahead of the others, allowing them to be trapped in a dry watercourse. Puemre never let him forget his error."

"Puemre made a costly mistake of his own."

"He blamed everyone but himself for that, while Senu has spent a lifetime blaming himself for his error."

A flock of swallows plunged from the sky, small winged missiles chattering with excitement. Wheeling in midair, they darted back and forth across the water, feasting on a cloud of insects too small for the human eye to see.

"Inyotef told me Puemre constantly reminded him of his age and his crippled leg," Bak said.

"I counseled him and Senu both to ignore him, pointing out that he'd soon use his influence to have himself transferred to the capital, where he could walk the corridors of power. The man who tried to hurt him would merely hurt himself.''

Bak gave him a long, speculative look. "You told me he wanted your job. One stepping-stone among many, you said. First you would fall to his ambition, and Woser and Commandant Thuty and the viceroy would fall behind you. He surely couldn't be in two places at once: here in Wawat and in faraway Kemet.''

A touch of pink colored Huy's pallor. "His climb to power on the southern frontier was my own personal dread, one I believed unwise to share. The strength of a garrison lies in the solidity of its troops. I wanted no internal warfare among the officers. There was enough bad feeling as it was.''

Bak, who also now and again tailored the truth to fit necessity, smiled his understanding. Huy was a good man, he felt, one any good officer would be proud to serve. "Do you have any idea why Senu or Inyotef would hate Amon-Psaro? I speak now of the past in addition to the present.''

"I don't know." Huy eyed a dragonfly flitting around the islet. "I just don't know.''

Bak saw a reluctance in Huy to speak, a truth hidden in his heart that he preferred not to divulge. While he waited for the disclosure he knew the officer would be honor-bound to make, he watched the swallows, their hunger satisfied, streak away to the west and the steep face of the escarpment where their nests were hidden. A movement caught his eye, the sound of laughter reached his ear. The stubby prow of a boat nosed its way around the island to the north, a cargo vessel making its ponderous way upstream from the fortress. He shot to his feet to stand atop the boulder, waving his arms to attract attention.

Bak knelt beside Huy, sitting cross-legged in the prow of the cargo ship, sipping from a cup filled with a heady brew of beer sweetened and strengthened with dates. The breeze had died soon after they rounded the long island and the crew had taken up the oars. An aging sailor sang an old river song, beating out the rhythm on a large overturned pottery bowl, setting the tempo for the rowers. The river was smooth and still, a sheet of copper blended with gold, reflecting the evening sky. Birdsong rose from the trees along the water's edge. Traces of smoke drifted from the city, teasing the nostrils, hinting of food and drink. A falcon soared overhead, alone and lordly in his heavenly kingdom.

Other than the sailors and their two unexpected passengers, the vessel was empty and riding high on the water. The cargo of food and materials had been unloaded at the island fortress; the men ferried across to work there would remain overnight. Bak, his spirits restored by a jar of the ordinary beer more suited to his taste than the sweeter brew, had been watching Huy since their rescue. From the older officer's troubled expression, he guessed the time had come to press him further.

"Have you thought yet of any reason why Senu or Inyotef would wish Amon-Psaro dead?"

Huy started, torn from his reverie. "I don't think . . . No! I can't help you."

"You've thought of something, sir, something that troubles you. Your expression betrays you."

Huy stared at the bowl, cracked and worn from use. "I call both of them my friends, Lieutenant."

"Did you not in the distant past call Amon-Psaro your friend?" Bak's voice was gentle, but firm. "Did he not once save your life?"

"As you did today." Huy rose to his feet and walked to the rail, where he looked out across the water at the distant city, lying in the shadow of the escarpment, and the massive fortress towering above, its white walls gleaming in the last rays of sunlight. Much of the pallor had gone from his face, but his eyes were deep-sunk, the flesh below them darkened by exhaustion. "Senu's wife is a woman from far to the south. He took her as his own many years ago when first he traveled to Kush. He cares for her above all others, and she cares as much for him. She's given him many children.'' A smile touched his lips. "How Senu keeps his sanity in so chaotic a household, I'll never understand.''

Bak, who had expected some momentous disclosure, was puzzled. "From what I've seen since I came to Wawat, men who take wives from the south aren't uncommon, especially the traders, but some soldiers as well.''

"This woman," Huy said in a voice made ponderous by reluctance, "is a member of the royal family of a Kushite king, Amon-Psaro.''

Bak stiffened. "No wonder you hesitated to tell me.''

"Such a position is often precarious and can sometimes be downright dangerous," Huy pointed out, "but I was told by one who should know that she's too far down the line of inheritance to be a threat to the throne. Nor would she feel menaced by Amon-Psaro's arrival here in Iken.''

"Who was your informant?" Bak asked, barely able to contain his excitement. "Can I speak with him?''

"He was long ago laid to rest in his tomb." Huy must have known the man well, for a sadness clouded his face. "Many years before his death he was an envoy of Akheperenre Tuthmose, our present sovereign's deceased husband. Senu accompanied him upriver more than once to the courts of the various tribal kings.''

Bak tamped down his excitement, cautioning himself to jump to no conclusions. Huy was right about a woman of royal blood. Unless she was a daughter or sister or one of more distant parentage who attracted the favor of the king, she would be one among many, a ewe in a herd of ewes to be handed over to the most tempting bidder. Yet what if Senu had stolen away a royal favorite? Unlikely, but as plausible as any other theory Bak could conceive. He must speak with Senu or the woman as soon as possible.

Vowing to hurry straight from the harbor to Senu's house, he asked, "Have you any . . . ?" His voice was lost in a flourish of drumbeats as they neared the quay. "Have you any idea how well Senu knew Amon-Psaro?''

"He's never spoken of him to me or to anyone else as far as I know, but neither do I mention I once befriended a king.''

Bak eyed the officer with curiosity. "Most men would be proud of so lofty a comrade.''

"Can I call a man my friend when I've not set eyes on him for more than twenty-five years?''

"You've mixed emotions, I see, about meeting him again.''

"I'll not draw attention to myself, of that you can be sure.'' A stubborn pride glowed in Huy's eyes. "If he chooses to recognize me, I'll be delighted. If he doesn't, so be it.''

The officer's modesty was a trait to envy, Bak thought, and one seldom developed to so great an extreme. Perhaps, if the occasion arose—and if he could keep Amon-Psaro alive—he might get the opportunity to whisper a word in the king's ear. "Are you prepared now to tell me more about Inyotef?''

"I know less about him.''

"But . . . ?''

"I've heard . . .'' Huy hesitated, sighed. "I've no way of knowing how true the tale. I was gone then, assigned to far-off lands.'' He sipped from his bowl, emptying it, and set it on the forecastle. "They say Amon-Psaro was a wild creature when first he went to our capital, a prince of the river and the desert, one who could never be confined within the walls of the palace. Oh, he studied like the royal children and played with them, they say, and he learned the ways of Kemet. But he valued his freedom above all things.''

"What was Inyotef's role in the prince's game?'' Bak could well imagine the kind of knowledge a young sailor could pass on to an innocent but willing child.

"First, Amon-Psaro took Inyotef's family as his own.'' Huy's smile turned inward. "A peasant family, they were,

much like mine. A mother and father to substitute for his
own lofty parents living in faraway Kush. A sibling or two
close to him in age, and Inyotef, like an older brother.''

Bak noticed a sailor standing close by, poised to take up
the mooring rope. He backed out of the way, drawing Huy
with him. "And then?"

Huy gave a cynical laugh. "Amon-Psaro grew to manhood. No longer in need of a family, he went out in search
of life. From what I was told, Inyotef helped him find it.''

Bak, born and raised near the southern capital, had grown
up hearing tales of hostage princes and young men of noble
birth slipping out of the palace, of wild carousing and un-
governed and licentious behavior. As he grew older, he had
learned to sort fact from fiction, but a few of those tales,
he knew, had been close to the truth.

"How old was Amon-Psaro when he went back to
Kush?"

"Fifteen years? Sixteen? I'm not sure." Huy gripped the
frame of the forecastle and stiffened his stance, ready for
the jarring bump when the hull nudged the quay. "The very
next day I said good-bye to him, I was sent on to the land
of the Retenu and from there to the island of Keftiu. I was
gone for close on ten years, and when I returned to Kemet,
he was gone."

Bak spread his legs wide, waiting for the thud. Inyotef
or Senu. Which of the two would want Amon-Psaro dead?
Many signs pointed toward the pilot, especially the way
Huy's skiff had been sabotaged. Only a man knowledgeable
about boats could've removed the dowel and butterfly
cramp with such expertise. On the other hand, Senu had
been on the island when Bak's skiff was cut free of its
mooring. And his wife was a Kushite, a woman of royal
blood.

"He could be anywhere," Huy said. "Probably at his
quarters, or more likely in the barracks. It's time for the
evening meal."

Bak stood on the quay, looking down at Inyotef's skiff, as sleek and pretty as any craft in the harbor. It looked much as usual: sail furled around the yards, lines neatly coiled out of the way, oars lying in the hull with several bound lengths of extra rope. As far as he could tell, nothing had been removed since he had last seen the vessel. Several items had been added: a pair of inflated goatskins; harpoons and other fishing equipment including a rod, a basket for the catch, and a pottery bowl containing fishhooks, weights, and extra line; and a good-sized reed basket covered with a lid. He dropped into the boat to peek inside. The container was empty.

If Inyotef planned to slay Amon-Psaro, he surely would make his escape by water. He knew the river well, the Belly of Stones. In fact, he had walked the shore only a few hours ago, seeing how high the water had risen, perhaps planning his escape. No other man in Iken knew the rapids as well. If he sailed down them, no one would be able to follow, and his way north would be clear. Not even a courier could carry the word ahead fast enough to catch him.

"Gone!"

Muttering a fervent curse, Bak held the torch high so he and Imsiba could study the small room at the front of Senu's house. It was clean, but far from neat. The sleeping platform and stairway to the roof were cluttered with toys. A reed chest standing open against the wall was stacked high with dishes, two other chests overflowed with bedding and clothing, as if the objects had been hastily dropped inside. An unused loom had been pushed against the wall, sharing the space with a tawny shield, bow and full quiver, and four spears. Seven large water jars leaned against another wall.

"They left an hour before nightfall, two at most." Senu's neighbor, a woman of middle years with thin gray hair and no shape to speak of, shifted a chubby, bright-eyed baby from one solid hip to the other. "A man came, a farmer he looked to be, and the next thing I knew they were leaving. The whole family. Senu, his wife, and all the children from the oldest to the youngest.''

Bak questioned the woman further, but she could tell them nothing more. She had come to live in Iken less than a week before and had had no time to get to know Senu's family. The other houses in the block, she told them, were either empty or housed traders, transients who neither knew nor cared about their neighbors.

"One thing we know for a fact, my friend," Imsiba said after she had gone. "A man who runs away has a guilty conscience."

Bak wandered around the room, walked through two other rooms as cluttered as the first, and stepped into the kitchen. Senu and his family, it appeared, had dropped everything, leaving all they owned behind in their haste to go. Vegetables, fresh bread, a vat of beer brewing in the kitchen; more than a month's rations of grain in an alcove beneath the floor; bronze and beaded jewelry in a chest in one of the rear rooms; Senu's weapons.

"To run away, leaving so much behind, makes no sense, Imsiba."

"I agree, but why else would they go with such haste?"

Bak, dead tired and discouraged, shook his head. "He has a farm somewhere, I've heard, but wouldn't they take food with them if that's where they went?"

Imsiba took the torch from his hand. "We can do nothing more tonight, my friend. Come with me to Kenamon's house, where you'll find food and a safe and comfortable bed."

A safe bed. Bak had never thought of himself as needing a safe haven, but now the offer came as a relief.

Bak lay wide-awake, watching the stars and the moon overhead, worrying. He had finally narrowed his suspects to only two men—and both had vanished. Senu and his family had abandoned their house. Inyotef's house, according to Kasaya, had looked as empty and deserted as his skiff.

Which of the two was guilty? Who would reappear armed with sword or dagger or bow and arrow, prepared to slay Amon-Psaro? The time of the attack, Bak could narrow down to a few short hours, for the king would only be vulnerable from the time he marched up to the gates of Iken to his arrival at the island fortress. *Tomorrow,* Bak thought. *Sometime tomorrow the assassin will strike.*

Chapter Seventeen

"Wake up, my friend!" Imsiba, kneeling beside Bak, shook his shoulder. "Wake up!"

Bak woke with a jolt. "What is it?"

Kenamon's apprentice, a bony young man shaven bald, wearing a long white kilt and a broad multicolored bead collar, knelt next to Imsiba. "My master sent me, sir, with news you should hear."

Bak sat up, moaned. His muscles ached, his throat was sore, his knees were bruised and skinned. Souvenirs of his struggles in the river.

"A courier just came from King Amon-Psaro, carrying a message for Commander Woser. I waylaid him, saying my master needed word of the sick child. The Kushite caravan set off before first light and they'll arrive without fail by midday. The young prince's health appears improved this morning, but yesterday he suffered greatly. The king is convinced every hour's delay carries the boy closer to death."

Bak glanced to the east. The lord Re, too near the horizon to be seen from inside the fortress, was thrusting yellow-gold arms high into a cloudless blue sky. The air was surprisingly clear and cooler than during much of the previous week. If the day remained temperate, it looked a perfect time for Amon-Psaro to march into Iken. The thought was oppressive, throwing a dark and gloomy shadow over what should have been a grand and glorious day.

"I pray Kenamon can save the child." Imsiba's face and voice were as grim as Bak's thoughts.

"My master looks to each fragment of news as a piece of a puzzle." The priest spoke with the serenity of one whose belief was total. "He's had many clues; now he must see the boy. If the lord Amon chooses to smile on the child, one of several remedies he's prepared will cure his malady."

Bak hoped Kenamon's skills would live up to the young man's faith. "We'll offer a fine goose to the god."

The priest, his face flushed with pleasure, murmured his thanks and hurried away.

Hauling himself to his feet, Bak eyed the Medjays scattered around the rooftop of Kenamon's borrowed house, sitting or lying on their sleeping mats, eavesdropping. At his glance, they busied themselves with getting up, dressing, rolling away their sleeping mats, gathering together razors, body oils, fresh kilts, weapons polished to the glow of mirrors. The men, accustomed to slipping in and out of their barracks at any hour of night and day, spoke softly to one another as they would in their own quarters at Buhen. Not a voice among them carried beyond the rooftop.

A nervous tension filled the air, Bak noticed, and a multitude of emotions showed on their faces: the excitement of serving as guard of honor to a powerful king from wretched Kush; the gravity of guarding that monarch from an unknown assassin; and the hope that their officer would lay hands on the criminal before he struck—and in time to take his rightful place at their head.

Tall and straight, strong and manly, an elite company that filled Bak's heart with pride. He longed to be with them when Woser presented them to Amon-Psaro, handing them over for the duration of the royal visit to Iken, but the possibility seemed remote.

"I have to find Inyotef and Senu." He clasped Imsiba's shoulders. "You know what you must do."

"I'll not take charge of the men until the last moment. You must stand at their head if you can."

"All who live in Iken will have heard by this time that the lord Amon is to move to the island fortress, making Amon-Psaro's daily trip through the city unnecessary." Bak picked up his kilt, scowled at the torn and dirty fabric, dropped it onto his sleeping mat. Although loath to do so, he donned the second of the two garments he had brought to Iken, the kilt he had intended to wear while leading the guard of honor. "Today will be the last time he'll be this exposed, this open to an attempt on his life."

"We'll stay close on his heels," Imsiba assured him. "If we all must die to save him, we'll do so."

Bak refused to dwell on so grim a possibility. "I think I know which of my suspects is guilty, but I must look to both to be sure. If all goes well, I'll reach a satisfactory conclusion long before he can strike Amon-Psaro." The words sounded good, but could he live up to the promise?

Bak hurried down the stairs to a house empty but for two servants. Kenamon and his fellows had gone to the mansion of Hathor to perform the morning ritual. A portly man was busy packing the priests' clothing and jewelry into woven reed chests, readying them for the move to the island fortress. He handled each object no matter how mundane as if it were worthy of the same regard as the priestly accoutrements of office. The woman, as plump as her husband and far more cheerful, was bustling around the open-roofed kitchen, baking bread and hovering over a thick beef stew meant to satiate the priests' hunger after their morning fast.

Bak slipped into the room Kenamon had used as his own. The chamber had been cleared of the elderly priest's personal effects. Only the furniture remained—a bed, two woven chests, and a table—and a statue of the household god Bes standing in a wall niche. Removing the ugly, bowlegged god, he revealed the four pieces of broken pottery he had found in the hideaway of the mute boy Ramose. He took the shards from the niche and sat cross-legged on the floor, studying the sketches in a patch of sunlight falling from a high window.

The sketches were no less confusing than they had been before, but looking at them with a fresh and more educated eye, they made a childish kind of sense. An army, men fighting on the field of battle, ships traveling downriver— all images of the war twenty-seven years before, and the victorious journey back to Kemet. The embracing man and woman, Bak felt sure, depicted an incident closely related to the other images, an occurrence Ramose had believed worthy of documenting. He put the shards back where he had found them and replaced the statue, confident that if the portly servant had not found them, no one would.

Bak detoured through the kitchen, where the woman handed him a flattish loaf of bread filled with chunks of beef and onions, and then hastened outside to the street. Eating while he walked, he hurried through the fortress, out the gate, and down the path to the lower city. Thin spirals of smoke rose from a multitude of houses, spreading the odors of burning dung, cooking oil, fish, and onions. Cattle lowed, begging to be milked. A flock of pigeons took wing, whirring through the air low overhead.

Aware of how fast news could spread through a confined community such as Iken, he was not surprised at the hustle and bustle in the streets and houses along his route. Men, women, and children were rushing through their morning tasks, singing, joking, fussing, ridding themselves of duties so they could enjoy a day of pageantry and celebration: the arrival of Amon-Psaro with his large and colorful entourage; the garrison troops presenting arms outside the gate; the procession through the streets of the lord Amon and lady Hathor, the priests, the military, and the Kushite caravan; the flotilla that would carry the gods and the king and his party across the river to the island fortress. A day never to forget.

Especially if Amon-Psaro were to be assassinated.

Offering a silent prayer to the lord Amon, pleading for the god's help in preventing the king's death, Bak hurried on. He left the main street and turned down a narrow lane that took him to another lane strangely wider but not as straight. He passed the ruined warehouse, now little more than a foundation, that Senu had suggested Minnakht's men mine for mudbricks. Three small boys, chattering like sparrows, were squatting around one of many holes in the earthen floor, poking sticks down its open mouth, teasing a rat, most likely.

He rushed past two older boys trudging up the lane, one of twelve or so years, the second a bit younger, both with yokes across their shoulders from which heavy water jars were suspended. A few paces beyond, he plunged through the door of Senu's house and bumped into a low stool, tipping it over with a clatter. Instead of being empty and uncluttered, as it had been before, the entry room was filled with baskets heaped with vegetables: beans, onions, peas, melons, radishes, cucumbers, lettuce. A tall, thin woman sat cross-legged on the floor with three girls ranging in age from six to perhaps fourteen, shelling peas and beans into large round pottery bowls. The woman was as dark as night, the girls lighter but thin like their mother. A dusky young man of fifteen or so years who looked much like Senu sat on the stairway above them, sorting through a handful of fishhooks.

In a single fluid movement, the boy dropped off the stairs, grabbed a harpoon leaning against the wall, and held it ready to throw at the intruder. The youngest girl sucked in her breath and scooted closer to her mother. The other two stared wide-eyed and afraid. The woman, whose name was Nefer, he had been told, rose swiftly to her feet, scattering a lapful of peas across the floor, and stood over her daughters, a lioness protective of her brood. A childish hiss behind him warned Bak to look to his back. The boys carrying the water jars stood at the door, trapping him inside.

He hastened to raise his hands, palms forward. "I'm Lieutenant Bak, head of the Medjay police from Buhen. Senu surely told you of me."

Nefer's mouth tightened. "You're not welcome here, Lieutenant. Go away."

Like her husband, she was no longer young. The years, the frequent pregnancies, had taken their toll on both body and face, but Bak could see she had once been a very elegant if not beautiful woman.

"I've no time to waste, Mistress. I need your help, and soon!"

"You're not to be trusted, Senu told me. You believe he slew that wretched Puemre, and he did not."

"Where is he?"

"Where do you think he is?" she asked scornfully. "He has a task to do, and he's doing it. He went to the fortress to make sure his men were prepared for Amon-Psaro's arrival."

Senu might well be doing exactly what she claimed, Bak thought—or he might already be positioning himself to slay the Kushite king. He glanced around the room, trying to think of a sure and speedy way to get her to reveal what lay in her heart. "Yours must be the one family in Iken going about its tasks as if this day was no different than any other."

She swept her hand in an arc, drawing his attention to the overflowing baskets. "If we don't prepare these vegetables for storage, they won't last through the upcoming months. We've worked too hard planting and tilling and harvesting to watch them rot before our eyes."

"These are newly harvested?" He frowned at the baskets, puzzled. "Couldn't the task have waited until tomorrow, giving you the chance to watch the procession?"

"I see you've never farmed an island," she scoffed. "We left the crops in our low-lying fields as long as we could. If we'd not harvested yesterday, we'd have lost them all to high waters today.''

Bak recalled the neighbor speaking of a farmer knocking on the door. He almost laughed aloud. A fellow farmer on the island, no doubt. And a hasty departure, not to hide from a prying police officer but to save a crop. Could the explanation for their disappearance be so simple? ''Did your husband go with you to help?''

Nefer glanced at the abundance of vegetables and laughed. ''What do you think?''

''A big job,'' he admitted. Grabbing the stool, he set it upright and dropped onto it. ''Go on with your work, Mistress. With luck, you'll finish in time to watch your royal kin march through Iken.''

She signaled her children back to their tasks and knelt to pick up the peas she had scattered over the floor. The boys at the door brought the jars inside and, with the help of their older brother, unloaded them from the yoke and leaned them against the wall. They joined the older boy on the stairway to watch and listen. To protect if necessary, Bak felt sure.

''Someone's told you of my relationship to Amon-Psaro, I see,'' she said.

Her composure, her utter lack of concern were disconcerting, not the way a woman would behave if she carried fear in her heart. ''I've heard you're a woman of royal blood,'' he said, keeping his voice noncommittal, giving no hint of how little he knew.

''I'm his cousin, a daughter of his father's sister. I was eleventh in line to be his queen.'' A smile played on her lips. ''Too far away to threaten those near the throne, but close enough to be kept in his palace as a spare.''

The quip was so unexpected, Bak grinned. ''I'm impressed. I've never talked with a royal princess before.''

Nefer gave him a wry smile. ''Save your awe, Lieutenant. The day Senu took me from the palace was the happiest

I'd ever been, and I thank the lady Hathor each and every morning for the life we have together."

She wore her happiness like a linen robe, warm and secure in its folds. To what lengths would she and Senu go if their life together was threatened? He approached the question obliquely. "How'd you manage to get away?"

"When first Senu came to our palace, he was guard to an envoy representing Akheperenre Tuthmose, who ruled Kemet at that time. My cousin gave a feast for the party from Waset, and I was one of those chosen to attend. Though I sat with the other women far behind the king, Senu noticed me. He didn't know I carried royal blood; he saw only a woman who attracted him. So he asked Amon-Psaro if he could have me."

Bak whistled. "That must've taken a lot of nerve."

"No man but Senu would've been so bold," she said, smiling at the boys on the stairway, sharing with them her fondness for their father. "At that time, there were no horses in Kush. Amon-Psaro, who'd had a team and chariot while a hostage in Waset, wanted a herd with all his heart. So he told Senu that if he could deliver a fine pair, one stallion and one mare, I'd be his." Her eyes twinkled. "I was sure I'd seen the last of him. But the following year, he returned with two lovely white horses and a six-week-old brown filly. Amon-Psaro handed me over then and there."

Bak laughed with her, but soon sobered. Each answer she gave raised a fresh problem. "How did Senu, a common soldier, manage to lay hands on animals so costly?"

Footsteps sounded in the lane outside. Nefer transferred her smile to the doorway, adding the special warmth long-wed men and women reserve for their beloved. Senu stepped over the threshold, spotted Bak, stopped dead still. He queried his wife with a glance.

Her smile never faltered, though she must have noticed how wary he was of the younger officer. "Lieutenant Bak and I were chatting about the past. I was just telling him how you won me.''

Bak, who had begun to feel the warmth of Nefer's trust, was irritated by her husband's unexpected appearance. On the bright side, though, Senu was not in hiding, preparing to slay Amon-Psaro.

Senu eyed Bak, his expression hard, intractable. ''Commander Woser told me to answer any questions you might ask, but he has no authority over my household.''

Nothing would ever make him a handsome man, but, decked out in ceremonial garb, his muscular body oiled to a satiny sheen, he was striking. Short white kilt. Broad collar and bracelets made of bronze and blue and red beads. Bronze belt clasp, armlets, and anklets. Long spear shined to perfection, dagger sheathed in polished leather, and a golden tan cowhide shield. Golden fly of valor suspended from a gold chain around his neck.

Bak was very aware of the six small faces turned their way, the large, dark eyes locked on their father. He had no desire to lower Senu in his children's esteem, but time was too short for tact. He stood up, facing Senu squarely, his expression as hard as that of the watch officer. ''I have the authority to ask any question I wish. Did not Woser make that clear?''

''You can ask.'' Senu's jaw jutted. ''We don't have to answer.''

Bak's voice challenged. ''You claim you don't like to see men die in battle. Well, I'm trying to stop a war, and I intend to succeed with or without your help.''

Nefer's eyes widened. She clapped a hand over her mouth and wrapped the opposite arm around the youngest girl.

Senu stepped back a pace, surprised and puzzled. ''You're not here about Puemre's death?''

''Indirectly, yes, but his slaying is no longer my primary concern.''

Senu looked at his wife, and an unspoken message

THE RIGHT HAND OF AMON 259

passed between them. He sat down on the stool Bak had vacated. "Go on," he growled. "I won't promise we'll answer, but try us."

"Will you see Amon-Psaro while he's here?" Bak asked Nefer.

"If we finish with these in time . . ." Drawing her arm from around her daughter, she nodded toward the vegetables. ". . . I'll go with the children to watch the procession to the harbor."

"Will you speak with him, I mean, while he's here in Iken."

She frowned, trying to understand his purpose. "If he summons me."

"But you won't go out of your way to approach him," Bak said, pressing the issue.

Senu leaned forward on the stool, his expression stormy. "Let me set you straight, Lieutenant. Nefer may be Amon-Psaro's cousin, but before all else she's my wife and the mother of my children. She's no longer a woman of Kush, nor does she want any part of her homeland."

Nefer hastened to explain, to soften her husband's belligerence. "We've five sons, Lieutenant Bak. They're no closer to the throne than I was, but they'd be looked at as a greater threat because they're male children. Neither Senu nor I want them to be involved in any life-and-death struggle for the throne should Amon-Psaro die."

"Believe me," Senu added in a fervent voice, "we pray each day he'll live many long years, and that the priest Kenamon will heal his firstborn son. The boy is the only child he's sired on the queen, the only child whose claim to the throne is unimpeachable."

Bak glanced toward the stairway, where the three youths were watching and listening with unflagging interest. He wondered what they thought about the life they lived in Iken as compared to the way they would live in a palace in the land of Kush. He dismissed the urge to ask. Both

Senu and Nefer were too protective of their brood to tolerate questions directed to their children.

"Would you not feel safer with your family in Kemet?" he asked.

"Why should we run away?" Nefer, her eyes flashing scorn, flung a handful of peas into a bowl. "You haven't been listening to my husband, Lieutenant. I'm not a woman of Kush. I've lived in this land of Wawat since I was fourteen years of age. I've a different name, one common to women of Kemet. I dress and cook and live like the women of Kemet. Amon-Psaro has no claim on me, nor has the land of my birth."

"This is our home," Senu said, giving his wife a supportive nod. "Oh, I grumble about a stalled career, claim bitterness at being assigned to this godforsaken land of Wawat, blame my youthful error for a lifetime of assignments on this vile frontier." He clasped his hands between his knees, smiled at Bak a bit sheepishly. "The truth of the matter is that my boyhood mistake, one I regret bitterly, had no influence on my career. To rise through the ranks I had merely to move north to Kemet. But we'd have had to leave this land of Wawat, a place our children have always known, a place Nefer and I love as much as life itself."

Bak had no doubt Senu would kill to protect his family—and so would Nefer. But neither would do so, he was convinced, unless he or she had no other choice. "I know nothing of the customs of the land of Kush," he admitted, his eyes on Nefer, "so my next question may seem foolish. Would Amon-Psaro . . . Could Amon-Psaro reclaim you, take you back to his palace as his own?"

"If he's the same man he once was," Nefer said with a laugh, "he thanks the lord Amon each night and morning that he had the good sense to trade me for those horses."

Bak and Senu laughed with her, dissolving the tension and the mutual mistrust. The children, most of whom were too young to understand, began to laugh, too, cautious, tentative, relieved.

Wiping the tears from his eyes, Senu said, "You spoke of preventing a war, and you question us about Amon-Psaro. There must be a connection between the two."

Can these people be trusted? Bak asked himself. *Yes. They've nothing to gain by the Kushite king's death, nothing to lose while he lives.*

"Puemre was slain because he discovered a plot to slay Amon-Psaro." He forced himself to go on, to voice the unthinkable. "Inyotef, I now feel sure, is the man I seek."

The full force of the pilot's betrayal struck him. For a betrayal it was. A personal betrayal because a man he had liked and trusted had deceived him with lies and smiles and had then tried to slay him. The larger betrayal, that of Inyotef turning his back on the land of Kemet and the company of gods, was no less hurtful.

"I'd not have thought it of him." Senu, hurrying along the lane beside Bak, shook his head as if to deny Inyotef's treachery. "We've never been close, but I've always believed I could trust him."

"My conscience prodded me each time I considered the possibility." Even now, after accepting the pilot's perfidy, Bak felt deceitful in voicing his mistrust. "He used that, I'm sure, to blind me to his wrongdoing."

In the distance, a trumpet blared. Three long blasts. It was the second signal they had heard since leaving Senu's house. They could see nothing from the lower city, but Bak pictured a herald standing high on the twin-towered southern gate of the fortress, his eyes on the distant caravan, invisible except for a huge yellowish cloud of billowing dust, making its slow way north along the desert track.

"How much farther to his house?" Bak asked.

"A few blocks, that's all."

Men, women, and children hurried along the street, not yet a stream but a steady trickle making for the path that would take them up the incline to the fortress. Eager and excited voices, laughter ringing out, an impatient mother yapping at her children. The crack of a whip, rapid hoof-beats, and the raucous braying of a train of donkeys made to hurry against their will. A gentle breeze stirred the air, easing the heat without raising the dust.

"From what I've heard, his anger can flare in an instant and only a quick retreat can save the one closest to him from the fury of his fists." Senu ducked away from a snapping donkey. "But for the life of me, I can't think why he'd want Amon-Psaro dead. As far as I know, they haven't met for years. I see no flame there."

"I think a long-dormant ember has come back to life." Bak stepped over a greenish pile of fresh manure, launching a cloud of flies. "Do you recall any special happening, anything unusual or suspect, when your paths crossed in days gone by?"

"We seldom met. I spent too much time traveling, guarding shipments of precious objects moving downriver or escorting envoys laden with gifts for tribal kings far upriver. He, too, spent most of his time on the water, but on warships rather than merchantmen. As far as I know, he never sailed much farther south than Semna."

"Strange," Bak said, frowning. "Huy told me Amon-Psaro and Inyotef were great friends while both were young and living in Waset. One would think Inyotef would've asked to voyage south. Not everyone can claim friendship with a king."

"It seems to me there was something . . ." Senu paused, giving himself a moment to think, then ducked around a woman trying to console her sobbing baby and strode on. "Yes." He glanced at Bak, nodded. "Yes, I remember a time . . . Oh, fifteen, maybe twenty years ago. Inyotef had been given his first command, a warship of moderate size. He brought it upriver through the Belly of Stones, lay over at Semna for repairs, and sailed on south with the intent of journeying deep into Kush. The mission was insignificant: a show of power, I think, and no doubt to collect tribute as well."

He paused again, listening to another blast of the trumpet. "I must hurry. My men will be wondering where I've gone."

He rushed around a corner, entering a narrow lane hugged on both sides by small houses buzzing with the voices of those who lived inside. A flock of ducks squawked in a derelict house, which reeked of bird droppings.

"The envoy I was to escort was slow to reach Semna," Senu went on. "I was still waiting for him three days later when Inyotef sailed again into the harbor. His ship had been turned back. He gave no reason, but a rumor went around that he was not welcome in the land of Kush."

Bak's heart surged. "Do you suppose Amon-Psaro was behind the rebuff?"

"I often journeyed upriver, yet I never learned the truth."

"Did you travel often to Amon-Psaro's court?"

"Four or five times, no more." Senu stepped around two naked toddlers, wide-eyed with wonder at his magnificence. With an easy smile, he answered Bak's unspoken question. "Yes, Lieutenant, he took me to see his growing herd of horses—and he never failed to ask for Nefer's health."

Bak grinned, forgetting for an instant the gravity of his mission. "I'm still curious. How'd you manage to lay hands on the pair you gave him? Their value must've seemed enormous to a common soldier with no wealth or power."

"I raised my problem to diplomatic status," Senu laughed. "I spoke with the envoy, and when he traveled back to our capital, he in turn spoke to the vizier. That worthy politician agreed that a gift of two horses, mare and stallion, would remind Amon-Psaro of his friendship with our king, not just once, but each time a foal was born. Later, after the trade was consummated, after Nefer was mine and the animals Amon-Psaro's, I felt bound to tell him the horses were a product of my ingenuity rather than

wealth. He thought my tale so amusing and my honesty so
admirable that he offered me a lofty position in his court.
I chose to remain in the army of Kemet.''

Bak laughed heartily, as did Senu, until another blare of
the trumpet reminded them of their mission. They hastened
across an intersecting street, passed a block of well-kept
interconnected houses, and veered into a dead-end lane
bounded on one side by a serpentine wall built to hold back
encroaching sand dunes. Kasaya stood before a door located near the far end of the lane. The Medjay's discouraged expression told them the house was unoccupied, and
none of the neighbors knew of the pilot's whereabouts.

Senu muttered an oath.

Bak had not expected the gods to drop into his hands the
solution to his problem, but his spirits dived nonetheless.
''If he's gone for good, I doubt he left anything of value
or interest, but I must search anyway.''

''I'll leave you then. The men on the battlements will
need further orders, and I must find Huy and Nebseny and
warn them as well. The men they've placed on the rooftops
along Amon-Psaro's route must be told.''

''You must also warn Imsiba and my Medjays. I'll send
Kasaya to the island to alert Pashenuro and Minnakht.''

''Consider it done.'' Senu strode a few paces up the lane,
paused, turned around. ''Amon-Psaro is haughty, imperi-
ous, cunning. But, he's a good man, Bak. Don't let Inyotef
slay him.''

Bak forced a smile. ''A prayer to the lord Amon, an
offering, might help.''

Inyotef's house was much too grand for a man alone,
five spacious rooms around an open court that would have
better suited Senu's large family. It was neat and clean but
had an air of abandonment. Two chambers were furnished,
and those not well; the remainder were empty. A few stools,
a couple of tables, several chests, a sleeping pallet. The
basics of housekeeping a wife might bestow on the husband

she was leaving, the remnants of a marriage.

Bak went from chest to chest, raising each lid and peering inside. He found a few sheets, a man's clothing, a few dishes and cooking paraphernalia. A small chest held eye paint, perfumes, and oils. A fine inlaid wooden chest contained jewelry, mostly of the beaded variety and of small value. He found no golden flies. A somewhat larger, unadorned wooden chest contained a few small weapons, including a hefty and powerful sling—the weapon used, Bak felt sure, during the initial attempt to warn him off.

Returning to the main room, he settled down to a long and tedious search, looking specifically for clues as to where Inyotef might have gone and the reason he wanted Amon-Psaro dead. Bak tried to lose himself in his task, moving systematically from one chest to another and on to the walls and floor, probing for a secret hiding place. The first room finished, he searched the next and then the next. The rich smell of braised lamb wafted through the open doors, rousing pangs of hunger, announcing the approach of midday. He longed to quit, to leave this dreary house and walk the streets of the city, searching for the man rather than some minuscule clue he could overlook as easily as find.

Finished with the interior, he had nothing to show for his effort but a growing sense of failure. When Senu's oldest son arrived with a leaf-wrapped package of grilled fish, a cluster of plump grapes, and two jars of beer, Bak could have hugged the boy. The food and drink, the cheerful voice, and the smile were welcome indeed.

"How far away is the caravan?" he asked, ripping the flesh from the bones, gobbling it like a man starved for a week.

"They'll reach the gate within the hour."

The youth reported that his father had relayed Bak's messages to Imsiba and the others. Extra guards had been assigned to Amon-Psaro's route, and every man who could be spared was searching for Inyotef. As far as anyone knew, he had not been seen all day. Bak, his self-confidence wavering, tried not to think how foolish he would feel if someone other than the pilot attempted to slay the Kushite king.

He could see the boy longed to be on his way, afraid he would miss the upcoming spectacle, so he dismissed him and went out to the courtyard to finish his meal in a sliver of shade beside the wall.

His hunger sated, he searched the court with its round oven, large water jars, and grain silos. He was sweeping up the last of the grain he had spilled when the sounds in the distance changed. The strident call of a single trumpet was lost in the blare of several. Now and then, when the breeze blew from the right direction, the faint sound of the accompanying clappers and flutes wafted across the lower city. A rumble of drums filled in the background. Amon-Psaro's caravan was approaching the fortress gate.

Bak was on the roof, almost finished with his search, when a flourish of drumbeats announced the presentation of arms to Amon-Psaro. Soon, the king would march inside the fortress. He and Woser would lead the slow ceremonial procession down the main thoroughfare to the mansion of the lady Hathor. There they would make obeisance to her guest, the lord Amon, and to the goddess herself. Then, with the priestly contingent and the gods joining the procession, they would march back through the fortress, down the cut in the escarpment, and through the lower city to the harbor.

Bak thought Amon-Psaro fairly safe inside the fortress. It was the latter portion of the march he worried about most. The descent through the cut and the streets of the lower city would be lined with hundreds of civilians as well as soldiers. More worrisome yet would be the harbor, the confusion of boarding the rivercraft in a place Inyotef knew better than any other man in Iken.

Tired and discouraged, he walked to the edge of the roof and eyed the low golden dunes outside the wall. Long fingers of sand, drifts deposited through the years by winds blowing in from the desert, reached out to a distant, ruined block of buildings.

His eye was drawn to the base of the serpentine wall and a wedge of golden brown close against the mudbrick. The end of a board, protruding from around a curve. It looked too sturdy to discard in the desert, too valuable. With his senses quickening, he stepped off the roof and, arms spread wide for balance, walked slowly along the top of the wall, following its curve. The board, he soon saw, was the side-piece of a ladder partly covered with sand. From the way the drift lay around it, he guessed it had been buried there and a recent stiff breeze had uncovered it. Consumed by curiosity, he dropped off the wall, letting the sand cushion his fall.

He shoved his fingers into the soft, warm sand, picked up the ladder, and stood it on end. It was almost new and tall enough to reach the roof of Inyotef's house. Had the pilot hidden it, meaning to return at a later time? Or had he used it to leave the house?

Turning his back to the wall, Bak studied the low dunes. The smooth parallel ridges were marred by the tiny footprints of birds and rodents, but no larger, deeper indentations that would indicate the recent passage of a man. A rough funnel-shaped disturbance twenty or so paces away could mean a small creature had found something of interest beneath the surface. Trying not to hope, but hoping anyway, Bak hurried to the spot, dug into the sand, and revealed a big, tightly woven reed chest. Practically holding his breath, he swept aside the sand on top, broke the seal, and raised the lid. It was filled with large pottery jars, each stoppered with a dried-mud plug to keep out prying animals and insects. A jar containing grain had cracked, inviting a mouse or rat to investigate. Elated by his discovery, Bak broke the plugs on all the other jars, revealing beer, food, clothing, small weapons, and jewelry including two golden flies.

Inyotef, he guessed, had dared not leave the chest of supplies on his skiff for fear every vessel in the harbor would be examined before Amon-Psaro set foot on the quay. So he had buried it here, intending to return after the search for him died down.

Bak saved the most intriguing item until last, a pottery cylinder plugged on both ends with mud. He broke one end away, reached inside, and pulled out a papyrus scroll. Sitting on the warm sand, praying for enlightenment, he unrolled his prize, which was stained and dog-eared, yellowing from use and age. Almost afraid to breathe, he began to read.

"To my beloved brother Inyotef," it said. "He's gone, the one I loved above all others. His many sweet words, his pledge to love me forever, were like chaff in the wind. One night he lay with me, whispering endearments; the next day he was gone. A message came, I've heard, a letter announcing his father's death. He boarded a ship for vile Kush without so much as a good-bye. I told myself he would summon me as soon as his throne was secure, but now four months have passed, and I've heard nothing. I can no longer bear the pain, my brother. The river beckons. Remember me always, dearest Inyotef, and forgive me."

It was signed "Sonisonbe."

Bak let out his breath long and slow. The words brother and sister were often used between lovers, but in this case he felt sure Sonisonbe was in fact Inyotef's birth sister. The elation he felt at finding the letter, the sense of accomplishment, vied in his heart with pity and sadness for the girl abandoned by Amon-Psaro and the dark legacy she had left Inyotef.

Chapter Eighteen

Bak stood on the northern quay, looking down into Inyotef's skiff. Nothing had changed since last he had seen the vessel. Sails, lines, oars, fishing gear were exactly as they had been the evening before. The pilot either meant to flee in another boat or intended to leave Iken in a manner Bak could not begin to imagine. Surely not by way of the desert. If he chose a path close to the river, he would easily be caught. To leave the river and its life-giving water was suicide.

No, Bak thought, *he's a sailor, a man of the river. He'll escape by boat.* The wording was too pessimistic, so he amended the prediction: *He'll try to escape by boat, and I'll be there to stop him.*

Clinging to the notion, he studied the vessels moored along the quay. Other than a fishing boat with a broken rudder and a raft built of papyrus bundles so soggy it was near to foundering, Inyotef's skiff was the only small boat remaining. The rest had been claimed by their owners and moved across the harbor to the southern quay. The barge of Amon was tied close against the revetment, rocking on the gentle swells, its gilded hull glittering in the midafternoon sun. On the warship moored close by, pennants of every color fluttered from masts and lines; its wood-and-bronze fittings gleamed. Sailors lounged on its deck and atop the cabin, awaiting the gods and the king, the priests and the local dignitaries. Their lively banter with the men on the decks of the two traveling ships, which would ferry the king and his party carried across the water.

Bak strode to the end of the quay and looked out over the river, its waters a reddish brown flecked with silver where the sun caressed the ripples. His abused muscles had loosened up, but he was tired and uneasy, his mood in need of continual bolstering. He had rushed from Inyotef's house to the mansion of Hathor, where he found Imsiba and the Medjays standing outside, awaiting their royal charge. Huy and the other garrison officers had been with them. He had exchanged his knowledge for theirs: Inyotef had not been seen since the previous evening.

Leaving the pageantry behind, he and six borrowed spearmen had hastened to the lower city. Kasaya, who had returned from the island to help, joined them there. The small party had swept through the homes and warehouses along the official route of march, warning the residents to invite only people they knew onto their rooftops and clearing away or blocking potential hiding places both near and as far away as an arrow could fly, praying all the while they would find Inyotef. The gods had failed to smile on them. The spearmen had gradually lost their spark and even lighthearted Kasaya had to work at a smile.

Bak eyed the southern quay, crowded with vessels of all sizes, their decks jammed with spectators. Nothing could hold the smaller boats back, he knew, after the official party sailed out of the harbor.

He hurried back to shore, passed through the line of sentries posted on the slope to keep the spectators off the quay, and stood at the lower end of the thoroughfare down which Amon-Psaro would march. The route was lined with men, women, and children, the buzz of their combined voices rising and ebbing, shattered now and again by a childish laugh, a yell, a hawker touting his wares. Soldiers dressed in ceremonial finery, their weapons polished to a fine sheen, held back the crowd. People from faraway Kemet wearing white linen and bright jewelry rubbed shoulders with poor, half-naked farmers who lived off the sparse lands along the Belly of Stones and ragged nomads who roamed the desert. Wealthy tribesmen and villagers clad in white kilts overlaid with colorful cloaks and jewelry stood among people from far to the south dressed in skins and feathers and fabrics, bejeweled and beribboned, their faces and bodies scarified or painted. Bak imagined the desert tracks and the river during the past few days dotted with people coming from afar to see the greatest of the gods and the Kushite king who had come to seek his help.

Shouldering his way through the spectators, he located a hawker selling beer and sweet bread. He negotiated a trade and, loaf and jar in hand, walked to a crumbling warehouse ten or so paces behind the people massed along the street. The spearman standing atop a ruined wall, watching the throng, jumped down to report that he had seen nothing of note. As he melted into the crowd, Bak climbed the wall and sat down, letting his feet dangle. From there, both the lower portion of the street and the harbor spread out below him. He spotted Kasaya and the other spearmen moving among the spectators, chatting, asking questions, studying faces.

Bak tore chunks from the bread, sweetened with chopped dates, and sipped the beer. He longed to forget Inyotef and enjoy the pageantry. The day remained temperate, the breeze as soft and gentle as the kiss of a goddess. The air smelled of the river and fish, of sweat and perfume. Fine dust stirred up by many feet settled on moist bodies and greased hair. Dogs tall and sleek or short and round, black, brindle, white, or dun-colored, trotted among the onlookers, sniffing heels, probing leaf packets emptied of food, exploring. A few donkeys tied well out of the way munched hay, stamped impatient feet, swished their tails to rid themselves of flies. A trio of crows called from the rooftops, their cawing raucous and persistent.

As much as he wished to forget his mission, thoughts of Inyotef intruded. And fear for Amon-Psaro.

"If he means to attack, he'll do it now," Captain Mery said, raising his voice to be heard above the roaring crowd, "before Amon-Psaro steps onto the quay."

The officer, a hard-jawed, muscular man closing on forty years, stood tall and straight on the prow of his warship, watching the priests at the head of the procession march to the quay. He was garbed much as Senu and the other garrison officers: short white kilt, broad multicolored bead collar, bracelets, armlets, and anklets. He wore a short, tightly curled wig, several rings, and carried a baton of office. Bak, standing beside him, felt like a common sparrow sharing a perch with some bright bird of passage.

For perhaps the hundredth time, he checked that all was secure. His eyes traveled from the priests—distinguished by their ankle-length white kilts, wide beaded collars, shaven heads, standards held high—down the sloping street and along the quay to the traveling ships moored at the far end. He scanned the harbor and studied the vessels tied against the southern quay, large boats and small crammed together in reluctant assembly.

"A man who can run with ease might escape in the confusion of the moment," he admitted, "but remember: Inyotef's hampered by a weak leg. And he's long been a man of the water, more skilled than most with a boat."

Mery's quick glance conveyed a grudging respect. "He's so agile on a ship that I forget his limp."

Bak looked back at the procession, the chanting priests, marching down the street while the enthralled masses pressed in from either side, shouting their adoration, jostling for a closer look. The priests passed through the line of soldiers posted along the revetment and stepped onto the quay. The rapture on their faces never wavered, but Bak could well imagine how relieved they must be to reach the open harbor.

While the lead priests marched past the warship, Kenamon walked onto the quay, waving his censor before him. As befitted his illustrious position, he was decked out in full regalia: long white kilt, short-sleeved tunic, fine linen robe, gold pectoral hanging from his breast. His face was calm and untroubled, free of such mundane worldly cares as the possibility of an assassination. Beside him walked the priest of the lady Hathor, a chubby young man, not as imposing but equally tranquil. A cloud of sweet-scented incense drifted around them.

The sailors pressed against the rail of the warship, their eyes wide with awe, their shouts lost in the overall clamor. Bak nodded at Kasaya, standing at the head of the gangplank, clutching a long spear, his eyes darting back and forth along the quay, his face tight with tension. The spearmen were on board the traveling ships, watching, waiting, but no less enthralled than the adoring spectators.

Four lesser priests walked behind Kenamon, purifying the deities' path with incense and libation. The lord Amon followed, his gilded barque carried high on the shoulders of four white-garbed bearers, his golden shrine open so all could view the elegant golden statue of a man wearing a twin-feathered crown. Four additional priests walked alongside, cooling the god with ostrich-feather fans. A second barque followed, not as magnificent but just as lovely, on which rode the gilded image of the lady Hathor in her human form, carried in her open shrine. She was accompanied by two fan-bearers and followed by seven women wearing long white sheaths and broad collars, each shaking a sistrum, a ceremonial rattle bearing the effigy of the goddess.

Bak scanned the shoreline, the harbor, the river, and found nothing out of order. But the evidence of his eyes could not drive away his anxiety. Inyotef was lurking somewhere nearby; he felt it deep inside.

The lead priests walked up the gangplank of the traveling ship on the downstream side of the quay. Kenamon, the younger priest, and the gods moved past the warship in slow and stately splendor. Behind them, ten men, shaven and purified for the occasion, carried the gilded, inlaid, and painted chests filled with ritual equipment and the god's clothing.

Next came a herald, his trumpet blaring above the shouts of the spectators, his cheeks puffed out, his face scarlet with the effort of blowing the instrument. The first contingent of Kushites marched onto the quay behind him: forty spear-men clad in leather kilts and wearing long feathers in hair dyed odd shades of red and yellow. Behind them, mounted on tall poles, waved twenty or so white-and-red pennants that Bak knew preceded Commander Woser and King Amon-Psaro.

The cheerful flags brought dread to his heart. He knew as well as he knew his own name that every vessel in the harbor had been searched, every man vouched for, yet he was equally certain Inyotef was somewhere nearby, wait-ing. Oblivious to the captain beside him and the seamen lining the rail, he climbed onto the forecastle for an overall view.

In the lower city, the spectators' shouts had increased in volume, losing awe in favor of enthusiasm, telling him the royal party had gone by and the garrison troops were pa-rading past their families. The merchant ships moored at the southern quay showed no sign of activity, but the smaller boats were preparing to move out. The moment the first traveling ship set sail, they would scoot across the har-bor like a flock of eager ducks.

Bak's eyes leaped to the end of the southern quay, and he muttered a curse. Two soldiers stood there, one pointing toward a small skiff floating just out of reach. Barely more than a rowboat, its mast lowered with the masthead resting on the prow, it was drifting in the general direction of the stronger current outside the harbor, where it would be swept downstream into the path of the traveling ships. Bak cursed again, his thoughts locked on Inyotef. But the vessel floated too high in the water to carry the weight of a man.

The soldiers stared at the craft, talking, probably deciding if it was worth the effort of swimming out after it. One of the men shook his head, and the pair turned around to walk back along the quay. The vessel must truly be empty and adrift, Bak told himself, but an image took form in his thoughts: the pilot clinging to the outside of the boat, guiding it through the water unseen.

Unsure of himself, worried, he glanced back at the procession. The block of Kushite spearmen had split apart, with the men now lining both sides of the quay. Three heralds marched between the two lines, trumpets raised high, faces looking about to burst, blasting the air with strident notes. Next came the men carrying the banners, a contingent of Kushites marching before their king.

Bak looked again at the skiff across the harbor, watched it drift, helpless to stop it, unable to make sure it held no threat. He had no way of reaching it himself, nor could he warn the soldiers guarding the quay. They were too far away to hear a shout, even without the clamor of the spectators, and by the time a messenger could reach them, the vessel would be closer to the northern quay than the southern—closer to Bak than them. Patience was not one of his virtues, but he had no other choice.

He tore his gaze from the skiff to look at the man who had been uppermost in his thoughts for close to a week. King Amon-Psaro, a tall, well-formed man with graying hair and a careworn but handsome face, strode up the quay with the set expression of royalty, his chin high, his eyes on the distant horizon. He wore a simple white kilt, a broad collar and bracelets made of gold and lapis lazuli beads, and gold anklets and sandals, his garb a conspicuous reminder that he had spent his formative years in the land of Kemet. On his head he wore the twin-cobra diadem of his royal house. Commander Woser, his face pale and tense, dressed in his ceremonial best, walked beside and slightly behind the king.

Four bearers carried the prince, a small shadow of his

father, sitting on a gilded palanquin. A fifth man walked alongside, fanning the child with ostrich feathers. The way the boy's chest heaved, Bak could see he was having trouble breathing. And no wonder, he thought. The odor of incense, close to overpowering, was nearly lost in the stronger, more exotic scents of perfumes and oils made from unknown flowers and trees grown in faraway lands.

Imsiba and the ten Medjay policemen marched close behind their illustrious charges, their faces glowing with pride yet alert to trouble.

The skiff drifted northward, unimpeded.

A shout and the rumble of a drum drew Bak's attention to the ships at the end of the quay. He eyed the vessel, more crowded than it should be, carrying the priestly party and the gods. He noted the captain at the prow, the sacred barques settled on the deck amid a flock of priests, the oarsmen in their places along the rail, the stout drummer beating out the tune that would set the rhythm of their strokes.

The captain of the second vessel stood at the foot of his gangplank, waiting to welcome the royal party.

Bak's eyes darted across the harbor, and he swore again under his breath. The smaller boats were pulling away from the southern quay, their owners paddling with all their skill to extricate their vessels from among the larger ships, each man determined to cross the harbor ahead of the rest and lead the flotilla to the island fortress. The empty skiff rocked on a gentle swell, barely moving, soon to be overtaken by the other craft. Overtaken and surrounded. Lost among them.

Amon-Psaro and the royal party marched alongside the warship. Mery saluted with his baton of office, and Bak made do with raising a hand. The king stared straight ahead with majestic disdain, but Woser glanced Bak's way, an unspoken question on his face. Bak gave a barely perceptible shake of his head. The prince came alongside, his great dark eyes huge and round, his face enlivened by a delighted smile. Sick he might be, Bak thought, but he was not too ill to enjoy himself or too regal to display pleasure.

Imsiba and the Medjays came even with the warship. The big sergeant raised his spear in an open salute to his sweaty, unkempt officer; the other men followed suit. Unable to smother a proud smile, Bak gave them the same salute he had given the king.

The rhythmic beat of the drum grew stronger, faster, tugging his gaze toward the ships at the end of the quay. The first vessel was slipping away, swinging into the current for the journey to the island. Heralds and flag bearers stood at rigid attention on the end of the quay, well out of the way of the royal party marching to the second ship. The captain fell to his knees before Amon-Psaro, his forehead on the stone, demonstrating the greatest respect. The prince grinned with delight. Imsiba and the Medjays looked discomfited by the unexpected pause, worried.

Marching up behind the guard of honor came the Kushite noblemen, each man strutting at the fore of his own small contingent of followers. Gaily bedecked in multicolored clothing, jewelry, and headdresses, each group displayed a tribal or provincial standard.

Bak glanced across the harbor, saw twenty or more small boats, most well away from the southern quay and skimming across the water where he had last seen the empty skiff, all speeding to catch the lead traveling ship. A flock of ducklings racing after a heron. As far as he could tell, every boat was manned and carried three or more passengers. Cursing himself for taking his eyes off the drifting vessel, he examined the river farther out and downstream. He saw no boats at all, only a few white birds riding the swells. His eyes darted toward the southern end of the long island and the rocky islets where the river split to enter the rapids, though he knew no boat could drift so far so fast. The only spot he could not see was the far side of the ship Amon-Psaro was preparing to board.

Bak's stomach knotted; he could not breathe.

*   *   *

The blast of the trumpets and the tattoo of the ship's drum rent the air. Amon-Psaro strode up the gangplank.

Bak dropped off the forecastle, pounded along the deck and, yelling at Kasaya to follow, plunged down the gangplank. Bursting into the exotic band of Kushite nobles, he shouldered men aside, trod on sandaled feet, ruffled feathers and skins and dignity. Kasaya ran close behind, face grim, shield and spear poised to kill. Men scattered like birds before a jackal, too startled to strike back, yelling in their own tongue oaths Bak could guess if not understand.

He burst through the foremost group of noblemen and yelled at Imsiba, who had paused on the gangplank to check out the disturbance. The big Medjay, confused by the melee and unable to hear through the din, jumped off the gangplank to come to Bak's aid. Bak glimpsed Amon-Psaro standing beside the bright-painted deckhouse with his son, staring along the quay, trying to see what the trouble was. He saw sailors on their knees scattered around the deck and rowers sitting with their heads bowed over their oars. He saw the captain hovering and a worried Woser striding toward the gangplank. And he saw Inyotef, carrying a long pointed dagger, hauling himself over the rail close to the stern where he would not be noticed.

Bak shouted again, but his words were lost in the blare of the trumpets and the beat of the drum. He dashed through the guard of honor, who were paralyzed by surprise, beckoned to Imsiba, and sprinted up the gangway. The sergeant swung in behind him, keeping pace with Kasaya. Bak hit the deck with a thud and raced toward Amon-Psaro. The king recoiled, astounded by what he no doubt believed was a raving maniac. Fumbling for his dagger, he took one pace back, another, and another, glancing now and again at Imsiba, plainly expecting the big Medjay to fell the lunatic. His steps carried him to the corner of the deckhouse. Inyotef darted around the bright structure, dagger poised to kill.

Bak leaped toward the king, shoving him roughly against the deckhouse, and rammed Inyotef with his shoulder. The pilot stumbled back against the rail. Bak stood before him, knees flexed, arms wide and loose, ready to grapple if he had to.

"You!" Amon-Psaro cried, coming up behind Bak. "Inyotef!"

With an ugly grimace, the pilot lunged at Bak, who ducked backward. The tip of Inyotef's blade drew a thin red line across Bak's chest and cut a deeper swath across Amon-Psaro's arm and ribs. Bak saw the blood spill from the king's breast, felt the sting of his own wound, heard Imsiba yell and the onlookers gasp. He leaped forward, trying to get inside the arc of the blade, too close for Inyotef to strike again. The pilot wheeled around, hurdled the rail, and dropped over the side.

Though staggered by his quarry's sudden disappearance, Bak was quick to react. He threw his legs over the rail, glimpsed the skiff below and saw Inyotef scrambling for the oars. He let himself fall. The pilot shoved off from the larger craft. Bak hit the water in the space between the two vessels and sank like a stone. By the time he fought his way to the surface, the skiff was skimming over the water near the ship's rudder and closing on the end of the quay. Once it reached the swifter flow outside the harbor, he would never catch it.

Gritting his teeth, swimming with quick, powerful strokes, he sliced through the water. A half dozen Medjays leaned over the rail above him. Their spears were positioned to throw, yet they hesitated. The pilot had rowed in among the few small boats in the flotilla that had stayed behind to accompany the Kushite king to the island.

Imsiba, who had dropped off the ship, raced to the end of the quay, waited until Inyotef cleared the vessels, then heaved his spear. It missed the pilot by the width of a finger and slid into the water on the far side of the skiff. Inyotef glanced up at him and sneered. Bak swam alongside. Imsiba jerked a pole supporting a long red pennant out of the hands of a startled bearer and hurled it at the skiff. Inyotef ducked away from the ungainly missile, but the banner slapped him across the face. He flung it aside with an angry snarl and rowed rapidly away from the quay.

Taking advantage of the distraction, Bak heaved himself into the stern. The boat bucked beneath his weight, throwing Inyotef off-balance. The pilot scrambled into the prow, where the sail had been stowed, braced himself between the hull and the lowered mast, and swung an oar in a hard, mean arc. Bak ducked, bumped the rudder stanchion, heard the sharp crack of splitting wood. He grabbed for the rudder, missed, glimpsed it sliding into the water. The boat rocked wildly, its stern swerving toward the half-rotted trunk of a palm tree carried along on the stronger current of the open channel. Bak half fell, half sat on a crossbeam. Inyotef lowered the second oar into the water to steady the boat. He was too far forward to row with any authority. An inflated goatskin lay midway along the keel, a hairy gray wall between the two men's feet.

Holding the free oar aloft, Inyotef eyed Bak along its length. "You always were a stubborn swine. I should've ended your life and your prying the day you set foot in Iken."

"Why didn't you?" Bak spoke automatically, his thoughts on the oar and how best to take it away from the pilot. It would do as a makeshift rudder until he could beach them on a riverbank well away from the rapids.

Inyotef snorted. "A man can be stubborn, yet not have the wit to be dangerous."

Bak noted the backhanded compliment, or was it meant to be an insult? "You've tried hard enough to correct your error. Your use of the sling, I took as a warning. But the snake in my sleeping pallet was meant to kill. As was my skiff when you cut the mooring rope and jammed the halyard, and Huy's skiff so cleverly sabotaged.''

"You've Nebwa to thank for giving me purpose." Inyotef laughed, cynical, mocking. "If he hadn't sung your
praises so loud and clear, I'd not have realized how formidable an opponent you might be."

"I understand why you wanted to be rid of me, but why
slay Huy?" Bak asked, shifting his weight so he could
lunge forward.

Inyotef looked at him with the wariness of a feral dog.
"Of all the men who traveled north with the hostage prince
Amon-Psaro, Huy was the only one who truly cared about
his well-being, the only man to ask questions in Waset after
he came back from afar. I feared what he might've
learned."

Bak vowed again to tell the king of Huy's presence in
Iken—if ever he had the chance. "I'm surprised you didn't
slay me long ago for what I did to your leg."

Inyotef lowered the oar as far as the edge of the hull,
husbanding the strength in his arm. "You're no more responsible for my injury than that wretched horse," he
scoffed. "It was I who stood too close to the gangplank
that day, I who laughed so loud I frightened the beast."

Bak let the news sink in, tasted it, savored it. Yet he was
not surprised by the deception. "I doubt your blade pierced
Amon-Psaro deeper than his rib cage, Inyotef. You've
failed to slay him."

"Perhaps." Inyotef glanced at the line of scratched and
bleeding flesh across Bak's breast. "But he knows now I
can reach him, and he knows I'll try again. I've nothing
left to lose."

The man's single-minded determination made Bak's
head swim. "Let's go back to Iken."

"You'll never take me prisoner."

Bak's voice hardened. "I'll not let you escape."

"We've reached a stalemate, it seems." Inyotef's eyes
glittered with cold amusement. "You're too close to throw
your dagger with any force, and too far away to drive it

into my breast. Nor can I use my dagger to good effect. If you come close, I'll brain you with an oar. Yet if you continue to sit there, holding me in the prow, I can't direct the course of the skiff.''

Bak eyed the river ahead, flowing swift and smooth, safe—at least for the moment. The ship carrying the deities and priests, and the flotilla of smaller boats, had swung into the channel that would take them to the island fortress. A quick glance back showed him Amon-Psaro's ship still moored at the quay and the smaller boats fluttering around, their masters confused by its failure to sail. Imsiba would follow, he knew, but how long would it take him to commandeer a boat?

The skiff appeared to be floating toward the southern end of the long island, a deceiving image, he knew. Soon the current would split apart, carrying the vessel to the left, down the western channel where the shoreline touched the desert north of the city, or to the right into any of several narrow channels with swift and angry waters and fearsome rocks, or into the awesome rapids below the island fortress.

A frightful thought, one Bak refused to dwell on. "Can I trust you to come near? to row this vessel? I think not. I've met few men as deceptive as you, as clever with a falsehood. You came close to getting away with Puemre's murder.''

A gloating smile formed on Inyotef's face. Bak lunged forward, grabbed the oar resting on the edge of the hull, and wrenched it out of the pilot's hand. Inyotef snarled a curse, tore the second oar out of the water, grabbed it with both hands like a bat, and swung. Bak ducked away and raised his oar. The weapons collided with a loud crack, showering them with droplets of water, striking with a force so strong it shook Bak's teeth. The skiff rocked violently; water splashed inside.

Inyotef laughed. "Do you wish us both to die, my young friend?''

Bak wiped the water from his face, the nervous sweat.

"If by chance you get away, where will you go? With the desert on either side of the river, with word spreading to north and south, how can you hope ever again to place yourself in Amon-Psaro's path?"

"Go?" Inyotef snorted. "I'll slay him here and now."

Bak swore a silent oath. The pilot had just wiped out any middle measures he might otherwise have taken. He had no choice but to capture or kill. "You hate him that much?"

"He destroyed my sister."

Without warning, Inyotef swung his oar. Bak parried the blow, rocking the skiff, skewing its path. The vessel swerved sideways to the current and drifted to the right, choosing the channel that could carry them to the island fortress. A likely source of help, Bak thought, trying not to hear the roar of the rapids blocking the first side channel, a siren song to a boat without a rudder.

"You'd cause a war merely to satisfy a misguided sense of family honor?"

"Misguided?" Inyotef's laugh grated. "He made her love him. While she dreamed of a lifetime in his arms, he walked away as if she didn't exist. He took her life as surely as I'll take his."

There was no stopping him. He had lived too long with his hate, spent too much time dwelling on revenge.

The fortress appeared beyond the long island. The traveling ship was moored against the landing, the priests passing through the gate and the gods making their precarious way up the path. Sailors and soldiers were unloading offerings and priestly accoutrements. Most of the flotilla had landed across the channel on the long island, where the passengers would have a good view of the king and his followers. The wait would be long and tedious; the vessel carrying the royal party had not yet set sail.

"Amon-Psaro will soon be safe in the island fortress," Bak said, raising his voice so he could be heard over the rapids in the side channel. "You'll never lay hands on him then."

"I'll die trying," Inyotef said doggedly.

The skiff swept past the two small islands at the mouth of the channel, sailing faster than before, drawn downstream by the maelstrom at the far end of the island fortress. Bak could no longer wait in the illusory hope the pilot would let down his guard. He stood up, setting the vessel to rocking, and waved to the men on the shore, yelling, hoping they could hear him over the thundering waters.

Inyotef scrambled to his feet, caught his oar in both hands, and swung. Bak, expecting the attack, practically inviting it, ducked away. The edge of the oar slid across his belly, taking a layer of skin, leaving splinters in its place. Bak caught his own oar in both hands, swung it. Inyotef blocked the blow. The skiff bucked like an untrained horse. They stood facing each other, legs spread wide for balance, weapons locked together, waiting for the craft to settle down.

Bak jerked his oar back, tried to step away to give himself room, stumbled over the inflated goatskin. As he fell, he swung the oar. It glanced off Inyotef's oar and smashed into the pilot's good leg, dropping him to his knees. With Bak on one knee, his other knee bent and the foot flat on the hull, with Inyotef on both knees, they lunged and parried time after time, swinging with all their strength, wearing themselves down. The skiff danced and bobbed and bucked, swerving to left and right as the weight inside shifted, but never leaving for long its course down the channel. A palm trunk, maybe the one they had seen earlier, floated ahead of them, its passage straight and true like a pilot fish leading them along the path of destruction.

Bak's arms grew heavy from swinging the ungainly weapon, his legs grew weary from holding himself upright, his belly burned, his teeth and skin felt loosened by the jolts of oar against oar. Out of the corner of his eye, he glimpsed men on the traveling ship, leaning over the rail, gaping at the passing skiff, and soldiers running down the path. Yelling, he thought. The silent voices alerted him to the heightened roar ahead, the cold sweat on his face, like mist blowing off the roiling waters, warned of the vicious torrent.

His body went cold, chilled by fear. He had to stop this insane voyage toward certain death.

Inyotef swung his oar. Instead of parrying the blow, Bak followed its arc with his own oar, letting momentum carry both paddles beyond the hull of the skiff. He mustered his strength and pressed Inyotef's oar downward, holding it against the hull. The skiff tilted beneath their combined weight, threatening to slide out from under them. Inyotef's face grew red with strain, the tendons corded on his neck. Bak felt his own face flush and his muscles scream for relief. He saw a wall of white ahead, water boiling and tumbling over and around the rocky barrier, black granite boulders glistening in the wet, the palm trunk smashing against a boulder, bits of wood flying through the foam.

Inyotef saw the look on his face and took a quick glance over his shoulder. "Give me your oar," he yelled, "I can save us."

Seeing no alternative, Bak warily released the pressure. Inyotef jerked his oar free and at the same time drew the long dagger from its sheath and lunged. Bak raised his oar, deflecting the blade, and swung hard and fast, slamming the pilot on the side of the head. Inyotef gave him a surprised look, the dagger fell from his fingers, and he crumpled over the side of the skiff. Bak reached out to grab him, saw froth on the water, felt the skiff strike something solid. Horrified, he saw the vessel's seams tear apart and frothing water rush inside. He grabbed the inflated goatskin, more from instinct than conscious thought, and felt himself slide into a river gone mad.

He was seized by the angry white waters, swirling, leaping, falling. His body was thrown and twisted with such force he was powerless to control himself, unable to tell upstream from downstream or even up from down. He was swept along like a pebble, tossed from torrent to eddy to cascade, scraping rocks and the jagged riverbottom and things he could feel but not see. What little air he held in his lungs was quickly knocked out of him. He was certain he was going to die.

The swirling waters buffeted him, lifted him and slammed him down, and lifted him again. Realizing he still held the goatskin, he clutched it tight against his breast and prayed with the fierceness of desperation to the lord Amon. His head broke the surface. He gulped in air.

Holding the goatskin close, he tried to swim, but he was flung against a boulder and dragged into a vortex that whirled him around and around, giving him a taste of what death must feel like. The eddy spat him out and flung him along the riverbottom, flipping him over and over. He hit another rock, smashed his left arm against a boulder so hard he tried to scream, but he sucked in water instead.

Gasping for air, coughing, he let the current sweep him along a fast but blessedly quiet stretch. When he surfaced, when he could breathe again and think rationally, he looked to right and left, searching for the river's edge. He saw nothing to either side but rocky islets, great craggy boulders, and now and then a pocket of sand supporting a few clumps of grass, or a stunted tree.

A growing rumble downstream and a fine mist rising from the channel alerted him to more rough water. His throat tightened and his mouth turned dry. Too exhausted to fight another rapid, his left arm afire with pain and close to useless, he set out diagonally across the current, swimming toward the closest bit of land, a tiny pockmarked boulder. The flow strengthened, sweeping him past the safe haven. Ahead the river vanished.

He sucked in a breath, clung to the swollen goatskin, and let the current sweep him over a foaming cascade. The plummeting water drove him down, swirled him around, and flung him out at the head of a stretch of fast but un-cluttered water. Gathering all that remained of his strength and willpower, he swam toward what he assumed was an island but prayed was the western shore of the river.

Then he saw Inyotef, limp and pale, beached on a rocky crag, lying across a shallow pool. Wishing he could leave him there to live or die at the whim of the gods, yet knowing he could not, he swam closer. He approached slowly, cautiously, aware of his own weakness, his exhaustion. If he had to fight, he knew he would lose.

He neared the boulder and, from a safe distance, studied the still, pale form. Inyotef was bruised and battered, his breathing labored. His pallor, Bak recognized, was the color of death.

He stumbled onto the rock and dropped down next to the injured man. How could the proud warship captain he once knew bring upon himself so awful a death? "Inyotef?"

The pilot's eyes fluttered open. He formed a weak smile. "I guess I didn't . . ." He paused, took the shallow breath of a man with broken ribs. ". . . didn't know the rapids as well . . ." Another pause. ". . . as well as I thought."

"Don't talk," Bak said, his voice rough and uneven. "You'll hurt yourself more."

Inyotef took a slow careful breath. "Better this way." Another breath. "I couldn't face . . ." A pause, a careful swallow. ". . . a judgment of death." His eyes closed, his head fell sideways.

Bak dropped his forehead onto his knees, saddened by the death of a man he had thought his friend yet glad the awful journey down the river had ended as it had. Inyotef had offended the lady Maat, upsetting the balance of order and justice. He had to die one way or another. To lose his life in the river on which he had thrived seemed fitting.

Chapter Nineteen

A soft light penetrated the white linen that covered the wood-framed pavilion in which Bak and Kenamon sat. The fabric rippled in the breeze, making fluttery, whispery sounds, and sent vague shadows darting across the scrolls, utensils, and bags and bundles of medicaments laid out on a reed mat beside the priest. The odors of frankincense and juniper wafted through the open portal of a connecting pavilion. Murmurs outside, men's voices softened by the presence of royal guards, announced the passage of soldiers and nobility. Distant laughter, the smack of spear against spear, an occasional bellow, told of soldiers practicing the arts of war. A low never-ending rumble spoke of the rapids outside the fortress walls.

"The swelling will remain for a few days, as will the discoloration." Kenamon rewound the linen bandage holding Bak's lower arm and hand firm against the wooden splint. An oily green salve oozed out along the edges of the fabric. "It's as I told you yesterday: The break should heal without problems, but you must treat the arm as you would a newborn babe: gently, kindly, making no demands on it."

"Rest assured, my uncle, I'll not try to use it again. It hurts too much."

The elderly priest, seated on a low stool in front of his patient, gave Bak the same severe look he had used when he was a child. "The pain is there to remind you that you must take care. You ignore it at your peril."

Bak, scooting back on the thick pillow he sat on, gave the old man a lopsided smile. "How can I stand in a guard of honor with my arm tied to my waist?"

Kenamon shook his head in mock disgust. "Guard of honor! Hah! You should see yourself."

Bak knew what he looked like: bruised, battered, and bandaged. A wounded sparrow. A man praised by all within the garrison and city of Iken, soldiers and civilians alike, for laying hands on Puemre's murderer and for surviving the rapids. A man who had knocked a king to his knees, a divine being who had not yet deigned to summon him.

"Perhaps it's just as well," Kasaya had said. "He was very angry when last I saw him on the ship. Better to hear nothing than to have your hands lopped off because you trod on his royal pride."

Kenamon, on the other hand, had counseled patience, saying the king had been busy, praying long and often for the health of his son, receiving people who had traveled great distances in the hope of an audience, and renewing past friendships with men such as Huy and Senu. Bak preferred to believe the priest rather than Kasaya. After all, Amon-Psaro had lived many years in Waset, learning the civilized ways of Kemet.

"Now let me look at your shoulder," Kenamon said, drawing close a bowl containing a brownish paste that smelled bitter like wormwood but carried other, more subtle, odors, too.

Bak turned around obediently and let the priest cut away the bandage he had applied the previous day, revealing an area of scabby, bruised flesh as large as the palm of a hand, one of several places scraped raw in the rapids. Kenamon cleaned the wound and spread the ointment over it, murmuring prayers while he worked, magical incantations that would drive away the demons of sickness.

Whether eased by the poultice or the prayers, the fire in

Bak's broken arm soon waned to a smolder, and he let himself relax under the priest's capable hands. Kenamon rebandaged the shoulder and went on to a deep, ragged cut on the arm, drawn together beneath a thin slice of fresh meat bandaged tightly over the injury. Removing the meat, he probed the wound in search of infection. Bak let his thoughts drift, his eyelids droop. A soft moan, as delicate as the mewing of a tiny kitten, roused him from his torpor and stilled the priest's hands.

"He's awakened?" Bak asked, glancing toward the connecting pavilion, trying not to show concern. He had heard rumors all morning that the prince seemed almost healed, but he feared the tales more wish than reality.

Kenamon quickly scraped the salve from his fingers to the edge of the bowl and wiped the residue on a clean square of linen. Hurrying to the portal, he looked inside. His face relaxed into a smile. "Amon-Karka is dreaming," he whispered. "Something happy. Come see the way he smiles."

Bak scrambled to his feet and hastened to the priest's side. The small bony child lay sprawled across his sleeping pallet, holding close against his cheek a wooden lion with movable tail and lower jaw. The toy was a gift from Aset. The boy's breathing was slow and easy, with no coughing or desperate panting or noisy and fearsome wheezing.

The room reeked of frankincense, juniper, wormwood, and beer. The pungent odor wafted from a bowl on the floor beside the prince. A reed straw protruded from an identical bowl turned upside down to serve as a lid. Kenamon, Bak knew, had dropped a hot stone inside, heating the liquid remedy, and the prince had breathed in the fumes through the straw.

Amon-Karka nuzzled the toy, smiling, and repeated the sound, more a contented sigh than a moan.

Bak laughed softly, half-ashamed of how worried he had been. "I know you're more capable than most, my uncle, but I didn't expect so quick and miraculous a cure."

"The lord Amon has guided my heart and my hands, young man. I'm his tool, nothing more." The reminder was gentle but firm, an adult telling a child a fact he should take for granted.

"Without sufficient knowledge and skill, you'd not have been able to obey the god's wishes."

"I blame your father for your impertinence." Kenamon's voice was gruff, but his eyes twinkled with merriment. "He should've remarried, taking into his household a woman who'd teach you the respect you lack."

Bak had thanked the lord Amon many times that he had been spared a stepmother. "Your apprentice said you had clues to the malady, yet how could you? Until yesterday, you never laid eyes on the boy."

Kenamon looked in at the prince, his expression a mix of self-satisfaction and compassion. "I asked many questions of the couriers who came from Amon-Psaro, and I talked with men who've lived in his capital. Through the months, I learned much of Amon-Karka's sickness and the way he lives and even the weather. I came to know as much about him as his servants do, and more, I think, than his father knows."

"And from among the details of his life, you plucked out the clues to his illness." Like a policeman searching out a murderer, Bak thought, though so illustrious a physician as Kenamon might not appreciate the comparison.

Kenamon walked back to his stool and sat down. "By the time we sailed into Buhen, I knew he suffers most during the months before the river rises, when the winds blow hard from the western desert. I knew he grows ill when he travels or when he drives a chariot or plays with his dogs." He took a daub of ointment on his fingers and waited for Bak to settle down on the pillow. "I thought I knew the cause—it's common enough in children—but I couldn't be sure."

Kenamon spread the ointment over the cut. "The reports I heard during his journey from Semna seemed to verify my diagnosis. When they brought him to me here and he responded so quickly to medication and prayer, I knew I was right. He has a breathing sickness that befalls many children. Most outgrow it; some never do."

Bak thought of the lord Amon and the long journey he had made from the land of Kemet. He thought of the great tribal king who had traveled from far-off Kush in the firm belief that the greatest of the gods would answer his prayers. "Have you told Amon-Psaro his son may never recover?"

"He knows I can do nothing but ease the boy's symptoms." Kenamon wrapped a bandage tight around Bak's arm to hold the cut together and tied the ends in a small, neat knot. "I've told him how best to protect the boy from further attacks. Other than that, all we can do is pray and make suitable offerings."

"Then I'll get well, won't I?" The childish voice drew both men's eyes to the doorway and Amon-Karka leaning against an upright, rubbing one leg with the other foot. Before the priest could answer, the prince's large dark eyes darted toward his patient. "You must be Lieutenant Bak, the policeman who saved my father's life. The one who went through the rapids."

Without thinking, Bak spoke as he would to an ordinary child. "How'd you guess?"

The boy laughed, delighted by the quick rejoinder. "Because you're bandaged all over, halfway to being a mummy."

Bak grinned. "Are all princes so impertinent?"

Amon-Karka wrinkled his nose at the smelly room behind him, sauntered over to the two men, and plopped down beside Kenamon. "Can I watch?" His eyes leaped from the priest to Bak. "Will you tell me about the rapids? And the man you chased? And how you knew he wanted to slay my father?"

Bak hoped, if ever he got to meet Amon-Psaro, that he would be as bright and open-hearted as his son.

*   *   *

"Lieutenant Bak." The herald's voice resonated with authority. "Son of the physician Kames of the southern capital of Waset in the land of Kemet. Lieutenant of chariotry in the regiment of Amon. Lieutenant of the Medjay police at the fortress of Buhen. Right hand to Commandant Thuty of Buhen."

The man stepped back so Bak, on his knees, his forehead on the floor mat, could no longer see his feet. All he could glimpse was the edge of the dais on which Amon-Psaro sat. The rough surface of the mat dug into his scabbed knees; his broken arm throbbed. A heavy perfume smelling of lilies and myrrh tickled his nose. He prayed he would not sneeze.

"You may stand, Lieutenant," Amon-Psaro commanded.

Bak rose as gracefully as his battered muscles allowed and stood at rigid attention. The king studied him in silence, taking in the bandages and bruises, the splint. Bak, clinging to Kenamon's prediction that the interview would go well, examined Amon-Psaro as closely as the king studied him, but not as openly.

As he had the day before, the king wore the garb of a royal son of Kemet: simple white kilt, multicolored broad collar, and bracelets, armlets, anklets, and rings of gold and precious stones. Twin golden cobras mounted on a golden diadem rose above his forehead, and he carried a scepter of gold. Spotless white bandages covered the cuts across his ribs and arm. He sat enthroned on a gilded armchair, his feet on a matching footrest. The royal backside was made comfortable on a thick red pillow embroidered with gold threads, and the royal spine was eased by a magnificent leopardskin draped over the back of the chair. Every inch a king, he was also a man: tall, muscular, leonine. Attractive at close to forty years; no doubt doubly so in his youth—especially to women.

Red-and-white banners fluttered from the frame of the

open pavilion in which he sat. Two of Bak's Medjays stood guard with two soldiers from the king's homeland. Other than a few lookers-on, only a half dozen functionaries stood nearby, murmuring together while they waited to obey their ruler's slightest command.

"I owe you my life, it seems," Amon-Psaro said.

"Yes, sir."

"Commander Woser tells me he looked upon Inyotef as his friend, and he had no suspicion of wrongdoing. He says only your tenacity unearthed the plot to slay me."

Bak suspected the king would prefer a simple yes or no answer, but if he did not speak up the mute child Ramose would soon be buried and forgotten in a desert grave. "The boy who died at Inyotef's hands, the one who served Lieutenant Puemre, left drawings behind pointing to a plot. Without them, I'd have been as blind as the commander."

"The boy, yes." Amon-Psaro's thoughts turned inward. "Younger even than my own son." He rubbed his eyes as if to rid himself of the vision. "I've asked Commander Woser to see him properly entombed. I pray the gods give him a voice and hearing in the netherworld, and he leads a better life than in the past."

"Thank you, sir."

"No, Lieutenant, it's I who must thank you. Not merely with words, but with all the good things of life." Amon-Psaro sat up straighter on the throne and his voice grew more formal. "I wish you to return with me to my capital in the land of Kush and serve as my right hand while I govern my people. I've few men I trust and I believe you'd be a worthy adviser. I'll give you a fine house, much land, and many cattle. And so you may fill your life with children, I'll give you my youngest sister, a woman of merit and beauty."

Bak was struck dumb. The offer was the last thing he expected—or wanted, for that matter. It was too generous by far, the task too demanding for one who had no experience in such lofty company, too precarious according to

Senu's wife. *But how,* he wondered, *does one say no to a king?*

Late that evening, Bak stood atop the fortress wall, looking out over the roaring waters that had come so close to taking his life. Seen from above, the rapids looked like a demon's brew boiling in a great cauldron, with the water bubbling and foaming and pounding the deadly boulders, teasing the eye with a multitude of rainbows trembling in the mist. The sight filled his heart with awe. How had he survived? He felt sure that walking the corridors of power would be equally dangerous.

"Do you often swim in such waters?" Amon-Psaro asked, his voice raised to be heard over the thundering rapids.

Bak swung around, startled, and fell to his knees.

"Stand!" the king commanded. "I'll have no bowing and scraping from you, Lieutenant."

Bak hastened to rise. "Yes, sir."

Amon-Psaro had abandoned the glitter and gloss of office, he saw, retaining only the royal diadem and the broad collar and bracelets of gold and lapis lazuli that he had worn during the procession through the city the day before.

"It's been many years since I've stood side by side with a man of Kemet and had the opportunity to speak the language of my youth. Don't steal the pleasure from me by placing me in a niche with the gods."

Bak heard loneliness in Amon-Psaro's voice and regret for a lost past. The thought had probably occurred to him at one time or another that a living god might share such basic emotions with ordinary men, but the realization surprised him—and touched him. "Would you like a jar of beer, sir?" he blurted.

"Beer?" Amon-Psaro hesitated an instant, laughed. "Yes, Lieutenant, a jar of beer would be in order."

Bak leaned over the inner breastwork and called out to a soldier strolling along the base of the wall. The man,

seeing the king beside the officer, hastened to the kitchen.
In no time at all, a ruddy-cheeked boy delivered a basket
filled with beer jars, dried fish the size of a man's finger,
and small round loaves of crusty bread.

The king, beer jar in hand, looked out over the wall, his
elbows planted on the bricks, his eyes on the rapids below.
The lord Re, a golden ball resting on the horizon, threw
streaks of red and orange and yellow high into the pale sky,
brilliant ribbons thrown out by the god in honor of the
Kushite monarch.

Amon-Psaro sipped through the reed straw, scowled at
it, dropped it into the basket, and drank from the neck as
his less refined companion was doing. "It seems you and
I have a mutual friend, Bak."

"We do?" Each time Bak spoke, he had to remind himself not to call the king "sir".

"Mistress Nofery, a woman of business in Buhen. I've
a letter from her, brought today by the courier who delivered dispatches from Commandant Thuty to Woser. She
calls you a good man, one of the best in the garrison of
Buhen, and a good friend."

Bak gaped. "You know Nofery?" Even as he spoke, he
recalled the obese old woman, sitting with him in her house
of pleasure in Buhen, telling him she once knew Amon-
Psaro. He had laughed, he remembered, skeptical of her
tale.

"I knew her well many years ago. I was a prince then,
a hostage in Waset." Amon-Psaro stared straight ahead,
looking into his past. "She was shapely and beautiful, the
most seductive woman I've ever met, even to this day."
He laughed softly to himself, the sound lost in the rumble
of the rapids. "She was a woman of pleasure then, and
now she runs a business. A successful endeavor, she wrote,
selling the bounty of the fields. I'm glad she's found good
fortune."

Bak opened his mouth to blurt out the truth, but changed

his mind. If Nofery chose to paint herself in bright colors, it was not his business to dull the sheen.

"I long to see her again," Amon-Psaro said, his voice wistful, "but I'll not take my son to Buhen and risk further illness. Nor can she travel, she tells me, with her business so brisk this time of year and her daughter too heavy with child to carry on alone."

Bak stared at the river below, hiding his face from Amon-Psaro, his racing thoughts. Nofery had no daughter. What was she up to? Why would she lie when, if she told the truth, she could see once again a man she liked and admired, a powerful man who might give her many precious gifts.

"She was a lovely creature." Amon-Psaro emptied his beer jar and, smiling at the memory, dropped it into the basket. "Slim, straight arms and legs. Breasts large and round and erect. Mouth soft and gentle."

The answer came suddenly, stunning Bak with its simplicity, showing him a sensitivity he had never imagined Nofery possessed. She had indeed been beautiful, just as she had told him that day in Buhen, and she wanted Amon-Psaro to remember her that way, not as the fat and aging old woman she had become. He admired her for the sacrifice.

"I've sent her a gift to let her know I've not forgotten: a lion cub and a young male slave to care for it and cater to her every wish." The king glanced at Bak, his expression anxious. "Do you think she'll like them?"

Bak pictured Nofery with a large new house of pleasure, a grand place of business with an exotic mascot and servant. "She'll be overwhelmed with joy." *An understatement, if ever I heard one,* he thought. *She'll parade them before me, never letting me forget I thought her tale untrue.*

Amon-Psaro relaxed, smiled, broke the plug out of a fresh jar, and handed the brew to Bak. He seemed friendly enough, open to questions, but Bak hesitated to ask the one uppermost in his thoughts. Curiosity finally nudged aside his trepidation. "Will you tell me of Sonisonbe, Inyotef's sister?"

The king gave him a quick look, and turned away to stare out across the river. "Sonisonbe. Yes."

"I don't have to know any more than I already do, but I'd like to understand."

Amon-Psaro let the silence grow, reluctant to speak. When at last he did, the words came hard, torn from a past long buried. "I met Inyotef during the voyage north to Kemet when first I was taken hostage. He was a sailor, barely a man but older than I, more experienced. A man of boundless ambition, and one who played as hard as he worked." He stopped, raised the jar to his lips, drank, set it on the wall. "Huy, who was as close to me as a brother, was sent north with his battalion the day we set foot in Waset. I walked into the palace friendless but for Inyotef."

He toyed with the jar, his thoughts far away. "I soon found a way to scale the wall, and I made my way to the harbor and the warship Inyotef sailed on. He showed me Waset that day, and I thought it the most magical city I'd ever seen. We roamed the streets for hours, and when we grew tired he took me to his home. His parents and sister welcomed me as one of theirs."

"Didn't anyone miss you in the palace?"

Amon-Psaro snorted. "That night my wings were clipped. But I refused to eat, so from that day forward they closed their eyes to my absences." He took another drink, but Bak doubted he tasted the brew. "One day Inyotef's warship sailed north, taking him with it. At first, Sonisonbe and I played as we had before, but our games soon turned to lovemaking."

He picked up the beer jar, set it down again, looked at Bak for the first time since starting his tale. "Inyotef returned a man of the world, filled with the desire for pleasure. By then I had many friends among the nobility, all with a like passion, so for months on end I spent my days and nights reveling. I drank too much, played games of chance, and lay in the arms of countless women. Nofery was one of them. She stole my heart.''

"What of Sonisonbe?"

"I loved her, too." Amon-Psaro drew in a deep, ragged breath and released it. "Long before my father died and I had to return to the land of my birth, I promised them both I'd send for them as soon as my throne was secure. Nofery laughed, taking my vow as a joke. Sonisonbe promised to follow me to the four corners of the earth if need be. In the end, when at last I took my father's place, my duties as king overwhelmed me: the need to wed my sister to keep the line pure, the squabbling among my cousins, the need to learn about a land and a people I'd long ago forgotten. I didn't send for either woman. I wanted no more burdens." He rolled the jar between his two hands, unaware of his action. "Some months later Inyotef wrote, telling me of Sonisonbe's death, vowing to slay me."

Bak felt an immense pity for Amon-Psaro, for Sonisonbe, for Inyotef. "I heard his ship was once turned back from the land of Kush, so I assumed you knew he wanted you dead." He frowned, bewildered by a new thought. "Why then did you come north to Wawat? Surely you knew he was a pilot on the Belly of Stones."

"I had to save my son's life."

"A prudent man would've sent a message to Commandant Thuty, asking him to send Inyotef north, well away from Iken."

Amon-Psaro shrugged, as if as much at a loss to explain as Bak was to understand. "Perhaps I wished to end his misery and mine, for we both mourned for her in equal measure. Or did I wish to appease my conscience by putting myself in his hands and letting the gods decide my guilt or innocence, my life for hers? I don't know."

Bak left Amon-Psaro at the entrance to Kenamon's pavilion, and Imsiba intercepted him moments later. Eyeing the broad gold and lapis lazuli collar around Bak's neck, the wide bracelets on his arms, the Medjay's expression plainly showed his concern. "What did you tell him, my friend? That you're going with him to faroff Kush?"

Bak took Imsiba's arm and aimed him toward the quiet corner where their men had set up camp. The camp was empty, the men somewhere across the fortress watching Pashenuro play knucklebones with the champion of the Iken garrison. Distant voices, laughter, and cursing announced the ebb and flow of the game. They hunkered down beside a thick fish stew, kept warm on a bed of coals contained within a tripod of rocks.

"I danced around the truth for a time," Bak said, "but finally told him how I felt: I'm content as I am and I have no desire to live a life of wealth and privilege. So he gave me this instead." He ran his fingers over the cool, smooth beads of the necklace. "He took them off and, with his own hands, fastened them on me."

"I thank the lord Amon!" Imsiba grinned. "When I saw you laughing together, I feared the worst."

Bak's smile was as broad as that of his friend. He was relieved the decision was over and done with, the temptation to climb to great heights a thing of the past. "He hid his feelings, but I suspect he was relieved. He talked too freely today, more than a king should, telling me the deepest secrets within his heart. I imagine he'll be glad to see the last of me."

"The prince, Kenamon says, is doing well. How much longer, do you think, before we can go home to Buhen?"

"Soon," Bak said. "The sooner the better."

LAUREN HANEY worked for some years as a technical editor in California's aerospace and construction industries. She now writes full-time. The Lieutenant Bak stories combine her enjoyment of the mystery genre with her passion for ancient Egypt. She presently lives in San Francisco and travels to Egypt at every opportunity.